Son of Soothsayer

SIMON A. SMITH

Son of Soothsayer

A NOVEL

LIBRARY OF CONGRESS CATALOGING-IN-PUBLICATION DATA

Son of Soothsayer
Authored by Simon A. Smith

ISBN: 9780999461709
LCCN: 2018935740

Acknowledgments

Thank you to my incredible wife, Romi, without whom this book would have never been completed. Her love for me, her patience with me and her belief in me, from the very beginning, have meant, and continue to mean, everything.

Thank you to my exuberant one-year-old son, Holden, whose silent inspiration and mute judgment in the back of my mind, drove me to create a book that will hopefully one day make him proud.

Thank you to my friend, Jeremiah Kniola, whose willingness to applaud and critique my work, even when the manuscript crept up close to 500 pages, is always greatly appreciated.

Special thanks to artist Judith Hoch for letting me use her fantastic painting, "Inside and Outside," for the cover, and to Ian Koenig who did one hell of a job crafting the overall design.

Finally, to my family whose steadfast support has always been my greatest source of strength, especially my father, Simon K., who was my first reader and also my biggest influence as an artist and free-thinker. I really wish he was still around to share in this accomplishment.

CONTENTS

Take off your band-aid 'cause I don't believe in touchdowns.
—JEFF TWEEDY (WILCO)

*How many legs does a dog have if you call the tail a leg? Four.
Calling a tail a leg doesn't make it a leg.*
—ABRAHAM LINCOLN

*Then came in the magicians, the astrologers, the Chaldeans
and the soothsayers: and I told the dream before them; but
they did not make known unto me the interpretation thereof.*
—KING JAMES BIBLE – DANIEL 4:7

I. THE SHORTCUT REVEALED

Look at It This Way or
It's Apparently Endless (2005)

I call my mother to tell her I quit my hazardous job as Zarek's townie busboy, and her response is to read me a story from the book she's assembled. The one she picks is a testimonial about a former "streetwalker" who has changed her life through positive thinking. It is not a short story but she reads the whole thing, and when she finishes and the tramp has made her transformation from street walker to wedding planner, she tells me that this is something emblematic of what I myself need to do now. It isn't literal, I gather. "Think only good thoughts," she explains, "and imagine yourself succeeding in a business that better suits your spiritual self. It's *the shortcut*," she whispers. I ask her to speak up, and she repeats herself, this time with a fanged response, louder than necessary. "The shortcut!" she says.

I can't see much harm in being more optimistic, and so over the next week, every time I send out a resume, I picture myself in one or both of the two occupations I consider my dream jobs. One image is that of a veterinarian, all dressed up in blue scrubs with a stethoscope around my neck, bandaging a fragile cat's paw. The other is a world-renowned magician, an outfit replete with a black top hat, silky red cape and matching cummerbund.

On the eighth day following our conversation, I take a walk through Leal Park and on the way out I look down to find a wounded bird on the ground with bloody feathers but still breathing. And as I bend to examine the heartbeat, I wonder if this is it, if this is what she (or the universe) would count as a double triumph.

Tantamount to the End (2006)

The Orange County Convention Center is, counter to what one might expect, entirely white. Its expansive front end is flanked by wide beveled windows framed by arching metal hoops resembling mammoth fans or giant eagle wings. Its trippy, aeronautic design gives one the impression that it could rise from the baking asphalt at any moment and blast off into the atmosphere. Much like the rest of the city of Orlando, it has a whimsical, enchanting feel, as if its primary reason for existence is to divert reflection away from the monotony of daily life and transform ordinary thoughts into generators of fabricated magic. This, of course, makes it an ideal setting for the "Night of Reciprocal Power," the colossal conference dreamt up by my mother to end her spectacular tour.

As I step outside the heat whooshes out at me, like opening the door to a broiling oven. It's late July, no doubt the worst time to visit the Sunshine State. I'm out back, huddled beneath the loading dock doors, lighting a smoke, nursing a painful longing for Sasha, when a crack of thunder splits the sky and a gush of angry rain comes dumping down. Before I can react it turns my cigarette to a wet blob. I toss it to the side, light another. Even Sasha, bless her, would forgive me this small transgression. If ever there was a time to allow yourself a little "cheat day" cigarette, it's after a phone call from your sobbing girlfriend telling you an old companion just had his throat sliced in prison by the head of the Aryan Brotherhood. Imagine. This Black guy who Sasha knows murders another Black man, then barely lives through the night, only to get put inside a prison where a deranged white man kills him anyway. This sort of thing goes on all the time with all kinds of individuals, and not a one of them is the root cause of the other's misery. It doesn't make any sense. What a mad and mixed up world... Anyway, it's over with now, right? What can you do? I knew the guy a bit, I guess, enough to be shaken up, and so knowing the little that I know about him it's not that I'm necessarily shocked by these events, but that doesn't make it any less poignant. The hostility I'm expressing now, I know, deep inside, is masking a real heartache I have about all the senselessness in the world. I'm a downright powder keg of emotions at the moment. Like I said, I'm smoking the hell out of this cigarette. This cigarette is getting burnt clear down to the filter. I might smoke the fucking filter.

The parking lot is swamped. Thirty minutes before show time and stragglers are still pushing in, praying for the serenity of one last spot. The possibility of defeat is setting in, becoming palpable. I see it happening, watch the ugly awareness mount like an ocean wave. The annoyance reaches its crest, then crashes down, manifesting itself in human frailty—raised fists, blaring horns, close encounters with mad, swerving drivers. Irony has arrived, and it can drive stick-shift. Here it comes, a high-strung mob threatening harm and discord at a rally for low-bar peace and order.

"Move your fat ass!" A doughy woman shouts from the window of her maroon hatchback, oblivious to her own self-mockery. "Moooooooooove!" she cows, her piercing voice swallowed by her own shrieking horn. On the bottom right side of her bumper there is a sticker, a small white square outlined in black.

"Get out of my way!" It's a caveman's holler. That's what it sounds like, at least, some Neanderthal moan. I can't see exactly where this voice is coming from, but it's sluggish and booming.

"Get out of *my* way," another baritone voice responds, followed by more horns and screeching tires. The cycle renews, repeats—"*my way!*" *horn, tires,* "*my way!*" *horn, tires…* The cumulative effect is terrible. At this frequency, almost all of the cars start looking the same. About every third one, I'm noticing, has a sticker on its bumper, a small white square, like a patch. It's a perfect white box, bright and clean, with some sort of unseen rays that seem to be sucking the viewer's eye straight into the center…

Shit. The rain is not letting up. If anything, it has the audacity to come on harder. Here's the thing; I'm virtually useless in situations like these. Instances like this are what have caused some people to label me a real doomsdayer. Tense, frenetic moments like these bring out my batty side. Truth is, in extreme cases, I start feeling like I am actually *involved* in whatever fracas is happening, like I'm in the middle of it. I mean, I could be thousands of miles away from some sort of random devastation in another country, a typhoon for example, and feel faint, claim damages, any insane thing! I've done it before.

This is all for comparison's sake. Because right now, my fear is that neither the repetitive argument in the lot nor the rain will ever end. We'll all just be gobbled up in some raging current, carried away, screaming insults, clawing one another for strongholds, until every last one of us drowns like the cockamamie mortals we all are. My heart thrashes against my chest. I'm taking puff after puff of my cigarette, like I'm trying to woof the whole damn thing down my throat when…

"Aaaaaaaaa!"

A screeching woman comes bolting out the side door. She is bent low, tenting her spindly hands over her head like some surreal umbrella. In a matter of seconds she serpentines the jammed cars, bounds for the safety of a shiny luxury car parked in the closest spot to the entrance. She attracts quite a commotion. Immediately, all the manic attention and venom spilling from the impatient motorists funnels toward her. She represents a possible evacuation, a vacancy, an escape from their unseemly frustrations. I move closer against the edge of the landing, squinting and wriggling about for a closer look. This woman, she's berserk. Even from my obstructed vantage point I can tell. I'm suddenly caught up in it against my will, flotsam in this odd but unstoppable momentum. It's nearly impossible to see through the downpour, like trying to look through filmy, double-paned glass.

The woman is fumbling with the lock on the car, jerking the handle.

She is losing it, screaming. "Aaaaaaaaaa!" Her keys slap against the door, little tinkling chimes ringing out above the chaos. As the door flies open I see the emblem of a jaguar leaping across the dark green paneling. And that's when I put it together. That's our rental car!

For the first time I notice that the woman is wearing a familiar scarf around her hair, red and white with black Chinese characters scribbled on top. And just as she manages to wrench open the door, she turns, and I see the big dark glasses purchased at the drugstore yesterday afternoon, meant to complete her disguise.

"Mom!" I yell. I cup my hands over my mouth and scream as loud as I can. "Maaaawwwww!" But the hermetic door swings shut behind her, the rain pummels the blacktop, the horns fill the swirling air and the pleas from the disgruntled crowd, just as I was afraid, drown out anything or anyone worth hearing.

In Death, Ronald (1992)

My mother's father, the self-proclaimed Korean War hero and valiant, beer-bellied entrepreneur, Mr. Ronald Patrick Blaine, died a week ago of what can either be called heart failure or death by a thousand grunts. My foggy recollection consists mainly of him knocking drunkenly about his Hickory Hills property, elbowing people out of his way in the kitchen or living room… the front yard. His boozy reach knew no prejudice, most especially for poor Grandma Shirley. What he was in a hurry to locate or latch onto in his clunky meandering, aside from a whiskey bottle, was always unclear. I cannot comprehend the oldfangled cliché of masculinity that he represents, not only because of my young age but because, though we lived less than an hour away, I only met him a few times in my life.

Grandpa Ronald, either bending to fit the clichés laid out for him or the other way around, looked precisely how one might imagine—bald, beefy, furrowed and liver spotted… In any case, other than the fact that he was obviously miserable and hard-hearted, he left no great impression on me. There are millions of sour old men like him out knocking about, suburban misanthropes ground down by manual labor and a gnawing feeling that they never lived up to the virile conquerors they expected themselves to be. I suppose it is that distorted vision for which he was forever grasping after.

His burial this afternoon, as if to conform to my villainous perception, comes with an accompaniment of fury and grief. Perhaps out of regular parental concern or maybe as a means of preventive maintenance, father positions me in one of the far back rows of mourners, maybe twenty or thirty feet from the casket. At any rate, perceptive children will not be denied access to disturbing or arousing sights. They have tiptoes designed to lift a small, audacious body high enough above adult shoulders to glimpse a rabid mother kicking and stomping at the grave. They see a frazzled, weary father clutching their mother's waist and tugging her away from the hole as she spits into it, crying and cursing.

Further, if you are both a budding voyeur and a timid, frightened child attempting to calm his two year old sister, Lindy, in the back of the car during the ride home, you have a problem. This is a preposterous undertaking for a kindergartener. Add to this a desire to remain obedient and mild in a sad attempt to alleviate the stress and pressure you know your parents are under, and you begin to see. The situation is unworkable in every way. There is no option to talk things out or express troubling emotions; not with the two unstable adults riding up front. Even at this young age you have enough experience trying to navigate that precarious route. So what you do, as all conscientious children from a broken home know, is you put the needling worry away in some brittle corner of your mind where all distressing items or concerns belong.

On the drive home Mom and Dad stare straight out the windshield, hands intertwined atop the center console. It is not often that their connection shines through, but in times like these, usually when one of them is in physical or emotional pain, a tenderness arises, and it becomes a little clearer as to why they married. Both of them, as if groomed to do so, come alive when they are comforting the afflicted. Their bond is one of mutual mercy rather than love, each performing better when the other is at their lowest. The funny thing, from my vantage point, is that as I sit in the back of our beat up Datsun, I'm thinking that the most likely cause of my mother's outburst was the upsetting fact that dead Grandpa Ronald probably always wanted a boy, and made no effort to hide his dissatisfaction when she was born, even going as far as to call her Roberta, a pathetic bargain struck with a wife who refused to name her only daughter Robert.

The Final Remains (1992)

My father, Neil Gregory Blaine, to his credit, waits about three weeks after the funeral to offer his final petition for relief before making his getaway. Nowhere in America is the excess of the early 1990s more pronounced than in our otherwise banal apartment. Throughout the first half of the decade our apartment is a dumping ground for Mom's torment. This era of my mother's hoarding should come with its own index of damages caused. Throughout these tumultuous years our floors stay perpetually littered in a smattering of cookie tins, cardboard boxes, clothes hangers and Mason jars. At night, trying to reach his bedroom, Dad crawls over piles of refuse like some kind of rabid homeless person climbing over soiled bodies. It's awful to watch him go, teetering and wobbling, falling onto sharp objects or stepping on barbed edges.

"Son of a whore!" he shouts. He is a very creative swearer. His all-time favorite is, "Mercy stroke!" or for added effect, "Fucking mercy stroke!" Which means please, dear Lord, finish me off, release me, for I can't stand one more second of this misery. Often he goes to bed with bloody feet, gashed knuckles or split kneecaps. It's unbearable.

Meanwhile, in a desperate attempt to keep mother's abhorrent habits from encroaching on my own personal space, I have become a junior inventor of sorts. What I do is I take a long plank of wood that I found in the alley behind our house, and I prop it against my door so that when she opens it the board comes sliding down and bonks her on the hip. It's unclear if she ever takes the measure as anything other than a juvenile attempt at slapstick.

One way or another, Dad makes it known that if they have any hope of salvaging their last-legged marriage, they will need to have a yard sale to rid themselves of the debris currently vandalizing the house. It is no longer acceptable, he makes it clear, for him to come home from work and find another heap of garbage adding to his already sullied life. So he comes home yesterday, after a long shift at the skinners, and he's finally had enough. Nothing's changed. He says, "I can't even make my God-damned-son-of-a-twisted-monkey-tit way to my own hairy-bastard bathroom!" Or something like that. *Fucking mercy stroke.*

Mom caves, and on the next sunny Saturday morning, Dad, along with my help, drags what amounts to about twenty trash bags full of random objects out onto the lawn and sets up shop. For better or worse, Mom balks on assisting with both the transporting and arranging of the belongings. It's probably for the better. For the time being she has locked herself in the bedroom and refuses to come out. It is likely that she is writing in her journal. She is always writing things down. In the back of her closet, a stack of filled notebooks a foot tall are tied together with large rubber bands, an implied promise that the contents never be unsealed. I am aware that whatever she is doing in there, whatever is in those journals, involves some sort of deep reckoning and private agony, but investigating or inquiring further is not an option. Just one look at my father's stony, intolerant demeanor is evidence of that. I watch as he rips her daffy little trinkets out of the bag and stamps them down hard on the tables, like stabbing holes on top.

We live in the Albany Park neighborhood near the Chicago River. It's a pretty bleak apartment—one bath, two beds, three drafty windows and four million summer born mosquitos. Dad nicknamed it the "Mite Bite Motel." It is a particular blow that the same murky river that offers us a scenic view, a small comfort, also brings us disquiet and infestation. But despite our less than appetizing living quarters, the surrounding area isn't altogether unpleasant. The streets are clean by city standards; the other renters are polite and affluent, and the majority of the owners in the community are politically conscious, which means plenty of flower beds and organic vegetable gardens to boost resale values.

We erect our little marketplace on the corner of Rockwell Street, which has a quaint view of the Montrose Bridge to the west. However, for reparations no doubt, in the universe's comical attempt to always find balance, our backdrop is the emergency room entrance to Kindred Hospital; a stark area forever clogged with expectant gurneys waiting just outside its ominous glass doors. Can't have everything. Anyway, a few card tables, some folding chairs, one or two makeshift clothing racks, and we have ourselves a little emporium. It really is a fine day. The sun flickers across the water, twinkling through trees, dappling the sidewalks. The birds, though nothing more than the Chicago variety of warblers or street pigeons, are singing their chipper songs. Good, hearty looking parents stride by with their handsome young brood, smiles and milkshakes all around… There is the occasional urgent bleating of a siren or the wails of Lindy's infant crying, but we have made a silent pact to not let it ruin this day of purging.

Things go well from the start. Right off the bat a tall, bubbly woman buys not only the toaster oven but a blender as well. Following that, a hefty man, listening to his Walkman and perspiring through his sweatshirt, purchases both of the workout machines Mom has been saving in the original boxes for over a year!

Dad's ecstatic! In only a little over an hour we've made almost two hundred dollars. I honestly don't think I've ever seen him in better spirits. He comes alive. It is not too bold to call what he is on today a "rampage." Whisking Lindy up out of her stroller in some foreign maneuver he's never performed before, he smacks a wet kiss on her cheek. He tosses her in the air, catching her giggling, drooling body as it plummets back down. He dances her about the streets, waltzing between cars, swooping around pedestrians. It's straight out a Broadway musical!

In a few moments he comes whirling back, gracefully transferring baby Lindy into my arms mid-spin. Unburdened, he stands up straight and proud, a puppet with its strings pulled tight, and pats me on the head. There is a stench blowing in from the marshy banks of the river, a sort of briny, fecal funk. Lindy smells it too. She wrinkles up her eyes and nose, nuzzles her head into my armpit for relief. Dad is impervious.

"Watch this," he says. He's swishing his tongue around, making a show of it, the way a dog licks its chops. "Yoo-hoo, Miss!"

I hike Lindy up on my waist, watch our father scamper out onto the curb, waving like someone hailing a taxi. This open enthusiasm, the jauntiness, is truly an odd sight.

"You," he hollers. "Yes, you." A lank, shapely woman in high shorts and a wide-brimmed hat comes to a stop on the sidewalk. She puts a hand to her chest. The hat bobs forward on her head. That hat! It is like Saturn around her blushing face.

"Me?" she says, flashing an alluring pair of blue eyes and an easy grin. Her long blond hair flows from the hat, flouncing against her narrow spine.

"Listen," Dad says, "if I may…" He sort of bows, beckoning her closer as he asks permission to proceed at the same time.

The woman laughs. "Yes, there it is, you have a lovely smile! Now, I can only guess that you are the sole caretaker of your house. You do all the chores, the cooking and laundry, the dusting and dishes, but your least favorite task is the floors, am I right?"

She giggles. "You're not wrong," she says.

"I knew it!" Dad shouts, nearly leaping with excitement. "Now, I am the last person to suggest that you should buy yourself a present that would only add to your burdens, but what if I told you that you could purchase something today that would make your inevitable duties less of a strain?"

"Tell me more," she says, humoring him. She breezes toward our display, her movements smooth and elegant.

"This," Dad says, "this right here is the Kirby 2000." He holds the contraption aloft, presenting it like a diamond ring. "This is the sleekest, fastest, most streamlined vacuum on the market today! And I say, I say, that if you are going to have to clean the damn floors anyway, you may as well do it with less effort and more style! Am I right?"

Dad's going for it, throwing all of his blue collar, Midwestern charm into it. The fact that this woman is well beyond his reach, seems suddenly inconsequential. We are all caught up in the pageantry, pretending not to notice his shortcomings. For example, how twenty years of butcher work in a Peoria packing plant has lent his skin a sort of gray, ashy quality. How, like many suitable butchers, he is hairy in all the wrong places—not quite enough up top, too much on the arms, neck and back. Nobody would trust a skinny man with a bone saw, he told me once. However, he has not gone all the way to pot yet at age forty-two. There is still a firm foundation of earned muscle waiting to be uncovered by a run of sobriety or a spate of increased exercise. For now though, through the blend of softer fibers and the fur of neglect, he has taken on the characteristics of an out of shape bear. Needless to say, that prior to this moment, it would have been impossible to conceive of him as the person he is currently impersonating, this fawning, flirtatious hambone.

In the end, he wooed the money right out of the beautiful big-hatted woman. He somehow manages to make the transaction seem inevitable, as if the vacuum has been meant for her always. The lady is so intoxicated with giddiness and the uplifting effects of father's dalliances that I half believe she is going to reach out and slap him on the ass as she wheels the contraption away down the street.

Now he is positively riding a high like never before. He flicks the money out of the shoebox and begins counting it up. From time to time he pauses, taking a moment to high-five me or Lindy or even the blank air for no reason at all. He hums something… what is it? It's melodic but not… rock-n-roll opera style… Meatloaf! It's Meatloaf's "I Would Do Anything For Love." Yes, he is immensely caught up in his own joyous revelry, which is exactly what makes Mom's precipitous appearance all the more jarring…

When I first catch sight of her, she's standing a few feet in front of the main entrance looking a little comatose. She's sort of bent over, all rumpled and limp, swaying on buckled knees. I've always thought of my mother as being very tall, but I realize now for the first time that it must be at least partly because of the many layers of clothing she always wears, even in the summer time. It is as if she's armoring herself against something, taking cover. Despite her buffering attempts, she is still a pretty woman with certain undeniable features; things like her naturally rosy complexion or her firm, resilient physique. And friends and relatives still go out of their way, perhaps as a conscious bolstering attempt, to comment on her luck at having what many consider an "ample" upper body. But there she is, a few paces beyond Dad and his jittery, offbeat dancing, looking willfully unaware, just kind of rocking there, letting the sidewalk hold her up.

"I would do anything for love, but I won't do that," Dad sings, woefully trying to reach Meatloaf's operatic range. Looking up at me, he stops. It's abrupt and clashing, a record scratch that threatens to cancel out all of the great music he's made today. He's noticed my eyes fixed on something behind him. He spins around, trailing my gaze.

"Oh!" he says, with a mix of fright and delight. "Hello, dear." He wafts a stack of bills in the air, wags his tongue.

Mom slouches there with her puffy eyes, listing and blinking, and she says, "I think I'm going to go for a walk."

"All right," Dad says, "Enjoy the splendid day. When you get back we can construct our pillars of gold, and then maybe go out for an extravagant dinner." He stands aside then, gallantly, allowing Mom to step gawkily around him, hands resting in pockets, head down, sniffling. And as she passes, he smiles at her with what can only be considered a genuine fondness. Oh, that look. It lingers...

Dad's buoyancy is still intact when approximately thirty minutes later we spot Mom returning, crossing over the bridge, approaching slowly, morosely. And as she gets closer, Dad stands up from his lawn chair. He rises shakily and crooked, gasping and gulping for air.

"No," he says. "Oh no." He staggers up toward the corner of the street, already panting. "No, no, no, no..." he whispers.

And there is Mom. She comes teetering across the arch, dragging a roll of carpet in one arm and cradling what looks to be a pile of old magazines, picture frames and Tupperware in the other.

Dad pauses, snaps around to look at me. There is a mixture of hysteria and rage in his eyes. There is a look that says, "This can't be happening. Son, help me. Tell me that I'm dreaming." He stumbles back to the lawn chair and plops down. "She... she went to the other yard sale up the street," he says. He gazes up at me, begging me to tell him that he is mistaken, pleading with me. He actually reaches up, clutches my shirt in his fist.

What can I do? I nod my head.

"No," he says. He scrambles back to his feet, frantic, unscrewed. I pick Lindy back up from the stroller where she has been napping. I cling to her, press her tight against my chest. Dad is now spinning in circles, desperately trying to decide what he is going to do next. I watch him consider running, then see him stop, yank at his hair, open his mouth and do a silent scream. When his jaw gets tired he comes charging at one of the tables. I hold Lindy, leap back. We look on as he curls both hands under the table, bends his knees, using textbook form. I cover Lindy's ears, wait for the crash of coins, of bins and lamps, silverware and crock pots. He growls. He's growling. He lifts the table maybe an inch off the ground then, perhaps feeling a plunge in his heart rate or waking from his fever, lets it drop back into place. He turns one last time to watch his wife, the catalyst for all his agitation, waddling across the bridge.

"JesusMotherFuckingChrist!" he hollers. He then pivots, soldier-like in his precision, shakes his head, and takes off. I observe his retreat as long as I can, all the way until he is maybe fifty yards straight north, and then I watch him hinge to the right, floundering east, out of sight. There is no particular anger or animosity left to his strides, just a deadened, passionless shuffle that I know won't end until he is sure everything, all of the delirium he's been feeling, the foolish ardor and zeal, has been extinguished for good.

Mercedes Benson (2006)

It's not her real name, but according to her it sounds like a "sex bomb" rumbling from the speakers as she takes the stage. That's what she tells me when I ask her if her Christian name was actually the make and model of a luxury car. I'm a "cutie pie" for asking, she says, but don't I "know nothing about the seedier side of stripping?" She gives me a prolonged, shattering wink of her eye, one that momentarily snaps me out of whatever spell I've been under for the past few hours. It's a clever, facetious gesture, something designed to tip me off. She's toying with me, playing a game. But I don't care. She can toy with me all she wants. I apologize for my ignorance, but offer a suggestion. Maybe, since we're playing interview and everything, she wouldn't mind telling me a story? I need something to take my mind off of all this heat and pressure.

"All right," Mercedes says, jumping right in. I like her style. She's a "Jump Right In" type of girl. She plunks her boots onto my crotch, the stabbing end of her heels mincing my privates. The pain is searing, but somehow I know that mentioning it will be the worst possible thing if I want her to like me, if I am to keep up this charade. "I had this one night," she says, unbuttoning the top clasp on her straining collar. She's settling in now, removing sympathetic bricks from whatever wall she's accustomed to building in these situations. Whether or not it's true, it feels as if she's doing it especially just for me. Despite everything one might assume about someone like Mercedes, there is a real depth and sincerity coming through. I don't mean that in an insulting way. It's not her fault. It's hard to gauge a woman's potential acumen when the only thing filling your mind is the recent memory of booming music pounding from the speakers and the two naked, arrowed breasts being squeezed up against your forehead. It's too dark and disorienting in a place like that to get a clear picture as someone as a whole human being. That sounds awful. What I'm trying to say is that Mercedes seems like she has the type of guile and genuineness that people can't just put on for show, and it's turning me on almost more than her heaving chest and sweet peach perfume.

"I was having one of those nights where everything just sort of vanishes except you and the pole. I was in the zone," she says, and there's the sincerity in her eyes; just glistening there all dewy and vibrant without even trying. It's partly because she takes her time. She has a way of losing herself in a story that makes you want to get lost with her. "Five dollar bills, tens, then hundreds, all of it showering down."

We are at a diner, far from the blazing, throbbing club we just left. The difference between west Lawrence and east Fullerton Avenues are lunar in scope. We leave the gritty ethnic crowd of Albany—hardheads, sharps and Mexicans—for the pallid, standard English set—college youths of Lincoln Park with pompous nicknames like Ted and Trixie. I should be ashamed of myself for bringing a girl like her to a place like this, but what do I know? She needs a pick me up, she says. So okay, no problem, I say. I need a place that communicates a certain level of class and panache… but this is not it. This is… Well, what chance did I have? Who would ever imagine that a lady like Mercedes, such as she is, would agree to go to a second location with a guy like me? There's no chance. None. And yet she doesn't even seem to notice. She might as well be inside her home-base bar in her own neighborhood with a close friend. That's what's so great about her. She's... of the earth?

Whatever, with any luck, so my current line of thinking goes anyway, the caffeine will carry us to a bar next and then... who knows what. I'm not trying to be blithe. I really wouldn't know what to do next. But tonight, for now anyway, I have a feeling that I'll figure it out. It's her. She brings something out of me, bravado, bluster... idiocy. Nobody knows we're together, which is horrifying and titillating at once. Nothing about this situation is in any way part of my normal manner of operation. It's Jerry's fault. Or I have Jerry to thank. Who knows. See, Jerry, my future U of I classmate, creates stunning replicas of state ID cards. They feature real photos paired with aliases he concocts for added effect. Mine reads: "Flynn Piccard," which always reminds me of some sort of World War I fighter pilot. Anyway, it's how I was allowed entrance into the "dance club" where Mercedes makes her living. It's the first I've used it, and the overwhelming success has resulted in a dizziness that is hard to conceal. I do my best. I fold my arms across my chest, try to channel whatever twenty-two year old Flynn-ness might look like.

"Toward the end of my show I start snatching up all the cash and sticking it in my g-string like usual, you know, only every time I turn around it falls out," she continues. "I tuck a five spot up against my right thigh and one second later it's gone. I slip a hundo down my backside and poof! Disappears in no time and reappears on the stage. Now, what the fuck! I'm thinking"

She removes her boots, and I realize I've been holding my breath the whole time. It's a miracle I don't pass out. I could have set a world record for all I know. Or died. I could have died, I suppose. It's frightening, but if everything continues as planned, I remind myself, then it will all have been worth it. Her eyeliner runs. It looks like mud slipping down her puffy jaw line. Then she starts smoking. I close my eyes. I can't watch for some reason, too real. A comingling image floats through my mind, an iceberg splintering loose, creaking, drifting away in the current.

"I go back to the dressing room," she proceeds, "and I have all the bills cradled in my arms, 'cause they wouldn't behave you know, and they're sticking out all over the place. I doubt I got 'em all, but I'm losing my mind and so I don't care. I think Jay sees me cursing and snorting as I dump it on the table, but I guess he doesn't. Jay's the club manager. He's this kind of guy who wears knock-off Ray Bans indoors, and I hate him because he somehow pulls it off. I could tell you a million stories about Jay, and I probably will if you end up sticking around. Anyway, he's walking around back there and I say, 'Jay, I can't hold onto my money,' and he tells me, he says, 'try burying it in your backyard,' because of course he doesn't have a fucking clue what I'm talking about, and I ask him what the hell he's talking about, and he just says it again. He repeats it. Something about sacrifice and bountiful returns or some shit. Then he leaves. Courtney comes in, and…"

"Wait. Is that her real name?" I ask.

She sighs, continues. "Courtney comes in, and I tell her the same thing, I can't hold onto my money, and she says come here. She's had the same problem before. She takes a wad of chewing gum out of her mouth and mashes it on my waist. It looks like a birthmark only it's banana-yellow and wrinkly. She picks up one of my bills and presses it there and voila! It stays. 'Hey, there we go, now. Lookie here,' I say. And I go over to the mirror and twirl around a few times and sure enough it stays put. 'Fucking, men,' I tell her, and she shrugs and says, 'why don't you just say, fucking fuck?' And she's poker-faced, which makes it even better. She smiles and struts out like nothing."

"Courtney said this?"

"Courtney."

The whole place smells and sounds like sizzling bacon grease. I imagine seeing all of the oil and grime and booze sloshing around deep inside the bowels of all the drunk patrons, a flooded junkyard of rubbish. Which of them will end up occupying the waiting paddy wagon parked outside on the curb? I saw it out there earlier and knew right away. Similar to a gun appearing in the first act of a play, if a police vehicle shows up outside an establishment at the beginning of the evening, it must be filled by the end of the night. Punishment must be levied.

I open my eyes. It's a little unexpected, but she's very pretty in a classic sort of way, and nobody would ever suspect a thing if not for her spiked heels and the cigarette she insists on holding like a Pocket Ruger. There's a smooth, waxy mat to her chocolate colored skin. Cutting through the smoke is that peach perfume that coats her neckline and makes me want to bury my face in her chest. Her smile is open, lots of teeth, and giddy, like she's always on the verge of breaking out into full laughter. It's too much. I can't go through with it. She sees it in me, the feeble hesitation and uncertainty. I can see she's seeing it. A bit of smoke gets in her eyes and as she waves it away it wafts up her nose and she starts coughing. The fit lasts several eye-watering seconds, and as it winds down she composes herself by putting out the rest of the cigarette, which is only half gone, in the ashtray.

"You used a fake ID," she says, letting some of the trapped laughter and coughing spill out.

The way she looks at me with both condemnation and arousal drives me into some kind of mania. There's a napkin in front of me, and I grab it and start playing with the edges of it, folding them up, mashing them back down again. On the corner of the table there's a small basket of crayons for little kids to draw with, and all of a sudden, when I look over at it, my vision goes all blurry and swirly. Each of the individual colors start morphing together into one blob, and I can't seem to separate them in my mind. To see if I can straighten things out, I reach for one of the crayons in the basket, but I'm not sure if I ever actually make contact with any one of them in particular. It feels like I'm trying for a quite a while, but time is starting to melt together on me just like the crayons.

I excuse myself to the bathroom and vomit. I'm not sure if it's the shame or pain or nervousness over what I've just done. I can't figure anything out. Is she into me or just acting out some role? Why did I think I could do this? Take a stripper out to eat? Is that even a real thing that happens? Not to me. Not to Clayton Blaine. Maybe to Flynn Piccard. Who the fuck is Flynn Piccard? I'm out of my mind. I've spent the entire summer trying to cultivate this new persona. I've tried channeling this sort of primal, king of the jungle type instinct. Have I become the lion I've so consciously tried to imitate? Or can she see right through me? Maybe she knows I'm only pretending, and she's pretending back, playing some perverted game of tennis or chicken. I try not to look at myself in the mirror when I wash my hands. I'm worried I might not be able to retain the illusion I've spent the past three months constructing. Afraid the mane I've been picturing around my flabby jaw-line will look more like a beard of fleas.

It's hard to say how long I've been gone, but when I come back out, Mercedes is missing. The ashtray still holds the half crushed cigarette with her lipstick on the end, and if not for all the after-hour kids with their cold eggs, popped collars and greasy faces ogling me, I'd stick it right in my mouth. Haven't they ever seen a scrawny white guy in a diner with a buxom black chick before? I should freak them out. I should put the whole cigarette in my mouth, chew it up, gulp it down. I should, just to get a small taste of her cherry lipstick, to get something of her inside of me. To make all the bleached-up girls gasp and squirm. I get as far as picking up the butt and spreading my lips. My tongue flicks out, all lizard lappy and ostentatious…

Aw, Christ. What's gotten into me? I know better. I should know better. Flynn would know better.

Back and Smelling of Pig's Blood: Part I (1994)

Early Saturday morning my dream takes a sharp left turn, and a grieving hound appears, howling at the moon. Lord knows what I'd been dreaming of before, but all at once I'm looking up at a gray wolf perched on a mountain top, head back, wailing like there's no tomorrow. It grows louder and louder, layered over sounds of whirring fans and melodious cries from somewhere down below. As I open my eyes and sit up, things come into focus. It's Mom. Mom is the wolf. I rub my eyes, roll out of bed. The fan noise morphs into the vacuum cleaner purring across the living room floor. The crying down below? Vanessa Williams' mournful voice piping out of the speakers, singing about "The Colors of The Wind." I open the door, catch the plank before it falls, and for an instant, everything makes sense.

Out in the living room, Mom's really deep into a zone. She's got her eyes closed as she saunters to the slow but flourishing beat. "Have you ever heard the wolf cry to the blue corn moon!" she bellows. The vacuum rolls swiftly across the rug, whizzing away. Mom shimmies back and forth, gliding from baseboard to hallway. Vanessa's vocal chords battle the vacuum's roar for supremacy as Mom fights for her own clarity over Vanessa's trilling. It's a cacophonous dance.

As I come around the corner I can hardly believe my eyes. What was just the night before a series of floors and pathways crammed tight with refuse, is now an open expanse of clean lines and unveiled surfaces. I am struck, startled by the greenness of the carpet. I have completely forgotten about the color beneath all of the casings and vessels and other dross that had acted as coats of gaudy paint for so many years. For a few seconds, I just stand there and catch my breath. It's too much to take in all in at once.

"The rainstorm and the river are my brothers. The heron and the otter are my friends," she sings.

It's quite an eye-full. The way she's bounding about, smiling and whisking, is having a sort of tingly, woozy effect on me. I gather myself to approach. She hasn't seen me yet, and I want to be very careful not to scare her. "And we are all connected to each other. In a circle, in a hoop that never ends," she continues, rising on her toes, prancing to the side. I step closer, slowly. I wave my hand out in front of her, jangle it there, sort of like jazz hands. Jazz hands are the least alarming thing, I figure. She makes a half little start at first, but then perks right up and gives me a nice grin. She props the vacuum up straight and taps the off switch with her foot.

"Good morning!" she says, still using her singing voice.

"Good mor…" I begin, but stop. My ears are ringing. "Can we turn the radio down?" I say.

"It looks good, doesn't it?" she responds.

"The radio!" I repeat.

"Decided that I needed to downsize, clean up my act!"

I walk over and hit the power button on the stereo. The song turns to sonic vapor, and in its wake an ear-buzzing reticence begins to bloom.

"Oh!" she squeals.

"I couldn't talk to you like that," I say.

She's wearing a pair of what look like my father's old sweatpants. They bag out around her thighs like a parachute. On top she wears a thin white T-shirt with holes dotting the armpits and hem. Her hair's tied up in some type of oriental bandana that I've never seen before. She leans forward on the handle of the vacuum. "This is my new style," she says, patting the top of her head, "hobo monk."

"What's gotten into you?" I ask.

"It's really what's gotten out," she says. "Last night I couldn't get to sleep. I saw this segment on Sixty Minutes right before bed. There's this little town in Kentucky. Beattyville it was called. Beatty, like it had the stuffing beat out of it, you know? Apt name. Anyway, the place was a disaster, barely enough residents or jobs to keep the town from sliding off the map." She tilts her head to the side, and I watch a far off glaze come into her eyes, like she's looking past me or through me to some other dimension. I glance over my shoulder to see if there is someone behind me, but no one's there. "I thought to myself, Roberta, you have enough clothing and food and sundries for every sad sack in that whole village." She pauses, lowers her head, shakes it back and forth. A few droplets of sweat come splashing off her forehead. Her face is red and swollen around the mouth. I wonder for the first time if maybe she's sick. Is there an illness that causes people to ferociously clean up messes?

"You realized something," I say, brightening. "That's great, Mom." I'm proud of her.

"I realized, it's all about materialism. I've been too greedy," she says, "that's my problem. If I just start giving all this crap away to the Salvation Army, I'll feel… everything will feel better."

I take a deep breath, try making my voice sound cutesy and pleading the way I've seen it work sometimes on old cartoons. "Everything?" I say. "Are you sure?" Something isn't adding up. At age seven I'm only beginning to feel my way through complicated thinking, but I have a budding intuition that solutions to problems are never as easy as they first seem. It's just a little prickle of concern, the way you might feel if the driver you are travelling with takes a turn that you are almost certain is the wrong direction, but you are too timid to say anything.

"It's all in the way you look at things. You have the power to choose," she says. She walks over to the stereo and turns the power back on. "Removal is my recovery. Starting tomorrow, after all this junk is swept away," she points down at some lint and dirt waiting by the dustpan, "I'll be a different person. I've decided."

"Decided?" I ask. "How did you decide? You talked it over with someone?" I wish she had asked me what her biggest problem was. I could have helped…

She turns the volume up even higher. The song is coming to an end. Mom closes her eyes again, sinks into the music. "You can paint with all the colors of the wind."

It's at this precise moment, at the final note, that I catch sight of the door behind her. It's… moving. The doorknob twitches, the frame rattles. Then, with great horror, I observe the door, like something out of a nightmare, come creaking open. Mom jerks up at me as I suck in a chilling gulp. In reaction to the dread she reads on my face, she turns around also, and we both watch in terror as Dad comes snorting through the door draped in his white butcher apron. The front panels are splattered in ripe blood. The collar is the only thing left white. There's a big pool of crimson on the left front pocket in the shape of Texas. It makes me wonder if there's a pig's heart still beating inside.

He enters as if he has not been gone for two years, like he'd just stepped out a minute or two earlier and forgotten to grab his lunch box. A gush of raw smells sail in behind him, acrid pork fluids, mucus and warm whiskey that's stewed too long in an unbrushed mouth or open pores. At the end of his pink fingers dangle the old set of key rings he'd never returned. Locks are the type of details people never think about until someone is standing inside their door covered in gore.

The color vanishes from Mom's face like it's running for cover. The red evaporates as if Dad has yanked up the mechanism acting as the plug to her drain. She flails back against the wall, screams. It's a herky, sustained cry with peaks and valleys but no end. At some point I realize that it has gone on for so long that it's lost its impact. Then Dad gently puts the keys on the table inside the door and clears his throat. It's a simple, proper ending, a fitting family portrayal. As with all seismic happenings throughout Blaine history, the reaction, inconceivably, is worse than the original incident. As if to prove the point, Lindy flings herself awake, echoing Mom's howl with her own mighty cry before even knowing why.

Something's Gotten Into Lindy (1995)

Determined to preserve Dad's favor, Mom spends a long stretch of time cultivating a sort of traditional, deferential flair for domestic living. The benefits include a cleaner house, less arguing and more routine. The negatives can be described as a gradual dulling of sensitivities and conscientiousness. This latter effect could perhaps best be exemplified by her lack of concern regarding Lindy's descent into a sort of perverted, delirious sexuality.

Several nights, most often either right before bed or a few minutes prior to Dad taking off for one of his scattered bar runs, Lindy performs what can only be defined as her masturbation ritual. Straddling the back of the sofa, both hands planted between her thighs like a child gymnast, Lindy slides her pelvis back and forth across the cushion, moaning and giggling. Though I am nowhere near old enough to comprehend the specificities of the act, I can only gather that if the response it produces is anywhere as unnatural as it looks, then it can't be normal. Eyes rolling back, tongue out, Lindy completes her gambit with a great gushing of squeals and shutters. How neither Mom nor Dad ever notice or fret over any of it is far beyond me; especially because it is clear that the main reason she is engaging in the conduct is to capture their attention in the first place.

Following her maneuvers, she lies flat on her stomach, splayed out over the backrest with a satisfied air. She folds her legs up behind her, crosses her ankles. She leans in, props her chin in her palm. While I gaze from the chair across the room, stupefied by my complete juvenile ineptitude, Mom rounds up toys from the floor or washes dishes. I see that it is Dad who is her target. She makes it clear, slithering up behind him and waiting for a reaction, anything. But Dad refuses to remove his focus from the television screen. He sits there, straight-backed and conked from work, legs stretched out on the coffee table. To his left, a tall boy of Pabst Blue Ribbon, and on his right an ashtray littered with cigarette butts. He alternates between the two, slurping and puffing until gradually, like the rest of him, each withers and dries up. The smoke hangs in a cloud, turning the air muggy and stifling as an old train station.

Lindy rocks forward on her elbows. Her mouth inches from the back of his head, she aims her lips at the side of his cheek and blows into his ear. When that doesn't work she sticks her tongue out, makes a hissing snake noise through her teeth.

"Stop. That tickles," Dad says, swatting her away. His concentration is unshakable. Rarely if ever does he remove his eyes from whatever show he's watching. Sometimes he watches "NYPD Blue" or "Walker, Texas Ranger," often "Chicago Hope" or "Law and Order." He likes shows with a strong moral center, as he puts it, something that makes him feel reassured about the righteous triumph of good over evil in the world.

"Come on Lindy," I say, forcing myself to interrupt the deadlock. The only thing worse than being party to the original spectacle is allowing the fallout to keep lingering.

Pulling her off the couch is no easy task. She clamps her fingers into the soft fabric and bears down. "Nooooooo!" she whines, legs whipping like flames in the breeze.

"Come on," I say, "let's go into your room and play Old Maid." She loves memory games. Still, it is always a long, difficult struggle for release, a grueling physical and mental tug-of-war. There is a look of grit and determination in her eyes that scares me. She is going to win the affection of her father. It is palpable. One can sense the intention, practically touch it. On the outside she is a kicking, screeching dervish, but in her mind's eye, you can tell, she's already accomplished the feat, is already safe and secure in his warm embrace.

When I finally calm her down and get her inside the bedroom, she collapses into a heap on the floor. "I hid my dolly," she tells me. "I put it somewhere, and I can't find it."

"Why did you do that?" I ask.

"I don't know," she says. "I guess I wanted to see if I could do without it, or no…" she says, reconsidering, "I think I wanted to see if I could find something that I'd lost."

"Really?" I ask. "What made you think to do that?"

She sits up, shimmies her back up against the bed frame. "Why won't he play with us?" she asks. "Do you think he knows how?"

"Maybe not," I say. "Maybe he never learned what playing is."

"I think he knows," Lindy says, leaning forward and licking her lips. "I think he's playing a game with us right now."

"No," I say, "I don't think so."

"Yes!" she insists. "He wants us to play hide and go seek."

"Why would he do that?" I ask.

"It's a secret," she whispers, "why else would somebody keep it from us?"

I have to think long and hard about this one, but I don't have time. Lindy bounces up to her feet, races for the door. "Daddy!" she yells, a second wind swirling through her slippery limbs. I lurch up, corralling her around the waist just in time.

"Hold on," I say. "Wait!"

"What?" she says, squirming against my grasp.

"We need to find dolly first."

"Why?" She asks. "Why first?"

"There's an order to things," I say. "You have to figure out one secret at a time. Dolly first." It's astonishing how this explanation comes to me, as if it's been waiting somewhere in the air, just biding time until I need the phrasing for something important. I don't even know if I believe what I'm saying. I don't think I do, but it doesn't matter. The main thing is to get her calmed down as fast as possible, and something makes me think that this tact, describing the benefits of structure or systems of symmetry might do the trick.

"Okay," she says. She stops moving. She tilts to the side, lets her whole body go slack and floppy in my arms. "But I'm not done with this mystery," she sighs.

Taking to the mission right away, she stomps over to her desk and rips open the top drawer. She is so cute, all twig and bones in her long baby blue nightshirt. In her pointed, deliberate movements, one can see a complicated adolescence approaching too fast. Already she is a conundrum, the flighty whims and desires of a child mixed with the pluck and cunning of a foxy adult. In a matter of seconds she has all of the pens, pencils and notebooks out on the floor. In a whoosh of exaltation she snaps her attention toward me, smiling and hopping to her feet. "She's not in here!" she announces, "the little rat baby!" And she spreads her arms like wings, whisking off to the next suspected location.

She swoops round and round, unstoppable and begging to be stopped. Taking a sharp detour, she throws herself onto the bed, bouncing and giggling. She has the same blue, deep-water eyes as Mom and the hale, piped muscles of her father, soft and strong, round and firm at once. Out in the family room the TV makes a flurry of noises, fake popping sounds from a prop gun. I hear Mom creak open the oven door, scrape out a pan from one of the greasy racks. Lindy yawns. She creates a tender portrait of a young girl, lying atop that pink spread with such vernal purity. This image will stay with me. It is this tableau that I will return to should she ever become, as I predict, less pure, more corrupt in the coming years.

For the next hour or longer we go sleuthing around the room, digging under coloring books and coats, climbing on top of shelves and cabinets. I even fashion a fake magnifying glass out of construction paper and a sheet of Saran Wrap. Around nine or ten o'clock, waist deep in a pile of dirty socks and pajamas in the back of her closet, I turn around to let her know I am calling off the search. "I give up," I say, yawning, "I'm beat. It's time for bed." But Lindy is nowhere to be found. "Lindy? Lindy!" I say. I get to my feet, a bit winded and off guard. She's gone. I run to the door, and there, sitting tight up against the stiff outline of her dad's unyielding body on the sofa, is little Lindy. A lamp has been switched on above their heads, a ghostly yellow light glowing atop their mutually tousled hair. It is obvious that she has taken great pains situating herself to mirror his exact posture, nailing his every nuance. She has her small feet stretched out on the coffee table, her hands resting limply in her lap, her head cocked slightly to the side just as he has his, as if this will do it, as if copying his movements might compel him to reveal all of his concealed intentions.

Back and Smelling of Pig's Blood: Part II (1994)

It is Lindy, in all her preschool whimsy, who offers the best reaction to the lunacy laid out before us. Having drunk in as much of this unknown, stinking man's profile as she can, she waddles behind my legs, pops a thumb in her mouth and whispers, "Hamton."

"Shhhhh," I say. I rub the thin baby hairs on top of her head and watch as Dad lumbers around the family room. First he stops at the rug in front of the sofa, lifting it with the toe of his boot. Nodding, he bumbles over to the end table and plucks up the lamp to check underneath. He moves over to the back door in the kitchen, runs a mangled hand up and down the frame, like checking to see if a secret compartment might come flapping open. Drawing the empty hand away, he brings it up to his eyes and blinks. He is expecting to see hair, dust, whole wads of skin and wax, a hollowed out rat carcass. Instead, he looks pleased. A smile blooms on his lips as he shakes with raspy laughter.

Judging from the looks of him ... his ruby colored jaw, the leaden sacks of skin around his chin and neck, he must have gained at least twenty pounds since last we saw him. His general appearance is that of a man who has been on a deranged drinking binge for weeks. All of the alcohol has begun bubbling up and weeping out the sides of him. There is a sort of burnt, charred color to his moist skin. His whole body has taken on the look of a plump, bursting hot dog.

When nobody responds to his queer chuckling at the door, Dad gets down on all fours and goes rooting around the floor like a curious hog. He noses his way down the halls, groveling around the entrance to the bathroom, pawing the ground, crawling about, checking his knees and elbows for signs of dirt. He comes to a stop in front of the master bedroom and clambers to his feet.

"I cleaned," Mom says. Still rocked by his appearance, the words come out in a warped stammer. However, whatever hesitance and uncertainty comes through in her voice, it is not reflected in the expression covering the rest of her face. The message has not reached the upper ridges of her face, where her beaming eyes gleam flush and spoony.

Lindy laughs a little under her breath. "Tiny Toons," she says. "Hamton J. Pig."

Oh! Ha, I get it. "Shhhh," I repeat. I cuff an arm around her neck and hug her to me.

"How…" I start. I have no idea if I can get out a full sentence. As it turns out, I can't. "How did you know… How did you know, um…" My throat feels clenched and mucky. There's no saliva, and then there's too much, gumming everything up inside. "I…"

"What is it?" Dad says. He says it with a deep inhalation of breath, then exhales. He puts his hands on his hips. "It's all right. Go on. Spit it out."

"I can't," I say. "I don't have any spit." For the next few seconds I just stand there trying to gather up some moisture in my mouth. I must look like an idiot, just smacking my lips, slurping my tongue all around like some kind of chewing mule. "Did you know she just started cleaning today?" I manage to mutter.

"That's one of those big, cosmic questions," Dad says. "Did you know she was going to start cleaning?" He hawks something up in his throat, but instead of getting rid of it swallows it again. "There's no good answer to that one. Ask me another question. Try it with a little more oomph."

I take a deep breath, puff my chest full of air. "Is that real blood on your apron?" I say, squeezing as much gravel into my tone as possible.

"Atta boy," he says. He makes a giant grunting sound from the pit of his stomach, comes at me from across the room. Lindy grabs hold of my pants so hard I fear she'll bring them down around my ankles. When he's a few inches away, I close my eyes, bracing for the worst. "You might still have a shot," he says, taking a full swing at my shoulder. The hand lands with more gentleness than I suspected, but because I was so stiff, it still knocks me off balance. There's a jolly quality to the gesture that I'm not used to from him. I wonder if this new attitude is coming from the intoxication or from the travels he's been on or both… or neither. Something has changed him, moved him in some way. I have so many questions. As I right myself and open my eyes he is standing right there in front of me, chest to chest. There's a single fleck of tobacco wedged between his middle teeth like a tiny wood chip. I try remembering the last time I saw him, the smiling and dancing, the way his eyes twinkled with hope and prosperity, but it is hard. While he seems relatively happy on the outside, the light has gone dim inside. All that's left is a huffing mouth wreathed in a coarse beard, a flattened nose and two stony orbs resting in cracked sockets.

"Your dad and I have a lot to talk about," Mom says. Already she has forgiven him, has transformed any anger or hesitation into trust and expectancy. She walks over, loops her small hand around his burly one. Dad backs away from me slowly, then turns to face Mom. His bulging chest rises and falls in full, expanding waves of breath. Mom looks up at him, all misty and swooning, and it's difficult to tell if you don't know her, but wheels are turning inside that head. This moment has done something to her, confirmed something beyond a basic idea or intuition. To her, she has been vindicated… somehow. She is set in motion now. The tumbling and cranking has begun, gears grinding fantasy and reality, blending them into one. She slips into that immense crevice where miracles seem not only possible but probable. *If this is what falling feels like,* I can almost hear her saying as she sinks down across from him, her hand cupping his fist atop the kitchen table, *well then take me to the cliff and push me, please.* Here we go.

Drew and Jerry's Airspace (2005)

Drew and Jerry, practically my two best friends, met at a Salvation Army near the campus in Champaign. They reached for the same swanky pair of white canvas loafers at the same time and bumped heads. They laughed it off right away and then, not even three days later, went to a Futureheads concert together at the UIC Pavilion in Chicago without me. I'd been at the Salvation Army with Jerry when they met, and so I felt like I had helped introduce them even though I hadn't. It did sting a bit that it took Jerry approximately seventy-two hours to replace me as his best bud in town, but we all get along together pretty well now.

A week after the first encounter we all bump into each other again at a bicycle rack outside a divey café on Wright Street. It turns out they both like sleek, angular racing bikes with only one speed and no brakes. Drew notices for the first time that Jerry has a tattoo of a big cartoon keyhole on his left forearm. He is wearing a dirty pink baseball cap that Drew knows he wears because it doesn't make any sense on him, which is perfect, and right away it gives Drew his own giddy idea about trying to find his old football jersey in the basement of his mom's apartment. Damn, he hopes it's still there. He can't stop smiling about it. I know all of this because we've all become very intimate very fast. We have a psychic connection built around our mutual desires to mold derivative and also non-derivative personas for ourselves. It's not easy. It takes a lot of practice, but it's hard to tell exactly who or what we're practicing for, which is partly how we've grown so close. For example, each of us has a very distinct way of noticing and processing information. Drew is a total aesthete, and so he thinks long and hard about all things fashion. Both of them are easy guys to like. There's something so casual and blasé about them, characteristics that sort of lull you into admiring them.

"What?" Jerry asks him.

"Nothing," Drew says.

During this encounter, I'm standing beside them, killing time before I go pick up my bus pass and class schedule over at Harker Hall. I'd met Jerry on the first day of orientation, and we've spent almost every day together since (except the Futureheads concert). I have my "killing time" stance going on—one hand punched inside my new jean jacket and one hand holding a Camel Light. If there was a wall to lean against, I'd have one shoe bent up against it while I gazed off into the distance looking like some broody type of rebel, like Albert Camus or something... At this point, I already know that I'm only pretending to be dark and cryptic, but it's a start. Basically, Drew and Jerry are already where I want to be eventually. They actually *are* high off of about six different drugs at once. I'm not sure if that's part of what I'm going for literally, but I think I'd like to craft the appearance, the essence. I want people to look at me and think that I'm the kind of guy who gets blazed or at least the kind of guy who'd be capable of blazing.

Jerry kneels to wrap his lock around the rack and his bike's front wheel.

"How those hot loafers treating you?" Jerry asks.

"Ha ha! Hot," says Drew.

"You sure do know each other," I say, hoping to sound like I don't really care. It doesn't matter anyway.

Jerry has a mangy orange beard and sloppy hair that almost looks accidental. He wears a droopy, tattered tank top with a faded palm tree emblem on the front and dissolved press-on lettering beneath it. Because he's sort of stocky and shaggy, he reminds me of my other friend, Max, from back home. Drew is much more lithe and hairless. Where Jerry has a forest of tangled leg fur, Drew has a panel of bald, shimmering skin. When Jerry walks he thumps the earth. Drew's feet hardly touch the ground. He's sauntering and flamboyant, which makes me think maybe he's a little… but then it doesn't even matter. Even if he is a little… So what. This is college, and Jerry and the other people I've met are much more open and accepting than the kids from high school, which is good. Progress is important. I'm thinking about all of this, and I'm realizing that despite all of their physical differences, they could still practically be twins. There's something about their attitudes, their outlooks on life that match so succinctly that it gives off the impression of sameness. They even have the same stiff Velcro mail bag. Both of them know, without saying anything, that their bicycles, with the stripped parts, missing decals and basic colors, make the riders appear more neutral, which is sort of nice, but weird because in some ways it isn't at all what they mean. Being a minimalist has become oxymoronic; it shaves meaning down to a single symbol, like a dangling exclamation point against a white backdrop. The bikes make them seem rugged and uninterested.

"Aren't our bikes nonchalant as hell?" Jerry asks. "And raw. People think we only eat uncooked meat or only vegetables. Only. And nothing else. Rrrrrrrrrugged, man."

"Where have you heard that before?" Drew asks. "I've heard something like that before."

"LaMonte Young?" I venture a guess. Last summer I got pretty heavy into the Velvet Underground and took a bunch of trips to the library. You'd have thought I was a real drug-head or something, but at the time I'd never even thought to wonder about the junk.

Jerry looks at me like I'm totally daft. "No, definitely not. You've definitely never *heard* those words before. You would never want to talk about something like that."

Drew watches Jerry snap the lock into place and sling his bag over his bare shoulder. Drew looks at Jerry's arm again. He stares. He takes his index finger and absently, almost unconsciously traces a circle on his own forearm, round and round and round.

"You forgot a word," Jerry says, pointing at Drew's bike.

"Huh?" Drew says. He stops drawing the circles.

"You forgot to blackout those two letters." Jerry leans over, makes his fingers into a V and presses them against Drew's bike frame, up near the head tube. "M.O." Jerry says. "You missed them."

"Oh yeah," Drew says. "Right."

"Paint over them. You don't want those showing."

"Right."

God forbid they communicate something.

"God forbid we communicate something," Jerry says.

"Whoa!" Drew says.

"What?"

Drew whips his head back and forth; he cocks it to the side, whacks his ear with his palm. "But we're nihilists, right?" he says.

"Nihilists wouldn't try so hard."

"Maybe they would."

44

Jerry straightens and arches his back. He looks up at the clouds, which are turning grey and ominous. A sharp breeze blows across their chests. He's got me staring now, too.

"Uh-oh, we're gonna get wet," Jerry says. I watch a small trickle of blood seep out from one of his nostrils.

"Your nose is bleeding, dude," I tell him, but he doesn't appear to hear me.

"Huh? Oh, what, you're a weatherman now?" says Drew.

"No, asshole. Look."

Drew follows Jerry's eyes skyward. "Oooooooh," he says.

"What else? Grey, ominous clouds… sharp breeze…" Jerry says.

"Just say rain," Drew says, clamping his hands over his ears. "No, don't say it, I guess. Don't say anything. I'm getting interference from someplace, static… doublespeak."

"Fine. Rain," Jerry says. "The clouds are like an advertisement for rain, a coming attraction."

"Wow, that's a good one," Drew says. He's serious. "Did you come up with that on your own?"

"I think so," Jerry says.

"That's deep," I say. They both shake their head, exasperated with me for reasons I can't place.

"What?" Drew yells, still covering his ears.

"I think so!" Jerry yells.

"I think so," Drew says. *I think so.* It keeps repeating in my head. I look at Drew and Jerry, and they are nodding along to the frequency as well, processing.

As we duck inside the café for cover, rain hammers the pavement, pushing old piles of garbage toward rusty drains, forcefully and carelessly, like a threat. A few blocks away: a movie theater marquee vandalized by someone who thinks it funny to flip all the letters upside down. Half of the time the joke is on them, letters like H, I, O and X refusing to lose their meaning no matter which way they're turned. Further away: a billboard outside the Urbana shopping mall has been painted over. Somebody slopped a coat of white paint all over the thing and then outlined the white with a thick black border. The thing is stubborn though, and if you look hard enough you can still see the message underneath: an advertisement for the same Dutch Boy paint the person used to cover it up with. The rain is barbarous. The rain might wash it all away, slap the letters loose from the Virginia Theater's marquee too, before anyone notices.

Back in the café, Drew and Jerry argue. It's like their old friends already. This is one of the main things I appreciate about them; their passion, the way they can get incensed about just about anything, no half measures. They are chill as can be, but when something gets under their skin, they know how to get fired up. It's hard to be uncomfortable or awkward around them. But sometimes it's hard to understand what they're saying. Like now. Their words are garbled and thick in their mouths. What are they saying? Jerry is literally saying…

"We're arguing! Take your hands away from your ears!"

And Drew is saying:

"Stop that, please! Don't be tricked. Just because I have my hands up like this doesn't mean I can't hear you!"

The Darkest Mare (2003)

Dad's friend, Randy Mullins, is an exceptional poet and artist. He's also been known to shit himself in the late morning or early afternoon hours following a big bender. Randy is one of Dad's butcher buddies from work, but he's not like most of the other roughneck guys. He's this very handsome, arty guy with these intense green eyes, a little stubble around his rugged jawline and this distinguished gray hair that he keeps swept back in a sort of youthful blowsy style. Lindy has the biggest crush on him. But Randy's an addict. It's a real unfortunate thing. If he isn't drunk on gin or high on cocaine, which is rare, he's about the nicest guy you'd ever want to know. Recently though, he's been clean, and he's back doing his kind, quirky deeds. For example, a few days ago he painted this magnificent picture of him and Dad fishing in the river. Dad's in the back of the boat, gazing up at the sky with his arms stretched out wide. He's reaching for something, (the clouds?) head thrown back in a pleading way. The canvas is rather large, maybe four feet high by three feet wide. Standing straight up, it stretches all the way to Lindy's breast line—something both Lindy and Randy may have taken too much pleasure in measuring. He made sure to paint Dad in his butcher outfit, gripping his old cleaver in his big hairy fist, shaking it at the heavens above. On the front side of the boat, Randy hoists a fishing rod with a dangling fish on the end. Unlike Dad, he's sporting his civilian clothing and a gleaming smile. There is some serious juxtaposition happening, for sure, but none of us know exactly how to decode it or talk about it. Randy is a deep guy. There's no way around it. He really has something. That's what makes him so tragic.

Everyone loves the painting except Mom. At first sight her reaction is one of reluctance and dismay. She doesn't say anything, she wouldn't know how to articulate it anyway, but she isn't good at hiding her emotions. When Randy looks over at her to ask what she thinks, she starts rubbing the back of her neck. There's sweat running down her cheeks. She keeps making these sort of pained, wincing expressions. It makes me feel sorry for Randy, but then it makes me feel sorry for Mom too, and so in an attempt to remove the discomfort I just pick the canvas up and carry it to Lindy's room where I hide it behind her dresser. When I come back and realize that it's gone and we don't have to talk about it or look at it anymore, it's a huge relief. It feels sort of like being worried you might get caught for some horrible crime, but then destroying the evidence right before the law comes knocking.

Anyway, here it is Sunday, and whatever Randy had working during the week, his sobriety jig is up. I mean, it's an epic collapse. He's fallen from the wagon with the force of a felled wildebeest. By the time he calls me and Lindy out of our rooms, he is half-unconscious and nodding in the center of the kitchen. We find him there, all Jell-O knees and whooping cough, with this crinkled piece of paper in one hand and a bottle of Gordons in the other. You can see right away by how his jeans are all brown and saggy in the back, and how the whole place is starting to smell like a sewer, that he'd made a total mess of himself. He sort of staggers backward, catching himself against our sliding glass door. He pins himself there, squatting and grunting like he isn't done going to the bathroom yet. The crazy thing is that Lindy is smack in the middle of her Violet Flame phase, which Randy is to blame for. For the past few weeks she's pretty much been doing nothing but praying all day and all night, so for the first few minutes, before Randy really gets fired up, she's just standing in the corner with her head bowed and her hands squeezed between her thighs. It's like some kind of church for the dispossessed in here.

Mercifully, Mom is not home. She's still out finishing her regular weekend trip to the shopping mall. Dad's outside somewhere… There he is. I spot him. Through the sliding glass door behind Randy, I catch him rummaging around on the patio. Not surprising. When he's loaded, he busies himself with a lot of mini reclamation projects; things like sharpening old knives or gluing vases back together. It's as if he's trying to repair things in the outside world that somehow coincide with all the things that are broken up on his insides. Today he's on his hands and knees scrubbing out the grill with his big wire brush. As usual, when he's good and sloshed, he's talking to himself and laughing. I watch as he leans forward to wash the bottom of the propane tank. His cigarettes go spilling from his shirt pocket. He starts cursing, pawing around the grass, smashing the pack with his useless fingers. When he moves to straighten up he bonks his head on the base. "Aaaaaa! You fucking piece of rat shit! Mercy stroke!" he hollers.

Randy puts his hand up, punches it through the air like a salute. Lindy looks up, unclenches her palms. No, she will not be able to evade this. Her zapped look says it all. She tried, but there's nothing she can do. The Violet Flame will have to be put aside for the next few minutes or hours. There will be no "over-dubbing" this moment.

"Get ready for this, kids," he says. He rips a huge belch, then thumps his chest, punishing it like he means to pound some sobriety and sense back into himself before beginning. It's no use. "I'm giving this to you when I'm done, Clayton. You need to remember this."

He doesn't have to worry about me or Lindy. We are mesmerized. Lindy comes out of her stupor long enough to whisper something into my ear.

She smiles, nudges my elbow. "We're going to call this, 'The Soiled Sermon From the Mount,'" she says.

I laugh. It's nice to see her show a little bit of emotion again. It's been awhile. She's even pulled out our old game. That was something we used to do all the time, give silly nicknames to people, places or things that left some kind of big impression on us.

Meanwhile, Randy launches in, delivering his composition in one pungent burst...

Relapse, you bitch. You, with your three fingers pointed backward, you wretched, ruined rambler. This is what you know about your flaccid, selfish self. Self, you'd lick the barrel clean and call it blasé.

You listen to Wu-Tang on your way to the barn because it drowns out your thoughts about Neil Young, the Damage Done, your wife's shared wishes, your childhood goodness and your near future regrets.

Your thoughts on guns: distasteful, freakish, frightening and dreadful. Horses? Fine, smooth specimens with soft eyes, warm hearts and anthropomorphic wisdom. Your wife, Wanda, agrees. Some of your most satisfying conversations have been about guns and horses, your anti- and pro-religious stances about no religion at all save the farmlands you grew up on. You don't even like rap music, which is why it pairs so well with your other horrors from which you can't keep your hands clean.

The last time you pulled the trigger you almost went to church. But you don't believe anymore so you wrote yourself a note about discipline and self-control and slipped it in your sock drawer. If you consider hitting up the stables again you'll read it, and it will be your paper savior, your painful reminder, your Jiminy Cricket. That's the plan. You scribbled: Wanda, whom you love more than anything, will abandon you and your pitiful self. The cops will find you. Your mother will know. Your body will fill with sweat. The heart can only beat so fast. You'll get cancer and die. You won't recognize yourself and you'll wonder if you ever have, and that will go on and on until… when?

The sock drawer is such a silly place to keep something so serious, and you allow yourself to laugh about it. You don't read it. You can't. The music has already started in your mind. It convinces you that your horse shooting problem is cosmetic. It's not a problem at all but more of a temporary blemish. And even though you've been shooting horses solo for years, you remind yourself about your horse shooting comrades from college and wonder how many things they've killed in the past ten years. Inside the barn the straw is a duality of sharp, piled food and a stiff pillow. The naked bulb is just that. It's a far cry from a heavenly light but it will have to do. The horse is pitch black, beautiful and inquiring, and his forelock shutter matches your shutters shutter for shutter as you bring out the pistol. You'll hate yourself in the morning. Hate isn't a strong enough word, but then neither must be words like release, compulsion, propulsion, erasure or… fuck.

A Synonym For Pity (2006)

The other day I'm hiding out at the Wooden Nickel Bar under my Flynn pseudonym, right as it opens around four, and this girl we'd met during orientation pops into my head. The memorable thing about this girl was that she had this horrifying hair lip. What made me think of her was that I started noticing that everybody around town was wearing mustaches. Not wearing them like a novelty accessory, but *owning* them. It had become a sensation, hairiness. I guess I was picturing that part of the face or mouth, the upper lip area, and Gina, that was Hair Lip's name, came into my mind. I should mention that Jerry is with me. He has a ginger mustache, too, which isn't surprising if you know him. He's drinking a High Life to go with the mustache. They're a matching set, I guess.

"Remember Gina Hair Lip?" I ask him.

"Of course," Jerry says.

"It looked like she had part of her lip attached to a fishing wire that was yanked back over her shoulder and hooked into a belt loop or something," I say. I'm acting it out, doing the motions. Slapstick.

"She wasn't attractive otherwise, was she, outside the lip?" Jerry says.

"What a shame," I say. "No redemption. That shouldn't happen."

"That's why there's *sal*vation," Jerry says. He burps, taps me lightly on the cheek. He is an extremely hairy man, and the fur around his knuckles tickles my face. There seems to be no end to his hairiness. That part is something he can't help.

Jerry gets up and heads for the bathroom. "Think about that while I'm gone," he says.

My cheek itches. I scratch it and think about Gina just like Jerry suggested. I'm thinking about her so hard that I start remembering things that never happened between us. All of a sudden I think I remember a time when she was standing in the middle of the hallway outside our classroom, naked. There's no possible way that happened, and yet it seems unbelievably real in my head. I can see her there, bone thin and pale with bluish skin and blond hair. She's just standing there outside our drawing class, I guess just sort of waiting to see if anybody will notice and say anything, but nobody does, which gives it this very stark horror flick feel. Then I start to wonder if maybe I saw a movie at some point where a hair lip girl was naked in a school, and maybe I was confused. It's amazing what bizarre leaps the brain can make.

I sip my gin and tonic. Jerry is taking a very long time. I guess I'm just about to move onto a different topic in my mind because I feel a transition coming, like a distinct *oh well, onto the next thing* type of vibe and the shift somehow seems to be in cadence with my arm movement as I bring my glass to my mouth, and all of a sudden Gina's standing right next to me ordering three Blue Moons.

I don't know how I stifle my scream, but I manage it. The impulse gets damned somewhere deep in my bowels. It's a dagger down there. Because we've never made any real connection, probably never even spoken at all, she doesn't recognize me, but I know it's her. I've just spent the past six minutes picturing her naked, and so I have intimate knowledge. She looks almost the same as she did that day a few months ago, still upsettingly skinny and still with the lip upraised like an old-fashioned shade on a window. I don't know why that would be surprising. It's not like she would have just all of a sudden changed her whole life in a single season. Her style of dress is more appealing though, more hip and city, but you wouldn't be able to notice anything past those blooming gums.

I sneak a look over at her, and I realize she's standing with two other women who also both have similar hair lips. It must be a support group, I think, and that makes me equal parts devastated and comforted, but I'm still recovering from my near heart failure so I'm mostly just breathing into my cupped palms like a paper bag. A small blessing is bestowed when the three of them gather their wheat beers and head for the far back room. I had left no clue, that I could think of, that would have alerted her to my sickness at her appearance, and that at least is something to be thankful for. The support group brushes by Jerry as they squeeze past one another going opposite directions in the narrow aisle. Jerry is smiling and rubbing his hands together. He's proud of himself for something and wants to tell me, but I have no time for it.

"Did you see Gina?" I ask him.

"What? You're starting to scare me," he says, "mellow out, Clay. You're obsessed."

"Keep your voice down," I tell him. "Shhhh, listen. Don't look, but you just walked past her," I say. "Don't look, motherfucker!" I yell because he's not listening and looking anyway.

"All right," he says, "calm down." He looks straight ahead like a good soldier. He's slicked his hair back while he was gone, and it looks overly wet. Maybe that was what pleased him so much.

"You wouldn't be saying that if you were here. It wasn't pleasant. Do you know what I'm saying? You think about someone you haven't thought about in a while and then they show up. Isn't that supposed to be … I thought she was dead."

"What? Why did you think she was dead?"

"I don't know. I have no idea what happens to hair lips. Maybe they get infected or something. It doesn't seem like they'd have a long life when you look at them. When you think about it."

"So, it wasn't what you thought," Jerry says.

"Exactly. That's it. It was one of the worst moments of my life. No joke. Stop laughing. I'm serious." I put my hand over my heart. I'm still trying to get it to stop pounding.

"The lip condition and the person are not interchangeable, you know? You don't call somebody 'a migraine,' right? Wow," he says. He puts his hands behind his head, exhales a gust of breath at the ceiling. He's really thinking hard. He sits forward again, looks me in the eye. "Next time," he says, "don't picture someone ugly. Picture somebody hot." He gives the bar a little rap with his fist. The tangled hair on his wrist jumps a little when he does it. "Another High Life!" he shouts at the bartender.

He's got a point. I can't argue with him. I start to, but I can't. There's nothing else to say. It's a disappointment, common as any other.

II. THE SHORTCUT MADE SIMPLE

Serenity is a Wheel On Fire (2003)

It's hard to believe, but in some ways Mom's even luckier than she imagines. For example, employment opportunities. Money has never been her main struggle. It's not that she's ever had a lot of it, but always just enough. Landing a professional, coveted job right out of high school and never letting go is a lot of people's dream scenario. In that way, Mom's been living the dream since high school graduation. Despite no official training or particular skill set, she got hired as a nursing assistant at the Ambassador Retirement and Rehabilitation Center in Ravenswood. The place itself isn't anything impressive, just a leaky brick square of a building with a couple planter boxes outside and a few browning Norman Rockwell re-prints hung on the inside, but many folks were actively seeking those medical type professions when she weaseled her way in. People go to school to gain admittance into the industry, and it was a solid job for a lost and lonesome girl like the eighteen-year-old Roberta.

It's not like she didn't earn it, though. She does know how to work hard. If nothing else, she's going to show up every day on time without a single day off and never complain. She's never been much for the solitude of downtime. In the beginning her initial duties were less than spectacular, primarily rinsing bedpans and replacing bath towels, but over the years, to the surprise of many, she was promoted. The added rewards and benefits just seemed to keep washing up at her feet. Through some combination of automatic persistence and a lack of qualified or sound bodies with which to replace her, I guess, she parlayed a simple desire to help people into a nice little career. Her first advancement came in the form of a rather unsavory position called Infection Control Nurse. This title lasted nearly a decade and led to several lessons on food safety around our household. I recall one in particular, a detailed practice scenario involving bloodborne pathogens around the home.

In 2001 she was offered the more seemly position of resident Geriatric Nurse, where she won the duty of dealing with erratic elderly patients who often forgot the names of their children, crapped on the rugs or swore their spouses were plotting to kill them in their sleep. While this may not appear to be a glamorous task, it does allow her to assist a set of devalued people who make her feel useful and wanted, a group of well-meaning, modest folks who, when not high on tranquilizers or off on delusional rants, can show real affection and charm toward the woman who cares for their various revolting ailments. The summer of 2001 was also when the Ambassador started letting me get to know some of the residents on a more personal level, too. They allowed me a part-time job doing some light-lifting duties like separating laundry, sweeping the lobby or taking out the garbage, never anything hazardous. It works for me. I enjoy getting out of the house, making a small amount of my own money, and like Mom, I take pleasure in the reciprocal appreciation that comes with caring for the aging. There are all kinds of desultory and depraved characters. People like Horace and Gail Matthews, two of the most overtly, grotesquely sexual octogenarians you'd ever want to meet. Can't forget Lance Owings, the man who believes I am his dead son back from the Vietnam War, among other bizarre things. And there's Maureen Johns, the gypsy woman who claims to have once eaten a private dinner with Vietnamese Zen Master Thich Nhat Hanh. But my favorite resident is one of the simplest men on the grounds, Dick Farber.

Dick Farber is a senile but amiable widower from Germany. His old world touches include huge silver-sprouted ears and eyebrows the size and color of gray cotton swabs. He's a very tall man with a crooked spine and wide feet. Despite his imposing stature, he is always reserved and considerate with a soothing timbre to his voice and an inviting demeanor. He's one of my favorites because he always has a smile and a piece of licorice candy waiting for me when I arrive. I don't even particularly like licorice, but it's the thought that warms me. Sometimes he'll tell me stories about the long, beloved road trips he took with his wife and son to places like Niagara Falls or the Grand Canyon. I remind him of his son, he says. There's something about the familiar lines in my forehead... or... He tries to explain but can't find the right words. Instead, he takes his large, knobby fingers, bends down and traces the length of my hairline with a jagged nail.

Today at work everyone is dragging, taking extra-long bathroom breaks or refusing to leave the air-conditioned sanctuary of the break room after lunch. It's one of those oppressive summer Chicago days where the heat covers the whole city like a damp and choking sweater; you just want to squirm out of it, get it off you. The shift is almost over when Dad drops Lindy off. Mom promises to take us both for ice cream as soon as we're off. I see Lindy coming, walking across the parking lot outside in the lobby windows. She looks agitated, sticky with sweat and maybe a little pissed about a bad nail job or something. She keeps picking at the tips of her fingers, shaking her head and blowing hot air. I'm bussing a few card tables just inside the foyer. The ladies had a pinochle tournament this afternoon, but nobody won because none of them were able to finish before their scheduled two o'clock nap time. They'll all wake up around four, forget what they were doing before they went down, and then eat a 4:30 dinner of soggy fish, spiceless potatoes and rubbery carrots in the cafeteria. Lindy has her headphones in. She's listening to Pantera probably or some other loud, aggressive band with lots of hoarse screaming. She's going through a whole heavy metal stage. Paradoxically, whenever she isn't engaged in prayer, she's usually holed up in her room shouting dark, blistering lyrics about cemeteries or heroin needles up at the ceiling. It isn't only in her room. She went off yesterday before work. We were walking in together, though she wouldn't have called it that. She would have said that I was going to work and she was going to April's house, which only happened to be on the way. Whatever. I was trying to make small talk. I kept trying to point out what a nice job the landscapers had done planting all the new tulips and daffodils around the entrance, and she kept singing louder, whipping her bright pink ponytail back and forth against her shoulders. She had on these skimpy cutoff jean shorts, black tank top, black sneakers, sunglasses and nail polish, black, black, black. Typical. The trees along the perimeter are shimmering in the sunlight, bushy green and blooming. It's a beautiful day, but you'd never know it to look at Lindy. Up on the porch, as we pass by, Gail and Horace were holding hands, making googly eyes at one another. They wave and smile when they see us coming. Lindy allows herself to come out of her depressive, pre-teen act long enough to wave back. "Gross," she mumbled under her breath. She refuses to occupy herself with anything that might appear either frivolous or corny, even when it might actually raise her spirits a little bit. The thing is, there are times when she eases up and you can tell that she's putting it on. She loves Horace and Gail, and even if she might try, she can't hide it. She comes out of character, gives them her own little peace sign wave, then slips into a perky skip-trot dance, before realizing what she's doing and reverting back to her bleak, somber routine.

Anyway, she reaches the entrance, and just as she is about to go through the sliding glass doors, she freezes. She pops the headphones out of her ears. A distant, garbled roaring spills from the tiny speakers dangling in her hand. She has this look on her face like she's just witnessed a kidnapping or something, and so I come up alongside her, and I look over to where she's looking.

"Isn't that, Dick?" she asks the second I turn to look. She props the sunglasses up on top of her head, points. There, resting a few feet away is a rusty blue Pontiac wedged diagonally between two parking spaces. The car is ancient and dingy, crusted over like a barnacled boat.

I move over in front of the bumper, lean in until my nose is practically touching the windshield. It's Dick, all right. He's slouched there with his hands ringing the steering wheel, all bug-eyed and gazing straight ahead. The windows are all rolled up and covered in thick steam. "Dick!" I say, rapping on the window, rubbing a circle clear in the glass. He doesn't even flinch. It looks as though he's dead, but he's still breathing. I can see his chest rising and falling beneath the dashboard. "Dick!" I holler, and this time he wakes up a little bit. He blinks a few times, then reaches out and turns the keys in the ignition. The engine comes sputtering to life. A puff of smoke coughs out of the tailpipe. "Lindy," I say, trying to stay as calm as possible, "go get Mom!"

Lindy dashes inside. I stay with Dick or the vestige of Dick, whatever's inside this death trap. I have my hands on the hood of the car, my feet spread wide, as if I could pull back and stop the vehicle from budging if he made a move. This is my half-cocked plan, all I can come up with. His eyes are dimming, turning blank and vacant, like somebody has flipped a switch off somewhere inside his brain and everything is on slow-fade. He just keeps staring. It must be over a hundred degrees inside there, just one big boiling stew of nerves and licorice and brain cells. The fumes come dumping out of the tailpipe in sickly charcoal plumes. The whole lot is starting to smell like gasoline. I clamor around to the side, try opening his door, but it's locked. His face is turning a pulpy red, like melting clay.

Behind me I hear the automatic doors stutter open and rattle shut. Lindy and Mom hurry outside, and lurch to a halt. Lindy's out of breath, hands on knees, huffing and panting. Mascara runs down in her cheeks in ashy rivulets of black. Mom looks the opposite, full of wind and vigor, standing confidently erect. I wonder how she made it all day, so undisturbed, so fresh.

Hoping to look concerned and heroic, but coming off more like a spastic child, I run over beside them. "Mom!" I say. "What should we do?"

"Step back," she tells me. "Move away." She slashes her arms out in front of me, reaches across my waist like a seatbelt.

She's wearing her stiff, baby blue uniform, the one covered in a pattern of tiny roses and other happy flowers. It's having the exact effect that I am certain it was made for. I instantly feel calmer, more sedate. Such brilliant design ... But alas, the fabric can only do so much. There still needs to be action

Bound by our mutual hesitation and ineptitude, we stand and watch as Dick places his hands on the gear shifter and yanks downward. The car heaves, making a creaky, groaning sound.

"Mom," Lindy squeals, "do something!"

"He's been talking about this for months," Mom says. "He said all he wanted was to take one more road trip."

"And you told him he could?" I ask.

"He doesn't have to get permission from me. I'm not the ultimate granter of consent," she says. "I told him to ask for what he wanted."

"Ask who?" Lindy says, anxiously hopping from one foot to the other.

"Anyone," Mom says, "everyone, anything, everything. If it's what you want the most, keep asking for it. Keep speaking. Put it out in the world."

"It?" Lindy asks.

Without so much as a thought to check his mirrors, Dick presses the gas pedal. In a wild burst of noise and smoke, the car shoots backward and spun sideways.

"It's got a flat tire!" I yell. It's obvious right away. The sound it makes is like a barrel rolling down a rocky cliff.

"He's going to die!" Lindy screams. She puts her hands over her cheeks, then slides them up to cover her eyes.

"Take it easy," Mom says in a gentle tone that is so out of place it almost seems alien. "He's making something happen. It's taken care of."

Out of nowhere Dick has sprung to life, some sort of automaton programmed to accelerate, to slice and carve his way around this random lot. The thing is, he's making it. He's doing it. For a moment it looks like he's going to be okay. It's a miracle. He may have continued to be okay except for the fact that not only is his right front tire flat, but it's worn so thin that he's now gliding across the pavement on a hot piece of metal that keeps throwing sparks up all over the place. He spins the steering wheel round and round, unconsciously, but also somehow artfully, dodging cars and trees. It's really something to see. Every time it looks like he's heading for disaster and his luck has run out, he twists out of the way and goes careening farther toward the edge of the parking lot. About the time he's cashed out, aiming straight for the ramp leading to the exit onto North Bernard Street, the other nurses and medics come launching out the door and take chase of old Dick and his blazing blue Pontiac.

"He didn't mention the flat tire, did he," I say as the orderlies push past us, sprinting out onto the road.

"I don't think he knew," Lindy says, removing the hands from her eyes.

"He knew," Mom says. "It just didn't matter. He did what he was called to do; trusted that it would carry him anyway. Good for him," she says. "It was one of the things he must have been asking for. Good for him."

"It doesn't look like he understands that the tire is catching on fire. Is he going to make it?" Lindy says.

"You're asking the wrong kind of questions. You have to ask *for* something," Mom coaches.

"Can I have a Xanax?" Lindy says.

"That's not funny," she says. "Where is your faith?"

"Wrong kind of question," Lindy says.

I put my arm around Lindy's shoulders and squeeze, just like I always do when I get scared that she's going to say something she won't be able to take back, then I put my other hand over my eyes, which is what I do when I'm freaking out and can't take it anymore. "Shhhh," I say, unsure if I'm talking to Lindy or myself.

Dick must see everyone rushing and panicking behind him, because he gets spooked and runs directly into a lamp-post. Peeking through my fingers, I see one of the sparks leap up from the shredded wheel well, and it must have been timed just right with some combustion from the engine because there's an eruption and the whole front end goes up in flames. He'd inadvertently created the perfect conditions for an explosion.

"What are we going to do now?" I ask.

"Good question," Lindy says.

"Mom!" I say.

"It will be fine," she says, "I bet he already thought of everything."

Gardening Techniques (1999)

My best friend's name is Max Lingle, but everyone calls him Bronco or just Bronc for short. He first earned the moniker in third grade after he started chasing girls around on the playground, tromping around on all fours, slobbering and begging them to ride his back. As disturbing and inappropriate as that sounds, and it was, if you knew Max you'd understand how earnest he was being in his attempt to simply make friends and entertain the crowd. In his mind, he was doing it more for the amusement of others. If there is anything he thinks he can do to brighten the spirits of his classmates and gain some affection at the same time, he'll do it. Anything.

There are benefits to having Max as a close pal, like how he always listens carefully to everything people say, and then has a really thoughtful response for them afterward. He's also big and strong to look at, and even though he's a total softy underneath, most people are still scared of him. They're frightened off by his enormous head and hands, his dirty clothing, unkempt hair and earthy odor. I overlook those things now that I know him, but there's other stuff about him that is hard to ignore. Today after school, I get a huge reminder. He wants to show me something in his bedroom, he says. It's a fingernail collection. Of all of the things somebody could guess or picture, I bet nobody would be ready for that kind of an announcement. It will blow your mind, he assures me. He asks if I want to see it. It's considerate of him to ask. That's Bronc for you, but I don't think he realizes that once you're standing in his house and he tells you about something like this, there's not much of an option. What am I going to say? Next thing I know he's walking me into his bedroom with an old T-shirt wrapped around my eyes for dramatic effect. When he takes it off me he's holding a mason jar about halfway filled with fingernail clippings. They look like dead mealworms, and I'm not sure why they all have to be so soiled up.

"I almost have enough for planting," he tells me.

"You're going to plant your fingernails?" I ask.

"Well, they won't be fingernails when I plant them," he says.

"How do you mean?" I say.

"Well, ever since my uncle read *Gardening Techniques of The Basqwa Tribe* to me last March, I've been living a magical life."

I look at the jar again. I take it from him and hold it up to the light coming through the window. Max stares at me staring at the jar, nodding. He's got this wide, warm smile. It's the first thing you'd notice about him if not for the heft and stink. What a strange guy Bronc is. He's so stout and muscular, but he doesn't really use it for anything. The nickname is a formality. Part of me thinks he should become a professional wrestler. Then at least he'd have something to point to when somebody asked about his identity, even if it didn't exactly connect. Wrestling isn't really supposed to link up with or match any other concrete attributes anyway. It would be the perfect career for him.

"I'm not sure you're using the word *magical* right," I say, turning the jar around against the glinting light.

"Look closer," he says, "You're not doing it right, Clay. See a plant." He's the type of guy who could demand just about anything from you and get away with it. I look again, this time with him hanging on me, his chin resting on my shoulder. After what seems like a long enough time, I tell him I see it. But he doesn't let me get off that easy. "Describe it to me," he says.

I clear my throat. "Um, well, it's got like really dark green leaves," I say. I'm not sure if I'm completely making things up out of thin air or if I'm actually starting to really see it now for the first time. It must not matter, because Max is eating it up. He just wants to hear me describe it. He trusts me. "There's a little purple bud on one of the stems," I say, and when I say it I really do start to see it in my mind. The image is there for a second and then dissolves. I caught just enough of it to improvise the rest. "The stem is long and thorny, like a rose," I say, and then I realize that I'm getting a little choked up. I'm trying so hard to call the vision back that my emotions are just coming out. I know how badly Max wants me to see it, and so now I want to see it with all of my heart. There's this totally innocent, anticipatory look in his eyes. He wants nothing more than for me to share his perceptions of the world. Luckily for him and for me, I'm trained in the art of magic and illusion. It's the one thing I've actually gotten good at, using my imagination. I wonder if I'll ever use it for a truer reason than this one.

Love Won't Settle For Hogwash (2004)

Mom's one foot out the door, and The Ambassador board brings in a new "Chief of Operations" named Harvey Douglas. She prints out and brings home an office memo regarding his hiring. At the dinner table she presents it to us, unfurls it like a grand unveiling. Squinting at the fine print, she holds it up to the light. She keeps raising and lowering her bifocals for official effect, intoning the thing as if she's reading from the constitution. "Mr. Douglas has been brought onboard," she reads, "to trim waste, track data trends and create a new branding model for growth." When she brings the paper back down onto the table it is with conscious intention. It comes down in a silent pat, neatly but curtly against the surface. This is our signal; she means it as a gesture for us to begin voicing our shared grievances, expressing our mutual dissatisfaction. Dad pipes up right away. He doesn't like the cut of this guy's jib, he says.

"I mean, what this guy's name again?" Dad asks.

"Harvey Douglas," Mom says.

"Who is he?" Dad asks.

"I just told you," Mom says, "the new Chief of…"

"No, but I mean who is he really?"

"My new boss, basically?"

"Who?"

"What are you talking about?" Mom says.

"Exactly. That's what I'm trying to say here," Dad says. "My point is, this guy doesn't mean anything to anyone. Nobody knows who he is. He thinks he's some big shot."

"He definitely does," Mom agrees, "you're right there." Dad has managed to say just the right thing. It pleases her, makes her body unstiffen in her chair. She smiles, brings her elbows in against her chest, lets her shoulders down.

"This asshole sounds more like some kind of small time corporate bully. Someone like Telecom would bring in to buy up another cable network. He's not the one for the Ambassador. What does he know about improving living conditions for people in pain?" There is an expression of confrontation and outrage on his face, a tense grimace that bends upward on the left side of his face in a hardened hook. It's been a long time since he's felt challenged in this way, threatened. I'd forgotten how fiercely competitive he could be. It seems odd that this would be the spark to light his fire, but for whatever reason, he's worked up quite a good heat. "Sweet hell on a ham sandwich," he adds, just because he wants to and why not let it out?

Mom has settled deep into her seat, sunk into it with a contented grin. This is precisely what she was looking for, some endorsement, some confirmation that she isn't nuts, doesn't have to explain herself anymore against accusations of instability. She leans forward, tilting toward Dad's face, and rests her hand on top of his. "What do you think I should do?" she asks.

"You don't need a jerk like him validating you. You're heading for stardom. As soon as you and Maureen finalize that book contract, you'll have people like Oprah Winfrey and Phil Donahue coming for you. Your name will be on their lips. Harvey Douglas may as well be a shoe salesman. Ignore him. You'll end up forgetting more about that job than he will ever know."

Mom stands; bowing over the table the way a piece of mistletoe dangles above a doorframe, and kisses him on the forehead. His eyebrows arch, partly in surprise, partly to emphasize the action. She sits back down but doesn't let go of his hand. In a sense the kiss is still lingering too, wafting between them like a warm cloud of breath.

"You don't work at some fucking factory," Dad continues, finishing off the argument with a flurry of straight jabs, "you're in the business of recovery. No," he reconsiders, "scratch business. Screw business. You're a recovery specialist. You help people heal. Real people. People. Not brands."

Over the next few weeks, Lindy and I eavesdrop on Mom's late night conversations with Dad. Harvey is worse than she expected. From what Lindy and I can tell, there's something creepy about the guy, something frightening. Maureen notices it, too. Maureen explains him best, Mom says. Lindy and I hide behind the staircase on the first landing, and strain to hear what she's saying to Dad in the living room. Most of the time she whispers, but sometimes she forgets or becomes animated, and we can make out some pretty racy details.

"It's like he's casually lecherous," Mom tells him. Lindy and I don't know what that word means, but just from the sound of it, we guess that it involves something close to murder. Just the vibration of the word makes it seem haunting and fanged. "That's how Maureen puts it. He slinks around all casual, drifts past us ladies, like one greasy, gropey ship passing another unassuming, objectionable ship in the night. Easy breezy molestation vibe. That's how Maureen describes it. It's like he's staging some kind of one-man pervert show. Eerie."

Lindy and I stay and listen well past our bedtime. My neck is cramped and my ribs hurt from being squeezed up against the railing where Lindy's been leaning all her weight against me. But I manage. Things would have to be about ten times worse for me not to want to hear what's coming next. There have been several shady situations involving Harvey in the past few days. For this, Mom whispers, but Lindy and I have grown accustomed to exceeding our listening capacity. Our ears, like eyes adjusting to dim lighting, have adapted to the lower frequency. We hear about the time Harvey asked Mom if she could peel a piece of lint off the rear of his pants. And then there was the time he told her that he would ask the maintenance man to turn down the air conditioning because it was clear to him that things were getting "a bit pointed" around the office, if she knew what he meant. She did. And she wasn't the only one who understood. There were several other women who had experienced different forms of harassment. Maureen herself admitted that he had once pinned her against the washing machines downstairs, and when she opened her mouth to scream, he put his hand over her lips and said he was only reaching for the detergent, and she should think twice before calling attention to things that she wasn't even sure were happening. He wasn't done "trimming the fat around here," he told her.

Monday morning, Mom comes home from work, Maureen trailing and gulping behind her, and just sort of explodes. She comes gusting through the door and storms right up to Dad in the kitchen. He is in the middle of something, crouched down, shaking an overloaded bag out of the garbage can. There is a look of utter pandemonium in her eyes. She is not in control of herself. I'm not even sure if she knows how much force and hysteria she's exuding. She twitches all over—hands, knees, lips, one big tic. Maureen is right behind her, stumbling in her wake as if she's been tethered by a gigantic rubber band. There's a supreme, towering energy zapping through the house. Lindy and I pick up on it right away, practically turn electric with it, start glowing. We practically crash into one another as we come running in from the family room. To be fair, we've been training to pick up on energies like this. We're finally getting to put our grooming to use. Despite Maureen trying to hold Mom back, grabbing onto the edge of her collar the way a mad dog might try taking a bite out of someone's coat, Mom starts in right away. The way Mom is moving, gyrating and bugging with adrenaline, I can picture the way she must have driven home. She must have flown home in a manic fit. I can just see her, stamping down on the gas, lips pursed into that creased dagger formation she reserves for these rare onslaughts of uncontrollable anger, arguing with Maureen about what was and wasn't prudent for the looming situation. Well, probably not arguing really, but likely just sitting there quietly, getting pelted by one of Maureen's classic lectures.

"Harvey went too far," she says, the words bursting from her breathless mouth.

Dad looks up from the garbage bag, wraps a twist-tie around the open top. He's pinched a cigarette in his mouth, and the smoke keeps steaming through his teeth, curling up and getting in his eyes. He takes it out of his mouth, exhales. This is done with a kind of fixed and abiding ease. Each measured moment spent straightening his bones, becoming erect, is like a little recitation on remaining steady under pressure.

"What'd the asshole do now?" He asks with a creaking cough.

"Now, Roberta. Calm down. You don't know if," Maureen says. Lindy and I are crowded in behind them. Lindy starts rooting her way forward, blazing a trail like some hawkish kid at a packed metal concert. We push right in close. From that vantage point, Maureen really looks her age. You can see all the lumpy wrinkles bunched around the bottom of her neck like a scrunched up sock. The makeup around her eyes is dark and runny, pooling around folds of tired skin below. From far away, she could fool people. It's possible the platinum hair might look real. Her painted-on smile could appear less like a garish clown's and more like the youthful, carefree girl she hopes to portray. But not up close. Up close there are no tricks.

"I was exiting the restroom," Mom continues, "I mean, I wasn't even all the way out yet!" Man, Maureen is tense. She has her hand balled inside the hem of her work shirt, and she's twisting it there, grinding and grinding. Her mouth's all screwed up, knees pumping. It's possible she has to pee. Something has scared the piss out of her.

"That's enough," Dad interrupts. Continuing his little pantomime, he uses decisive motion to communicate his objection. He snaps up the trash bag, throws open the side door and marches out. We all hurry to the window, watch as Dad makes a beeline right on to the car. Mom and Maureen race after him. Lindy and I track right in behind them. In his mind, Dad is already in the process of settling into the car, already plotting his course of action. As he comes around to the driver's side, he wings the trash bag at the dumpster in the alley. It splatters against the side, spewing the contents all over the street. He still has the cigarette in his lips, the goddamn champion!

"Neil!" Maureen shouts. "What are you doing? What do you hope to accomplish?"

Dad has the car door open, one foot inside, one out. "Yeah, you should probably stay here, Maureen," he says.

"I'm coming with," Mom says. She scampers to the passenger side, arms akimbo, and whirls herself inside. Before anyone can even protest, she already has the door slammed shut and is working on buckling the seatbelt.

"I want to come, too!" I say.

"Me too!" Lindy says.

We charge the back doors, but Dad puts a stop to it quickly and fiercely. "You two aren't going anywhere," he says. The tone is biting and barbed, likes he's chomping through the cigarette as he says it. "Stay here and wait. This won't take long. I don't want you getting involved."

"But Dad," Lindy pleads.

"Discussion over," Dad says.

"Stay here, sweetheart," Mom says. She's hanging out the window, looking feverish and full of anxiety. She is a regular portrait of alarm—elbow sticking out the side, hair all frizzy and wild.

"Roberta!" Maureen calls, but it is already too late. She's only about twenty feet away, but she has her hands cupped over her mouth like she's hollering across some great divide. "Remember our discussion," she shouts, all dramatic and echoey, like, *Remember the Alamo!* "You're acting out of dread and worry. You are about to fight against something you don't want. You *don't* want Harvey bothering you anymore."

Dad shakes his head, shifts into drive and holds the brake. "That's a good enough reason for me," he says.

"No!" Maureen bellows. "No, you never fight against something you *don't* want. You only endeavor to act on something you *do* want, like peace. This is the wrong motivation. It's all wrong."

"We don't have time for this," Dad says.

"Just a second," Maureen says. "Remember Mother Teresa?"

Dad takes one last drag from his cigarette and flicks it to the curb. He pulls himself inside the cab and swings the door shut. Mom is in the passenger seat, nodding her head out the window. There is an implied apology in the watery lids of her eyes, but also a finality. She is resigned to this.

This is when Maureen goes into her guru mode. It begins as a very gradual, very deliberate stroll toward Mom's window, a slow motion pageant. "She said, remember…" she continues, her voice becoming dreamy and low, "she said she would never go to a rally against war. She said she'd only go to a gathering for peace. There's never a reason to protest out of anger or frustration, only love. You want peace, right?" Mom is still nodding her head. "Good. Good. Neil? Mother Teresa," she says. "Think of Mother Teresa."

Dad rolls down his window, yells over his shoulder. "That's hogwash," he says. "She isn't even a real person, Maureen. She's dead. She doesn't count. We're human beings. We're alive." He cranks the ignition, steers out onto the road. Mom whisks her head inside the window. As the car speeds away, Mom waves at us, shouting something that none of us can quite make out. It sounds like, "We're all in this together!" but it could have been, "We'll call you again never." Either way, they are gone, disappearing out of sight in a mélange of dust and smog.

While Maureen and I just stand there, holding down the grass together, I guess, shell-shocked, wondering what to do next, Lindy darts off somewhere. I'm angry that she has abandoned me, but I don't know what I can do about it. It feels like every option for relief or suspension has been exhausted. If Maureen couldn't halt the thing with all of her jargon and witchery, what is left to be done? Maureen flops down, sort of falls onto the lawn like she's been pushed. "What are we going to do?" She moans. "This could ruin everything we've been working for." It seems strange that she would ask me.

She knows that I'm not good at that this sort of thing. I'm just about to offer up whatever lame, comforting remark I can come up with, something about how everything will work out in the end, when Lindy goes whizzing by us with her hair flagged straight out behind her.

"Come on. Look!" she yells, each word coming out choppy, riding on the strides of her rapid feet. On the way past she slaps me on the back hard, then kicks it into an even higher gear and takes off like a gazelle. Wham! "The bus! The bus is coming! Come on!"

First she creates the whirlwind, then she sucks me up in it. She has her ways of propelling people into motion, especially me. It's her enthusiasm, and also her keen method of insisting something without taking no for an answer. There has always been a kind of world-weary deliberateness and exactness about her ideas, a confidence and conviction that throughout time she has come to fully harness and own. One just simply does not go against her plans for fear of either missing out on something grand or losing out on something fundamental for survival. She has practiced and perfected that kind of serious-ness. I don't even know how much practice is involved. Most of the time it seems as if she has been like this from birth.

In any case, her cunning and persuasion is important to understand, so that it won't seem odd how quickly I take off after her, chasing her down the street. Here her older brother comes, nipping her heels as she jumps and hollers for the bus to stop at the corner. I can't help myself. Suddenly I'm just moving, romping up the steps behind her as the bus doors pop open. There is a complete mindlessness, a programmed motion to the way I reach into my pocket for money as she puts her open palm out and demands that I "hurry the hell up."

Automatically I give her the money, pay our fares and sit down. All of this before she even looks over at me and says, "We'll get there for most of the good parts." And the next thing I notice or comprehend as the bus's huge engine roars into action is Maureen. Out on the lawn she has wiggled her way up to her feet, which is apparently a process that has left her sapped and frightened. Pale hands cupped to her even whiter cheeks, she yells in the direction of the bus as loud as she can. She may as well be whispering into a paper bag, for there is no way we can hear a single thing she is saying neither over the bus's motor nor the pulsing of our own hearts. Whatever she is going on about is causing her quite a lot of disturbance, forcing her to flail and buck about like some kind of rattled animal. Lindy and I watch out the side window as our neighbors come staggering out of their apartments, swarming Maureen in various states of wonderment, dread or consternation. There she is sputtering out in the middle of our lush, sprawling yard. Her added presence, like a drop of oil in a glass of water, diminishes the fullness and splendor or our home. Our three-story "Prospect Palace" is an ill-fitting backdrop for her crackup, too elevated or grandiose. And much like our hesitancy at having purchased the property, its façade casts a wide, chilly shadow of doubt around the whole idea we've been trying so carefully to build.

The next thing I know, Lindy is basically dragging me off the bus and sprinting for the Ambassador parking lot. It comes into view fast, approaching as if it too has been rushing to meet us halfway. There are some ambulances outside with the lights on, swirling red and blue across the trees' budding spring leaves. My mind speeds toward worst case scenario, Mom, Dad and Harvey all lying unconscious inside the metal doors, hanging onto whatever fading life they have left.

"There they are!" Lindy says.

As we enter the property at a full gallop, my lungs burn and my feet ache from pounding the pavement to keep up. The entire neighborhood must be out in front of the entrance— night shift workers, shop owners from across the street, small children lost from parents, haggard residents in bathrobes, police officers in all their formal bullet-proofed regalia, every-one! They're all lined up like they are watching a house go up in flames. As if to confirm this, a fire truck races up alongside the curb, and a horde of fireman come charging out.

Lindy bashes her way through the mass, tossing people out of her way, barreling into anyone who dares not budge. All I can do is try to trail her, following the path she clears, apolo-gizing to everyone for her, feeling zonked on some unknown cocktail of panic and adrenaline.

"Dad!" Lindy yells. There is one last woman impeding her progress, a mammoth sculpture of a woman, an obelisk monument to obesity. I watch with marvel as Lindy virtually lifts this lady off her feet, shucking her to the side like nothing, like she isn't even there.

Through the parting of foreign bodies, Dad appears. He's standing in the middle of three police officers, one of which is taking notes as the others look on, their muscular, blue-clad arms folded across bulging chests. I am elated to see that he is still upright and speaking, neither lying on the ground nor splayed out on a gurney, as I had feared. In fact, he looks completely fine, calm even. The way he points and gestures, how he lightly nods or shakes his head in response to the stern questions being asked, it's as if he's describing some mundane aspect of his job, how to prepare a prime cut of roast beef.

"Are you hurt?" The Irish sounding one with the notepad asks him.

"Not really," Dad answers. He bends his elbow, raising his fist, and checks his knuckles. That's when I notice that there is a small gash on one of them, a thin line of blood trickling down his wrist. Following its crimson stream, I look down and spot Mom huddled on the stoop at his feet. She has her thighs drawn up against her chest, her head buried in between. Neither one of them has seen us yet. Because of this, because of Lindy's daring, we are getting to see them in a context we've never seen them before, someplace raw and vulnerable. This realization makes me simultaneously captivated and repelled, unable to look away.

I look over at Lindy, hoping she knows what to do, but she is out of range, her mind off somewhere remote, somewhere deep and swimming. When I call her name she gasps, and I catch what's been tugging at her concentration. Over by the curb, sitting on the back fender of one of the ambulance is Harvey Douglas. His torso slumps forward, head propped against one of the medics who is standing there trying to get a read on his blood pressure. Once again pursuing Lindy's lead, we walk together for a closer glimpse.

"You should come in with us," the medic is saying. He's a young and handsome man with radiant white teeth and smooth, hairless skin. "You probably have a broken jaw."

"I'm not going," he says, but because his jaw isn't working right, it sounds like he says, "Awm, rot bowing."

"Suit yourself," the medic tells him. "You'll have to sign some papers."

Harvey sits up, nods his head wearily, rustily. He massages his chin, trying to coax the slanted jowls into cooperating.

The way he's slouched there, all withered and crumpled in defeat, he looks pitiful, infantile. Gone is the upright, arrogant demeanor he's worked so hard to achieve. No longer will he be revered or longed for by even the most damaged or attention-starved women on duty. Whatever power he's been holding over his employees, whatever fear and control he's been wielding, has been beaten out of him. This is who he really is beneath all that bullying, a small man who understands that things will never be the same around the halls of the Ambassador or likely even in his own home ever again.

A man's gruff voice startles us. "So, you're sure you're not pressing charges?" Lindy and I turn around to find not only a husky officer with a crew cut and a wiry moustache, but Mom and Dad also.

"Lindy, Clayton!" Mom says. She's been swaddled, wrapped inside Dad's hearty embrace. Her frame sits doll-like against Dad's hip, narrow shoulders cinched close against his armpit. When she tries to leap out at us, Dad hugs tighter, reining her back in.

"Jesus Christ," Dad says. "I told you to stay home." He shakes his head; grumbles some more curse words under his breath. "Mother of fucking pearl…" But there is also a pride lurking behind his eyes, a concession of respect he has for our spunk and pluck. He lets a faint chuckle escape his creased lips. I know Lindy notices it. She's been staring adoringly into his eyes since she first spotted him, hoping for some kind of recognition. Dad allows a small salute, a little winky smirk in her direction and then promptly turns away. Lindy jolts to life. She bobs back and forth on the balls of her feet, looking ready to do the fight all over again. She swivels about, darting looks back and forth from Dad to the officer to Harvey.

"Awm, not pessing chawges," Harvey mumbles. He lowers his head, unable to look anyone in the eyes.

"You should ask the rest of the ladies around here if they want to press charges," Dad says.

"I already did," the officer says. "They don't want to take a side."

"Oh, for fucks sake," Dad spits. He whirls around to face the rest of the women circled together by the entrance. He flings his arms out wide in an imploring fashion, as if to say, *Really? Not one of you, after all this, has the guts?* "None of them?" He asks, shaking his head.

"Nope," the officer responds, shrugging as he snaps his pen into his breast pocket, giving Dad a little pump with his elbow in the process. There is an air of resignation and intimacy to the way he nudges Dad's arm. He too is disappointed.

Together they scan the group; asking, pleading with their eyes for someone to come forward, do the right thing. Dad snorts, shakes his head. He cranes his neck down to take one last look at his bundled wife. Maybe she'll take a stand. Does she have any of the gumption or moxie she somehow passed onto Lindy? He nestles his head down under her chin, compelling her to look up at him.

Mom keeps her head hung low, closes her eyes and sighs. "There's already been enough negativity and sorrow for one day," she whimpers.

"Well, shit," Dad groans. "Why did I come down here?" He seems to be asking the officer mainly. The officer doesn't have an answer. The man just clucks his tongue and whistles; a calculated response meant to say, *Man, you're preaching to the choir*. They make mirrored shrugs. Dad throws his arms up in the air, letting go of Mom's shoulders. He keeps the arms up, spread full, holding some imaginary globe up to the sky. He looks exactly like the way Randy had drawn him in the painting. The resemblance is close enough to be eerie.

Then Dad does something nobody sees coming. He looks over at the dejected Harvey still sitting and cradling his crumpled mouth in back of the ambulance. "Do you know why?" he asks, trying to meet his eyes. Harvey refuses to look up. He's pretending to not even hear him, but it's a poor pretending job.

"Okay!" Dad shouts. He lets his arms come slamming back down at his sides. "Thank you, officer," Dad says, brusquely. And that's it. He's done. "Have a good night. Come on, everyone," he says. He aims himself toward the car, sets his shoulders and heads downhill. After a brief pause, we follow him.

"You know, if Mother Teresa were here, she'd have a goddamn conniption fit," Dad says. He's a few paces ahead of us, his voice sailing off toward the road.

"Nobody said anything because we didn't want to make things worse. We need healing and harmony more than anything else," Mom offers, sheepishly.

"You need a fucking union," Dad says.

Mom breaks down then, starts sniffling and whimpering. Dad halts, turns around. "Aaaaaaack," he sighs, pivoting, doubling back to meet her. He puts an arm around her again, squeezes her close. "It's okay," he says. "All right. Okay," he says. He guides her forward unsteadily, snared together like a singular, four-legged blob. It's clumsy going, and a few strides in Dad steps sideways on a rock and loses his balance. "Fucking mercy stroke," he mumbles, teetering back into position. He says this one quietly, softly, and almost gets away with it. But Lindy and I hear it.

I peek over at Lindy. She has one of the biggest, goofiest grins I've ever seen on her, which makes me smile, too. "Stop it," Lindy says, but I can't. I start laughing.

"Stop it," Dad repeats up ahead, imitating Lindy's huffy voice. Then we hear Mom start to laugh a little, too.

"Stop it," I say, and then Lindy starts laughing also.

"Stop it," Lindy says again, but this time, this one time, I can tell, she doesn't mean it.

Immaculate Contraception (2002)

Lord help me, whenever April is over, I hide outside Lindy's door and eavesdrop. To a puberty stricken boy like me, a sister's older friend may as well be a giant bowl of naked pink candy. Okay, so that doesn't make any sense, but that's what happens. You can't think straight… Let's be honest, when your entire body is on fire with hormones, spying on your sister's hot friend is pretty much the sexiest thing a kid can do besides maybe hiring a prostitute, and I've only ever heard of one kid doing that. It was probably a lie, but still. I fantasized about that one for months. I think April's even older than me, maybe fifteen or sixteen, but she and Lindy are like these deranged, kindred sisters. They are soul mates. Today I hit the jackpot. They're literally talking about virginity and what a mind-boggler the whole ordeal is.

"It's like moving a bookshelf that's in the way of the TV but then realizing it's blocking the window now instead," April says.

I have one of Dad's old pint glasses pressed up against the outside of the door. The wide end's facing my ear; just like I've seen kids do in movies.

"Totally," says Lindy, "like when you rescue a dog from a shelter, and you bring him home and all he does is piss and bite your arm."

"You wish you'd just let him die, right?" April says.

"Exactly," Lindy says. It doesn't sound like they're talking sex at all, but more like figuring out the answers to complicated riddles. They're voices are both enthusiastic and irritated at the same time.

"You know there's a surgery that makes it back to how it was before?"

"No way. You're joking."

"No, it's called Hymenoplasty," April says. "It's a real thing."

"Gross," Lindy says. "That doesn't sound real. How much is it?"

"I have no idea," April says. "There's this place or this person… I'm not sure which one, and it's called something like the Hymen Ridgewood. It's a technique I think."

This is fast becoming one of the most unsexy conversations I've ever heard. Surgeries and ailments? They may as well be discussing retirement villages.

"Could you imagine?" Lindy says. "A new virgin again."

There is a considerable pause. "I know," April finally says. She says it dreamily, like longing for an expensive gift she's always wanted. "It would be like those air-fresheners people buy for their cars, like 'New Car Smell,'" she says.

"New hymen smell," Lindy giggles. "You could tie it there over the hole with some hair." They laugh hard.

After they're done laughing it gets very silent for a while. It gets so quiet that the absence of sound starts to make me uneasy, and I start to feel guilty and ashamed. I back away from the door.

"Well, I don't think you'll need the procedure because I'm the only one you've told and you don't really act like a you-know-what, and so it doesn't show on you, and also, you already sort of convinced yourself that it didn't count," April says.

My heart knocks in my chest. It's a hammer inside a dryer. I don't want to know this. This is more than I want. And yet I can't pull myself away.

"That's true," Lindy says.

"You're lucky," April says.

"Yeah, I guess so. Thanks."

I hear what sounds like bed sheets being removed and then a tearing sound.

"What are you doing?" April asks.

"This'll make it official," Lindy says.

"Oh, okay." After another minute or two, during which time I jam my ear so hard against the door that it almost falls off, April says, "Well, I really have to go."

"Okay," Lindy says, "see you tomorrow."

"See you tomorrow," April says, and then right away, before I can unfold or unglue my ear from the door, she wings the thing open, and I go slamming backward.

When she brutes her way out I'm trying to scurry to my feet. I've only made it to my knees, and so there's this comical scene they come out to, me kneeling on the carpet with my arms and hands in the air looking stupid, like I'm being robbed or something.

"Whoa!" April says. "What the fuck are you doing?"

"Nothing!" I say. It takes everything I have not to shout, *Don't shoot!* "I was picking up some money I dropped."

"You don't have any money, perv! I'm telling your mom," she says.

"Yes I do. I have lots of money. She'll tell you how rich I already am."

April storms her way past me and flees right out the door. And because I'm not only embarrassed but still wildly turned on, I try to catch what she's wearing, maybe grab onto some enticing scent or appealing gesticulation. I don't really have time to see anything, but in my bonkers adolescent mind she's wearing a short plaid dress, knee high socks and pigtails. Her white Oxford is tied in a knot around her navel, a little wisp of blonde fuzz trailing downward. *Hit me baby one more time…*

I make it to my feet, and realize that I haven't heard anything from Lindy. I'm shocked she hasn't yelled or thrown something at me yet. I creep over to her door, still expecting a shoe or fist to the face, and I see her there, hovering over her bed. All the blankets are stripped off, and she's stacking paper towels in the middle. There must be fifty squares already piled there, and she's ripping more off from the roll, each sheet drapes right on top of the next like a tower in the center of the mattress.

Then, without even turning toward me, she shouts, "Get out of here! Get out, Clayton! You're not wanted." Her head is down, facing the towels, like she's not really talking to me but addressing the bed instead for some reason. And I think about asking if she's okay, but I'm too nervous, and so before I can think about it too hard, I hightail it out of there just in case.

The Tragedy Theorem (2003)

It's just past her curfew, about 10:05 on Friday night, when Lindy comes home looking like she's been caught in some sort of deranged street fight. Her eyeliner streaks her cheeks like muddy rainwater. The slinky tank top she normally wears with great audacity and dexterity has been stretched so vigorously it looks more like a scarf around her skinny neck. Her breathing is out of control, husky, whooping gusts. She throws her purse on the couch beside me. For a few moments she leans her palms against the backrest, concentrating, trying to slow her heart rate.

"That was like the most crazy night that has ever happened," she says. She's been spending so much time with April her voice is starting to take on that valley girl drawl all the popular girls are adopting.

"What…" I say. I draw myself up against the cushions, lowering my voice to a whisper. I take a hard, purposeful glance at our parents' bedroom door, then back up at her, meant to remind her to keep her voice down. They've gone to sleep early, told me to wait up for Lindy. This is something they've been doing more of lately, trusting me to be in charge. It's sort of a self-fulfilling prophecy. In return for their confidence, I become the square, upright guardian that they envision anyway. This is a win-win for them. Lindy, of course, acts older than her age too, but not at all in the same ways, not in the way they covet. I think Mom and Dad think we might cancel each other out. "What happened?" I rejoin. On the TV, a *Seinfeld* rerun plays at a respectable, parent-friendly volume.

Jerry is explaining something sensible to Kramer about how his home security system won't work if the door is left wide open. Hushed, canned laughter rings out. I pick up the remote from the coffee table and turn it off.

Lindy comes around the couch, plops down next to me. She smells of sweat and fruity perfume. Her hair and clothes are drenched in it. I watch her gaze as it dims, quivers and collapses inward for memory recovery. It's the kind of purposeful, pointed cognition that comes with accompanying eye closure.

"April and I are getting ice cream at Georgie's, right?" She's keeping it down, but still speaking in a brisk, wired tone. Georgie's is the local place for teens to sit around and look bored with life, maybe lick some soft serve in whatever seductive manner their hormones dictate.

"Okay," I say. I try using a level, impartial tone, one that keeps a safe distance while enticing open communication to fill the gap. My aloof posture on the couch is intended to do the same.

"We're sitting there, and like we're surrounded by all of these little kids. Just swarms of them. Four-year-olds, Five, six, seven-year-olds, whatever... they're everywhere. There weren't even enough parents for these kids. Like, there must have been eight kids for every adult. It was like they just appeared there, like they'd landed some alien ship and come waddling out to take control of the place."

"Well, kids do love ice cream," I say, not meaning to sound disagreeable.

"That's what April said," Lindy complains. Her eyes pop open as she lets out a rankled moan. "She was like, whatever, Lindy, it's a Friday night. What's the big deal? But I don't know, it seemed strange to me. And I started telling her that I think little kids freak me out a little bit, like they make me a little jittery or something." She arches her back, bracing for the shiver that sends her back into spasm. "I don't think I like little kids," she says. "I think I just realized that tonight!"

"That's weird," I say, "but, I mean…" trying to correct myself, "they're not for everyone."

"You sound like April," She says. Every time she says April and I have something in common, I get these lusty pictures of us together in my mind. They cycle through in fast-forward mode, anything from falling in love to humping, even getting married. I almost get a hard on. "But listen," she continues, "I'm telling her all this, and I'm explaining how dirty and slimy and snotty they all are. I point at this one kid who has somehow managed to drag his ice cream through his hair like a comb. He's got like chocolate pudding hair. It's gross! Look how sticky they are, I'm telling her. Look! I point out another kid, a little girl who like literally was so sticky that she had glued her hand to her shirt with like caramel sauce. She couldn't get it off. She was just sitting there, hand pasted to her shirt, bawling like an idiot!"

"They're not idiots," I say, trying to channel something like April might have said, "they're just kids."

"I don't think I like them, Clay." She whines, sort of weeping a little now. "I mean, I don't think I want to have kids."

"You're only thirteen," I say. "You shouldn't say that." I've abandoned my cool, laidback attitude. There's no fighting off this Dad inside of me.

"I know!" she barks. Something dark and angry passes into her eyes. "Don't you think I know that?" she says. I must have repeated something April said again. I get another jolt, a mix of fear and excitement. Lindy calms herself by closing her eyes again, clutching her heart while she breathes. "So," she says, gulping, taking a long final exhalation. "So, I finish telling April all this stuff about my little kid phobia or whatever, and then we're just quiet for awhile. I have no idea what April's thinking about, but I'm still thinking about those messy kids. I can't even imagine having to go home with them and wash them up, put them to bed, make sure they don't cover the sheets in syrup or their own drool, and I'm getting more and more and more sick. I was losing my appetite."

She stops talking, takes a deep, stuttering breath. Her face falls. I watch as she lowers her head, lets her shoulders go limp and noodly against the backrest. All the life just seems to ooze out of her. Her pupils go rushing back, rolling up under her eyelids.

"What happened?" I say, reaching over to steady her torso before her whole body goes the way of those flapping, rolling eyes.

"I'm sitting there," she starts, and then she begins crying. Tears come leaking out of her eyes, and she just lets them come, softening her expression with their warmth. She makes no attempt to stop them. "And, all of a sudden we like heard this horrible scream," she sniffles. "It sounded like someone starting up an ambulance siren right in back of you, like the siren was like inside your ears." She pauses, wipes some tears away with her wrist. "I look over," she says, and stops again, gasping. "I look over at the exit and there's this huge truck plowing out of the parking lot. It's like one of those monster trucks, and underneath it, like stuck to the bottom of the bumper, is a little kid. He's like jammed there, smacked to the bottom like a wad of bubble gum! I can't tell what part he's pinned to... how? All I can see is his legs bouncing the pavement, the little kid jeans with elastic at the bottom and baby little kid sneakers. One of the sneakers comes off and tumbles down the street … It's white and so small, like it doesn't even look real. None of it looks real. April drops her cone on the ground, and everyone starts running after the truck. Moms are bonkers. Kids are wailing. Somebody knocked me over," she says. She grabs the strap on her top and pulls it back up on her shoulder like she's trying to fix or preserve whatever dignity she has control over.

"Oh my God," I say, "that's crazy! What happened? Did he die? I mean, is everyone okay? Is anyone?"

"I don't know," she says, shaking her head. "I couldn't watch. I just like started running. I ran all the way home. I've never even run like two blocks before, but I ran like two miles," she says. She pulls her legs in against her chest, coils herself into a ball.

What could possibly be said? If I'm supposed to be the adult in this situation, I am clearly failing. There are zero adults on the sofa. Lindy and I are the only ones. I place my hand on her bare knee, but not with any sort of firmness or compassion, just kind of rest it there like a damp cloth. "I'm sorry," I say.

Lindy glances up at me in a deep, pleading way. "I kept thinking all the way home, like what if I did this? What if I made this happen with my obsessive thoughts?"

"Wow. Yeah," I say, shaking my head. I hadn't even put that together. "I mean … Wow."

"No," she says. She reaches out, clinches my hand. "Do you think I did? Tell me! Did I do it? Is it true?" she begs. "Does one thing lead to another?"

Sixteen year olds are prone to all kinds of whacky thinking. We can be tricked into any number of outlandish notions, from urban legends about vanishing hitchhikers to postulations about malicious insects burrowing into your brain. It's what gullible, wondrous youth are programmed for. But I am not a kid tonight. That is not what I was charged to do. I am in command, and that confidence makes me think I know what to do.

"It's not like that," I tell her. "It's not like a one plus one type of thing. It doesn't add up." I invent everything as I go along. There is a gnawing in me that I ignore, a deviousness that wants to shine through, and I feel a partial tingle of adventure, wanting to break script and indulge in some bizarre, nightmarish scenario where we scare each other so much we can't get to sleep. Like we used to do when we were kids… still are kids… I have one foot in each world, halfway between adolescence and adulthood.

"It's not like math?" she asks, her moist, childish eyes twinkling up at me.

"Exactly," I say. "It's not like math."

Somehow, out of pure luck, the answer has been the right one. It works. I can tell, can see it was working, watch the cooling sensation burrow its way in. Something about the logic in the words cool things, manage a stark restorative effect to her frayed moorings. She heaves forward, collapsing into my arms. Her tears turn my shirt warm and damp. And we just sit there, tangled together, trying to figure out our roles, our physiology; two old children too young for complicated equations.

An Easy Going (2002)

Maureen has a way of greeting people that is both bracing and rousing at once. Imagine an unannounced visitor ringing your doorbell on a quiet afternoon. You obey the signal, approach with requisite wariness and agitation, and as you peek outside the window you glimpse a woman with a wooden, ramrod posture. Her cavernous mouth is filled with a gaping, preposterous smile. Her wave is like a creaky hinge, more forearm than wrist, set in time to some unseen metronome. It's a scene out of some creepy movie with a circus theme. Doubtless you identify this peculiar woman as a salesperson, thus setting in motion your natural fight or flight response... This is the odd experience I am forced to reckon with every time I encounter Maureen Johns no matter how big or small the occasion. Take for instance my casual drop-in at the Ambassador for Saturday lunch with Mom.

"Hello!" Maureen shouts as she spots me coming through the doors of the downstairs lounge. She shoots up from the table, and right away snaps into the eerie saleswoman routine. Mom has been sitting facing the wall, and she whips her head around, a little spooked by Maureen's vehemence. The sheer combustion of the whole display always girds me at first. I almost drop my lunch.

"Hi," I say, catching the paper bag before it hits the floor. Mom stands up and meets me with a hug; she squeezes extra tight for some reason, like she's happy to find that I am still alive. We sit down side by side on the bench.

"Yes, yes," Maureen sings, "sit down. Join us." She stays standing long after I have settled into place, casting down on us from the other side of the table.

The space, like most basement break rooms, is bleak and cheerless; a few fluorescent ceiling lights, a faded poster of a drab sunrise, some fake plants arranged inside a cheap golden pot and placed at the center of a folding table.

"I was just telling your mom about Red," Maureen says. She finally sits down, settling so softly into place that her motion doesn't make a sound.

Mom puts her arm through my elbow and presses down hard against my bicep, like a warning. I flinch. "Oh, I think we should save that story for another time," Mom says.

"Who's Red?" I ask, trying to wiggle some feeling back into my arm.

"No, really, Roberta," Maureen says, "it'll be fine. I think Clayton should hear this. It will be good for him. You're never too young to learn about the essential laws of surrender."

Mom releases some pressure on my arm, but does not let go completely. The tender grasp has the warm, ruminating feeling of a gesture that was more for her benefit than mine. Maureen has some psychic hold on Mom, and everyone knows it, Maureen especially. She knows that Mom cannot resist anyone with a commanding personality. Maureen must have also figured by now that Mom doesn't have the luxury of resisting much of anyone. Maureen is her only friend. Loneliness, she is just savvy enough to understand, is one hell of an agent.

"We were on vacation in Mazatlan, me and Red," Maureen starts right in, disregarding Mom's wishes. She smiles primly, but not necessarily at the story. It seems to be directed at some inward, private tickling. "He'd always wanted to go to Mexico. We were pretty young when we got married, and it was almost two years since the wedding, and so much had happened already, and I guess it was sort of like our belated honeymoon. He wouldn't have wanted to call it that because of the circumstances, but what other word is there?"

I slide a ham sandwich out of my bag and begin unwrapping it. The plastic crinkles, causing a slight rift in the communication. I want to show Mom how I've made it just like hers, with lettuce and tomato and a little bit of salad dressing, but she isn't paying attention. She's busy trying to hang on, power through Maureen's account. With Mom holding my arm so tight, I have a hard time getting the sandwich to my mouth. She and Maureen are locking eyes, engaging in some sort of battle, a telekinetic showdown. I kind of want to ask what the circumstances are that she is referring to, but I don't care enough to disrupt things any further than they already are.

"See, I think Red had waited so long, too long, to release all of his... well, stress. That's the tamest way to put it. He needed a vacation. Vacation! That's the word I guess. I don't know. Anyway, that was part of the problem from the beginning. Everything he did and said was coming out too big, too extreme," Maureen pauses long enough to make a gesture like she's hoisting an enormous ball in the air, then continues right on. "So when he finally got in the ocean, it was like whoa! He couldn't just go for a little swim, he had to go on some sort of huge quest, you know, like push the limit."

I take another bite of my sandwich. Some of the dressing oozes out the side, and I have to get a napkin to wipe it off my cheek. I wrestle out of Mom's clutches. In a few moments the story will be over, I think, and I can ask Mom if she wants to go for ice cream when her shift ends. Bullishly, perhaps miffed by my overly casual reactions thus far, Maureen shifts her gaze from Mom to me.

"He was just swimming and swimming," Maureen says, watching both of us out of the corner of her eyes, "stroking away like there was no tomorrow." She flaps her arms about, frantically paddling her way through imaginary waters. "Within about four or five minutes he was so far out, I could hardly see him. He was just this distant speck gliding through the water, like one of those blips on a radar screen. The lifeguard noticed, and he started blowing his whistle. 'Come in! Come in' he was hollering, but it was in Spanish, and so it was, 'Adelante, adelante!'" She stands, leans over the table and cups her hands over her mouth. "But Red didn't understand Spanish. What did he know? Here's this Mexican guy looking at me, and he's wondering why my husband won't stop, and I'm like, 'hey, buddy, he doesn't know what you're saying; maybe you could speak his own language at least. What do you expect?' And this guy looks at me like I'm nuts. Like *I'm* nuts. This guy, he looks at me, and then he looks out at Red, and back at me…" She gets a far off look in her eyes, sits back down. Somewhere buried behind those eyes she is still on that shore, imploring Red to turn back. "And I'm just staring out at Red. He looks so peaceful, like he knows exactly what he's doing. And his body is getting smaller and smaller, and after a little while I'm not even sure I can see him anymore. And then the lifeguard grabs his little orange floaty device and starts to go charging out into the water, but I put my hand on his shoulder and stop him. This guy, he looks at me and he can't understand what's happening. I don't know a lick of Spanish, and so all I say is 'No! Stop!'" Maureen pauses. She's gazing off toward the door, lost in the memory. "I told the guy, I said, if it's meant to be he'll wash back in. There's no use fighting. We can't hold back the waves. Struggle? Struggle?! That's the worst thing we could do. Are you crazy!" she says. She pounds the table, then seems to reconsider quickly and reins her emotions back in. "And there he goes," she says softly. "There he goes. I'd never seen anything more serene in my whole life. For a second I thought I could feel him letting go, trusting the current or whatever else might be meant to carry him wherever he was meant to go." I can tell she's picturing it in her mind, following the stream. "He's just… poof… whisk, off into the horizon. And… and the sun is shining and the gulls are swooping. It's an unbelievably gorgeous day. The water is this emerald green and royal blue, and… and Red is gone."

I stop chewing my sandwich, unsure if I still have the ability to swallow, and put the sandwich down. Mom releases her grasp, unable to use any of her sapped strength to hold on.

"See, that's what Red would have wanted," Maureen says. "The people in Mazatlan, the police and the surfers and the ocean authorities, they didn't understand. They couldn't. How is a poor, Spanish speaking man going to understand all of the things that Red and I talked about before that moment? Could you imagine if everyone had started screaming and carrying on? What good would that have done?"

She is looking straight at me, Maureen, with this serious, prodding look, like she really wants me to answer. With great effort I shake my head no. I manage to start chewing again, but not too well. Instead of swallowing a few small particles, I end up ingesting a solid rock of dough and vegetables that hurts going down.

"Should we have ruined everyone's time, possibly traumatized them for… forever… the horror. No…" For a few more seconds she just sits there shaking her head, mouthing the word "no" over and over again. "There is no reward for that. If something is meant to happen it will or it won't. That's it. That's your prize, that knowledge of deliverance."

Despite all of my wishing and yearning, she isn't finished. Somehow I can tell, can sense the bundle of tension surrounding us has not yet been uncoiled all the way. I don't dare move.

"This is important, Clay," Maureen says, as if there is any possibility I am still taking any of this as a joke. "One of the first steps to enlightenment is letting go. You have to understand that, *life!*" she says, spiking the word on a stick, "life will always give you something better than what it asks you to give up. Do you understand?"

It is clear that she is not going to release me from her glaring until I agree, and so I am all too happy to nod my head.

"Life is one beautiful, whole movement. Red knew this. We talked about it often. He was proving something to himself and to me and the universe. Life, Clayton, life cannot contradict itself or be in conflict. The earth is in harmony with us, and us with it. We are part of the same ground. All of it!" She spreads her arms wide, trying to fit the entire room between her hands. "When I lost my first job as a dry cleaning assistant back in Kentucky, Red said to me, he said the most wonderful thing… he said, 'Maureen, this is exactly how it should be. Who and what you were up until this moment of upheaval was but a seed to the flower.'" She shakes her head, then lowers it into her hands, and rests it there for a long time. I am certain she is crying, but when she raises her head again she's beaming. She reaches out across the table and puts her hand over mine. There is fervency in her, a compulsion to reach forth, lug people into her sphere of influence. "It's a story of rebirth and renewal," she whispers. "Energy, both negative and positive, will clear space for us if we let it. It stirs us so that we can recognize a higher purpose." She lets go of my hand and leans back against the wall behind her, satisfied but also winded, spent by the treasonous weakening effect of her own passion. When she rolls her head to the side a grease stain in the shape of a Rorschach Test blots the peeling wall where the hair used to be. "And now here I am."

She has spoken with such tranquility, such certainty, that I almost expect a bell to chime the way a prayer or sermon is sometimes ended in church. A shiver needles its way down my spine. My fingers go limp around the ham sandwich, and it sort of just wilts from my hand onto the table. I don't want to look over at Mom because I'm worried that she might be too scared and won't want me to see her that way. I'm afraid that she is afraid, and that makes me move very slowly as I turn my head to look at her. The gradual motion is meant to give me time to figure out how two people might go about comforting one another under these circumstances. How can we share some brief signal of distress and then move to get out of the situation as fast as possible? But when I meet her eyes, I do not see any signs of flight or concern, but instead a look of detached reverence and wonderment. Her gaze is fixed and placid, but behind it, inside, she is adrift, already gone like Red.

Baptism By Fire (2003)

Lindy's crying has reached a level of intensity that can no longer be ignored. I've already been to her bedroom twice to check and see if she wants me to help with anything, but her attitude toward my sympathy both times is best defined as dismissal and agitation. My opening of the door seems to only act as a widening of the funnel through which her anguish gushes. The fact that Randy has come over again for one of his morning walks with Dad is only complicating matters. He sits at the kitchen table, waiting for Mom and Dad to get home from the bagel place, sipping coffee and pretending not to notice Lindy's wailing. For the past few weeks Randy's been dropping by early every Saturday and Sunday for what he calls his "sobriety strolls" with Dad. From what I can tell, they're working. I haven't seen Dad take a single swig of alcohol in almost a month.

Following my second visit to Lindy's room, I walk back into the kitchen and grab a seat next to Randy. He takes a loud slurp of coffee from his mug. The mug is so full that every time he blows on it another slosh of coffee splashes onto the wooden tabletop.

"What's up with Lindy?" he asks. There's a serene quality to the way he hunches forward over his drink, eyes hardly visible above the rim, shoulders relaxed. If not for the stream of coffee dripping down his wrist, staining the cuffs of his flannel shirt, he's the picture of calm and stability.

I can't tell him about how Lindy witnessed a small child being dragged beneath a truck last night at an ice cream shop, so I just say, "she had a rough evening."

Lindy's crying shifts into a higher, whinier register. It sounds like the shriek of a fire siren.

"Maybe I should go talk to her," Randy says. He sweeps a hand back through his silver hair, bunches the end in his fist and releases it so that it falls into a luring curtain just above the shoulder line. Lindy's crying fades down, idles to a dull whimper in the background.

"No," I say, "I think she wants to be left alone." Lindy must be lying in wait, using our conversation as bait, because upon hearing my response, she takes her screeching to what can only be the loudest register she is capable of reaching.

Randy puts his cup down. He raises his eyebrow at me. There is a heavy helping of skepticism in that eyebrow. It lifts more than just skin and muscle in its arching. It's then that I realize maybe Lindy's plan has been to capture Randy's favor all along. It's Randy's coltish reassurance she wants. Of course. She's trying to coax him out, force his leathery hand. This is about a different kind of attention, the type an effete brother can't possibly offer.

Randy stands, cracking his back on the way up. He pushes the chair in softly, with an air of competence and resignation. This is surrender. He lets Lindy win at her own defective game, even though he's already figured out all of her strategies and could easily defeat her with a simple dose of evasion or disregard if he chose.

I follow Randy as he walks to Lindy's room. She is still howling, but Randy approaches it not with concern or trepidation, but with tact and prudence. He sort of half knocks as he nudge the door open with a sly knee.

"Can I come in?" he says, pretty much already all the way in.

The crying comes to an almost immediate end, like someone cranking off a garden hose. Randy pulls out the small white chair in front of Lindy's little-girl vanity. He removes the fluffy teddy bear from the seat and puts it in his lap as he sits down. Lindy looks from me to Randy then back again, and it is clear that she doesn't want me waiting around, soldiering the door. I step outside and close it tight, but I don't latch it or leave the hallway.

Through the door I hear Lindy tell Randy everything, the whole story, from how she and April were licking ice cream cones to how the boy's body looked limp and lifeless as he banged and flapped around under the wheels of the truck. She spills it all, how she felt responsible and guilty, how she was certain that something inside of her had made it happen, maybe *wanted* it to happen. There is such coolness and articulation in her voice, as if she'd been remaining clear-headed and lucid all along. Had she ever even been tormented or conflicted by any of it?

Randy listens to everything. Not once do I hear him respond, not even during prolonged pauses that call for a reply. He waits them out, and every time Lindy comes back in, deletes the silence with more words. Randy knows he can count on this, can milk it. He doesn't speak one time until Lindy is all the way finished. When it is all over, I hear Randy stand up from the chair. He moves closer to Lindy, and I estimate, based on his trajectory, that he's about to sit down next to her on the bed, but I don't think he does because there are no sounds of springs folding or sheets rustling, and then I hear Randy come to a stop. I hear the floorboards squeak, and then I hear him take a crinkly piece of paper out of his pocket and fondle it for a while before offering anything.

"This is a prayer," he says. There is another a pause as he hands the paper over to Lindy. Lindy sniffles and smooths the paper, and then there is silence, which I can only assume is her delicate moment to read the note. "It's called the Violet Flame," he continues after a while.

"What is it?" Lindy asks. Judging from her tone, she's nervous, maybe shuttering a little bit as she struggles to hold the paper straight.

"Well, it's kind of hard to explain, but basically it's a prayer that when you say it everything bad you've ever said and done, any mistake you've made or any negativity you've ever produced, it goes away."

"How does it work?" Lindy asks. I have to put my ear extra close because they're both starting to talk very low and sultry.

"There's something called karma and there's good vibrations and bad vibrations in life, and…" he pauses, "the thing is everyone has things they've done that they wish they hadn't. It's a part of growing up. This prayer, it's a… it's like an eraser of bad spirits and deeds. I mean, I could try to explain to you about the physics of light and darkness and about something called the alchemist's dream, but all you really need to know is that if you say this prayer often enough, like over and over again all the time, God and the universe will forgive you, and then you can forgive yourself." It is quiet for a stretch, and then Randy does go over, he must, and he does sit down next to Lindy on the bed. Each creek is like a separate warning, a cautioning that goes unheeded. "You understand, don't you?" he asks.

"I think so," Lindy says. Her words are coming more aggressive now, dripping as tigerish bites. "How do you know it works?"

"Well," Randy says, backing away, and then coming closer again in his body language, "you see me don't you? You see I'm smiling and I'm healthy, right?" There is no response to this, only imagined space, vacant space waiting to be plugged. "Well, I'm living proof."

"How will I know if I'm doing it right? Will I feel something move or change?"

"You can keep that paper," Randy says. "It has everything on it about how and where and when you should practice. It takes all the guesswork out of it so all you have to do is repeat the words over and over again. They call it a celestial script. Can you say that? Try."

"Celestial script," Lindy repeats. She's already preparing, drafting a mental list.

"That's right," says Randy. "Celestial means it belongs to another plane of consciousness, something high and mighty. See, here on earth people are flawed but up there," he says, "up in the sky, there are no such things as errors or slipups. You can't go wrong."

"I want to start," Lindy says.

"Go on," Randy says, "give it a try."

"I am the violet flame," she starts, reading line by line, "to light alone I bow."

I hear Dad's keys rattling in the lock. Randy hears them too. He springs up from the bed, leaps for the door. I run for the couch. And then Randy is bursting free, firing out of the room.

"Neil!" Randy says as Dad comes through the door. "There you are. Ready for our walk?" His voice comes out loud and rushed, falling syllables trying to catch themselves before they crash to the ground. He rubs his hands down his pants to dry the sweat.

"What's going on?" Dad asks. He's still standing in the doorframe, the paper bag filled with bagels dangling from his hairy fist.

"Nothing," Randy says. His hands make zipper noises on the thighs of his jeans. "Nothing."

Lindy's voice grows rowdy and demanding. "I am the violet flame!" she shouts. "I am the light of God shining every hour!"

Dad closes the door hard behind him. Mom must be standing right behind him because as the door goes slamming shut in her face, I hear her call out, "Hey!" Instinctively, reacting to the rattling slam and the castigating echo it leaves behind, Randy backs away. Dad rumbles toward him, a dogged boxer stalking his opponent across the ring at the sound of the bell.

III. HOW TO USE THE SHORTCUT

Listening Plus Waiting Equals Distance (2003)

The first time April comes to the house when Lindy isn't home I think it's an innocent mistake. The fact that she doesn't look innocent in her super short shorts and tight tube top doesn't necessarily set off any alarms. April's always dressing for beach weather or worse. What does make me jumpy is that when she sticks her hand up under my shirt and squeezes my nipple. We're standing on the porch, the door halfway open from my residual uncertainty. It isn't even noon yet.

"Ouch!" I yelp.

"Don't be a pussy," April says, "it's only a spider bite."

"Why did you do that?" I ask.

"I'm bored," she says. As I rub my nipple she stares straight into my eyes, either hoping to melt my confidence or bolster it. It is what can be considered a seductive gaze, but that sort of thing has an opposite effect on me anyway, so it really doesn't matter.

"I guess I'm not familiar," I say.

"You wouldn't be."

I'm still massaging my chest, hoping she'll go away so I can have some alone time to sit and process what just happened.

"Don't be a gentleman and invite me in. You're going under the bridge with a lady," she says. She makes it sound like some kind of ritual passage. Before I can respond she's already bounding down the steps and heading for the sidewalk. "You're coming," she says. "Put some shoes on."

The bridge I know she's taking me to is the one about a mile away beneath the Lawrence Street overpass. The area's a known wasteland, a place where derelicts and outcasts get stoned and screw their scummy girlfriends. There used to be a torn skirt hanging on a tree branch down there. It must have been there for three years. I remember it was small and pink and the way it dangled there was like a warning or some of kind of crass conquering, which always scared me.

Trying to keep up with April as she trudges over the rocks and roots covered over by prickly weeds along the riverbank, I realize maybe sandals are the wrong choice of footwear. My hair is unwashed and gnarled, as is my T-shirt and athletic shorts I wore to bed last night. The afternoon heat is building. It rained all evening, and the air is pasty with warm mist.

The journey is fast paced and insistent, an ambiguous race across the asphalt of shadeless city streets. Along Lincoln Avenue people sit outside under umbrellas sipping coffee and nibbling on pastries. It's unclear if they note anything strange in seeing two teenagers bound for wilderness, the larger one panting and pumping to keep up. It's forty-five minutes of huffing and very little speaking.

There's no discernable reason for us to repel our way down the dicier part of the bank on all fours instead of walking down the smoother mud path on the other side, except April's leading and for that liberty there is no questioning. She's always in the lead, hiking over crooked, slippery stones, tearing dandelions up from her path like it's a requirement for reaching our destination. My toes are caked with dirt and debris, the nails wedged with russet earth. From time to time a leaping beetle, its shell the color of oil, alights from the reeds, hurls free of its slumber and spins into the air.

My armpits pool with sweat. There is no opportunity to wipe away any sediment from my neck or shoulders, and even if there was it wouldn't help. My fingers are useless anyway, all damp and soiled. Ahead, April crawls. Two identical streams of perspiration wash down the back of her firm, bronzed legs. When she takes an extra long stride, the cushiony skin around her butt cheeks dips below the denim line of her shorts. The desire to reach out and cup them, to stuff them back inside her underwear is almost unbearable. Her underwear. My God. I try not to think about what type of panties would allow such ample slippage of flesh; afraid my inability to hide my eagerness will show too prominently on my face. In the past year I've pictured her underwear a thousand times, and now that I am this close I can't handle the looking. It's one of life's great quandaries.

We were ascending for a while and then descending, down into a small canyon that opens up onto the teeth of the river, the part where the current comes biting out at the edges as if it's hungry for dry land. This is the spot where derelicts come to smoke cigarettes or worse, where transient children come to practice deviant behaviors no doubt modeled by absent parents. It has a chilling effect. There are all kinds of remnants down here, old beach blankets swarming with flies, stained pillows with the stuffing sliced out; some drunkard's idea of a sex den or something. The air smells of garbage and swamp gas.

When we reach our destination I sit down on the grass to rest. I am exhausted. The rushing water is inches away, close enough that I can lean forward and drink from it if I want. The passing traffic overhead shakes the bridge, their muffled tires rumbling over the bumpy pavement. April stands, hovering over me, her hands resting on her hips. She has barely broken a sweat.

"What, are you like a workout queen or something?" I ask her, trying to catch my breath.

"You need to exercise more," she says. "You're practically a man now."

It is maybe the best compliment I have ever received, and yet my mind lingers on the latter statement more than it should. And does she mean that my manhood is being defined and determined by this voyage as we speak? Is there some implication in her wording meant to infer that we are about to embark on a different kind of exercise?

With her slick brown hair cinched into a ponytail, her face looks stern but lovely. There is something of automatic control in her piercing green eyes. Everything about her is rigid and blustery, like she's ready to dole out punishment at the slightest indiscretion—a naughty principal in a cheap porno.

From where we are positioned, low in a slight hollow, we can see a few stray walkers standing by the railing up above, but they cannot see us. What stretches out in front of us is shrubbery and dirt trails leading to a small inlet area with only a few houses, johnboats and high wooden fences meant to keep people like us out. The traffic is light, but consistent. Aside from the river, the sounds of her feet smoothing the ground beneath us and our own breathing, everything is silent. I put my ear down close to the water and listen to it surge. The soft bubbling sound has a gentle but also unstoppable quality.

"If this was a railroad track," I say, lifting my head, "you could listen carefully to the vibrations." We are learning about sound waves in physics class. "People can predict when trains are coming by just listening. If you are patient, you eventually hear some kind of ringing sound, I guess, and you can tell how far away a train is."

"No, you're off. That doesn't sound right," she says. April doesn't have good grades in school, but they're not horrible either. From what I can tell, she gets by mostly on some kind of internal guilt reflex. She'll slack off for weeks on end, neglecting several smaller assignments, and then when she feels she's gone too far, there is a switch that is triggered and she turns it on, an operation that pulls herself back from the cliff just in time. It's a tug of war between her natural instincts and the person she knows she's expected to be.

I straighten up. "Two rings and one vibration means the train is fewer than two miles away."

"One ring equals a mile or two vibrations equals two?" she asks. She shakes her head. She crouches down beside me, her stout breasts almost resting in my lap. She presses her ear up against where mine is, the bend in her torso creating a perfect crescent.

"You multiply," I say.

"Of course you do. Everyone multiplies these days," she says. "I can hear the ocean."

"That's not the ocean. That's a seashell you're thinking of, but that's wrong," I say. "It's only ambient noise from around you, anyway. I mean, it's only because the shell is shaped like a big lobe or tube, and it picks up on whatever sounds are in the area and loops it back to you."

She rises higher on her toes, forcing her hips and waist into a point and her ear closer to the river. The butt cheeks again, intensified by her flexing. "There's no need to ruin it," she grunts.

I wonder how many takers she's escorted to this exact spot. She has a reputation, one that I've conjured into a myth beyond all reason. There are rumors that she's slept with the entire hockey team at her previous high school; members of which I am certain shared no resemblance to me.

"Explaining and ruining don't have to be the same thing."

"You are so wrong about that."

"I can prove I'm right." It takes everything I have not to reach for her.

"That doesn't mean a thing," she says.

"Oh, you think thoughts have frequencies," I say. I'm taunting her. "You can measure thoughts."

"What's wrong with you?" April asks. She collapses her legs and wiggles down beside me. At the same time her hand comes down and lands right on top of mine. She tries to make it seem like an accident, but it's a botched attempt. There is this thing I've always noticed about April. She is an enraged girl caught between two worlds. In one dimension she wants men to see her as desirable, irresistible, and in the other she wants respect, wants to be viewed as decent and wishes to punish men who covet her sex appeal. This is where she dwells all her life, stuck in this infuriating crevice, perpetually working to screech and claw her way out.

"That's what my mom says, about the frequency part," I stammer.

"Roberta loves me," she says, squeezing my knuckles in her palm.

"She really does," I say.

"You use a ruler for this measuring or something?" she says and laughs.

"Well, I mean, not like one you have in grade school," I say.

"What other kind are there?" she asks.

"I better not. This probably isn't the right… You wouldn't… I don't want you to think I'm insane," I say.

"Maybe I'll like it," she says, and then her mouth is on mine, her lips prying mine open. She pokes her tongue inside, jabbing first at my gums and then in the gap I make for her.

Her lips are cool and juicy, the way I imagine the river might taste, but the inside is sweet and sticky like honey. This is everything I have imagined and more. It's an overload of sensations, too much to handle. I can't quite settle it up in my head. My mind and hands are all over the place, little boiling atoms. It's like I'm here and not here at the same time, stuck between present and future tenses. My thoughts are already racing, outrunning my brain. I can already feel my mind seeping into some time, some dimension that is ahead of this one. I'm locking away the memory before it has a chance to form, saving it for inspiration or recovery for some unknown deficiency in the distance. When I try settling down, taking my time, I only feel panic at realizing the slippage of more seconds, the loss… the sensations are outstretching my capacity to hold them in the moment…

I run my palm down her back, slide it in under the crease of her shorts. There is nothing there but more warm, rolling skin. We are coming together, pushing against the pulsing momentum of our own bodies. April grabs my penis, and I think it's all over. I am going to burst. A rustling sound, someone whipping through tree branches, rings out behind us. We both hear it and unlock ourselves as quickly as possible. Standing there with a look one can only describe as a cobra ready to strike, is Lindy. She has one hand in her back pocket, and with the other she scratches the side of her nose, then spits onto the loam beside us.

"I followed you," she says. "I had a feeling. I knew I couldn't trust you." It's unclear which of us she's talking about. Then, as if to clarify, she looks right at me. "Benedict," she says, enunciating every letter, stabbing her eyes at me. Then she snaps her gaze over, latches it on April. "Arnold," she says, and storms away.

Windfalls and Tailwinds (2003)

It's getting late, and Dad and I are still the only ones home. I'm in my bedroom reading one of the books assigned for American Literature class, trying to block out the sound of the TV and Dad's phlegmy coughing coming from the family room. It's six thirty, which means *Monk* is on, Dad's favorite show. I hear Tony Shalhoub's panicked voice scream reprimands at somebody for touching his food. It's his OCD acting up again. On the screen, plates clatter to the floor, and Dad follows it with his own hacking laugh track. There's another noise too, a sort of rhythmic whisking that I can't fully make out. A light cloud of cigarette fumes has drifted through the cracks of my door, making my throat itch and clench. Outside, the whole place looks like a sauna, only with smoke instead of steam. I pull the bed sheet up over my nose and inhale. For about the hundredth time in the last ten years, I promise myself that I will never so much as pick up one of those cancer sticks once I leave the house after high school. Anyway, both of us are doing whatever we can to take our mind off of the fact that our other family members should have arrived over an hour ago.

When the door finally opens, it's past seven. Whatever Mom and Maureen had gotten into between the end of their shift and now is unknown, but as soon as they enter everything is forgotten. What overtakes any discussion or inquiry regarding the lateness is that for some reason Maureen is dressed like she's fresh from a role as a servant woman at the local Renaissance fair. Her shirt is bright white and billowy with kinked sleeves around the elbows. Over top she wears a red velvet vest tied fast with leather that makes her boobs rise and point like two stout bullets. Lining each side of her ribs are more ropes and hooks. Then, as if to prove that she is seeing the outfit all the way through, she's added a skinny gold crown, cocked sideways atop her orange hair.

As they shuffle down the hall Maureen is right behind Mom, almost on top of her. She steers her by the shoulders, talking fast, saying something about how the Jewel grocery store didn't have the right Japanese variety she was looking for, but whatever it was would have to do. Mom is stooped and panting, weighed down by the two sagging plastic bags in each hand.

As they pass through the family room, Dad looks up from his recliner and lets out a raucous laugh. A fit of wet, raspy coughing catches him good, but he recovers. He leans way back until the springs make a thunking noise against the carpet, then bungs forward, hacking and slapping his knee. Drawn out by the sound of the commotion, I stand in the doorway. At first sight, unable to get a beat on what is happening, I laugh too. But based on Maureen's serious look as she pushes Mom straight passed us and keeps right on talking, this isn't meant as a joke.

"We're making you dinner," Maureen says. "Just sit back and relax." Dad leans forward, plants his feet on the floor. He puts his hands over his face and roars. Tripped up by Maureen's impatience, Mom almost takes a tumble as she enters the kitchen. Unimpressed by any of it, Maureen asks, "Where's Lindy?" Dad is in no position to answer.

"I don't know where she is," I say.

"Figures," Maureen snorts. She snatches the bags from Mom and heaves them up on the counter. "She'll have to get her blessings another time."

When neither Mom nor Maureen responds to our looks of confusion or hilarity, Dad and I drop it. We just let it go. We've both seen Maureen act in outlandish ways before. That it is a random Thursday night, that they are late, and that she has not been invited, doesn't much matter. There isn't anything you can do once Mom lets her take over and come inside. Unless you are in the mood for a lot of crying and arguing, you just concede and move on.

Dad goes back to what he is doing. Now I can see what the other sound was I couldn't quite place before. He reaches down between his legs, retrieves a jar of polish in one hand and a small brush in the other. With his big black shoe wedged in his knees, and his Camel between his lips, he commences his shining and TV watching.

Back inside my room, I sit on the bed. In my book, the main character, Holden Caulfield, has just arrived at a sleazy hotel in New York City. He's talking about how there are perverts and maniacs all over the place, which he can at least appreciate. Up until this point, he's been surrounded by phonies. The kid just wants people to be real, say what they mean and mean what they say, but everywhere he looks people are pretending to be someone or something that they think they ought to be instead of who they really are. Only in cities do you find people willing to really let loose, totally come out. That's where all the freaks end up. If they aren't born there, they find their way there on a bus, they hitchhike or they walk the three hundred miles because they are nuts, and they just can't take it anymore. They'd do anything to escape their backward hometowns where everyone looks at them like they just flew in from Mars. I've never been to New York City, but I bet it's just like Holden describes it. It's the best thing I've ever read.

Every few pages I stop reading and look at the clock. It's almost eight o'clock and still no sign of Lindy.

About an hour later, Maureen hollers that dinner is ready. The table looks good; there's no denying it, and the kitchen smells of fresh bread and spicy soup broth. They've draped a nice linen cloth over the table that I've never seen before. In the center are two tall candles flanked by simmering pots and fancy serving dishes with ceramic ladles. Dad is already seated at the head of the table. He's got some sort of plastic coil in his hand that he keeps digging his finger into and then bopping on the table.

Maureen gestures for me to sit in one of the middle chairs, then waves her arm out over the table. "This is cornbread," she says, indicating the tin pan in front of Dad. Mom pulls out the chair at the opposite head and takes a seat. "The pot has Japanese... well," she corrects, "*Asian* long noodles. They're delicious. We have King Cakes and a little Chiacchiere if they actually managed to turn out okay." She looks over at the oven and shrugs her shoulders. "Anyway, I hope you like everything. Enjoy," she says.

Before Maureen can even take a seat, Dad grabs a square of cornbread with his bare hand and takes a huge bite. "Ouch!" he says. He drops the bread on the table and grabs his jaw.

"What?" Maureen says. "What is it?"

"What happened?" Mom asks.

"My tooth! I think I broke it. Damn."

"Oh," Maureen says, "that was probably a pomegranate seed. Shoot! I thought I got all of those out. Sorry, sorry, sorry. Be careful, everyone. Sorry."

"Why is there pomegranate in my cornbread!" Dad demands.

"I was going to explain that," Maureen says.

"Let us explain," Mom says.

Dad cradles his mouth in pain. His words come out garbled through his fingers. "Go ahead," he says.

"It's good luck," Maureen says.

"Huh?" Dad says, "what is?"

"All of it," Mom says.

"All of what?" Dad asks.

"The pomegranate," Mom says.

"All of the food," Maureen adds.

"Not if I break a tooth," Dad says. "You think a dentist's drill is good luck?"

Mom lets out a little whimper and drops her fork on her plate.

"Take it easy, Neil," Maureen says.

Dad has already forgotten about the tooth. He has the plastic tube back in his hand. He holds it up to his eye; looks through it like a telescope. Unsatisfied with whatever he sees, he pulls it down and knocks it hard against the table two or three times.

"What are you doing?" Maureen asks.

"I could ask you the same thing. You look like some of kind of two-bit Gypsy."

"Neil!" Mom cries.

"What?" Dad says.

"Can you please stop? Please. We have something to tell you."

"That's not even sanitary," Maureen says, leaning in for a closer look at the tube or whatever it is. "What is that? Is there mold in that?"

"There might be," Dad says. "I'm trying to find out. It's a hose from the water pump. Something has been blocking the air. The thing can't breathe. Hasn't anyone else noticed how hot it is in here? The air conditioning has been broken for days." He picks up his pack of cigarettes from the table and slides one out.

"Neil!" Mom says.

"Come on, Neil," Maureen says.

"Dad," I say, softly. I give him a pleading look, but don't say anything else. I make a little nodding gesture toward the pack, like *can you please just wait?*

Dad sighs, clears his throat. He shoves the cigarette back in the pack. He picks up the hose and throws it on the floor. Then, hands raised above his head like a police suspect, he edges back from the table. "Okay," he says. "Okay. Lay it on me."

As Mom and Maureen look back and forth from one another, wordlessly trying to communicate their next move, Dad reaches over and spoons some noodles into the large bowl sitting in front of him. He brings a strand to his mouth and slurps it up. Half of it goes down but the other part, flailing like a hooked fish, slaps his chin and wiggles off onto his shirt.

"These fuckers are long," Dad says.

"That's the point," Mom says. "That's why they're called long noodles."

"That's the luck, huh?" Dad says. "I've always thought size matters."

"Okay," Maureen says, "listen."

"I'm listening," Dad says. He takes another forkful of noodles and slops them into his mouth. He makes loud sucking and sloshing noises as he wags them in and swallows.

"This," Maureen says, tugging at the corset around her chest, "is a traditional cassock worn by many Irish nomadic wanderers in the seventeenth and eighteenth centuries. It is known to bring luck." Her explanation is interrupted by Dad who is laughing and trying to eat noodles at the same time.

A mess of broth and noodle splatters his shirt and placemat. Maureen takes a deep breath. She puts a hand up to Mom, signaling that she's got this. "It's good luck," she continues.

"You said that already," Dad says.

"The noodles you are devouring, along with the cornbread and the pomegranates and the dessert, all of it is known to bring fortune, health and profit to those who indulge in its offerings."

"Okay," Dad says. "Get to the punch line."

Following a few attempts by the ladies to talk together and then over one another, Dad jumps back in. "Let Roberta tell it," he says.

"We're writing a book," Mom blurts.

"You are?" I say.

"Yes, we're writing a book, and it is going to change the world forever."

"It already has," Maureen says.

"It already has. It is shaping and defining and improving the world even as we speak," Mom says. She looks at Maureen with a giddy, impish look as if to say, *am I doing it? Am I doing it right?* Maureen gives her a proud nod.

"You wrote a book," Dad says.

"We are," Mom says.

"You did?" Dad says.

"Did you really write a book?" I say.

"The question to ask," Maureen says, "is when will the book be ready to take the world by storm?"

"So?" Dad says. "Tell us."

"We are writing a book about…"

Maureen halts her for a second. "*You* are writing a book," she says, "I'm just here for guidance and moral support. Roberta has all she needs to make this happen.

"Yeah," Mom says. "That's right." She stops briefly, trying to remember what she was saying.

"What it's about," Maureen says. "Go ahead. You got this."

"Right," Mom says. "It's about… it's about how to harness the power of positive thinking and transform the world into a collection of doers, believers and realizers who are able to craft and mold their most perfect dream from their own minds."

Nobody does or says anything for awhile. Dad has his mouth open. Bits of noodle dot his lips. A yellowish drool seeps from the corner of his mouth. He has his hands spread out in front of him on the table, his neck stiff on his shoulders, not moving a muscle.

"Tomorrow we start writing, but today…" Maureen starts before Mom cuts her off.

"We bought a new house!"

"What?" I shout.

"We have the most gorgeous, unbelievable house that anyone has ever seen!"

"Remember that house that you and Roberta looked at last year and fantasized about one day owning? The one on Greenview, over by Irving Park?" Maureen is so excited she can't keep her tongue in her mouth. She keeps licking her lips over and over again, waiting for Dad to answer, but he doesn't move. "Neil?"

"Shouldn't you wait until you already have the book?" I ask. I start to talk again, something about trying to be practical, but Dad chops his hand out and whacks me across the chest. I gulp.

"How much?" Dad says.

"We made an offer," Maureen says.

"We took out a loan," Mom says.

"That's one of the most expensive streets in the whole city," I say. I can't help myself.

"How much?" Dad repeats.

"One hundred thousand," Mom says. She says it with a kind of confidence and clarity that is uncharacteristic for her.

Dad plucks a cigarette out of the pack and lights it. He tosses the lighter on the table and leans back in his chair.

"We have the credit," Mom says. She tries to look him right in the eye, but Dad is looking all around the apartment, everywhere but at her. "The man at the bank said we've got the credit of royalty!"

Dad blows smoke. He looks down at the hose on the floor. He puts the cigarette back in his lips and crosses his arms. There is a steely determination in his eyes. He looks over at the closet door that has broken free from its hinges. Looking up at the ceiling, he studies the brown water stain that's been there since the last heavy rainfall a few weeks ago. A fly buzzes the air over by the sink. Up in the cabinet where he is staring now, his toolbox sits waiting for the next project.

"We've been saving for years," Mom says. "We haven't even taken a vacation since Lindy was four." She is restless, fervent. Something changes in Dad. There is something unexpected in his demeanor, something elastic, possibly even flexible about his posture as he sits up straight. "We deserve this, Neil," Mom says, her eyes turning red and watery. "We've been modest so long. I haven't even bought a new dress in years." She looks back to Maureen for fortification, and she responds by waving her on, the way a third base coach does when sending a player home to score the winning run in baseball. Dad is off balance. I see it, and so does Mom. She goes for it. It's an incredible, invigorating sight. "The book is going to bring us millions," she says, and then with added, robust assurance, "millions!"

Dad stands up from the table. He takes the cigarette out of his mouth, replaces it with the remaining hunk of cornbread on his plate. He walks over to the sofa and picks up his Cubs hat from the cushion. Snugging it down against his ears, he swallows and looks back at the table. "Okay," he says, "this is on you." He stands still, his gaze split halfway in between Mom and Maureen. "I have to go meet up with Randy at AA. I'll need it tonight." He turns and opens the door to exit. Just before closing it he says, "I bought a new dress for you for your birthday next month. If you want it now, you can go under the bed where I hid it and try it on." And then he shuts the door. In a few seconds his footsteps can be heard descending the stairs and then there is silence.

I think about how he's been putting in ten, twelve hour shifts over the past year, about how he comes home many nights with gashes on his hands, blood on his apron, blisters on his feet from standing on the concrete cutting floor. I think about how he won't go to AA at all tonight, but a bar instead. I wonder how much he'll drink before driving home inebriated. I wonder if he'll see Lindy at all while he's out. Will he take the time to search for her or maybe just bump into her by accident while stumbling through a dark alleyway or parking lot? I think about all of the reasons I know for why he drinks, and I think about how this new information will sit on top of the pile like a piece of kindling on a bon fire.

"I think that went well," Maureen says. She stands up, grabs her own plate, then Mom's and then a butter dish in one hand. On her way to the sink she hums a little tune.

"That went very well," Mom says. She smiles at me, pats my hand, then leans forward and blows out the candles.

Evening Advances (2006)

Jerry spends a string of libidinous nights with a Ms. Cadillac Deville, one of Mercedes's co-workers, and acquires a madness I've never seen in him before. A few days later he shows up at my door, soaked from the rain and looking beaten. It is pouring. There is nowhere else for the water to go. Leaking droplets from his nose, hair and fingertips, he regards me with a miserable frown. The weather is of no consequence, anybody can tell. It could have just as easily been a desert dryness that brought him. The weather, despite its tyranny, is not the point. Cadillac is on his mind. None of us has heard from him in a week. I invite him in.

"We were really in love," Jerry says first thing. "We are so in love. We are." I grab a towel from our closet, and he takes it and wraps his head. He takes another and loops it around his waist as he takes a seat on the sofa.

"How did it happen?" I ask. I am gathering us some tea from the kitchen.

"Easily. So easily. I caught up with her after her show. I looked her right in the eyes, no place else, and told her she would never regret getting to know me. I wasn't the same, I told her. Zero sameness, whatever that meant to her. I thought it would mean something. I wanted to know what that was but later not now. There was nothing about her that I was fixated on. I had no preconceived notions or ideas. I was empty. Everything. Regrets, that's the thing. You shouldn't wonder, I told her, it's a plague. Please, I said. I was a gentleman. That's what I meant by it, you see, but it was not plainly there for her. We were playing a game."

"That sounds… difficult," I say.

"It was damn near impossible," he says, "I wouldn't believe it myself, but then we were in her car, and she was driving me back to her place. She was quite a competitor. What a poker face! I guess I should have known."

I hand him some hot tea. I bring mine to the recliner across from him and sit down. "You shouldn't kick yourself. What you did was buy something not for sale. That's impressive to me like you would not understand." I do not tell him how badly I wanted to sleep with her before getting to know Sasha.

"Nothing you say will make it hurt less," he says.

"I'm sorry," I say. "Of course not. What went wrong?"

"Can I tell you a story?" he asks.

"Why else?" I say. I raise my mug to him like a toast. "What else are we here for?"

Jerry puts his mug on the coffee table. He sits back against the cushions, breathes into his hands, then shoots forward again with his elbows on his knees. "Okay, so the first night afterward… Wait, no. I refuse to go into details," he says. "You'll have to imagine. The first night as we slept she had a nightmare. I don't know what it was, but she was flailing around in the bed, tossing and turning, groaning something wicked. It woke me up. I thought there was a prowler or something horrible. When I saw her there, writhing in the grips of the terror, I rolled over and put my arms around her. At first she leapt up and screamed, but when she noticed it was only me comforting her she wrapped her arms around my arms and would not let go. She sucked me into her and whispered thank you. Can you believe that was one of the most awesome experiences of my life?"

"I can see why, yes. It was an accomplishment."

"As I fell asleep curled around her I wondered if this would be a sensation that I would ever be able to relive again. I wanted to make it last forever."

"I can imagine," I say.

"Yes! Imagine. Use your imagination. You're good at that. That's why I came. You see, the next night the exact same thing happened again. You can imagine my elation. I was allowed to reenter heaven twice in two nights. We needed each other. We were saviors, nothing less. Sooth somebody who's in need of soothing. I dare you. You will never be the same. Trust me. Beware. The feeling was overwhelming. Drugs? I'd never had any better before or after this. It was love. We were in love, really. Truly. You can't argue it. Don't even try. I'm begging you."

He's losing his mind, pleading with me this way in the middle of my living room, I think. This isn't like him. Something fundamental to who he is, some central cable, has been snipped. There is a real concern that he will not return again, not fuse back together. But then again it could just be me. I'm always worrying that things will not return to normal, especially people. It's a horrendous curse.

"Okay. I'm with you. I'm here. Then what happened?" I ask.

"The third night nothing happened. I mean, the nightmares. There were no nightmares. It was awful, like something being taken from you, something priceless that can't be replaced, you know. Like your parents suddenly telling you that the pet dog you cherish so much is no longer your pet anymore. Do you see what I'm saying?"

"Yes, I think I do. You were deprived."

"Yes, and so I did what any deprived man would do. I created a pet dog where there was none."

"What do you mean? You lost me."

"No I didn't. You'll see. I pretended she was having a nightmare. I went through the identical motions that had transpired the previous two nights. I woke her, wrapped my arms around her. Told her that everything would be okay, that I was there for her and that there was nothing to fear. And viola! Same results! She recovered. And even though the nightmare wasn't real, my embrace still was. My grips were on fire with truth! Don't believe me. I dare you." He suddenly wraps his arms around his chest, hugs himself like he means harm.

"She allowed you to save her," I say.

"You tell it better than I do," Jerry says. "Why don't you finish it?"

"No, no, go ahead. Please."

"The fourth night when nothing happened, I faked a nightmare of my own. You've never seen such thrashing and wailing. It was a magnificent performance. And like I had hoped and envisioned, she was there, squeezing an arm around my shoulders, nuzzling my neck. We were one again. I tell you we were in love beyond love. There is no word for it. We were in love. We are in love. We are in love. We are in love…"

"The repetition," I say. "You fill her cup, she fills yours, on and on and on."

"It could not be sustained," he says, and collapses back against the cushions. His arms drape the backrest, his belly drops, sinks to his waist. He's a boxer knocked out against the ropes. "Okay, there. I said it. You will never hear me say it again." He claps his hands together to show that it is done with. "Poof!"

"It was the fifth night."

"It was the fifth, sixth and seventh when things did not go well," Jerry says.

"She was on to you," I say.

"I told you what an adversary she was. I've told you that already."

"She figured it out."

"I don't even know if there was anything to figure. That's the headspace I'm in right now. I'm treading water. Are nightmares real? That's where I am. Nightmares are dead, Clay."

"You are torturing yourself."

"Not for long," he says. "I'm on my way out."

Jerry stands up from those metaphorical ropes, ready for round two. He's pacing, circling the ring. "We are in love. We have been in love forever. We will be in love afterward. Love is owed to us. We are entwined. There was a love that was waiting, and we tapped into it. We awoke love, we lived inside of it. There is no exit. We are really, really in love. It's already written…"

"Are you all right?" I say.

"You are already all right. Say it. Say 'you are already all right.' It is written. Say it."

"It is written," I oblige.

"Say the whole thing! 'You are already all right. You are in love. She is your girlfriend, she is your wife, she is your destiny. We are good together, made for each other. Say it! You are already all right…'"

A few times I try to chime in, give him what he wants, but he won't stop and so I can't keep up. The list keeps growing. It is quite a list, but most of it is the very same things said in slightly different ways. He is having a breakdown. Anybody can see it. Nobody knows what to do with these people. Beware. It will be the person in the throes of one of these mental mishaps who will promise things… Don't try telling them, I've learned, that they don't have the answer, that they are off. I've seen the mistake before, been a part of a few myself. It is something to behold, and not in a good way, in a shattering way, like a broken mirror. When someone is convinced beyond all horizons, it is best to be a piece of furniture. Stay still. They say never to wake a sleepwalker. And nobody does. Blind obedience. But really, who wants to be the person to buck the trend? There are reasons for compliance in some instances, I think. I'm still figuring things out... but one thing is for sure. If one does decide to go against the multitudes, to threaten the pervasive thinking of the times, everyone will know what that person has done. Whoever that rogue is will just be dangling out there, some smelly fish on a hook. Nobody wants that, right? Some maverick type, right? So I just nod my head and look empty. No one gets angry at the absence of logic, only the other way around.

Divination For Beginners (2001)

On my thirteenth birthday, I receive my first magic kit. It is a deluxe package with 100 different tricks, an official top hat, false bottom rings and sliding coin boxes. The whole thing comes in a big leather suitcase with brass locks and hinges. When I set it on my bed and swing it open, I fully expect a glowing light to come pouring out, followed by a leaping white rabbit. These magic companies, they know exactly what they are doing.

"Okay!" I demand. "Everyone out!" I am being very theatrical, waving my arms, squaring my shoulders, projecting my voice. It seems like the right position to take under the circumstances. It's practice for a later stage routine. No self-respecting magician would ever allow even the slightest possibility of a civilian uncovering any of the trade secrets. After a few playful attempts to pretend they are going to stay and try to figure out the tricks, Mom and Dad leave. I have to throw a shoe at Lindy, who won't stop feigning her exit and then hiding behind my dresser, before she eventually scrams too.

And then I am alone, just me and the shiny trunk filled with power, wonder and delight. The first thing on top is a waxy deck of playing cards, and directly beneath it, held in place by the box's subtle weight, is the list of directions. I unfold the sheet, and spread it out on my bed. Smoothing it out with my palm, I begin reading out loud.

"Step one, warm up the audience."

Beneath this direction, there is a cartoon drawing of a young boy greeting a crowd of people by blowing them a kiss.

"Tell the audience how amazing they all look this evening. Point out a few particular people in the audience and comment on something specific about their appearance. Make them feel lovely and special."

A watercolor of an old woman smiling and clutching her heart is painted alongside these instructions.

"People want to be astonished. They want to be impressed, but they do not want to feel duped. People feel fooled and belittled by people they distrust. They feel honored and esteemed to be tricked by someone they like," I read. "It is your job as the magician to make your observers feel lucky to be in your presence. The more fortunate and flattered they feel, the less likely they will be to question anything you are doing. You want your followers to feel guilty and ashamed for even daring to doubt your abilities! The ultimate goal is to build such a devout gathering of admirers that they will attack and destroy any newcomers who so much as deign to challenge your true skills as sorcerer."

Attached to this bit is another picture, this one of a large bald man hulking over a cowering teenager. The enraged man's meaty hand is pumped into a fist; his mouth flung open, spitting fury.

The first trick is a simple sleight of hand.

"Put one of the small red balls under the cuff of your shirt. This ball represents hope, light and escape," the instructions say.

This is not at all what I expected to find. These directions are so strange, so esoteric. What do they mean by this? I flip the box upside down. On the bottom is a small white square with dark, bold lines bordering each side. The lines are unbroken save one tiny opening where the outline ends on either side; a miniscule opening wide enough to slip a fingernail through. Beneath the shape is the company's name. "Whole Pie Inc" it says.

"Take the other red ball, and place it in your opposite hand. Hold it up to the crowd. Hold it in the very tips of your fingers so that the entire orb is displayed for their satisfaction. Flaunt it about like it is some kind of rare, precious jewel. They want this jewel. They need it. You need them to believe that this is the only ball, and they need to believe the same thing. It's a match made in heaven. If you have prepared the gathering properly, if you have greased their desire to accept, you have already won. Test yourself. Following the trick, ask the audience if they would like to have the secret revealed. When you get to the point where they are threatening to kill you for your even suggesting such blasphemy, you have become a master magician."

Below this frightening directive is an ornate painting, a huge image that takes up the entire panel. It appears to be a portrait of an African American family. The mother and father, painted in various shades of brown, each have their arms stretched high above their heads, hands reaching, touching. Their fingers are laced at the knuckles, forming a cross design. Next to the parents, the daughter character is bent over her brother, trying to wrestle a gun from his hand that is pointed at the stage.

"Are you ready to put on a show!" Dad yells from outside the door.

I jump. "No!" I shout. Out of some delirious reflex, I wad the directions up and toss them under my bed. "I mean," I say, trying to recover, remembering the first rule of magic tricks, "I'm waiting until your beautiful, smiling faces are fully ready to relax and give me your undivided attention." I cringe. I have never in my life said anything so stagey or phony. They're onto me now, for sure. I wait for Lindy to call out, "shut up!" Or for Dad to say, "what's wrong with you, son?" but nothing happens for awhile.

"Okay," Dad says, clearing his throat. "Well, we'll be waiting in the living room whenever you're ready."

"Yeah," Mom says. "You've got us champing at the bit out here."

Yes, I think. *Yes.* It's working already.

The Reptile House (2003)

The new house is so shimmering, so plush and ornate, that it appears as if it wasn't constructed for humans but for figurines instead. You can picture a tidy little elf living there— dapper comb-over, polished shoes and a tiny bowtie. It's like a dollhouse, but with real stone pillars, a real chimney and a garden full of flowers out front that looks big enough to swim in!

When we pull up along the curb at 4122 North Greenview Avenue, I put my palms on the window of the moving truck and shout, "That's it? It's so green!"

"I told you!" Mom hollers over me. She drowns me right out. "What did I tell you?" she asks Tony. Mom and I are crowded inside the cab of the moving truck with the driver, Tony, and his two helpers, Mitch and Eduardo, both of whom are humongous. They have mountainous shoulders and thick, round arms like tree trunks with saucer shaped moles and tangled hair.

The wheels on the truck are enormous, too, and we ride high above the road. As if we need such a grand vehicle to transport such modest belongings from our Albany Park apartment. It's more for show, anyway. We don't want to show up on the block, all the neighbors watching as we roll up in a singular car with the back window crammed full of trash bags full of clothing and old beer crates stuffed with dishpans. The truck at least makes us seem legit. With the diesel engine rumbling and the air brakes grinding, it makes me feel strong and mighty, like we can just roll over the other parked cars if we want to and not even feel anything. I look in the rearview mirror and see Dad and Lindy pulling up in back of us. They look so puny and low sitting behind the windshield of our crappy Oldsmobile. Black smoke seeps out from under the hood, which is held shut by a series of bungee cords hooked to the front bumper.

"You called it," Tony says. "A spot right out front. How'd you know it would be there?"

"I asked!" Mom cries, lifting her palms, tilting her head skyward. "I simply asked. You should try it sometime. Open yourself up to the possibilities!" Tony nods his head, a new convert. He seems to be contemplating the notion as he removes his cap, itches the back of his ear with the brim.

Mom cranks open the door handle and leaps out without any regard for her surroundings. She hits the ground flat and hard so that it must have rattled the teeth inside her head.

"Whoa," one of them says. "Easy there."

In an instant she disappears. There is an *ooof* sound as she touched down on the sidewalk somewhere out of sight. It is like she has just dived out of an airplane and been sucked under the belly of a roaring Cessna.

I crawl my way out next, and when I reach the pavement, Dad and Lindy are there to greet me. Dad's standing right outside the gate, feet spread, shoulders slumped. He props his hands behind his back, down around his belt. He rocks his weight backward into them and groans. "Wow," he says.

Lindy saunters closer. She approaches the iron fence with catlike strides, like she means to seduce it. Fearless, she leans her arms right on top of the spikes that crown the top of the railing. Resting there, she tries to take it all in. I walk up beside her, but instead of pressing my skin forward against the metal spikes, I stand back, clasp my hands in front of me. What we were are both taking in is a full acre of lavish, verdant realty the likes of which we have never imagined before. From the front it is quite a sight, immense in both its length and width, so that it is hard to see all at once. There is a high arching roof, a shady porch trimmed by planter boxes on every post, a stone path with steps leading to an entrance swept so clean you can almost see your reflection in it. But what catches the eye first are the colors. Blended into the cedar shingles covering the facade are shades of green and yellow with little specks of gold that sparkle in the sun. Because each panel is square and thatched together, it makes it look like the house is wearing some kind of scales.

"It looks like a big lizard," I say. "The red door could be like the tongue. Do you see it?" I move closer to her, taking a chance. "We could call it the reptile house." It is a sheepish statement that comes out more like a question. Lindy doesn't answer it. She just stands there, wide-eyed and mesmerized. Her hair flags in the breeze. "You know," I add, "you know... like how we always name everything something different...?"

"I heard you," she says, but she doesn't blink or lift her gaze from the lawn.

Dad comes through the gate and strides over to where Mom is standing next to a short Mexican man covered in a mixture of potting soil, grass and sweat. This must be the gardener we were told about. We have a gardener now. Maureen mentioned it, but I didn't believe her, couldn't picture it. I've maybe seen the type of people who can afford hired help on shows like Beverly Hills 90210 or Richie Rich, but never in person. The man is looking at Mom with a blank expression, sometimes nodding, sometimes shrugging his shoulders. But that doesn't stop Mom. Her mouth just keeps moving, and her arms keep moving too, big, wheeling gestures that look almost frantic from where I stand. I decide to follow Dad. As the gardener sees Dad and I approaching, he looks toward us in a pleading sort of way, begging us to help him. It is then I realize that he speaks no English, and has been trying to communicate this to Mom who is not understanding why he won't respond the way she wants him to. A singular piece of mulch sticks in his bushy black hair, and as Dad gets close enough he plucks it out for him. At first the man flinches, ducking and swatting, but when he sees what Dad has done, he laughs and says, "gracias."

"De nada," Dad says. "Roberta," Dad says, and he grabs Mom by the elbow, foisting her to the side the way a forklift moves merchandise in a warehouse, the force of which knocks Mom off balance.

"Hey!" she says, "whoa!"

"Lo siento," Dad says to the gardener, not to Mom. Then he turns to Mom with a brisk flurry of movements before tamping his intentions, idling back. He wants to tell her something on the side, alone, but there is no time or space for it. "I'm sorry," he says to her, clearing his throat. There is a little shame and embarrassment in his tone, but he's trying to keep his composure. "Listen, this man doesn't understand a word you're saying."

"Well, what I was trying to tell him was that he is a true artist!" She is very animated and jumpy, which makes everything come out like anger. I can see why the man is put off.

"Okay," Dad says, exhaling, "Calm down."

"I was being nice," Mom says, but this too is spoken with an edge. "I asked him what his dreams were. I was trying to tell him that anything was possible. Anything! Look. Look!" she bends down, points to a cluster of pink, orange and white flowers standing out against the bright emerald of the yard. "He's like a painter. I was trying to tell him that he should quit doing this little side work as someone's servant, and go get his degree in fine arts or something. He could be the next Bob Ross… or… or Diego Rivera or whatever, you know what I mean!"

"Maybe we could share some of your father's inheritance to get him started," Dad says. Though I don't catch all of the finer details, I understand that Mom takes this aside as it is intended, which is with a large dose of sarcasm.

Mom's expression lurches from enthusiasm to betrayal. She drops her head, shakes it at the ground. I know inheritance has something to do with money, but the particulars about how it can be used as a weapon against Mom or why it makes her crumble the way it does, this is not fully within my comprehension.

"No," she mouths. "No, you know I don't want to talk about… You know I don't want to talk about that man."

"I'm sorry," Dad says, backing off. He sort of scolds himself, gives himself a little reprimand by biting into his bottom lip until it turns pale with teeth marks. He moves in close to her and wraps his arms around her shoulder. He embraces her, hugging tightly until she stops struggling and gives in. "I'm sorry," he repeats, "I shouldn't have said that. That was cold blooded. Why don't you go inside the house, and I'll talk to the gardener, okay?" Mom's face is buried in Dad's shoulder, but I can see her head nod up and down in agreement. Slowly, she unglues herself and backs away. Reinvigorated, she spins around and sprints up the stairs to the entrance.

When she is all the way inside, and not a second sooner, Dad reaches his hand out to the gardener. "Hola," he says, "mi nombre es Neil."

"Juan," the man says, brightening, "mucho gusto."

This is the first time I've ever heard my father speak Spanish, and it comes as a jolt, a deception. There is a duplicity in this fresh discovery, a withholding, like finding out for the first time that you've had an undisclosed brother your whole life. I look back at Lindy to see if she is getting any of this, but she is unreachable. The movers have her attention or maybe the other way around. One of them, Eduardo, I think, is leaning up against the fence beside her. His hips rock back and forth against it, a swollen belly mashing between the bars. The others mosey to the side and gawk like they are taking in a sporting event. They laugh, whisper, probably wondering if Lindy is sixteen or seventeen or twenty-two, unaware they've already been outplayed by a girl who will never allow the score to get close.

Dad is staring Juan dead in the eyes, like he's trying to decide if this is the man he once knew in some intimate way, like he's asking confidential questions about his origins with only his eyes. Something about the intensity and familiarity is too much for me, and I look away. The whole street is like something straight from a postcard, each house more opulent and palatial than the next. A few houses down someone has an authentic World War I cannon in the yard. When I look back at Dad I find that he has a flustered Juan trapped, fixed with some kind of deep, reverent gaze.

"Que Suenas con?" Dad intones. In an instant Juan's expression changes. Whatever he's said has worked to unlock a vault of trust within him. Juan steps back; he puts his hand on his heart and takes a deep breath.

"Tengo una hija en Mexico," Juan says. He moves his hands to his hips, looking relieved but also exhausted for the first time, as though he's been waiting all day for just one person he can confess to, unburden himself, and now he has found his confidant. He exhales a long, mournful sigh. A tear comes into his eye. "Quiero bailar con ella a Luis Miguel. Quiero ir a Acapulco con mi esposa y mi hija. Podemos bailar juntos por una noche. Seremos felices juntos. Por una noche." He dries his eyes with the side of his soiled T-shirt.

"You are a beautiful man," Dad says, "hermoso hombre," and now he looks sad and weepy, too. As a means to prevent the flow, he turns away from the man and spits. He makes a deal with himself, expels the saliva instead of tears, a poor man's substitute, but distinctly a man's choice nonetheless. He straightens back up, pulls himself back into himself. He sucks his teeth until they make a hissing sound. "Hermoso," he repeats, "you are simple and pure… Eres simple y puro. América será no gracias por tu inocencia, pero lo Hare. You are better than all of us." Then, with great conviction and zeal, Dad grabs the man by the back of the neck, tugs him forward, and kisses him hard on the top of his head. As if completing some fantastic cycle, in one, astonishing movement, he releases Juan, clears his throat, and bounds up the steps. With a singular gasp and sniffle, he charges through the door, slamming it shut behind him, leaving me, Lindy, her pitiful competitors and the gardener to speculate about our new surroundings, this enclosure in the middle of some new vast, unidentified habitat.

IV. POWERFUL PROCESSES

The Shortcut Summit (2003)

It's Sunday night, one of the only times the Blaine household is mellow and subdued, an occurrence Lindy and I have called "The Sunday Blues" for years. It is the dark feeling of a storm closing in, a transfer of energy. On one side the bright cloudless sky of weekend buoyancy, on the other the gray promise of Monday's burdens. Though neither Lindy nor I have ever been able to put the sensation into words, we share it, have almost managed to make friends with its consistent arrival. We sit alone, seeping into its murky embrace as night approaches. But that peace is broken when Mom comes bouncing through the door with her stack of notebooks and a tittering giggle that brings all of us out of our various reposes.

"Hellllllooooooo!" Mom sings as she claps the door shut behind her.

Lindy and I both come to the precipice of our doors, poking one shoulder and one foot outside to investigate. Our eyes meet, and through a series of practiced nods, winks and clicks, we decide this occasion will be worthy of our presence. As we converge on the living room, Dad opens the patio door and steps inside. He's wearing his white tank top and red bandana, a sure sign that he was out "working on the Oldsmobile," which we all know is code for drinking and smoking under the cover of car parts like suspension mounts and jack points. His bloated belly is covered in a mixture of axle grease, Pabst and sweat.

Mom drops her journals on the coffee table, plops down on the sofa. "Well," she says, "it's official!"

"We're ordering pizza for dinner?" Dad says. This gets a chuckle from me and Lindy. I'm starving.

"I'm going to be an author!" she says.

"What kind of an author?" I ask. I come around the sofa and take a seat in Dad's Lazy Boy. Lindy follows. She settles in next to me, balancing one butt cheek on the armrest. Dad hunkers in over at the kitchen. He plants his palms atop the counter and leans in like *this is going to be good.*

"A spiritual writer," Mom says, "like a spiritual guide."

"What does that mean?" Lindy says, asking the question on all of our minds.

"It means," Mom says. She thrusts forward, delighted to answer. "It means writing about how to harness the power inside ourselves and inside the universe to produce a scientific reaction of light to light."

Lindy's same question could have continued forward, like some kind of repetitive riddle or knock-knock joke, but instead, I take my standard course, one of support and compliance. "So, the meeting with Maureen must have gone well then," I say, knowing that's what she wants to hear.

"Yes it did, Clayton, thanks for noticing. What a get together. What a meeting of the minds! It went so well. I met all kinds of people, Metaphysicians, Homeopaths… I already have four different co-writers and an agent!"

"They all liked your writing," I say, keeping up my end of our unspoken arrangement.

"Yes!" Mom squeals. She lifts one of her journals from the pile as proof and shakes it up at us. "They said I had the talent of a true artist, a born author!" She holds the notebook aloft, bobbing it back and forth in front of her the way a lord would do with a sword on the shoulders of a newly crowned knight.

"I am the chosen one, Maureen said. And Lawanna!" Mom shrieks, "Lawanna even said that I could have been a composer or poet in my past life! Lawanna is the one who already has a publisher in mind. We're thinking of calling it The Shortcut."

"Wow," Dad says, "I could use some of that, some timesavers. Take dinner for example. I could use that faster!" Nobody laughs this time, and he changes angles. He coughs. "So, this Lawanna. She's got the connections, huh?" He's got something caught in his nose that he can't dig out with his finger. He turns, grabs a paper towel from the rack by the sink and blows. "She and Maureen know people at Random House or Simon and Schuster or what?" he asks, then honks again into the towel.

"Better," Mom says, tossing the book back on the table. "She knows people from the Centers For Rejuvenation."

"Aw," Lindy says, "the good old CFR." She's being a smart ass as usual. I take my elbow and bop her one in the arm, only I miss and catch a boob by accident. "Ouch!" she says, "that was my tit!" Mom frowns but doesn't say anything.

"The CFR," Mom continues, shooting Lindy a defamatory smirk, "is a leader in spiritual symposiums. They take you on retreats, teach you about tapping the metaphysical and reaching your psychic potential. Maureen just went to one last year in Sarasota, which is where she met Lawanna, Tammy, Tina and the rest of our crew. But anyway, CFR is not the publisher really. They're under some other umbrella company. What's it called? I forget. Something pie industries. Lots of pie incorporated? I don't know." She sits back against the couch with a wry smile. She folds her arms, props one foot and then the other up on the table and crosses her legs.

"Tell us about Tammy," Dad says. He flicks the trash can open, throws the paper towel inside.

"Tammy," Mom says, directing her glare over at Dad who is now back at his regular counter-leaning post, "Tammy is a visionary... A visionarian."

"Oh," Dad says, giving a surreptitious nod in my and Lindy's direction. "That sounds official."

"I know," Mom says without a hint of sarcasm. "She is something else. For one whole year she lived in Tibet and studied everything there was to know about intuitive healing and got her degree in dream orientation." Her voice is soft and airy as if she's just returned from a romantic date. "Oh, and she spent another few months in Africa learning about rocks and gems like abalone and carnelian... she's like a real guru!" She flings her head back onto the pillow, fans a hand above her hairline.

"Mmmmm, I see," Dad says, keeping up his little charade. "And Tina?"

"Tina!" Mom says, snapping back up straight. Her eyes zap wide, brimming with intensity. "She's got her masters in past life regressions!" she explodes.

"So, she's a Harvard grad then," Dad says, and Lindy loses it. She rolls from the armrest, landing on all fours. She pounds the carpet, each strike of her hand releasing another yowl of hysterical laughter. Dad watches with great pride. He's accomplished what he set out to do. Mom turns on him with a vicious scowl. "What?" Dad says.

I'm trying to pry Lindy up from the floor, but she makes her body go floppy and dead like a sack of cement, and I can't get a good grip.

"I swear!" Mom says. She punches her fist down in the couch cushions, uses it as a lever to stand. "You'll all be sorry. You'll see." She slides around the narrow aisle that leads past the coat closet and into her bedroom, stopping to face Dad. "It's your low money consciousness and your stupid practicality. You never believe in anything. You never believe in me. Well, I guess I won't share any of my millions once this book takes off." She takes one last look at Lindy who is still convulsing with laughter, fluttering on the ground like some kind of beached fish. I try to tell her with my eyes that I'm sorry, but it's too late. She lets out a sob and runs for her bedroom where she hooks the door and slings it shut behind her.

I let go of Lindy and scamper to her door. I pound on it. "Mom," I say, "Mom!"

"I'm sorry!" Dad hollers. "I didn't realize we were being serious. I thought this was for humor… for entertainment." He catches my eye, shrugs. I look back at him, head cocked to the side, eyes arched at the ceiling, trying to shame him. He knows what he just did. He knows better. I'm trying to communicate this disappointment, this frustration with my glowering expression and curling lip. And it works. Dad can't hold my gaze. He reaches for the dishrag on the faucet and whips it onto the counter.

"Fucking shit balls," he sighs. He slaps the rag down on the counter and mops it across the granite top. "Ouch!" he screams. A mosquito has landed on his forearm. He pinches the skin around the intrusion, grits his teeth. When he feels that he and the insect have suffered enough he lets go, grabs the rag again. He mashes down hard, scrubbing like he means to grind it straight through to the wood beneath.

Christian Names (2006)

All weekend I've been sitting on the toilet, grunting and pushing like a cow in labor. It's Drew and Jerry's fault. See how fast you can slam this Guinness, Drew says. Let's see who can take the most Jameson shots in one night, Jerry suggests. Christ… Here, have another smoke, they offer. Because of them I've been relegated to my dorm room, unable to venture too far without the fear of revenge from my merciless bowels. For the third time in the past few hours I assume the humiliating squat, tethered to the can, chopped in half by my roiling stomach.

Here's a first. For the first time, I notice there is something caked to the back of the door, a smear of old tobacco or dried vomit. You tell yourself over and over again that once you depart your parents' home you will leave behind all of their bad behaviors and discouraged practices, but the moment you leave the property the inborn struggle begins, that inherent tug toward familial norms and centrifugal tendencies. All it takes, apparently, is a little peer pressure, not even outwardly, from some delinquent friends or a pretty coed, more outwardly suggested from the feminine lot, and right away you are losing your hold on your promises; the center slips and you find yourself smoking squares in the park with a pack of other young wanderers breaking their own set of values for a good time. There was that whole ten months with April, too, that wicked detour, but I've already made a deal with myself about not counting any of that. I've succeeded in blocking most of that out, taking my mind elsewhere… And this brings me back to the stain.

I'm staring at this disturbing blemish, trying to remember what happened, what devilish state I must have been in … when my cell phone rings. If it isn't for the worrisome fact that I haven't heard anything from Drew or Jerry in a day or two or the urge to find out what else might have been wiped from my memory, I ignore the call. However, the weight of that curiosity is so heavy, that I answer the phone even when I see that the number is unknown. It is perhaps the added mystery that spurs me on. I pick the phone off the sink, flip it open.

"Hello," I say, trying to hide the strained sound of my thrusts as my anus clenches tight.

"Hello?" the voice says, and then there's a pause. Something has halted my response. It's a woman … the delivery familiar in some way but not placeable, a sort of low, erotic tone. She begins to laugh, and then I remember. I know who it is. "Is this Flynn?" she says.

In my panic my bowels loosen, release a flood of diarrhea into the water. I grab as much toilet paper as I can, wrap big mounds of it around my hand and wipe. And then I'm standing, commode loaded behind me, underwear down around my ankles. "Um," I say, "hold on a second." I can't wash my hands or flush the toilet for fear of giving myself away, but I can at least pull my pants up. I clamp the phone between my cheek and shoulder, reach down and fix myself. The belt buckle clatters as I cinch it tight. On my way out, I click the fan on, and shut the door gently behind me. "Is this Mercedes?" I manage to ask. My voice is high pitched and hurried.

"If this is Flynn it is," the voice says. She laughs again, and this time it relaxes me, lets me unwind a little.

I'm floating, drifting through the family room on autopilot, when my brain gives the signal to land. My body obeys, independent from anything, and then I'm plopping down on the sofa. "How did you get my number?" I ask.

"You gave me your number," she says.

"I did?"

"Yes, you left it on the table before you went off to the bathroom for like a half an hour," she says, and follows it up with more soaring laughter. "You wrote the number on a napkin with a yellow crayon, so I could barely read it."

This time I catch the laughter, and respond, "Oh my God. I didn't even know. I wondered how long I was in there."

"It was a looooong time," she says.

"I guess I wasn't sure," I say, and then I have no idea what to do next. "Why did you call me?" I say, and right away I realize how bad that sounds. "I mean… not that I didn't want you to. I mean, I thought… Wow," I say, "I don't know. I'm sorry."

"You left a couple playing cards on the table, and I picked them up."

"Oh," I say. "I did? I wasn't doing magic, was I?"

"Oh, you were doing magic all right," she says. "You did something called the Ace Shake Surprise."

"I did?"

"You sure did. And then you promised me you were going to make me light as a feather or something, like… stiff as a board? You said you could make me rise from the table and float away."

"Okay, that I kind of remember," I say. "I was trying to get you to…" I don't know how to put it, "come with me, I think."

"I thought so," she says. I hear something creak in the background, bed springs maybe. "Look," she says, more creaking as she stands. "I was wondering if you wanted to meet somewhere to get your cards back."

"Oh, well, I have like ten more packs. You can just keep those."

"No," she says, "I mean," and I notice for the first time that I am not the only one who is a little nervous. Her voice gets caught in her throat, and as she clears it, I feel something like anticipation rise up in me. "I didn't just call you to return your cards."

"Oh," I say. "Um, okay." I sit up straight, scan the room like I'm searching, trying to find something, only I haven't lost anything. "I don't… I should tell you that I don't have much money."

"Flynn!" she says. There is a brief pause, and then she's laughing again. "I—"

"And my name isn't Flynn," I say.

"Oh, Okay," she says, her voice rising at the end of the word. I've upset her. "I was getting to that. I mean, I know… Jesus, Flynn, I mean…" She takes a deep breath. "It's not like that."

"You're not a prostitute?" I say. It just shoots out of me.

What?" She hollers, and I have my stupid answer.

"Sorry," I say. "Sorry sorry!"

"You are unbelievable," she says.

"I'm an idiot," I say. "I'm just so flustered. I had no idea you were going to call me. I can't believe I'm talking to you!"

"Did you want to talk to me again?"

"Of course, but it was the furthest thing from my mind. Women like you don't call me. Ever!"

She's laughing hard. When she catches her breath, she says, "I think that's partly what worked in your favor."

"My idiocy?" I say.

"You are too funny!" she says, but she doesn't miss a beat. "Now that hooker stuff," she snaps, "that comment, that was fucked up! That wasn't cool."

"Well, yeah! I'm sorry. I don't know," I say. "I'd never been to a club before. I'd never spoken to someone like you, and I don't mean that in a bad way, I swear. I was just very, very… naive."

"I know," she says, "I could tell. I could tell that you were trying in your own way, trying to be comfortable, and, and even more you were trying to make me feel comfortable," she says, and then she let out a little sigh. "You were so cute! You were talking to me, and trying to get to know me, asking me to tell you about myself, and you didn't try to like touch me or anything, and honestly, guys don't do that with me. You were being real, that's all. You were yourself. Real."

"Wow," I say, "I guess I am. I'm really something, huh?"

"Okay, take it easy," she says.

"I wish I could remember so I could do it again."

"You're doing pretty well so far."

"So my plan worked."

"What plan?" she says.

"The one where I get drunk, somehow convince a stripper to get coffee with me, do magic tricks that I can't remember, leave my number and a few cards on the table, blackout in a bathroom, become certain that I made a huge fool out of myself and that I'll never have another chance with an amazing girl like that ever again, and just sit back and not wait for the call."

"You really nailed it," she says, "let go and let God!"

For a few seconds both of us lose our minds with laughter, just roll around with it, roar. "Speaking of God," I say, coming around, "what is your Christian name?"

"My what now?" she says.

"Isn't that what they call it?"

"Who's they?" she asks.

"The Christians? You're the one talking about let go, let God," I say, and I brace myself, hoping I haven't gone too far.

"Oh, I don't know, baby," she says, "that's just an expression. We call it our government name."

I exhale, feeling a great relief. "Okay, good," I say, though I'm not sure who "we" are. Strippers? Black women? "Can you do that again?" I say.

"Do what?" she says.

"Call me baby," I say.

She laughs. "Only if you tell me your real name first."

"My real name is Clayton," I say.

"Oh, okay, baby," she says, "I like that. That's a nice name. Clayton," she repeats, and I can tell she means it. I feel a warm sensation tingle through me.

"What's yours?" I say, and I wonder if she can hear my smile through the phone.

"Sasha," she says, and there is such a shyness, such a bashfulness in the way she says it, that I wish I could reach through the phone and stroke her hair, maybe even give her a kiss if I could pull it off. She makes me feel like I could.

"That's a beautiful name," I say, and I really do mean it. I hope she can tell. I hope that whatever illusion or trickery got me this far won't wear off before I can get the chance to see her again.

Itchy Bones (2004)

Horace and Gail Matthews hate Maureen. They tell me this in between open mouth kisses and timeouts for feverish scratching.

"She told Gail that she has manifestation infestation," Horace says. He pumps Gail's knee with his knobby hand, then works his fingers down her leg, dragging his nails across her shin like a rake through arid soil. "She doesn't know what she's talking about."

Horace and Gail have been coming for treatments at Ambassador since 2000. At times they've lived there for long stretches, claiming they can't go home without anyone around to check on their blisters or keep an eye on their recurring hair loss.

"I told her," Gail says, "to mind her own business. She thinks I cook up all these welts and pustules with my brain." She lifts her leg from Horace's lap, dangles it out for me to assess like some kind of dead animal. It's covered in pink rashes, silver scabs and a swirling constellation of tiny white dots. "This," Gail says, "this Maureen says I bring upon myself. Like I want these bloody boils. I used to have beautiful skin. What does she know? Her skin looks like Greek yogurt." She lets the leg drop back onto Horace's thigh where it folds in half like an old bath towel.

They are forever amusing and adorable, Horace and Gail. Never have there been two people so old and so in love. What this love looks like, in the Matthews case, is two skinny, shriveled bodies tangled together on a padded window ledge in the day room of a dismal recovery center. Gail wears a dingy gown with faded moons on the front. It spreads twice her size, and she shares it, stretches it to fit over Horace's legs, too. Horace's crotch has become a willing pillow for his wife's veiny, disagreeable limbs. His arm, draped around her delicate neck, is another link in their chain. They are like aging Siamese twins who prefer their mutual bondage. The vent above their heads releases hot, gusty air into the room. The force flattens their hair, mats it down. Wispy strands of it lift free from their heads, and sail off into the current like plucked feathers. It's a comical sight, this love of theirs.

"It's not just the skin," Horace says. "The itch goes deeper than that. It's like the femur itself is prickling. My bones are on fire!"

"Oooooh, dear," Gail coos. She raises her chin to him, puckers her lips. Horace pulls her face closer, and they are making out again, moist, smacking kisses that sound like two raw steaks slapping together. Glass rattles in the frame behind them and they unstick themselves. It's cold outside, maybe twenty degrees. All the windows are covered in large rippling patterns of hoary frost.

"Brrrrrr," Gail says, shivering. Horace squeezes her tighter, fluffs her arm. She wiggles her legs. "Scratch it," she commands, pointing at her kneecap. Horace slips a hand under her gown and goes to work. I can smell the cortisone ointment radiating off of them, a blend of menthol and hot candlewax.

"See, honey. You need more of those..." Horace trails off, thinking of the words. "What did Maureen call them? Essential oils. Essential my ass. They ought to rub them on her big fat butt," Horace says. We all laugh. We grow louder and more animated until Horace cuts us off. "What was that? What's that sound?" he says. His head whips back and forth. Gail takes her legs down, puts her feet on the floor.

"What?" she says. "What is it?"

"I don't know," Horace says. His eyes are bugged and grazing; something invisible and haunting races behind them. And then the itching is back, this time his elbow. He moves with intention, rapid, furious strokes. Gail follows in unison. They both dig their nails into the red, swollen flesh blooming around the joint.

"It was just the wind again," I say. "Nothing to worry about."

To my great relief they believe me, and things begin to mellow. Both of them drop the itching and unfasten their fingers. Gail looks up at Horace with big, hopeful eyes. She grabs his collar in her fist. "It's okay," Horace says. He nods his head a few times and Gail unwinds. She lets go of his shirt and slowly glides her hand down his chest.

Gail and Horace have both been diagnosed with severe panic disorder. This means that fairly often they experience things like suffocation, the sensation of being choked by someone or something. Sometimes they perspire so much the moisture drips off of them like a swimmer fresh from a pool. Or their hearts drum so fast they start calling for nurses to come put their hands on top of their chests and press down until one of them decides the beating has ended and the other agrees. I've helped the nurses before, but Maureen refuses. She thinks the disorder is made up, a product of festering resentment from their childhoods or an overwhelming desire for attention. She believes in super fruits, lavender and acupuncture, she says, but not Lorazepam. Last week, the Matthews had their prescription of Lorazepam raised to eight milligrams per day, a dose that keeps them from feeling attacked by percussionists and stranglers but leaves them feeling plagued by bouts of intense itchiness. Imagine the choice, I tell Maureen, but she scoffs. "Which of them chose to get this quote/unquote disorder first?" she says, "hm? Imagine that. Ask yourself that." But why worry about that, I say. They're here and they need help. They feel each other's pain, so sue them. "The pills won't help," she says. "Never pills. Pharmaceuticals are manmade. Stick to plants," she says, "that's what the Indians did." I want to ask her what happened to those guys, how their tribes fared against modern methods of defense, but I don't have it in me.

I'm helping remove Horace's watch for him so he can scratch his wrist better, when Gail gasps. My instinct is that the medication is wearing off, and I should go find the nurses, but when I turn around I see what she's gasping about. Dick Farber has dropped by. He's standing just inside the door, cradling a mug of hot tea. He teeters, straining to bring the cup up to meet a set of flayed, melted nostrils. We're to understand that he is inhaling the steam, enjoying its aroma. A smile cracks his shrunken lips. It's a marvel he's able to hold anything at all, a real triumph. He's got the handle clamped inside the folds of what used to be his hand but now looks more like a carved ham hock.

"Hi, Dick," I say, cutting the tension. I hear Horace gulp, catch his breath.

"Oh," Horace says, "Yeah, that's him." He blinks a few times, cleans his glasses with his shirt, and puts them back on. I'm suddenly very proud of his recovery speed. "How are you, Dick?"

"I'm fantastic," Dick says, but he's hard to understand. Since the accident he can only open his mouth about a quarter inch wide.

The last time Gail or Horace saw him was probably the night he crashed his car into the telephone pole and burst into flames. That was a Dick who had a moustache, a solid set of chompers and a pair of biceps that made most other old men jealous. What they see in front of them now is a charred and brittle man festooned in deep crimson scars.

"What are you up to?" I ask.

"Treatment time," Dick says. He tries to put the mug down on the table, but it's stuck inside the flaps of his meaty flesh. He has to knock the base of it against the wooden top a few times before it pries loose. "Have you seen Maureen?"

"Not for a while," Horace says, and I know what he's doing. He's trying not to stare at Dick's neck. It's all saggy and raw, pink and bloody as an old turkey wattle.

"She's amazing," Dick says. "She's got me on tea tree oil and hypnotherapy." He takes a break, massages his jaw with the back of his ham hock. "She's going to cure me," he says. "It's working already."

I watch Horace look from Gail to me and then back again. All he can do is nod his head. His eyes settle back on the wattle again.

"That's great. Well, I'm sure you'll find her," I say. "Check in the basement. I think this is her lunch hour."

"Okay," Dick says, "good bye. It was nice seeing you."

Horace and Gail are mute all of a sudden. A series of nods and waves is all they can muster.

"You too, Dick," I say. "Good luck."

It takes what seems like an hour for Dick to pick up his tea from the table. It spills all down his chin and stomach. It must be scalding hot, but Dick can't feel it anymore. When he is through, and he leaves the room, Gail turns to me in a state of discombobulation. Her head still nods, independent from her control. She licks her lips, runs her tongue across the rim of her gums. "We need another round of meds," she says. "Mine aren't working anymore."

All The Way South (2006)

I follow Sasha's directions down Lake Shore Drive. Of course my nerves are shit, and so I'm smoking again, careful not to get too much of the smell on me. With all the windows down the car's a virtual wind tunnel, old fast food wrappers fluttering in the backseat, textbook pages flapping all over the place. I pass the imitation steamboat and white sands of North Avenue Beach, take the bend at Michigan Avenue, anchored in place and time by the glowing marquee atop the castlesque Drake Hotel. I travel through Hyde Park with all of its solemn Victorian homes casting their gothic shadows, and I'm still going, winding south, when I realize that I've only been down this far a few times in my life. It's a beautiful stretch. Past the Museum of Science and Industry, after the glistening boat docks at South Shore Harbor, the land levels out. There is a lushness to the scenery, a gentle sway to the low current of the lake, a divine glimmer to the reflection of a fading sun rippling across the water in shades of orange and indigo. It's much more tranquil and bucolic than many would expect. For decades the south side has been portrayed as a wasteland, a place of turmoil, murder and ruin, a place to fear. I wonder how many of those purveyors have been to this location at sundown on a Friday night, anxious to visit a woman who makes their heart skip, makes their insides flip and dance like the classes given at the grand Cultural Center on the corner of Lake Shore and 71st Street.

She lives a little west on 72nd Street in Jackson Park, a neighborhood known for its Dutch Colonial architecture, an eighteen-hole golf course and a legacy run dry by white flight following World War II. I'm going to see a black girl. A black woman. On the phone she told me she turned twenty-two last month. My age, nineteen, starts feeling extra diminutive and inconsequential when contrasted against the dimensions of our individual experiences and burdens so far in life. So, okay, I grew up in Chicago. It's not like I've never seen black people or spoken to them, I have. But this is not enough. There are always *things*, I don't know... perceived distances and frictions, invisible barriers, forces, telepathic signals sent through particular gestures, native scents or private lexicons that act to sever any legitimate bonds before they have a chance to form. Like the 63rd Street L stop or other covert dividing lines in the city, we are compelled to communicate through a haze of hesitancy, literal and figurative walls of distrust, forged by long histories of segregation.

There are some people who are better than others at navigating these borders, bridging the gaps between the two worlds. In junior high I had a friend named Johnny Bishop, white as a bar of soap, who wore his hair in a bandana, played dominos with the black boys in the BP parking lot and French kissed girls with cornrows named Chantelle and Pookie out by the busses after basketball games. I always admired his cultural flexibility, wondered how he did it. I used to want so badly to be like Johnny, which in part made me want to be black, I guess. It's confusing. Wanting to be black is a bad thing, right? Black people don't like it because you're encroaching on their territory, trespassing without permission. White people hate it because you're a fraud, a traitor to the race that got you this far. It's like there is no way into the scene on either end even if you are sincere, even if you genuinely feel like you want to join in. Going the other direction, black to white, is even more treacherous. The possibility is open, most people seem to think now, but everyone knows that the entrance is a big white door barely cracked, with a set of brittle, ancient hinges long since painted shut. It's just nobody ever really has an honest talk about it. If people don't speak of difficult issues out loud, the thinking goes, then maybe they won't be true. Anything is attainable in America as long as you don't ask too many questions or go digging for too many answers. *Shhhhhhhhhh…*

My parents have always been down for the cause, basically. Both are pro unity, acceptance, equality. They made it known, more or less, through their cordial interactions with people of color, and their emphasis on empathy extended to all comers. Their messaging was clear: racism is wrong. But, aside from Dad's stories of colonialism in Mexico or Mom's courting of African American audiences for her book, we never had any direct discourse, no big talks about bigotry or discrimination, all of the deeper implications related to social or economic policies. It wasn't until last fall, my senior year at Lake View High School, that Mr. Goodwin, our Black history teacher, led me to start making more profound connections. He gave us books to read like *Savage Inequalities* and forced us to write papers on issues like the tragic disparities found in urban housing, unclean drinking water or educational reform. It was a mind-altering experience, one that leaves me curious about how my parents would feel about my visiting Sasha if they knew, or, more intriguingly perhaps, what Mr. Goodwin would think.

Her apartment building reminds me of the one in Albany Park where Lindy and I grew up. The street parking out front looks onto a standard brick building, three stories high, bordered by a rusty metal gate, a fractured sidewalk and a few small shrubs leading to a splintered door. Sasha lives on the second floor. I find her last name, Wheatley, on the buzzer and press the button. Waiting her reply, I try to catch my reflection in the window, check the status of my hair, my armpits, palms, any outward thing that might give away my internal feelings of awkwardness or ineptitude. In a few seconds I hear the sound of feet descending stairs, the soft rumble and creaking of wood coming closer. And then she's there, bounding down the last step and lunging for the door.

"Hi," she says. She opens the door and we are face-to-face, so close our noses almost touch. There is a horrible moment where my lizard brain kicks in, and I almost lean in for a kiss. Sasha rescues me. She moves fast, coming in for a hug before I make the kind of bumbling mistake from which there is no turning back. We embrace and I smell the strawberry shampoo clinging to the ends of her tall, blooming hair. This is not the long, silky hair I remember from the club. This hair spouts like a bush, domed and wiry with a thousand tiny curls, and I have to fight back the urge to stick my clammy palms in it. We hold each other longer than is normal, both of us unsure when the other will let go, but content to feel each other's warmth longer. My face nuzzles her neck, sleek and creamy with lotion.

"You smell amazing," I say, releasing her to arms length. I step back, inadvertently gripping both her hands in mine. I guess I wasn't ready to let go all the way. I run my hand down and through her fingers, exchanging our different moistures.

"Thank you," she says, swinging my arms, "you look very nice."

I've worn the only respectable outfit I have, a white collared shirt tucked into black pants and finished off with a pair of Kenneth Cole shoes my Mom bought me for prom a full year ago. Seeing as how I own so little and know so little about date fashion, she's lucky I didn't just wear the whole corny getup, bowtie, cummerbund and all. *I'm* the one who's really lucky...

"Thanks," I say. We stand there for a while, smiling and batting eyes at each other. We're so shy and nervous, so cliché, it's almost relieving.

"I didn't dress up," she says.

"You look great," I say, and I couldn't mean it more. Counter to all of the preening and posturing I've done to prepare, Sasha looks totally natural. Everything, from her Afro to her plain gray T-shirt, to the blue jeans that trace the curves of her shapely legs like a second skin, it really knocks me out. She's done something, maybe on purpose or maybe without knowing it. She's conveyed to me that she is comfortable with my arrival, with my presence, and that goes a long way toward putting an out of place white boy like me at ease. I have the desire to reach out, to thank her for her kindness...

"Come on," she says, stepping in where needed once again. She keeps one of my hands in hers as she turns to lead me up the stairs. Her nails are painted a color I've never seen before, a sort of pastel green that when mixed with the hue of her skin reminds me of a mint Oreo cookie. The rooms we pass are alive with music or television chatter. There are children's voices too, little kids giggling, teasing one another. It's dinner hour and the place is suffused with potent aromas. There are so many I can hardly hone in on any individual scent.

Fried potatoes maybe… barbecued meat of some variety. Corn bread? A bare-chested, tattooed man opens the door across from Sasha's and bounds inside. He's carrying a brown paper bag under one arm. "What it is?" I hear him say in an animated tone. "What's good?" another man responds with equal enthusiasm. Such an interesting way of speaking; two questions equals one answer. I'd like to know more about that kind of communication, have a discussion about it, but how?

We reach Sasha's door. Above it, a flap of beige wallpaper hangs loose, peels down over the entrance like a used Band-Aid. Inside, she lets go of my hand, walks over and turns the volume down on the stereo. A woman's singing is dimmed, something jazzy and theatrical. I catch a couple lyrics… something about what goes up must come down. Next to the speakers, a stick of incense burns, a tropical, coconut scent. A long column of CDs and DVDs lines the top of the cabinet. There are two high bookshelves crammed with books on either side of the cabinet. There must be over a hundred books of different sizes and shapes. I spot a cardboard box sitting next to one of the shelves filled with an entire pile of Seinfeld cases, which makes me do a double take.

"Do you like Alicia Keys?" she asks. She glides her finger across the top of the player, moves her hips in the same fashion as she pivots and sits on the sofa. She tucks a leg under herself as she settles in.

"Sure," I say, still standing inside the door, waiting for some kind of instructions, I guess.

Sasha laughs. "You don't have a clue, do you?" she says.

"I know who she is!" I say, defensively. "I've heard of her."

"Oh, it's okay," she says, "I'm only joking." She pats the seat next to her on the green fluffy couch. "Come here."

I'm happy to oblige. There's a big rug between us. It's green and yellow and black, and right away I think of Africa. I'm not sure if that's what I'm supposed to do, and then I'm nervous all over again. She pats the seat a second time, this time with more vigor. "Come on," she says. The coffee table in front of her is glass, and underneath are teetering stacks of magazines. I see a *TV Guide*, a *People Magazine* and a couple others I don't recognize featuring many glossy photos of black women with various styles of hair and lipstick.

"You have a nice place," I say. I sit next to her, but not too close. Is it the right distance? The cushions are plush and comfy, but I fear I sink into them too far when I shift my weight, like quicksand. I feel small and puny, like I'm disappearing, and I'm struggling with where to place my hands. As I try to figure all of this out, she shimmies closer.

"I'm glad you like it, because I was thinking we'd just hang out here for a while. Maybe we could go for a walk a little later to get something to eat, and I could show you the neighborhood if that's okay with you."

"That's sounds perfect," I say.

She's doing everything right. Here she is flirting and staying cool, inviting me into her world with such graciousness, such … I'm not holding up my end. This is my job too … But she looks so *good!* She is something else. There is a slope of coffee colored skin peeking out just below her neckline, a sliver of flesh that slants down toward the most superb set of spherical breasts I have ever seen … Okay. Okay, I have to pull myself together. Breathe. I wriggle my back against the pillow, sit up as straight as possible. I exhale, force my eyes forward. I blink them a few times, and as they clear they settle on a coat rack across the room. It's off in the corner, a skinny oak pole cloaked in bright scarves, wool hats and winter jackets with fur lined hoods. Along the same corner is a potted plant with lanky palm fronds, and next to that is a rolled up yoga mat. I squint, shake my head. A yoga mat?

"What are you looking at?" she says.

Of course, *now* she asks. "Oh, um, nothing," I say. "Is that your bedroom?" I ask. Next to the yoga mat is an open door. Through it I can barely make out the edge of a mattress covered by a purple comforter. I see what looks like a scattered array of multi-colored underwear draped over the side.

Sasha smacks my shoulder. "Damn. Slow down, dude!" she says. "Really?"

"Oh," I say, "no, I was just taking the whole place in, you know, being inquisitive. Like, is that your bathroom over there or is that your kitchen behind us?"

"Uh-huh," she says, raising an eyebrow, "I'm sure."

I can't take my eyes off the underwear. One of the pieces, a slinky red thong with lace trim… I think it might be the same one she wore the night…. The pair I saw her slide off around her high heels at the strip club and throw across the stage. Sasha catches me staring. A flash of recognition comes into her eyes, and she makes a grunting sound.

"All right," Sasha says with a huff. She scoots away from me, locks her hands in her lap. When she starts speaking again she's aimed herself straight ahead, talking to the wall. "If you're here because you just want to get a lap dance from me or you think I'm easy or… or," she's getting worked up. Her voice rises, words crash together. "Or if you just want to fuck me so you can tell your friends you made it with a stripper…" She claps her hands together in anger. She turns back to face me, looks me square in the eyes. Her eyes are a clear, sharp hazel.

They stab right through me. "Then please, please, please go home now."

It's a direct hit. Man down. The force feels physical, a searing slap to my psyche. I'm surprised I don't go tumbling backward off the couch. The effort ahead of me would be no less daunting than scraping myself off the floor. "No, Sasha," I say. "It's… It's not like that at all. That's the furthest thing from what I'm trying to do here." I try to look back at her, meet her troubled gaze with a more consoling one of my own. I try to hold it, cradle it, bring it back down slowly, gently. What I'm trying to do and what is actually happening could be totally different. I don't know, but after a few seconds her eyes soften. They turn watery, and she coils away. Her shoulders go limp. For a few seconds I watch her grapple with her concern, uncertain what to do. I want to touch her, put my hand on her shoulder, but I don't know if that's what she needs or wants… In a few moments I hear her sniffling, and I know I have to make some kind of move. "Sasha?" I say like a question, like is it going to be okay if I touch you? When she doesn't answer I lean closer. I put a light hand on her elbow, which seems safer, less controlling. "Sasha, I'm so sorry," I say, "please forgive me. I'm just new to this. I want to make you feel safe and comfortable, but I'm trying to feel that same way myself too, and, and man, you are very attractive, very… You are, but, but I want to get to know you on some deeper level, you know. Like, like I want to get to know you like as if we grew up across the street from one another, like we ate the same food, went to the same movie theater. Or, or not like… I don't mean like I'm the same as you, but just that I want to know what it feels like to be you." I stop myself, a little dazed. I feel I've hit a pothole, blown a tire…

This is not what I planned to say. I don't know where any of it is coming from or where it might go. "I guess that doesn't make much sense," I say, and then I know I've got nothing else to say next. If I keep going I know I'll only make it worse. "If you want me to go, I will." I back off a little, take my hand away. Sasha moves when I take the hand off, a little shrug, a little like she registers the absence of weight, misses it, wants it back even. I think I see her shake her head. Is she saying no, that she doesn't want me to leave or no, she doesn't want me to touch her again?

Sasha turns around, and to my utter relief, there is a smile on her face. It's a slender one, one of at least half suspicion, but I'll take it. Based on what just happened it's one of the prettiest, most rejuvenating things I've ever seen. That seems like an exaggeration, but it's not.

"Oooookay," Sasha says, elongating the O, putting me back on my heels again. "I think I know what you're trying to say, sort of, but you're going to have to pump the brakes a bit."

"Yeah, I know. It didn't come out right, did it?"

"Not exactly sure what you were going for, but naw, not really."

"I just meant that I want to get to know the real you, and that I want to be a part of your world, and I want to see if I can earn the trust of you and, like, the whole community, and—"

"Yeah, that. That right there," Sasha says. She has her hand up like a stop sign, but she still has that faint smile, which is the only thing keeping me from losing my mind.

"What? Still wrong? I just want to talk about things, experience things, you know? I want to be honest and open."

"I get that, Clayton. That is coming through loud and clear, and you are lucky that I'm the kind of gal who doesn't mind discussing those tough issues, but you should know, like for real, you're being real forward."

"I am?" I say. "I guess I'm just anxious. I'm sorry."

"What you're attempting to do, on date one mind you, is the cultural equivalent of trying to rip my clothing off and get on top of me in like ten seconds."

"Yeah," I say, and then I just sit there for a while and let that soak in. She's totally right, of course. I should know better. The truth is I do know better. Who else knows more about keeping challenging concepts and controversies locked up inside? I guess I'm just suffering from fatigue. I don't feel like doing it anymore, not with someone like Sasha, but she's right. I'll have to slow down.

She hasn't left or moved off the sofa completely or insisted I leave yet, and so I count that as at least a minor victory. In fact, Sasha's body language is beginning to come around. I'm in the middle of feeling the pressure drain from my chest, congratulating myself for rebounding somehow, growing even more excited as Sasha moves to rock back toward me, reaches her hand out to me … when I see a cat run out of her bedroom. It's a huge spotted cat with a booming meow to match. I jump a little, and this makes Sasha flinch, too. She sways back against the armrest, eyes flared, waist and hips retracted. There is a distinct irritation marked by her withdraw, a reprimand for having been so fitfully perturbed.

It's now that I realize everything I observed before about her casual, mellow style, her gallant choice of hair fashion, the laidback clothing and mannerisms, they weren't choices designed to console me. They were signboards worn to alert me, inform me of her no-nonsense, serious attitude toward me and any unfounded or perverse ideas I may have arrived harboring. This is what people mean when they talk about refusing "to put on airs." The cat peers up at me, unfazed, and meows again. Like his owner, he is stalwart, not easily deterred.

"What?" She says, wobbling forward, reaching down over the edge of the couch. With a hurried swat of her hand the cat is dispatched. "What? You spooked by him? That's just Henry. That's my cat." She gives me a look like, *what, you've never seen a cat before?*

"Oh, right," I say, "a cat. What's a cat?" We laugh a little, and it feels really good. She curls back up beside me, our legs touching, and puts her arm around me. That's when I know that if this is going to have any chance at all, I have to tell her what I'm thinking.

I tell her that I'm ashamed that I don't know more about Black people. I didn't know they watched Seinfeld or went to yoga classes. I didn't know they owned cats! Why, she asks? I don't know, I say, whenever I see them on TV or in the movies or on the street, they usually have dogs. She asks if I wear a long night shirt to bed that hangs down to my knees. Do I wear a cap that goes with it, a droopy thing that comes to a point and has a ball on the end? She saw it once in "The Night Before Christmas." We laugh and laugh. We talk about everything, from different ways white and black people throw family reunions to the similar ways in which they each have hilarious stereotypes about one another that never get cleared up. And then we laugh some more. Oh, how we laugh. It's addictive. It's the best conversation I've ever had in my entire life. It's true. It actually is. And then she gets all solemn and grave on me all of a sudden.

She looks me dead in the eyes again, and she says, "I'm going to go to college."

"Okay," I say, but she's still staring at me like I don't get it. "What? Is that weird or something?"

"No it isn't weird!" she says. "It's totally normal. It's a totally normal, logical, reasonable thing that everyone should do to improve their life."

"Okay," I say, still missing something. She lets me off the hook a little with her eyes, but her posture is still rigid, firm.

"What I'm trying to tell you is that I'm going to college so I can stop being a stripper. It was a means to an end. I had a plan all along."

"Okay. That sounds understandable," I say. This gives me a mixture of feelings that I haven't anticipated. I hadn't thought about this possibility at all. On one hand, there is the deliverance from the inevitable jealousy that would certainly arise, and it allows her to be clear of the danger and threat that she's constantly under, but on the other there is the perverted but nonetheless real disappointment that her days as a trained seductress are coming to an end at the same time we are getting started. I'm being ridiculous again…

"I want you to know," she says, and then she presses her face up real close to mine and this time our noses actually do touch, which makes it a little hard to stay serious. "I *need* you to know that this is not about you. You are not rescuing me, you are not my hero, you are not my father figure, got it?" She mashes her nose into mine and we Eskimo kiss. I laugh a little bit and she pulls away. "I'm serious," she says. "This is serious."

I get it. This is important to her. I nod my head, suck my teeth. "I get that," I say in the most sincere voice I can.

"I've had other people play that game with me before, and it never works. There's this guy on me right now, Deion," she freezes. She shakes her head, wags her finger. "I'm sorry," she says, "You don't have to worry about him, forget him. Never mind about Deion, just know that he's not in the picture at all anymore."

"Shoot, Deion who?" I say. "I've already forgotten."

"I mean, he wanted to rescue me, his mom wanted me to rescue him," she says, shaking her head. "Shit, it was a regular hero jamboree."

I'm feeling good. Nothing she could say right now would make me upset, and so I'm hardly even paying attention. I tell her not to worry, and then I change the subject. I ask, and she tells me all about her aspirations. She astounds me with her knowledge of books and authors. She wants to major in Comparative Classical Literature when she enrolls some-where next fall. I tell her about U of I, and she scolds me for thinking that she hadn't already considered that as an option. According to her it has one of the best departments in the state. Her senior year in high school, she tells me, she wrote an essay contemplating the similarities between *The Color Purple* and certain sections of *The Canterbury Tales*. This astonishes me, and then the more I think about my reaction, the more it bothers me. Why astonished? Why shouldn't she be a scholar of literature? Is it because the last time I saw her she was grinding her arched and naked spine against a steel pole, gripping it down between her ankles, dropping to her knees and cat-crawling across a stage? Is it because later at the diner she used the long nails on her fingers to stroke the straw of her milkshake, spoke to me in the hushed, carnal accents of a ready minx? No… this is not the same. She is not the same. The woman in front of me is composed and dignified… but why could she not have been before…. She is transformed… This is all very confusing, but I want to figure it out. I'm not going to give up. I want us to get to the bottom of each other.

"Do you know what I mean?" She says.

"I do," I say, even though I don't. I need to bring myself back into focus. I put my hand under my knee and tweak the skin between my fingers until tears almost come to my eyes. It works, and I'm right back in the flow again.

She is a marvel. I tell her she is, but leave out the part about how her expertise came as a surprise. I do tell her that *The Color Purple* might be the only novel I've ever read that features more than two or three black characters. She reminds me about *A Raisin in the Sun*, which she says is *everyone's* only black text in school. Sure enough, with a little work I am able to remember the movie version with Ruby Dee. There is something about her long white dress and short hair that sticks in my mind... I'm so weird, Sasha says, and we laugh some more. When the laughing dies down, she grows somber and thoughtful again. She reiterates her concerns about my handling of her independent desires and ambitions. They are independent, she intones, not dependent. I am not her savior. She makes me repeat after her. And then she keeps going...

I nod my head some more, letting her know that I am absorbing everything she is saying, letting it all sink in. I'm a sponge. And then I get an idea, one that could only be made possible by how much we have shared already up to this point. I put my hands on my hips, thrust out my chest. "Okay, so does this mean," I say, "does this mean I can't dress up like Superman when we go out and carry you around in my arms like I just saved you from Lex Luther?"

Sasha bursts with laughter. She punches me two, three times in the stomach, then buries her forehead in my chest and breathes. "This is what I like about you," she mumbles into my shirt.

"What?" I say.

"You know how to talk. You aren't afraid to be silly, and you aren't afraid to be serious. You don't pretend to be… anything but you. You keep it real."

If she only knew. If she knew the amount of fear I had to navigate… the abyss that I had to swim my way through to arrive at this destination, this conclusion. I know that "keeping it real" is only an expression, but I think it's an important one. I wonder if it meant the same thing in her household as it did in mine growing up. Did she have to fight for every scrap of every honest word spoken, claw her way toward dry, practical land, drowning in a bog of nonsense and absurdity? No, it could not have been the same. Her battle was different but no less harrowing, I'm sure. I guess that if all of that hesitancy and apprehension, all of the time spent masking my genuine perceptions in the Blaine household was preparation for the release of this moment, then it was all worth it.

"The crazy thing is," I tell her, "I'm not always like this. I don't really talk like this to anyone but you."

"Really?" She says. She picks her head up, looks into my eyes again. Her head and hair zip upward and hover above me.

"Really," I say. "At home or when I'm with my friends, I talk the way they want me to talk. Or the way I think they want me to talk, I guess. I put on a show."

This really makes her beam. She pops up to her knees. "Oh, I think I know exactly how you feel!" she says. "Remember?" she says, and then she downshifts, decides if this is the right time to proceed with what's on her mind. "Well, remember how I was after the club with you, at the diner? I've been wanting to tell you about how…" She's starting to squirm a little. I put a hand on her shoulder to steady her, let her know it's okay to continue. "That wasn't… I mean, that isn't how I… It's not who I want to be with you."

This feels like the right time, and so I go for it. I stroke her hair, more like crimp it in my fingers, and I'm shocked at how natural it feels, like this isn't taboo, like it isn't the first time I've ever felt a Black girl's Afro.

"Whoa!" she says, whipping her hair out of my grasp.

"What?" I say. "What?"

"Baby, we are not there yet," she says. "That is another sensitive issue!"

"Damn it!" I say. "Shit. I'm sorry."

"You need to calm down, and you need to get yourself under control," Sasha says. "Let that be the last time you apologize tonight. I can't take much more of this explaining tonight. Not tonight."

"We can save that for another time."

"You sure like to get right to it."

"You make it sound like I'm ripping your clothes off."

"What did I tell you?" She says, but she's smiling again now. I've made her smile again. "What did I tell you about that? We're not there yet."

"I need to just appreciate how far we've already come." I say.

"That's right. We've revealed a lot of our true selves tonight. We've still got a long way to go, but we're working on it. We're on our way." The way she says it, it's as if she's not only talking about me and her but like an entire population of people trying to understand one another, like the whole human race. This makes me very happy. This is something I can work with.

I nod, smile. "We know who we are, and we know who we are not," I say. "I'm not Flynn, and you're not Mercedes."

"And we're not there anymore," she says. We take each other's hands. Together we sort of sink down, lower ourselves toward one another against the cushions.

"And now we're down here instead," I say, nuzzling myself into her. She responds, wiggling her warmth up against me, fitting ourselves together.

"We're down here instead," she repeats, and that's when I kiss her. Me, Clayton Blaine.

V. THE SHORTCUT TO MONEY

The Future Inside (2006)

All the way north along Ashland Avenue, Sasha won't stop fiddling with the knobs, dials and gears inside my car.

"What does this do?" she says, pressing a blue button on the dash. A blast of cold air fans our feet, filling the cabin with the sound of jet engines.

"Sort of answers itself, doesn't it?" I say.

"It does!" she laughs. She's like a little kid. She digs her fingers in under a panel by her knees, tries to take it out.

"Hey! Don't do that," I say, slapping at her hand. "You want to tempt death or what? You have a death wish?" I feel conflicted about what I've just said. It's just an airbag. There's too much eeriness in those words, too grim. I don't want her to think I'm morbid, but I do have a dark sense of humor. Are we at the stage yet where I should be coming clean, revealing every bit of my true self?

"Why?" she says, rolling right along. If she's concerned about my macabre tendencies, it doesn't show. "Is it for an ejector seat? Are you going to go flying out the moonroof? Wait, is that a moonroof?" And then her fingers are all over the ceiling, clicking and dancing, setting off flashing lights and motorized window rollers.

"You're freaking out," I say. "I've never seen you like this before."

"Oh, you know me, baby? You know me now? You better get used to this!" She giggles, swats my hand, dodges my play-ful attempts to grab her knee. I swerve a little bit, lose my lane for a second.

"Whoa! I told you. You're going to make us crash."

"Wait, seriously," she says, halting our little game. She puts a finger up to her lips. She turns the fan off, listens carefully like she's trying to discover the location of some loose lug nut under the hood. "What is this?" Her finger hovers a few centimeters above a small square featuring the letters PCS. It's in a discreet location at the very bottom of the console, which no doubt leads her to believe it's extra important and full of mystery. I can play this game, too.

"Oh, that?" I say. "You don't want to know about that. That's some top secret shit right there."

"Stop it," she says. "Tell me."

"PCS stands for Pre-Collision System." I let it go at that, as if that explains everything.

"And?" Sasha says. She grows wildly impatient. She pounds her seat. "Come on! I'll push it. I swear, I'll do it!"

"Go ahead, but only if you want to have the whole car implode on us. It dismantles the whole thing. All that will be left is my seat and the steering wheel I'm holding like in a Wile E. Coyote cartoon."

She pushes it and the car starts to shake. The brake begins to compress on its own and the steering column locks up. "Shit!" I say. "Push it again. Push it again!"

She does it fast, one quick jab, then recoils from it like it might explode. A horrible clunking sound rings out from beneath us, like we've just released some kind of barbell that had been clinging to the undercarriage. "I'm sorry!" She says. "I'm sorry, I'm sorry, I'm sorry!" She puts her hands over her ears and brings her shoes up on the seat.

"It's okay." I say, but she can't hear me with her hands up. "Hey, Sasha." I place my hand on top of hers, try to pry it loose from her ears. I trace the back of her knuckles, tickle her wrist. "Hey," I say again, and this time she takes her hands away. "It's okay. Look, we're fine."

"We're fine?" she says. "Are you sure? How do you know?"

I take my hands off the steering wheel, shrug. "We're still alive." I say. The car is humming along as usual again. It has corrected itself just as the manual promises. "Car's still moving. No fires. You still look great over there. And I'm over here… well, driving, doing my thing… we're fine." For the third or fourth time I admire Sasha's outfit. As usual, she's picked just the right one for the occasion. Her top is silky and flowing, a merlot color with a slinky bow suspended down in the middle. The black jeans are sleek and pencil cut to show off her ankles. When I start to think about how even her ankles are lovely and alluring, my mind starts to tilt and there's a fear that whatever self-assurance I've managed to locate inside of me might forsake me, come tumbling right out my ear hole. And so I shake myself out of it. Still, I'm having a hard time not reaching over and tugging on that bow, unwrapping her like a present on Christmas morning.

"What was that?" she says. "What happened?" She slides her whole body closer to my seat, almost climbs on top of it. She's got a serious, probing look in her eyes.

"It's a sensor system," I say. "It's got something called a low-speed tracking device or something like that. It'll try to sense if you're getting too close to another car or if you're in danger of driving off a cliff up ahead. It takes over if you haven't noticed some kind of danger on your own."

"Take over," she says, She swings back against her seat, like trying to elude a punch. "How do they, how does it know if you're too close?"

"I knew you were going to ask that!" I say.

"Well, what… it can predict the future? That's crazy. That's not possible, baby!"

This new name, *baby*. She seems to be trying it out, seeing how it feels. Does it fill the space just right, does it have the right resonance? Her smile and the repetition tells me she is leaning toward approval. I like it, too. It has such a sweet sound in my ear. It has the ring of relaxation and warmth, the music of authentic connection.

"Funny you should say that," I say.

"Why?" she says. Her eyes widen, pupils dilate. "Oh, you know the future? You're some kind of quantum physicist or something. You know string theory! Why didn't you tell me?"

I laugh. "It's actually the opposite."

"What does that mean? You know the past? You're a history teller?"

"I'd like that. That sounds fascinating, but no. It's hard to explain."

"Well, you should probably tell me now. We only have about twenty minutes before we're there."

She's pretty much spot on with her estimate, maybe a little over. We pass under the green sign reading Grand Avenue, and trees start to appear. The landscape has changed from vacant asphalt and open fields to dime store bodegas to gas stations mixed with Subways and Taco Bells. Now we're in Wicker Park. A young man walks by dressed in five different layers of clothing. His style seems to span all styles of dress, ranging from business casual to backyard barbeque circa 1996. This man marks our arrival. He's either homeless or on the cutting edge of fashion. This confusion, this concept does not exist on the south side of Chicago. There is no time for this type of irony in Jackson Park. The blurriness of the notion is so odd and whimsical as to be almost luxurious in its indulgence. We've made it. Welcome to Wicker Park; the boyish, concocted land of bohemians. We are approximately three miles away from the house on Greenview.

I've been to Sasha's place maybe six or seven times already in the past month. I take the train from Champaign each weekend, drive the three hours on Monday afternoons and stay until my next class on Wednesday evening. In a few weeks, after she gives her notice at the club, she's going to start coming down and visiting me on campus. It's been an accelerated courtship in pretty much every way. Already we've talked about meeting each other's parents. Actually, she talks about it most of the time and I nod. She's given me quite a few details. Her father, Roy, was a minor league baseball player in the nineties. There's one picture of him she showed me where he's in a Philadelphia Phillies uniform swinging a bat. His neck and shoulders fuse together in one solid block of flesh; forearms thick and sturdy as plumbing pipes. There was a moment, about thirteen years back, when it looked like he was going to make it to the big leagues, but it just wasn't meant to be. First he broke his wrist, then he started drinking every night, and soon after that he fell in love with some waitress at his favorite 24-hour diner. Last she heard, he was living somewhere in Reading, Pennsylvania where the Phillies have their farm team. When he calls, which is rare, he tells her he's still trying to get to the majors, but deep down they both know how out of touch he is. She went to visit him about a year ago. He's over forty now, she says, with gray hair and a belly the size of a wrecking ball.

Her mother, Deborah, still lives in Lyons, Illinois, the small suburban town where Sasha grew up. Deborah is where she got her love of reading. It didn't matter what was going on in their lives, she always found time to read. There was a little bench on the window ledge inside their family room where Deborah sat and read every night after dinner. She read everything from trashy tabloids to Charles Dickens, and when she was finished she always discussed everything with Sasha. Sasha was her little reading buddy, her partner for practicing her book reviews that she hoped to one day write for the Brookfield Sentinel. In the meantime, she was a bus driver for PACE. According to Sasha, she is the happiest bus driver the world has ever seen. The way she says it, she makes it seem like her happiness is the saddest part about her. Sasha directed me to a photo of Deborah hanging on the wall outside her bedroom. In it, Deborah stands on a set of steps outside a large but dilapidated church. Half of the place is burned down. Behind her, a sagging roof is covered in green tarp, one charred wall down to the studs. A few other churchgoers descend the steps beside her in their big, Saturn looped hats and doily collars. The others all have their heads lowered, frowning down at the sidewalk, while Deborah has hers pointed straight up at the camera. Like Sasha, her beauty cannot be denied. Her radiant smile, her lustrous skin and sculpted figure stand out like flashbulbs against a cloudy backdrop. Sasha says there is everything I need to know in that one photo; it explains everything.

Sasha has also confided in me about some of her own private apprehensions. She's an only child, which makes her whiny and cranky and also makes her a jealous person because of how envious she was growing up of other kids who had siblings. This bothers her and is something she is trying to work on. I have kept my secrets secret. Outside of their names, my parents and Lindy have remained enigmas to Sasha. This is something she can't take. If we are to make this work, she says, she has to know more about my family. This is a topic I try to avoid at all costs. The thought of it is something insurmountable in my mind, some colossal mountain I evade climbing for lack of strength, for the preservation of my own sanity. How do you explain the unexplainable? Acquaint yourself with the unknowable? I haven't even been able to figure out who my own family is yet or how to at least describe their complexities. How can I explain them to someone else? Having distance between us while I'm living on campus in Champaign has been helpful, but most of the time I still feel I'm not much closer to putting things together. Sometimes it feels as if I'm majoring not in botany or biology, which is what I think I want, but in the history of family illnesses, and still… The only way I can think to describe things to Sasha is to show her in person. So here we are, on a quest to see if whatever bleary, inscrutable images I can present, will do the work of all the evasive words I have been unable capture.

"My Mom thinks she can tell the future," I say. Here it comes. There's no putting a cork in it now. "In a way. That's why she bought me this car, as a gift for future success."

"Clayton," Sasha says. She sits back in her seat, stretches the seatbelt out in front of her and lets it snap back down across her gift-wrapped chest. "You're not making a lot of sense."

"It doesn't make much sense, that's why. That's why it's so hard to explain."

"You better pull over," she says. "This might take a while."

She's right. We're only about fifteen minutes away, and I've only just begun to give her context about the people she is moments from meeting. I put my turn signal on, coast over to the curb at the intersection of Ashland and Division. It's a bustling hub, a six cornered junction that shares its borders with Milwaukee Avenue, the behemoth First National Bank, and the Ashland blue line stop. Outside the station a diminutive water fountain doubles as a toilet for a thousand flocking pigeons. I turn the engine off, leave the keys dangling in the ignition. Sasha reaches over, takes them out. She caresses them with her fingers, fondling their contours with heightened concentration, the way a blind child might try deciphering a foreign object, relying only on the vibrations against her palm.

"What is up with this car?" Sasha says. She runs her hand down the wood grain paneling that covers her door. "I mean, this is a nice-ass car."

"My Mom," I start, but something grips me, an unwillingness to admit certain things to myself or others. It's a gag reflex of sorts. I sigh. "My Mom believes that people should desire and emit and sort of manifest abundance in their lives. She thinks that the more you indulge yourself, surround yourself with luxury, the more you are likely to attract those things into your life. If you want to be rich, you act rich, you talk rich, you… you drive rich. This car is like a beam of light, a signal to the world. I'm ready world! It says. It says I'm ready, send me my rewards, oh universe…" I realize that I've been clutching the steering wheel, aiming my words up at the moonroof like talking to God.

"Oh my God," Sasha says. Something in her voice scares me, a new tone of hesitation or doubt.

"See," I say, "this is why I didn't want to tell you."

"And so, she buys you this car, and then what? You automatically fulfill your dreams. You'll become the next… the next… Damn it, Clayton! You haven't even told me what your major is."

"I become the next General Educationalist," I say. It comes out angry, retribution for the way Mom, just the very idea of her, is already pushing people farther from me before ever having met them.

Sasha laughs, which lets a little air back in. "What's that?"

"Exactly," I say. "I'm undecided. I have no idea what I want to be. I always liked science, but that's part of it."

"Part of what?" Sasha asks. It's like she's already getting angry at me for things I haven't even spoken of yet, hints she uncovers, reasons she senses below the surface.

"Mom," I say. "Her influence. She is like an anti-chemist, a dis-examiner… I don't know. It's very confusing. I've tried for a long time to deprogram it out of me." I take a deep breath, release some tension I've been holding in my hands and shoulders. "If like attracts like, which is what Mom always says, I'll bring nothing but indecision and failure back upon myself in some sort of merciless loop of hell." I turn my face to the window. Suddenly I feel like punching something. I make a fist.

"Oh, Clayton!" Sasha says. "That's crazy." She unbuckles her seatbelt, cranes her body over in front of mine. She puts her arm across the steering wheel, folds her fingers over my fist. She makes these googly Sasha eyes at me. It's this charming thing she does where she sticks her tongue out and lets her eyes sort of twirl to the sides of their sockets. It's designed to appear that the slant of her head makes the pupils roll in that direction. But it doesn't work this time. I'm not feeling it. Just as I feared, I don't like this conversation one bit. I can't handle it. I twist my fist loose. "Come on, Clayton. So she's superstitious," Sasha says. "What's the big deal?"

"Superstitious! Ha! That's hilarious. You have no idea," I say. "She won't respond well to that," I say. "Don't say superstitious to her, not if you don't want her to think you're one of those self-defeating type of people."

"Self-defeating?" Sasha says. She moves over to her own seat, presses her back to it. "What's that supposed to mean? What kind of people, exactly?"

"It means," I say, "that she'll think your cynicism will bring you nowhere but down. She'll think you don't have what it takes. You're negative people," I say, "Whiny people." As soon as I say it I know I'm screwed. I cringe. "Shit," I whisper.

"Really?" Sasha says. "Those kind of *people*? Really? And so, she thinks *people* bring bad things, bad luck upon themselves." Her voice rises, reaching a boiling point. I can see her edging forward on her seat, ready to do that clapping she does when she needs to accentuate a point. I know where she's going with this. This. This is exactly what I fear most. This is my worst fear. I put my hand up to ask her to wait, but she blows right through my stop sign. "So she must think tremendous things about me and *my people* then, am I right?"

I wave my hand back and forth. I can't look at her. "Sasha don't, please. This is why—"

"Who the hell does she think she is?" Sasha says.

"I know, I—"

"What is she?" she says, and here comes the clapping. It fills the car, cracks through the depleting oxygen we share. "Let me guess, she's like a pet whisperer or something, right? She's Miss know it all, huh? I know the type. Miss look at me! Oh, look at me, I'm a dog walker. I can tell what Fido is thinking. Oh, look at me, I see the Wicked Witch in my crystal ball. I'm a grocery store manager by day, Nostradamus by night!" A smirk creeps across my face. I can't hold it back. I roll the window down. As she talks I shake my head outside the window, trying to whip the anxiety clear before it becomes a full-blown attack. "What?" she says. "What?"

"She's a millionaire," I say out the window. The wind is brisk, refreshing. It clears some of the mist from the windshield.

"What?" Sasha says.

I pull my head back inside, roll back the window back up to a crack. "She's a millionaire," I say again. The sound of it coming out of my own mouth braces me, turns me stiff in my seat. I'm not sure I'll be able to talk again when it's my turn.

"What the fuck, Clayton?"

"I know," I say. My mouth is dry. I need water.

"What does she do?" She tips her head to the side. Her hair moves atop her head like it might fall off.

"The Shortcut," I say.

"What does that mean, Clayton? Speak English."

"It's a book," I say.

"A book," Sasha repeats. "What kind of book? She's an author?"

"A best seller," I say.

"She gets paid," Sasha says.

"Just got another check for ninety-thousand dollars last week. It's the fourth one this month."

"What's it called again? How come I never heard of it?"

"She's been on Oprah," I say.

"Oh, shit!" she says. She does another handclap. This one may have injured her palm. She shakes it, clamps it between her knees. "Okay. Okay. Oprah! Are you serious?"

"Yes."

"And that's why you thought I had heard of her?" The head tilt again, this time hands on hips. It's deja vu.

I shrug one shoulder, bite my lip. "Yes?" I say, under my breath. I wonder if she's even heard me. I'm readying myself for an assault, but nothing comes. Instead, Sasha turns silent. She sits perfectly still in her seat, stares out the window. After a while her face starts to pucker and twitch, and I begin to mirror these movements in my own expression, shuttering in anticipation.

"Hahahahaha!" she erupts with laughter. She slaps her knee, throws her head back in a theatrical, overblown performance. In the midst of her extravagant production, a line of drool leaks down her chin, and she catches it with the back of her hand. "Oprah is a fraud. She's an Aunt Jemima! Her Horatio Algers, cockamamie corporate bullshit has done more to mystify and disarm Black people than food stamps and public housing." She flaps back hard against her seat, folds her arms. "Shit," she says. "She's actually worse than all that; you know why?" I shake my head, but there is no need. It's a rhetorical question, and she continues right along. "Because we trusted her, and all she offered us was a fake path to happiness, free marketing for designer duffle bags and some shitty remake of a Chaka Khan song. What we needed," she says, nearly rising to her feet along with the rise in her voice, "was someone to lead us down Wall Street with pit bulls and baseball bats. She rocks us to sleep instead of waking us up!" She shakes her head, mumbles something more that I can't understand. There's a kind of cabalistic argument playing out between her and some invisible opponent

There is nothing I can say to this. What can I add? Never have I heard anyone speak this way about a woman with such a hallowed reputation. Here is a woman, Ms. Winfrey as I have come to think of her, who I have only heard mentioned with the greatest of reverence. This is a woman, I thought, someone who has taken on the extreme hardships of a people, emancipated an entire race from the strictures of lower class fiefdom, released them hurling out into the light of her studio audience, her brand… No, I can't talk about this. I know I'm not allowed.

"Say something," Sasha says.

"No thank you," I say.

"Respond!" she says.

"I'd like to know more about your thoughts on Ms.… uh, on Oprah. For now, until then, I have no comment."

"You plead the fifth?"

"If I could plead the fifth to the fifth power, I would."

This gets her to laugh a little, and I feel bolstered again. Something about making her laugh makes me feel like I could do anything. "I think I've said enough," she says, relaxing a little. "Okay, so tell me more about your mama, then," she says.

"Okay," I say. "You know how to get a man to talk."

"I know," she says.

"We have a huge house," I say.

"Shiiiiiit," she says.

"That makes things worse, doesn't it?"

"It doesn't make them better."

We both laugh together then, and this seems to lead us back to a place where we have both become comfortable. She does most of the talking, animated and boisterous as always, and I nod my head, agree. This is a routine that I have grown to crave, lust after the way one might after sex. It's reaching the status of a drug. If I don't get her to rise up, get loud or stomp her feet, I go through something like withdrawal. I'm serious. I get all fidgety and tense waiting for it. And I do not agree with her out of timidity or uneasiness. In fact it's just the reverse. I've never felt so firm in my concurrence with her or in our mutual collusion against the outside world.

And so I tell her as much about Mom's book as I can. I owe her this. Halfway through my analysis of quantum mechanics, she interrupts me. She already knows more about it than I do. Not only does she understand the defective science better, but has somehow also apprehended the underlying debilities of my family as a whole, our dynamics. It's like somehow she's already had time to think and process; as though she's been doing some investigating of her own, some figuring... She's figured out the roots of all my neurosis, and she begins telling me about a regiment she's laid out for me, exercises I can do to recover and improve some of my fractured faculties. It all makes sense to her now.

It goes on, expands. Her comprehension on all things intellectual or experimental consumes me, washes over me like a giant wave. Like the way she draws comparisons to *Dianetics* and the *Shortcut,* how she sees Maureen as some kind of villain like Shakespeare's Iago in *Othello.* I don't know these things like Sasha, but she teaches me. She wants to double major now, the classics and abnormal psychology. She tells me she just decided. I tell her that sounds incredible. Then she makes me really get serious. She asks if I'm ready to have my mind blown. If you weren't already sitting down, I'd ask you to sit down, she says. The problem with my Mom and Oprah is that by pumping everyone full of rainbows and happy sauce, she says, they actually displace what's really important. As phony contentment and achievement flows in, genuine thought and genuine discovery flows out. By removing everything negative from your life, she says, you end up removing any real possibility, she stresses *real,* of actually removing it the legit way, which is through dissent and revolution. And ain't no White people, her words, want dissent and revolution. Oprah may not have white skin, for my information, but she is working for their team. She calls them The Washington Whiteskins.

"Wow," I say. "Well, I'm not sure my mom will like you, but I sure do."

Sasha chuckles. "I'm sure you're right."

I pull my hand out from under my butt where it's been sweltering away, and Sasha looks down at it there, all red and clammy. She puts her hand on top of it and squeezes. She stretches her other hand forward, etches her index finger over the logo on the glove-box one letter at a time. She skims over it like it's braille, then she removes the finger and turns on me with a force.

"You're telling me," she says, "that your mother is rich as a bitch…" she starts to laugh. I can see it bubble up from her gut, but she holds it back, stifles it in her throat before it comes out. "You could have had any car you wanted and you chose a Buick LaCrosse?"

The laugh is all the way in her face now. It makes her nose twitch. "What can I say." I tell her, "I'm a practical guy. It was on the list of the safest, most fuel-efficient models on the market. And it was rated best buy two years in a row by Car and Driver Magazine." She's past holding it in. Before I get done she's already in hysterics again.

"You are something else!" She says. "Your poor mother. You don't have an abundant bone in your body!"

"If you are looking for a family to test out your psychology skills, mine is a winner."

"Oh, I don't know about that."

"We're pretty abnormal," I say.

"You got that right!" she says.

We pull a U-turn and head back down south toward her place for another night. Sasha agrees. Meeting the parents will have to come later. Our conversation alone has scratched whatever itch she had for meeting my family in person. She is assuaged now, more included in my life, and that makes me feel good. She puts her head on my shoulder, and with that gesture buoying my spirits, and with my fix in place, neither of us notice as we move in rewind down Ashland, the scenery changing from the blind extravagance of Wicker Park to the extravagant blindness of South Shore.

Make It So (2004)

When I hear Mom singing, I check in on her just to make sure she's not about to lose it. She has a history of singing, sometimes whole songs belted in remarkable pitch, during times of heightened tension or mania. In my experience these episodes often portend the coming of some imminent crash. During her manic hoarding restoration she sang entire albums at a time, seemingly pulling chords and lyrics from some mythological well of knowledge that sprang to life as she went along. And then there was the literal example, the time she crashed her car into the side of an exit ramp after fleeing the scene following her discovery of Barry and Lindy huddled together under her bed naked. That time she was singing "Who Can It Be Now," by Men at Work.

Now she's singing "Here Comes the Rain Again." Her boisterous trilling seeps up from the break room and reaches me all the way in the upstairs cleaning closet. I take the mop with me. It could come in handy. What if I need a prop, a weapon or an excuse? Using it as a cane, I creep down the stairs. I stop just above the upper landing, using the ledge as a blind for my lookout. My knees crack as I squat, but Mom's really reaching for a high note, and so she doesn't hear a thing.

"So baby, talk to me," she sings, "like lovers dooooo." She's sitting at the head of the table in her nursing dress. It isn't often that she wears anything other than her regular scrubs, but she's lost about ten pounds recently, and she figures why not show off her skinny legs. As she sings she runs one finger down a long list of items on a sheet of notebook paper. With her other finger she punches keys on an electronic calculator. Between beats of her singing, the sound of clacking and ticking can be heard as rolls of receipt paper come scrolling out the top. "Raining in my head like a tragedy. Tearing me apart like a new emotion!"

Meanwhile, rounding out the commotion, Maureen is grunting and growling by the enormous chest freezer over in the corner. Their dueling shrieks compete for dominance. "Aaaaaaaaawwww," Maureen roars. She will not be outdone. She wins, at least momentarily. Mom takes her singing down a few notches to a quieter register. "Why won't you help me?" Maureen says. She has her back pinned to the side of the freezer. Her butt is flat on the ground, feet flexed against the wall. Sweat pools around her throat.

"I'm working," Mom says.

Maureen stands, hops up and sits on top of the freezer door. A squeak issues from the rubber seal like a delicate fart. "Oops," she says. "You're supposed to be writing."

"I wrote all through my break yesterday and Monday. I'm already on chapter four. You wanted me to be on chapter three by Friday. I'm ahead of schedule." She crosses her bare legs under the table, tears a sheet of paper from the spool. "I want to walk in the open wind," she starts back up again, "I want to talk like lovers do," There is a speed to her singing and clicking, each stroke hastier than the next, like hitting a fast forward button.

"Well, that doesn't mean you stop," Maureen says, "do you want your fortune now or later?"

"I need it three months ago," Mom says. "Right now I'm trying to figure out how we're going to pay all our bills for August."

"Oh no, don't do this," Maureen says. There is foreboding in her voice, something ghoulish. "Don't lose your will now. This is the worst time to doubt. Doubt will spoil the whole thing."

"I'm not doubting," Mom says, "I'm working." She puts a barbed emphasis on *working,* slams the next key instead of poking it. I'm not used to seeing her strike a confrontational pose like this. I lean closer. The mop is like a whaling harpoon in my grip. It's just what I need.

"You don't need to work," Maureen says, giving the word a dismissive tone, adding her own spin for emphasis. "Working is for the disconnected, the unenlightened. We talked about this. The belief that hard work and struggle is necessary to achieve some kind of prosperity is a lie. The truth is that life is just as easy as you want it to—"

"I know!" Mom snaps. She pounds the table with her palm. "I know. So, I'll work softer," she says. "I'll work lighter. It'll be like I'm not working at all. Money comes from purpose, purpose from money. Work smarter not harder. Manifest, manifest, manifest…" She picks up her pen from the table and begins whisking it across her notebook, wispy, airy brushes as if she's not touching it at all. "I want to walk in the open wind. I want to talk like lovers do." She picks the singing back up, louder this time, more aggressive.

Maureen has to scream to be heard. "If you want more money!" Maureen hollers. "You'd help me move this humongous freezer. Every second that this thing stays under this horrible beam," she says. She points above her head at an exposed eye beam in the ceiling. "We are all losing money. We're losing everything. Stagnant chi flow blocks the law of attraction."

"My back hurts," Mom says, and then keeps right on going with the verse. "I want to dive into your ocean. Is it raining with you?"

"Moving this monstrosity will help with that too."

"My back hurts!" Mom shouts. This brings everything to a halt. Her voice seems to still be hanging in the air, the fury ringing, vibrating out… "It's wearing off. I mean you're wearing off. You're wearing off on me," she says. She stands. "The freezer is not the problem," she says. "I have to use the bathroom." I've never seen her talk to Maureen like this. Her eyes are wired, fiery with irritation. For a second I think she might use the restroom upstairs and I flinch, but she decides to use the one down the hall instead.

"You'll regret this," Maureen says, calling after her. "You'll learn your lesson. Never underestimate the power of energy flow."

I stay perched just as I am. From here I have a perfect view of Maureen. I watch as Maureen slides down off of the freezer. The door to the bathroom opens down the hall and hinges shut with a hollow thud. That's when Maureen goes into motion. She scampers for the chair where Mom was sitting. She moves like a prowler, darting looks back and forth as she ducks low to the ground. In one furious movement she snatches Mom's purse up from the floor and rips it open. Her fingers fly, racing as she jams a hand into the outside pocket, then the inside, then the zippered pouch in the middle. *No!*

I ready the mop, thrust it out in front of me like a jousting lance. She's going for it. She's really doing it. I witness her fork a small fold of bills from inside the purse and wedge it into the front pocket of her apron. *You'll learn your lesson.* Her apron has tiny crosses and yin-yang symbols all over it. I don't know how she got it. Must have been tailor made just for her. It's an atrocity. She zippers everything back up, rushes to tidy whatever she's disrupted, then places it back on the floor and scurries back to her station on the freezer chest. The faucet turns on in the bathroom, and then Mom comes back out. She's wiping some excess water on her dress, the nice navy one she wore to feel special at work today. She's humming the refrain from "Here Comes the Rain Again" as she comes back into view.

"I'm sorry," Mom says as she settles herself back in her chair again. "I don't know why I got so testy. When I get finished with this in a few minutes, I'll help you move the freezer."

"That's the spirit," Maureen says. "It's not for me; it's for the negative radiation. I'm looking out for you."

"I know," Mom says. "I've been all out of balance."

My whole body is shaking. The mop trembles in my hands. I want to end this. I want to charge down the stairs in a frenzy of war cries and pugilist tactics, put a hole right through Maureen's stupid apron. If Mom knew she would come apart. There would be no putting her back together. It is impossible to tell her about what has happened. Maureen has done it, goddamn her. She has created a situation where hiding an outcome is worth more than unveiling it. She means to teach Mom one of her twisted, inconceivable lessons. This is her unfathomable idea of karma. This is her botched idea she passes off as rational thought. And the saddest thing, the worst thing, is that Mom will take something from this. She'll "learn" something. I loathe Maureen for this convolution, this wretched miscarriage of justice. I tighten my grip on the mop handle. I squeeze harder and harder until it feels like I might just melt the whole thing like a stick of butter in my wringing grip. I'm bearing down so hard I lose hold of it. It goes flinging out of my hands, banging every step on the way down. I have to think fast. Bounding to my feet I reach up and jiggle the doorknob like I've just arrived.

"Bombs away!" I shout. I come hurtling down the stairs, taking two, three at a time. I practically bust through the stairs with my stomping. When I get to the bottom I jump and holler. I'm laughing like a freak, cackling like a madman. I really must look insane, like a loose screw, like the way my mind must look inside right now. It's a triumph! It's Maureen's lucky day. She should be proud. Twice she's left her mark today. I've done it. I have manifested my own festering disgust.

Smoke Gets in Your Eyes (2006)

As a final hurrah of sorts, Sasha invites me to her last show at the Admiral Theater. She warns me that a lot of people will be there to see her off. There's no need to worry, she says. Some people will be happy for her and her new path in life, and others will be salty, jealous. There's no getting around jealousy and envy in the stripper community. No matter what, certain types of people will always want to see you fail. They'll say I think I'm too good for them, she says, a bourgie snob. Misery loves company. I understand, I tell her. Oh, and Deion will be there.

Deion. The way Sasha explains it Deion was a regular customer for about a month and a half before she agreed to go out on a date with him. He was very nice at first. He bought her flowers, opened doors, paid for things, treated her like a lady. The problem was, as she explained before, he didn't want her to work at the club anymore. He wanted to minister to her, protect her. It was a man's job, he said, to take care of a woman. Sasha didn't want to be cared for, she told him. She wanted to be her own woman, take care of herself. This didn't jive with Deion who insisted that she was just confused, clouded by her time in such a filthy place like a strip club. She had been changed by devilish men, his theory went. He was the angel to rescue her, change her back into a princess or whatever. What Sasha called him on, of course, was that if the guys at the club were all so tainted and fiendish, then what was he doing there? And so that was Deion. A little mistaken about gender norms, but not a bad egg really. Just a friend who hung around. Nothing to worry about, she said. Harmless.

I pull up in back of the Admiral at around ten o'clock. She told me ten-thirty, but I get bored and antsy, jump the gun. Traffic is light tonight, and the drive turns out to be a slim fifteen minutes. It can't be helped. In any case, I'm here. I'm more nervous than I even thought I would be. Meeting your girlfriend's friends is pressure enough, but meeting a group of exotic dancers on their turf, in a foreign habitat of unabashed nudity and unleashed desires is downright jolting. I've never stopped to take in just how imposing the club is from the outside. It's quite impressive actually, monolithic even. If you didn't know better you'd just think it was an elegant Shakespearean theater, a massive stone-pillared structure meant to showcase the greatest actors of our time. The irony is part of its appeal, I guess. Perhaps a second layer of irony, if you really think about it, is that the girls inside might actually be among the best actors around, able to convince every horny man in the audience that they strut just for them. Either way, there's an impression of classiness, an attempt to distract, that I am certain works for both the ladies and their admirers alike.

The back door reminds one of the iron gates inside a castle wall. Everything about it is fearsome and ominous, meant to send a message of warning and castigation. I do exactly as Sasha told me. Three raps on the door in a secret rhythmic pattern. The first two are slow and feathery; the final one is to be tough and booming. It works. In no time at all the door opens and a man wearing sunglasses and a Hawaiian shirt leads me inside. This is Jay. He doesn't say his name, doesn't even offer a hand, but it's him. Sasha has described him so well that I feel as if I've already gotten to know him on some deep, cosmic level, that I have access to things about him, his inner workings, that he doesn't even know about.

The halls are cold and cavernous. Everything echoes. As soon as the door vibrates closed in back of us I hear the throbbing bass coming from the stage on the other side of the wall. People hoot and holler. It sounds like a riot is going on, lots of roaring and clamoring about. I hear something crash to the floor and break. More cheers erupt. The walls reach what seem like fifty feet in the air. Their slate panels are hung with framed posters advertising sexy themes and contests from throughout the club's history. One of them reads, "Amateur Night at the Admiral: You might not be trained, but at least you're house broken!" It features a sketch of a naughty looking girl in nothing but fishnet stockings and leather boots. She has one finger in her mouth, the middle one, and she's licking it. Her legs are doing some kind of karate kick. In her callous disregard, her boot has ended up smashing the frames on some nerd's glasses who is pictured sitting at a table in the front row.

Jay is practically jogging ahead of me. It's just like Sasha said; he has to walk four or five strides faster than anybody with him, just in case they might think they were tougher or cooler than he was. A dangling chain connects his wallet to a belt loop somewhere on the frontside of his jeans. Every time he speeds up, the chain whips his thigh like it's spurring on his pace. As we get closer to the dressing rooms, I hear the sounds of joking and giggling, loose banter. A woman's high, tinkling voice says something about how she has to replace her transmission. Bobby blamed it on her, she says in a simpering whine. I lose my breath a little bit. I stop for just a second to collect myself, and Jay keeps right on going. He turns the final corner and as he does a puff of smoke comes wafting out after him.

This is it. Here goes nothing. As I turn the corner, I try to adopt a sort of casual, laidback walk that says *So what, I'm dating a stripper and I'm backstage. Big deal*, but it probably looks more like I have something caught in the leg of my pants, and I'm trying to shake it out. *Get out of there you pesky thing…*

"Hey," somebody says as soon as I enter. It's another stripper. This is the lady with the bad transmission problem, the one with the friend named Bobby.

"Hi," I say, trying to keep my voice from cracking. Jay closes the door behind me, and I realize how thick and leaden it is. The room goes immensely quiet and dense, like being sealed inside a vacuum. Jay walks to the far end of the room and takes a seat in a dark corner by an alternate exit. The lady looks a little concerned, but her eyes are kind and inviting.

She smiles, offers her hand, all the while acting normal and polite, like she's not standing in front of me wearing nothing but a witch's hat and a pair of skimpy green underwear with a screeching black cat printed across the crotch. This implies that one will be bitten or scratched if they get too close, but also sends the message that if you're the right kind of daring and dangerous you should still try. I go with the regular introduction, and she says she's heard a lot about me. I'm early, she tells me. Her name is Talia. Talia looks tall, but it's partly her six-inch heels. She's still pretty tall, though. That's what I'll say if Sasha asks what I think. Talia is tall, I'll say. Tall Talia…

Surprisingly, the place looks almost exactly how I imagined it would. I don't know why this shocks me so much, but it does, like I've predicted some kind of monumental event nobody could have ever seen coming. One whole wall is taken up by a large rectangular mirror. Set in front of it are seven or eight red velvet stools about two feet off the ground. The floor is littered with lumps of clothing, purses, coats, tanktops tossed aside like dirty laundry. A nagging fear forms around the mixture of odors in the room. Either the stifling scent of heavy perfume will get you or the other the other smells will... something like burnt cookies set aflame. The air is so fragrant that you begin to wonder if you'll escape without either a ferocious sneezing attack or a full loss of consciousness.

Talia steps aside, ushering me forward like a carnie. It is only then that I notice Sasha has been sitting right behind her the whole time. It must have been the cat underwear that distracted me. Or it could have been the perfectly pear shaped tits. One or the other ... Who could say? What I also notice is that Talia's body has been acting as a curtain, some type of partition between me and the enormous cloud of smoke that comes billowing toward me now. Sasha coughs, waves her hand in front of her face. She keeps curving her lips to blow, but all the smoke has already been expelled.

"Clayton," she says in a clipped, hoarse voice, "you're early." And as she says this another fog of smoke comes funneling out around the joint resting in her fingers.

"I know," I say. "The traffic was good."

"I'll let you guys have some time alone," Talia says. She grabs a cape, a broom and a fake plastic nose off a counter by the door, and exits the room.

"You guys" includes four of us. We're four, I think, if you count Jay. Jay is slouched in a big lounge chair over in his shadowy corner, looking intensely uninterested, trying to pick something out of his nails. There's Sasha, of course, sitting there all scented and shimmering, looking like a movie star in her fake eyelashes, glitter all over her neck and breasts... She's got her long, straight black wig on again, the one that almost makes her look Asian. It's the way she paints the lines under her eyes, too... Standing beside her is someone else, another man... Deion?

I hold my hand out. "Clayton," I say.

First, the man tweezes the joint from between Sasha's fingers and curls it behind his back, then he accepts my hand and we shake. "Deion," he says in a low, mumbly voice. His grip is weak, careless as an old sock.

We stand there for a few moments sizing each other up. I probably don't want to know what he sees, because whatever it is makes him do a little half smirk and a shoulder shrug which, real or imagined, seems to confirm all of my worst suspicions. I don't think he wanted me to see it, but there it is. He brings the joint to his lips and inhales. What my eyes see is a lean black man wearing a black do-rag and an extra-long white T-shirt down to his knees. The way it hangs, big and saggy like a wet blanket, makes him look even shorter within the excess fabric. He's not unhandsome, but not really good-looking either. He too, like the dressing room, is just as I pictured. I don't know what that says about me or him, but it does somehow make me feel exposed, off balance and naked in his presence.

"I was going to tell you about this, honest," Sasha says. She's still fluttering her hand in front of her face, trying to clear the smoke away.

Something about that phrase, about honesty, makes my heart speed up. What does she mean? She already told me about him, right? Deion takes another drag from the joint. He winks, and as the smoke comes pouring out toward me, I realize that she's not talking about him. She's talking about the marijuana.

"Oh," I say, "that? That's no big deal."

"Yeah, Mercedes, that's nothing for Clayton," Deion says. His words, like his handshake are careless and uninviting. He doesn't mean what he says. And I don't like how he calls her Mercedes. That's not her name.

"Okay, Deion, that's enough. You don't need to say anything," Sasha says. She's getting upset already. I didn't see this coming. This is supposed to be a night of a celebration, of release. Deion's supposed to be cool…

"It's all good," I say. "Don't worry about it." I step closer to Sasha, and she grabs my wrist. She sticks her fingers inside mine and we clasp our hands together. I'm feeling extra guarded all of a sudden, extra possessive. I hope Sasha doesn't take offense.

"Come on," Deion says, "it's not like that. Here, have some." Deion reaches the joint out to me. He holds there, lengthwise like a hoagie, and nods at me. "Go ahead," he says.

"No, Deion, don't," Sasha says. She's really worked up, and I'm not exactly sure why. We've never talked about drugs before, and that can be a dicey topic, I guess, but there's something else going on.

"What?" Deion says, "I'm being genuine. This is a gesture of respect and fraternity. Brothers offer their weed as a sign of kinship. Isn't that right, Clayton?" He's giving me a wide, toothy smile. I'm not convinced it's as genuine as he says it is, but I take the joint anyway.

"No, Clayton," Sasha says, "You don't have to do that."

"It's all right," I tell her. "It's cool." But I don't take a hit yet. I'm waiting to make sure it's not going to really set her off. If she's going to freak out, I won't do it, but I don't understand what the big deal is. For a while we all just stand there, like we're frozen in time or something. I start to feel a little stoned before I even take my first puff.

"All right, look," Deion says. "Can I tell him?"

"No," Sasha says. "I wanted to tell him myself."

"Well, you're right here, go ahead," he says.

I look from Sasha to Deion, still holding the smoking joint like some kind of moron. "I mean," I say, "somebody say something, please. This is making me feel weird."

Deion looks at Sasha. He puts his hands on his hips, arches his eyebrows. Sasha balks, looks away. He makes a clucking sound with his tongue, then lets out a groan. "Mercedes don't think Black people should smoke weed," he says. "There I said it. She's embarrassed or some shit."

I look down at Sasha. She looks sad and dejected. "Is that true?" I ask sheepishly.

"Not exactly," Sasha says. "There's a lot more that goes into it."

"Well, like what?" I say. "I want to know. You can tell me."

"Tell him, Mercedes," Deion says. He's all exasperated, huffing and sighing… and I wish he would stop calling her Mercedes!

Sasha turns toward me, looks up into my eyes. Her features turn soft, puppyish. As she looks up at me her eyes become doting, almost loving. When she starts to speak it's as if she's just talking to me, like we're the only ones in the room. "Well, it's a lot that goes into this. You know how I am. I don't have time to talk about the deeper issues below the surface right now, but I want to…" she trails off. I let her know with my eyes that it's okay to keep going. "It's just that when White people smoke weed it's all about peace and love and harmony. It's seen as some kind of recreational thing, like it's no big deal."

"Uh-huh," I say. "Okay." We're falling into our natural routine now, just me and her. I stroke a few strands of her wig hair, more to get a feel for the texture than for any amorous reason. I've learned my lesson about frivolous hair touching. The satiny ends feel dry and coarse, like straw. I don't know why anyone would prefer this fibrous mane to her normal consistency.

"When Black people smoke weed it's criminal. We're seen as dangerous and thugs. If the cops came in here right now and saw you holding that joint, they'd still tackle me and Deion to the ground before they even looked at you. It's not right, but it's true. I don't like it, but that's the way it is. And because of that, I always told myself that I would stay away from it. I didn't want anyone thinking that way about me, that I was just some common old, no good, corrupt Black girl." She's looking at me like she's begging for some reason, like she's asking for my forgiveness.

"It's okay," I tell her. I bend down and kiss her on the forehead. "I wouldn't judge you like that."

"I know," she says, "but it doesn't change everything. It's ingrained, you know?"

"Okay," I say. "I get it. I get it."

"I guess I just like it from time to time is all," she says. "I just don't like the stigma. It makes me feel all dirty or something."

This moves me, touches me somewhere deep down inside. I put my other hand on top of the two of ours that are already joined. One more heartbreaking thing to consider, to ponder about the injustices between White and Black worlds. But it can't be argued. It's the way things are. You start to see it more and more once your eyes are opened. I wonder how many people never even think about this stuff. I know I didn't before I met Sasha. We share a long, tender moment, just sitting there like that, two people who have put in the time, built a real appreciation for one another. It must be obvious to even Deion.

"You shouldn't have told him like that," Deion says. "He's going to think you're all crazy now. You sound crazy," he says.

He laughs. He's got a phony kind of laugh, the kind you use when you want to mock someone.

I just look at him. I try to communicate that he should back off. I try to tell him with my eyes that he's off base, and I think it actually works because he quiets down a little, turns off the little affected laughter track. He doesn't back down necessarily, but he lets off the gas a bit. He's just standing there, swinging his arms.

"Here," I say. I hold the joint up, but before I take a hit I look right at Sasha and I say, "I'm just going to take one drag off of this to show you that it's cool or whatever. It's just one hit out of, you know, solidarity," I say, and I look back over at Deion. When I turn back Sasha nods okay, and I bring the joint up to my lips. I try to inhale like I'm an old pro, which I kind of am now. I take a pretty big hit, but nothing extreme, and I let it out nice and slow. It tastes good and smooth. It's different than the stuff Jerry gets, much sweeter and sort of more minty in a way… like cookies… it's hard to explain.

I offer it over to Sasha next, but she shakes her head, so I pass it back to Deion. He sort of snatches it out of my hand, like he's pissed off or something, but I just try to ignore it. I don't care. I want the rest of the night to be about Sasha, not Deion.

"Hey!" I say, putting on a happy face. I take my hands out from between hers and give her shoulders a little shake, a little pep! "You look amazing!" I say.

"Thank you," she says, playing all shy and stuff. She's adorable. You can tell she's taken a lot of time and effort getting ready for tonight. Her vanity is a mess of lotions, polishes and lipstick. It's like a little village made of cosmetics.

"You are going to slay tonight," I say. "I mean, don't slay too much, but you know, slaaaaaaaay!" I put my tongue out and make a punk rock symbol with my fingers, like I'm in the band Slayer or whatever.

"Stop it!" Sasha says. "You so crazy!" She whisks something onto her cheeks with a mini paintbrush. It gives them a peachy glow. She puts the brush away, snaps shut the case and stands up. "I'd ask you to give me a hug and a kiss, but I can't," she says. "I'd get this shit all over you." She really does look tremendous. With Sasha there's no kinky nurse's costume or some wicked witch getup, it's just basic and straight to the point. That's part of what's so great about her, she's no nonsense. All she needs is her bright red bra and panties with the tasteful fur accents around the waistband and straps. She's a class act all the way.

"Hey, that's fine. I'll just give you a little love tap on your butt instead," I say, and I do. I give her a swat right across the ass. "Go get em, tiger!" I say.

"I'm going to kill you," Sasha says. She tries to hit me back on my butt, but I leap out of the way. She laughs, and I feel good again. "Look," she says, "I have to go meet up with the girls for a little bit before I go out on stage." She looks over at the digital clock on her table, "I promised them we'd have a little huddle before I went out for the last time. I'm already a little late."

"Okay," I say. "You're going to be great."

"Thank you, baby," she says. "You okay staying here for a bit until I go out?" she asks. She peers over my shoulder at Deion who is pacing in the corner, taking quick little pulls on the joint, and sort of grumbling to himself. I look over too, and we share a little moment of silliness, like, *Shoot, I don't know what he's doing, but I'll be cool.*

"I'll be fine," I say, "you just do what you got to do." This comes out the way I want it to, confident and smooth, which is the opposite of how I'm feeling.

She puts her palm to her lips, and blows me a kiss. We take one last look at Deion together. He's plopped himself down on one of the stools, and he's moving all around on it, almost like he's dancing in place. His body is going through some kind of hyper twitching. From head to toe he's jittering all over the place. With Jay's inert, half-dead body on the other side of the room, they make mirror opposites of each other. I grab Sasha's hand, and we look into each other's eyes. We seem to both be thinking the same thing. They'll balance each other out.

"See you later, Deion," Sasha calls to him.

"Yeah, okay," Deion says without looking up. He's really going through something. We can barely understand him with how low he's talking. It's like he has rocks in his mouth or something.

"Okay," Sasha says to me, "can't wait to see you after the show. Wish me luck," she says as she skips for the door.

"Break a leg," I say.

"You got it," Sasha says. She fakes like she twists her ankle, plays it up as she goes hobbling out the door. Then, with one last theatrical wave, she's out.

With Sasha and Talia gone, all the luster is sucked out of the place. It's dead. Suddenly, it doesn't matter that we're in the dressing room of a strip club. We may as well be in our aunt's walk-in closet or some other place where women gather in private to transform into their public selves. Jay certainly agrees. The way he's yawning in his chair over there it's like he got shot with a tranquilizer dart. Deion has stopped bouncing around so much, but his fingers are still moving. He's tapping them on his knee as he crushes the joint out in the ashtray beside him. I take a deep breath. There's an open stool beside Deion, and I decide it'll be a good idea to sit down and see if we can kill some time with small talk, make peace with one another.

"That stuff was pretty good," I say, nodding toward the ashtray. "I'm not too familiar with that kind. It was sweeter than I'm used to, like candy. Where'd you get it?"

Deion scoffs, shakes his head. "That's hybrid, son," he says, but it comes out garbled. I can hardly hear him. He takes out a small rectangular baggie from his jeans pocket, unrolls it, and dangles it out for me to see. It's a black baggie instead of clear, which stands out right away. On the bottom right corner of the bag is a small white sticker in the shape of a box. There looks to be a slight outline to the straight sides, but it disappears into the dark background. "OG Kush. Shit's like mint Girl Scout cookies. What you know about that?" He puts his hands behind his head and reclines back against the table. He stretches his legs all the way out so that they almost touch mine. I pull my feet in.

"Hm, not much. That's interesting, though," I say. "Never heard of that."

"Yeah, well, you probably will now. You'll probably be the next pusher." He folds the black bag back up and squeezes it back into his pocket.

"Hey, what was that sticker on the bottom of the bag?" I ask.

"I don't know, nigga'!" He says. The entrance of the new word carries its own supercharged impact, like someone smashing a huge glass vase. "I just buy the stuff and smoke it. You want to know all about some sticker. Ain't nobody has time for that shit," He clucks his tongue, grimaces. "That don't even make no sense."

"Yeah, I guess it doesn't matter," I say, and then quickly, disorderly, "Sorry. Sorry!" I say it in a hurry, realizing its importance as reparation, as if I'd almost forgotten to apologize for making him lose his temper, for forcing him to use that new word. "It was something new, a new experience, that's all."

"Shit," he says, gratefully acknowledging my attempt at a curative response, "I bet it was, I bet it was." He chuckles to himself, and something about his inner thoughts seems to have a mellowing effect on him.

He looks me over again, but this time his reaction is even less approving, and he doesn't bother trying to hide it. "How you meet, Mercedes?" he asks, but in a way that I know he already knows the answer.

"Sasha?" I say.

"Okay," he says, "suit yourself."

"Same way you did, I guess."

"Nah," Deion says. He pulls himself up to a more erect posture on the stool. He leans forward, puts his elbows on his knees. "No, see, you met Sasha somewhere else. I met Mercedes here."

This is not the territory I want to be in with him. This is precisely what I was trying *not* to do. I look over at Jay, but he's no help. It appears that he's started to doze off a little bit, but it's hard to tell with his glasses on. He keeps one hand rolled into a fist just in case someone might make a sudden threat to his position. It's just like Sasha said it would be. "Look," I say, "I don't want to get into this. I don't want any trouble. Let's drop it."

But Deion has other plans. "You don't get what I got," he says.

"What's that supposed to mean?" I ask.

"You get the White boy treatment," he says. "You don't notice the way she acts with you, but I do."

"Man, whatever. I don't even care about that."

"She thinks she's smart," he says.

"She is smart," I say.

"No, no, she's smart for a Black girl. She wants you to think she's smart smart."

"She's plenty smart—"

"You think I'm dumb, don't you?"

"I never said anything like that."

"You don't have to. I can see it. It's the same way Sasha started looking at me. I think she got it from you."

"I have no idea what you're talking about."

"See, not all Black people are stupid and lazy."

"I've never—"

"You all think I'm stupid, but I'm not. I know things. I see things." He closes his eyes, like he's trying to conjure up the image inside his mind. "Yeah, I know what's going on," he says. This is said in the clearest tone I've heard from him yet, plain and enunciated. He's still got his eyes closed. It's like he's speaking to the insides of his own eyelids. "You live on the northside, don't you?"

"Yeah," I say.

"How'd I know it?" he says. His eyes are still closed, then he pops them open, licks his lips.

"Chicago is a segregated city."

"Nah, nah, not anymore. Tell me something," he says, leaning in even closer. "Why is it that just down the street from my block on 75th, we got a Whole Foods going in, and then, and then up in Edgewater they have a Harold's Chicken up there now?"

"I don't know," I say. Uh-oh. Where's he going with this?

"Aiight, tell me this. Why is it that I drive around my hood now, and all I see is some fake ass niggas doing jack shit? We got prissy ass niggas with glow sticks wearing pink shoelaces, watching Sponge Bob, acting all Fresh Prince… Soft! People trying to rap about candy shops, and let me hold you, and shit. You know about this lame? And then on the other side of things we got Insane Clown Posse! Man, what you think about that? Those boys are rough! They look like they're going to merc somebody, G, just out of nowhere, like gah-jaw, blam!" He pretends he's holding a rifle in his arms. He cocks it back, then blasts himself off his feet with the invisible kickback.

"Man, I don't know anything about any Insane Clown Posse," I say. I put my hands up like "I surrender," like I don't want any association with that. I want out of this one. I've seen what the bleak suburban kids look like who listen to ICP, huge jeans, all pocked up with zits, zonked on Faygo soda, and not a one of them any shape or shade other than doughy and white.

"Okay, but here's the thing." He pauses, scans the ceiling like maybe something is written up there. He takes his hand and uses it as a cleaver, slicing it down against his opposite palm like an exclamation mark. "I drive I-90 and I'm passing Black people heading north, looking all worn out and weak, like they're lost and looking for an open project. I drive south and I see a bunch of White motherfuckers with their hats broke off to the side, grills on their teeth, looking happy as a pack of clams. We got the south side turning into a strip mall, and the north side getting ghetto as fuck. They're just moving us around, moving us around… And we just pass each other back and forth, and ain't nobody says or does a damn thing." He looks at me sideways, bewildered. "Motherfucker, somebody's robbing somebody else! Things just aren't real anymore, no sense of up or down, black or white. I got

Caucasians living in Lake View welcoming me in, and folk in Burnside telling me to get lost. Shit's got me fucked up. That's twisted. Now, you tell me what's going on with that."

I don't have an answer, and I don't dare try to make one up, not now, not on the spot. My head feels airy and swimming. All I can do is shrug.

"See, I told you I see things, didn't I? I'm no dummy. Here, here," He says, but he doesn't have anything concrete to offer me. What he's doing is using his empty hands like theoretical objects, some representation of good in one, and something bad in the other. "North side," he says, wagging his left hand, "south side." He does the same with the right. "I'm trying to work my way north, because that's where the money is, right? I have a plan to open my own strip club up north. So, that's where I go. I travel. I'm not one of those crab in a barrel type bitches. I take a ride up to Lincoln Park where the real cash is." He waits, looks at me to make sure I'm with him. I nod my head. "Okay," he continues, "so I'm up there looking around, and I don't run into some rich White guy with an ascot or whatever. I don't meet some guy with a stock portfolio and some bank accounts like I think, I see the same fucking niggas I saw on the south side last week!" He tosses his hands up in the air, leans his elbows back on the counter behind him. "They're scavenging for scraps, man! I go back down south, and that's where I see these pasty-ass crackers. I see the White dudes in their suits and briefcases, building real estate in Englewood, looking like some kind of dressed up construction worker in their ties and yellow hard hats. Now, ain't that some bullshit?" he asks. Just in case I thought it was a rhetorical question, which I do, he raises his hands up, shakes his head. "Well, what do you think?"

The thing is, I don't know exactly what he's talking about, but I get the feeling lately like anything is possible. What he's saying doesn't sound any crazier than the rumors I've heard about how cops have a secret warehouse somewhere on the west side where they beat the shit out of Black suspects or how aldermen intentionally let the crime rate rise in certain neighborhoods to push the property value down, only to turn around and buy up all the cheap real estate and gentrify it into the new hotspot in town. Maybe that's what Deion is saying… I don't know. My brain feels a little fuzzy and floaty, something from the weed, no doubt. He might be onto something. This is tripping me out. I think maybe checking in on Jay will give me some stability, some anchor, but when I look over at him, nothing much has changed. He's taken the sunglasses off, but it's unclear if he's done so out of concern or interest or… his expression is just as blank as before.

"I'm really not sure," I say. It comes out all sluggish, like slow motion.

"Okay, then, I'll tell you." This has a relaxing effect. There's a breeze of satisfaction now that I know he'll pick up my slack for me. I don't have to talk right now. He squirms around on the stool, making himself as comfortable as possible. "See, the prime real estate on the north side is gone. Whitey gobbled it all up. He's filled his belly with all that, and now he's coming for us, for our land." He's talking in a sort of shallow, hissing tone, like a snake. "And you know what?" he says, but this time it's rhetorical because he continues right along. "We're going to let him. We're going to roll over and say, oh yes sir, master, you can have our share, too! We weren't going to use it anyway. We were just waiting for you to come and take it. We're just sitting here twiddling our thumbs because we're a bunch of simple-ass niggas with no goals, no ambition and no backbone."

It's taken a dark, unexpected turn. I thought I knew where he was going, almost thought that I'd be able to contribute if he kept going the way he was, but this new information, this theory, it seems off to me. He's putting all of the blame on Black people for their apathy, their lack of drive and motivation, but that's not the whole thing. That's not what I've been learning, not what Sasha has been saying. I almost want to argue with him, but that seems ludicrous at this point. How would a White man argue a Black man about his thoughts and feelings on his own race, his own people? It's like a cat trying to tell a dog how to bark… but… What about the system, I want to say. What about the systematic oppression of black people over hundreds of years? What about the neglect, the bait and switch…

"Well," I say, "I mean, what about… what about the fact that the land was never yours to begin with? I mean, what I mean is… it wasn't like the choicest land that you would have wanted, your family, given an option, you know? You were more or less put there, or like *left* there, right? In the middle of nothing…" I cut myself off. Deion's face has been souring throughout my attempt to answer. He's got his nose curled up like he smells something foul. Even Jay has chimed in, so to speak. I hear him make some kind of sigh over in his lounge chair. He sits up a little bit, more alert, but then cancels it right out by putting his shades back on again.

"You really messed up," Deion says. "You and Mercedes are perfect for each other. You sound just like her. Put all the criticism on White people. Sure, go ahead. Give me a whole stack of complaints and some gub'mint cheese, please. I'll be just fine with that. It's too hard to pull myself up, so I'll just sit here and collect like the bottom feeder I am…"

"It's the distance, though. How far is the pull up? It's different—"

"Oh, you got it, White boy. You just go ahead. You pull Mercedes up. She's got it backward though. You're the one playing savior. You go ahead, White Jesus. You're all alike."

"We're not all alike," I say. "That's the thing."

My voice is hot, angry. I can feel my blood pressure rising. It's getting harder for me to hold myself back. I want to say something. I want to tell him that thinking everyone's alike is the problem. Everyone, given an equal chance, has a shot, but things aren't fair as it stands. We're not alike, he and I. We've never been allowed to be on the same footing. If anything's the same, it's the system, the same rigged one that's been in place since our forefathers, and…! Oh, I'm losing it. My nails are clawing into the velvet beneath me. My head is spinning. Unclench, Clayton. Calm down…

But there's a fear there, too. Fear and anger. A current of fright and terror runs just below the surface like troubled waters. I wonder if it's real or manufactured, something authentic or synthetic, something sinister given to me by the media or formed by my own preconceptions about the tendencies of a race rumored to be menacing and untrustworthy? The sensation is like groping, searching for some ground sturdy enough in which to anchor your mind in place but touching down on nothing but vapor or mercury. There are no absolutes or solids to rely on, only liquids. The slick, sagacious look on Deion's face seems to acknowledge my mental discordance, as if he understands its origins better than I do.

"Like attracts like," he says.

"What's that?" I say. All my thoughts come to a screeching halt, like a car crash. "What did you say?"

"I was watching Oprah the other day, and she had some lady on there talking about a book." All the color drains from my face. If I wasn't pure white before, I am now. I'm ghost white now. I must be. I think I might be ill. "Yeah, see, this author, she understands. I can't remember her name. She wrote this book, I think it's called the *Short Cut* or whatever. It's about how with the right kind of thinking and goal setting, you can accomplish anything. Forget about all this who has it worse bullshit. With enough gratitude and positivity miraculous things can happen. There's this one man in the book who used to live in a cardboard box. He used to eat out of dumpsters in New York City, and through this method, through the book's teachings, he became a millionaire. He attracted good things to himself because he thought good thoughts. The universe is a magnet. Yeah, so you don't know about that. People can become whatever they want. Nothing else matters."

There is bile and saliva rising in my throat. I feel hot and dizzy. I've got to get to a restroom. "It does matter," I say, and then I stand and head for the exit. "Excuse me," I say.

I'm passing Jay's lifeless body on the chair, when I open the door to leave. It's extremely heavy, and I almost trip as I push. A surge of noises rushes in upon me. It's forceful enough to stop me in my tracks. I can hear the pulse of drums and the rumble of claps coming from the showroom. They echo throughout the vast, yawning hallway, creeping inside of me, rattling my bones. I have to get out of here… I hear the announcer's voice bellowing from the speakers. "Ladies and gentleman," he blares, "Get your money out. Lay it down, and please welcome, for the final time in her illustrious career, the one, the only, Mercedes Benson!" The place goes bananas. People yowl and whoop like it's the second coming of Christ. The audience must be stomping their feet because the whole floor is shaking. I need to grab hold of the door handle to keep from throwing up.

"You'll see," Deion shouts. I see him stand up from his stool, lean into it. "Keep thinking your negative thoughts. We don't need you!" he screams at the top of his lungs. "I'm going to be rich! Fuck you, Clayton. Fuck you!"

I release the door behind me, and it swings shut with the force of a hell-bent stampede. The whole place is rocking. The roof might cave in. And still I go toward it. I follow the sound, stumble to the thrumming of a ravenous, wolfish crowd. I can't stop myself. I'm going straight for it.

See Green (2003)

Mom and Maureen talk Dad into letting Lindy paint her bedroom walls with her fingers. Actually, it's more Maureen than Mom. Dad knows what he's up against, and wisely throws in the towel. His only recourse is evacuation. He leaves the house, unwilling to standby while his daughter renders his plain, clinical walls a "mother-squirting abyss of rubbish." To him, the neutrality of the walls, the basic beige color, was one of the few things left in the apartment unsullied by "balderdash," as he put it. The color, or rather the absence of it, had been giving him some fraction of calm. He simply could not bear to watch one more aspect of his life shift from impartial to impractical. *Fucking mercy stroke!*

Maureen's argument goes like this. Lindy is expressing herself in the most productive way possible. Her perpetual recitations are a good thing to be applauded. If you take away her painting she will turn to drugs. Let the art become her medication, she says, before the pharmaceuticals do. It's not bad reasoning in some ways, and Mom goes along with it. However, I note that while Mom concedes, she does so, not with conversation, but instead through a series of nods and bashful aversions, protective lowerings of the eyes, head and shoulders. In the end, she gives in the way a flower submits to death after a month without water.

All of Lindy's furniture is piled into a mound in the corner of her room like some kind of refuse awaiting a bonfire. She stands in front of the open wall, fingers dripping with green paint, and recites her prayer.

"Om shrim maha lakshmiyei swaha," she chants in a hushed, reverent tone.

"Isn't she beautiful," Maureen whispers. She's leaning in the doorframe outside Lindy's room with her arms folded across her chest. She inhales deeply, exhaling the breath directly into Mom's face who is standing right behind her.

"What is she saying?" Mom asks. There's pride in her voice, but also reluctance.

"Oh, don't worry about the particulars," Maureen says, "focus on the essence. She's performing the abundance prayer."

"Well, phonetically," I say, nudging my way in between them, "it's pronounced om shreem mah-hah lahk-shmee-yay swah-hah." A few days ago Lindy let me read over the prayer sheet Randy gave her. There was something about it, I had to admit, that was mesmerizing. The next morning I practiced a few times in front of the bathroom mirror before I got into the shower. I was trying to get my eyes to take on the pasty zombie quality that Lindy seems to achieve each time or the mechanical jaw hinging she does, but I could not master it. Lindy is on another level. Her devotion is absolute. After weeks of rehearsal, she acts out everything with unwavering grace and duplication, as if she were born to deliver endless incantations. "Translated it means—"

"Love the color choice," Maureen interjects.

"It's very naturalistic," Mom says.

"Oh, yes, you would say that. I suppose you could go that direction," Maureen says, "but that's not what I was thinking."

"What were you thinking?" Mom says

Lindy gets on her tiptoes. She splays her fingers so that when she smears the paint on the wall it creates starburst designs with oozing contrails. Her legs are sinewy and smooth beneath her shorts, bulbous calf muscles the shape of swelled hearts.

"What she's doing is trying to give a visual representation of what the prayer looks like to her," I say. "According to the scripture, you're supposed to turn the unseen seen through some kind of ritualistic art movement. Get what's inside out."

Mom nods her head, thanks me for my commentary. Maureen is not as grateful.

Maureen does not react. She is motionless, save the subtle movement of her lips. I think she's trying to imitate what Lindy is saying. It's not going well. Her mouth is too stiff; eyes stray and roaming. If this were a game of follow the leader, Lindy would be hopping on one foot while Maureen knelt on the floor.

"Om shrim maha lakshmiyei swaha," Lindy repeats. It's happening. The effect of her litany takes on a rhythmic, hypnotic quality. When she does it right, it makes you feel like you're gliding, like the way it feels to fly in a dream. This is when I start to understand. It almost makes sense.

Lindy plows her hands down the length of the wall until all the paint has run dry from her fingers. Hunched low to the floor, she looks almost simian in her meditative squat.

"So, this is her mind's eye?" Mom asks me. She says it the same way someone asks a question of a seatmate in the middle of a silent, crowded movie theater.

"Kind of," I say. "It's a representation. Whatever was going through her—"

"It's what *is*," Maureen says. "She's already flush with green. You can see that coming through. That's obvious." She nods toward the green splashes on the wall, satisfied with her interpreting skills. "This is just a way of letting the universe know that she has already tapped in. She's prepared to receive what is already ordained."

"Well, the actual translation is, 'Om and salut—"

"Salutations!" Maureen blurts.

"Yes," I say, "salutations to she who manif—"

"Manifests!" Maureen says.

"Manifests every kind of abund—"

"Abundance!" Maureen barks. "Making the unseen seen," she says. "I get it. I'm always one step ahead. That's the point. We already get it, me and Lindy. We see what's coming before it comes."

"She's reaching out," I say, "trying to make it visible for everyone. It's supposed to be a cooperative act."

"Oh sure! Right. Okay, then why isn't it blue or red or yellow then?" Maureen says. "You just quiet down."

Lindy submerges both of her hands in the paint and rakes them all over the wall in a chaotic pattern. She makes floor to ceiling circles with both hands, creating a swirl of green planets and constellations that cover the whole space. Her chanting is growing louder and faster at the same time. It's gushing out of her.

"Look what you've done," Maureen says. She looks at me with disdain, shakes her head.

But my attention goes elsewhere. I'm not worried about Maureen because right now Mom is having an episode. Her eyes lock in on Lindy's and she goes faint. Their mutual turbulence passes between them. Mom clutches the wall for support, lets out a gasp. Her eyes are zapped with alarm. Lindy's furor courses through her and into Mom, and then Mom's volatile reaction transfers to me. And then we're snarled up in it together. We've broken the trance.

"Om shrim maha lakshmiyei swaha, Om shrim maha lakshmiyei swaha, Om shrim maha lakshmiyei swaha," Lindy shouts. Her movements and words have cracked free from whatever flimsy apparatus held them in place a moment ago. She is a wheel shucked from its struts, rolling wild down a steep hill.

"Lindy!" Mom shouts.

"Mom!" I say.

"Clayton!" Mom says.

"Oh, for God sake," Maureen says. She turns and storms out of the room. The farther she gets from us, the more Lindy simmers and her warbling winds down.

In a few seconds Lindy settles, sinks flat to the floor. Green paint covers the walls, the ceiling. It surrounds her, pools the ground beneath her butt like a lagoon. It's on the dresser, her shoes, her shirt. Some has even managed to get caught in the rims of her nostrils. The cleanup won't be cheap.

The Flora of Chicago (2005)

Zarek's Greek Restaurant is a campus hotspot. The owner has put a lot of effort into making sure it stays that way. Every wall except one is decorated in University of Illinois paraphernalia. The wall right inside the entrance is decked out in newspaper clippings showcasing various sports highlights from the school's history. The back wall is covered in orange and blue pennants, flags and artwork starring the team's obscurely offensive mascot dressed in a splashy headdress and carrying a spear. The frame above the kitchen window is festooned with photographs featuring students in various states of merriment and satiation. Because so many of the boys and girls are so pumped full of their own zinging hormones, and because they dress in a fashion that exposes those appetites, there is something vaguely erotic about the whole mural that cannot be helped. Overall, the intention is to create a welcoming atmosphere without too much corruption, an inclusive style meant to make everyone feel at home even if they're far away from family comforts. The décor screams: "Here is a place where any Fighting Illini member can come to get a decent meal at a fair price, and maybe a little action if you're lucky," which is really the only thing teenagers, at this juncture in their unformed lives, are asking for. It's also a place that employs a lot of alumni. Jerry was the first one to land a job here as a waiter. He got Drew a job as a host a few days later. Next, they got Max a job as one of the short-order cooks in the back. Max doesn't even go to school at U of I. He doesn't go to school anywhere, but he's been to visit several times and Drew and

Jerry have really taken a shining to him. That job only lasted about one week. Max got angry at Fred for chewing him out over a series of wrong orders and threw a cherry tomato at the back of his head as he turned to leave the kitchen. Long story short, by the time they got around to helping me out, all that was left was a lousy spot as a deadbeat busboy. It's fine though. Whatever. I'd have taken anything. Much like my lackadaisical approach to choosing a major, I'm willing to do anything that keeps me afloat and enrolled. There are much worse jobs, I think. The owner, a husky fifty-something with a scruffy goatee named Fred, takes pretty good care of us most of the time. He does have a tendency toward a quick temper, and he does insist on always backing the customers in every single situation no matter what the cause, but he likes to joke around and doesn't get too bent out of shape if you arrive five or six minutes late for your shift. I've seen other students accept jobs as envelope stuffers or van drivers, gigs that pay about the same but offer far less excitement. It's possible that I'm just being defensive. Is cleaning slop off of tables less demeaning than something like stocking shelves at the campus bookstore? Probably not, but what am I supposed to do? At least I have Drew and Jerry to keep me company, and some nights, especially weekends, we all get treated to front row seats at the revolving freak show that is college circus life. Last weekend we saw three girls throw soda and salad all over their boyfriends then smack the shit out of them with their plastic dishware. Fred didn't know which customer to side with that night, but he did make me and Drew stay an extra hour to mop up the fallout.

Things are particularly slow and somber for a Friday night. It's still early, only six-thirty, but usually by this time we've already catered to numerous coeds looking to get a little grub in their systems before a hard evening of boozing and lechery. I'm cleaning off a table in the corner, taking my time. There's no reason to rush. This table happens to be positioned next to the lone façade not plastered in U of I adornments. This side is furbished with a huge painting that stretches almost the entire length of the wall. The whole thing is an expansive portrayal of Greek landscaping and agriculture. The first panel features golden fields and rolling hills merging with the brilliant blue of ocean water. Which sea is it that borders that seductive countryside? I'm trying to remember from our world geography class. The Aegean? Mediterranean? Maybe it was both… So much water in that region… So cleansing. There is a way to get lost in this painting, the endless span washed in what seems like a hundred different runny colors. All along the banks women are portrayed as laborers with an old world flair. What time period is this depicting? The women are dressed in bland gowns, draped in flowing garments and all-consuming scarves. They wear satchels of some variety… What are they collecting? Wheat? Actually, on closer inspection, it's not a very good painting. The lines around both the people and property are blurry and faded, all bleeding together in one murky mass. It's hard to tell where the clothing ends and the soil begins. I wonder if Fred thinks this is a stellar piece of art. He must like it. It's the centerpiece to his entire business. Perhaps a friend or family member created it. This makes me reconsider Fred… Is Fred even Greek? He looks plainly Midwestern to me—overweight, unkempt, earthy and starchy white… I bet Drew or Jerry would know. They always seem to have the inside story. Speaking of Drew and Jerry, where are they? Weren't they on the schedule tonight? They usually start at five. I hope nothing happened…

"Yo Clay," a voice ruptures my daydreaming. It's Eduardo, the other busboy. Eduardo is a good natured, carefree Mexican with only one real flaw, as I see it. He tries too hard to come off as some kind of savvy veteran of the restaurant business, but the kid can't be older than sixteen. When things are really humming on a busy night and he's in the zone, he works quicker and more adroitly than anyone I've ever seen. He's got moxie, but he also has the creamy pubescent skin and enthusiastic disposition of a high schooler. What I mean is that he seems too cheery, too robust and easygoing to have conquered any major milestone even pre-adulthood has to offer. Lots of the college girls who come in find him highly attractive, but it's easy to be likable when life hasn't sunk its dreary hooks into you yet. Overall, I guess he's not a bad guy, though.

"Aye, Eduardo," I say, hoisting my slimy dish tray from the table. "What's up?"

"Nothing much," he says, shrugging. "Clearly." He gestures to the vacant room, accentuating its emptiness. "This place is dead as ever," he says.

"Yeah, I know," I say. I carry the clanking tray over toward the kitchen. Eduardo hurries over in front of me.

"Bro," he says with that childlike glee in his eyes. He doesn't say anything for a little while, just stands there blinking. What am I supposed to do with all of these flickering lashes? Am I supposed to have some kind of decoder? One blink means come with me. Two blinks means stay where you are? "We need to spice things up," he finally says, and he stops blinking. I'm not clear on what this phrase means exactly, but his body language is apparent. He doesn't want me to go anywhere until I talk with him more. His locked hips and torso act as a roadblock to any notions of escape I might harbor.

"Yeah?" I say. "Okay. What do you have in mind?" There's something precarious, something slippery on his mind. I've seen this act before. I'm not that concerned or really even interested in whatever he's selling yet, but I could be enticed. Eduardo isn't someone I necessarily see as an instigator, but I do have a track record with types who are. My record is a losing one if you score me based on my ability to stand my ground in the face of conspiratorial or reckless ideas.

For the next ten or twenty seconds, Eduardo just stares into my eyes and sands his hands together. He nods his head, each bobbing motion cranking a larger and larger smile across his face. He licks his lips, giggles in a very wily, cagey type of way. It's the kind of dubious laugh I've seen Drew do after one too many beers, right before he takes off his shirt and dances on a table.

"What?" I ask, trying to remain deadpan, unassuming. I don't want to egg him on, but I'm also curious. I've seen situations like this go both ways before.

For the next few seconds, Eduardo cycles through some kind of decision making rolodex in his mind, some kind of flowchart or cheat sheet that might reveal to him whether he should propose to me whatever it is that's been churning in his crooked little head. Following a couple starts and stops, a few hand wrings and mouth rubs, Eduardo ducks his head in close to my ear and whispers, "Come back into the kitchen, bro."

"I'm heading that way anyway," I say. This answer seems to strike the right note, seems noncommittal enough. It transmits neither full compliance for nor total denial against whatever plan he means to set in motion. I follow him back through the swinging doors. I follow his jittery strides back past the fryers and prep stations, back past the dishwashers and on to the rear exit that leads to the dumpsters. There, to the side of the door, is one of those stock, stainless steel tables on rollers that every restaurant needs for transporting miscellaneous goods from one location to the next. Atop its shiny surface rests a small mound of white, crystalline powder. To the right of this snowy peak lies three skinny fingers of the stuff. A stray credit card sits angled in the upper corner, tipped in a frosty chalk.

When we reach what amounts to a dead end, Eduardo turns on me with the same twitchy, effervescent smile from the dining room. "This will make the time pass faster," he says, "liven things up." He runs his tongue along the gums of his upper teeth, makes a popping sound with his lips. For the first time I realize that he's been doing this a lot, playing with his mouth and teeth in conspicuous ways.

"Eduardo, I don't' know," I say, and I'm not sure if this line, this excessive use of his name, comes out too much like a reprimand, but it probably does. The long, involuntary sigh that follows won't help my cause either.

"Call me Eddie," he says. He pats me on the shoulder, and everything comes clear. He's applying the buddy tactic, the recruitment strategy. "We're friends, right? I got a good vibe from you, man. I don't know, but I do." This was his strategy all along. It's not a bad one. "It just seems like you're down for a good time. I can trust you. Right?" He asks. He dips his chin when he says this, glances up at me with hope and expectation in his brown eyes. "Right?" he says.

"Sure, Eddie," I say, "but..."

"Dude, there is nobody else here. No customers, barely any other workers, and you know Fred isn't coming in on a Friday night, not after that shit last weekend."

"Yeah, but I don't think so," I say. "I think I'm good." This is all happening so fast. It's hard to say what I would have done in a similar situation with more warning and a safer environment, but right now the only thing I feel is caught off guard. But there's that thought, that possibility. I *think* I'm good, I said. I think…

"Come on! It's fun. Nobody else will know. Nobody is even around!"

"Yeah, I know," I say. "Speaking of which, where are Drew and Jerry?"

"I don't know, man. Why? Do you think they'll want some too?"

I think about Drew, how I'm certain he's definitely dabbled in the stuff before. Sometimes he stays up all night with this feral, racing look in his eyes, telling everyone he loves them and threatening to jump off our dorm balcony into the shrubs three floors below. "I can do it, assholes!" he says, hollering and clawing as he attempts to climb the railing. Jerry and I always pull him down in time and force him to go inside. We've talked about putting a lock on the sliding glass door that only we have a key for. I'm not going to lie; I've thought about trying it out before myself, but I don't think this is the time or place to do a mind-altering drug for the first time. I barely even know Eduardo, and as I mentioned he doesn't seem all that wise or discerning when it comes to matters that require a more mature thought process. If I'm ever going to do it, I want to be with Drew and Jerry. Where the hell are Drew and Jerry? They're supposed to be here. They'd know what to do.

"I'm all set, Eddie," I tell him. "I appreciate the offer, and no judgment, dude. You have fun, but I'm going to lay low tonight." It's already happening, I notice. He's pulled me right into his peppy colloquial way of talking. Eddie has this way of speaking in slang almost every single word. It's addictive in a sense, has this manner of reeling you into its breezy nonchalance.

"Bro," Eddie says, "Come on!" He uses a tone with such disdain that it startles me a little. "You are weak, man. Lame."

"Haha, okay, whatever," I say. I'm not going to let this guy peer pressure me. He doesn't have the clout or notoriety that it would take to make me surrender to his taunts. I'll be honest, there are people out there, folks who I could potentially look up to or feel threatened by, who could lead me to do it. I'm not above persuasion. My self-esteem isn't so strong that it can withstand all forms of mockery, but not him, not tonight.

"Aren't you from Chicago?" Eddie asks.

"Yeah, so?" I say.

"So? Aren't people from Chicago supposed to be all rough and gutsy? I thought you were a tough guy. I heard dudes in Chicago are like rugged gangster types and shit. I've seen the movies."

"Well, that's not always true," I say.

"You're no fun," Eddie says and shakes his head. This admonishment, slight as it is, gets to me for some reason. I feel like I'm an older sibling letting his brother down. He looks totally dejected and disappointed.

"Hey, come on," I say, trying to buck him up a little bit. This quickly I've shifted into nurturer mode. It's always lurking just below the surface. "It's all good. Don't get upset."

"I got this from my cousin. I'm pretty sure he got it from Chicago. The big city is where it's at, bro. That's why I thought you'd be down. I thought you were cool, bro. Chicago is where all the good stuff happens. They have the best drugs and shit."

To my surprise, he finishes up this little plea by swooping low to the table and taking a fierce snort of cocaine. He sucks it right up like a pro through a rolled dollar bill that I guess must have been laying there the whole time. I hadn't even seen it there before. Yanking his head up, he completes the endeavor with an invigorating "Woo-haa!"

"You know, not everyone is who you think they are, man." All of a sudden I feel like giving him a lesson. Somehow I take this to be the perfect time for a lecture on acceptance and stereotyping. "Not everyone is the same. Chicago gets a lot of bad raps, and I'm not down with that. You shouldn't assume that everyone is like you picture them in your mind. It isn't fair. It's not right!" Perhaps I'm taking this angle because of the conversations Sasha and I have been sharing recently. We've talked about how people should speak up more if they feel someone is expressing an ignorant idea about already marginalized groups of people. Maybe it could stop them from being so casual about it next time, make them think twice. It's worth a shot, anyway. And Eddie, with his mediocre reputation and his non-threatening demeanor, is not a bad subject for a trial run. "It's like flowers," I say.

"Flowers?" Eddie says in a skeptical, high-pitched voice.

"That's right, flowers," I persist. "Most people think that all flowers are lovely and they all smell great."

"Are you saying that Chicago stinks! What are you even talking about?"

"No, Chicago doesn't—" I bite my lip. I don't want to get too excited. This will probably work better if I can keep my head, maintain. "Listen, I'll tell you what I'm talking about. Many flowers aren't what you'd think. They're still amazing and beautiful in their own ways, but some of them smell like shit! There are literally flowers with names like Stinking Corpse Lilly, Western Skunk Cabbage, Carrion Flower! I mean, these aren't their scientific names, but—"

"Bro, you are freaking me out! You've got me upside down and tripping!"

"Good! Good things happen when you're off balance," I say, not knowing what I mean by that exactly. This occurs to me like a line from a commercial, a slogan I've absorbed somehow without knowing it. I am so worked up; I've been spitting all over the place. Sprays of spittle dot the wall, the floor, the table with all of the coke. I don't even care. I'm glad about it.

"Dude, what does this have to do with anything?" Eddie says. He is laughing, snickering through clenched teeth, then licking them clean with his hungry tongue. He jams a finger up against the gums and brushes it across the rim.

"Of course you wouldn't understand," I say. Wait. Am I the one being racist now?

"I don't know much about flowers, but I do know what kind you are. You're a pansy, bro!" This realization hits him hard. It's as if he's been saving this joke for a while, and now he's on fire with the execution of it. He is beside himself with laughter. He pivots back and forth, scanning side to side, wishing someone else was there to share in this hilarity.

"You don't know shit!" I holler. "Cocaine comes from coca leaves that are mostly found in regions like South America or Africa. Did you know that? Huh, bro? You think this shit came from Chicago? There are no coca leaves in Chicago, bro. What you're snorting there is most likely pure grade Johnson's baby powder, bro."

"Man, just stop," Eddie says. The humor is gone now. He is worn out. "You are totally ruining my buzz. All of this mumbo jumbo about fucking plants and shit, it's completely killing any good time that could have been had. You really know how to explain away a good thing. You think too much. Just stop, man."

Something takes over me, some gut reaction to his rattling accusations. I mean they are juvenile, but they are also not without merit… Damn it! Like some kind of cunning boxer, he's managed to get into me, back me against the ropes. I am so angry that I've allowed him to bully me like this… I've let my guard down, allowed him to get a few jabs in on my body, locate my weak spots.

Shit! This all just seems to have sprouted up out of nowhere. *Sprouted.* Jesus. I do sound like a nerd. I should blow a line right now; just inhale the whole fucking load of it up into my nostrils. Fuck it.

"Man, where are Drew and Jerry?" I say. I'm yelling and trembling, and I don't know why. "They are supposed to be here. They are *always* here!" I've got to punch my way out of this corner. When people are cornered there is no telling what they are capable of doing. If Drew and Jerry were here they would calm me down. I do the same for them. They do it for me. We have that type of relationship. They should really be here now. I need them here. Why aren't they here?

"Man you need to chill on Drew and Jerry. You're losing it." Eddie is yelling back now, throwing flurries. We're both out of control, possessed by our own separate catalysts.

All of a sudden I'm leaning forward, grabbing the dollar bill in my fingers, sliding it over in line with my right nostril. "I just don't know why they aren't here. They are always around when I need them. They should be." Wow, I am getting so loud! As I dip closer to the table, I can hear my own voice booming back up at me, ricocheting off of the polished tabletop.

"Yes!" Eddie screams when he sees me going for it. "Yes! All right! Do it!"

The door whips open up front. "What's going on back here!" It's Fred's deep, raspy voice.

In a heartbeat I fling the dollar at Eddie and jump back from the table. I knock the leg with my knee, and half the cocaine goes flying off onto the ground, most of it ending up on Eddie's black sneakers. Eddie gasps. He's gone and caught the bill in his hand, involuntarily no doubt, and there's a little bluff of powder clinging to the baby fuzz moustache just below his nose.

"Eddie!" Fred shouts. "What in the world are you doing?" He comes charging toward us, his heavy footfall jiggling the pots and pans hanging overhead.

"Nothing," Eddie says, but it's useless. He may as well be bathed in the stuff from head to toe. I don't say a single word. I couldn't even if I wanted to. But judging from Fred's neutral, sustaining look in my direction, I guess I don't have to. Fred looks at me as if I've already spoken. It's as if he only glances toward me long enough to confirm whatever scenario he's already cooked up in his head. He's already sized up the situation and decided that he has enough information. According to his assessment, I've already exonerated myself. I'm the clean one in this. Surely, I'm only back here to admonish Eddie and counsel him against this fiendish behavior.

Fred stares at the cocaine on the table, then down at Eddie's shoes, then pauses and turns to look back over his shoulder. He lingers in that position, gazing out toward the dining room. He turns back around and faces us again, then lifts his wrist and checks his watch. There is a clock posted beside the door, the one that we use to punch in and out each day, and he cross-references the time with its digital screen.

"Where is everyone else?" Fred asks. Because he is staring at the clock and not at either of us, it is impossible to tell which of us he's addressing. He seems to be questioning the clock in some way, interrogating the very concept of time.

"We don't know," Eddie says. "We didn't think you were going to be here."

"You weren't supposed to be here," I say, dumbly.

Fred rests his right elbow on the pad of his left palm and sort of gnaws on one of his raised knuckles. It appears that he is calling up some vision, conjuring some reminiscence from his memory. "I should have known," Fred says, glaring and grunting in Eddie's direction.

"Hold on," Eddie says, backing away from Fred's wingspan. "Wait."

"No, no, no," Fred says, shaking his head. "I know what's going on here. I could've guessed it."

"Please, Fred," Eddie pleads. "Please don't tell anyone. You know I'll be in trouble. I'll get deported. Please. You know my father. You know my family, bro."

"The only reason I'm not calling the cops right now is because I'm certain you're not the one who brought this filth into my restaurant." He wipes a finger across the table, comes away with a small dusting of coke. It's implied that this gesture means something. There is something final and decisive in this movement. He's figured out the culprit, cracked the case.

Eddie looks at me and I look back at him, both of us prepared to go to war over whatever haphazard allegations he is about to level against us.

"It was Drew!" Fred yells. "I knew it. That little fairy goes to those fruity nightclubs over on Taylor Street. All those queers do cocaine. I should have known better. He's walking around here, swishing his butt, talking all girly and whiny. I should have canned his ass weeks ago. What a fag." He's made the graceless decision to do his Drew impersonation. Eddie and I watch as he prances around the table, one hand curved to his hip the other droopy above his head like a ballerina, I guess.

I elbow Eddie in the arm, but he only responds by nodding. "Yeah," he says. "It was Drew. You know me. I wouldn't do this to you. I wouldn't hurt your family like that. We're family, Fred. Come on." Eddie is practiced in this art of family referencing. Someone has schooled him on this technique of using one's kin as a bonding agent nobody dare unbind. He has acquired that useful but troublemaking skill of drawing a connection between doing the wrong thing and loyalty.

"I saw him two weekends ago standing outside that dirt hole, Chester's. Him and that long line of doped up sissies wearing those spiked dog collars and disgusting makeup with—"

"I'll take the blame," I say. I don't want to hear anymore. I've heard plenty. "I did it."

Fred doesn't want to believe this, but he also wants an easy solution. He wants this all to go away. "You'll take the blame or you did it? Which one?" he asks.

"It really doesn't matter," I say. "I'm leaving."

Fred and Eddie are both silent as I begin untying the strings on my stupid white apron. My hands are all shaky and so I can't do it. I keep fumbling and fumbling with the stupid fucking string in back… Fred is definitely not Greek. He was never Greek. We're all bunch of idiots to fall for it. Nobody even questions it. He doesn't even have to try. Where's the olive colored skin, the large circular mouth, that chiseled, Statue of David nose? None of it. He doesn't even serve Greek food! The only thing on the menu that's Greek are those mealy fucking Gyros that would taste like nothing if not for the deluge of garlic powder he's not fooling anyone with. Only he's fooling everyone… All the rest is hamburgers and French fries! Fuck Fred. The fucked up thing is that when I tell people about what just happened they won't even believe me. *Not Fred. Not Greek Fred! He wouldn't do that.* Well, at least now I know how he feels about gay people and minorities. It's always exhilarating and disinfecting when someone reveals their true self. One more sleaze ball dragged out from the darkness. Life is sensible, simpler the more assholes are exposed. If nothing else this has been an interesting gauge for where we are at this moment in terms of social progress. Apparently, in the hierarchy of bigotry, Hispanics are slightly above homosexuals. Neither are preferable, of course, but one is clearly favored over the other. If we compare this case or these circumstances to those of malodorous flowers, Mexican people would be like the Dead Horse Arum, while the gays would represent the Stinking Root Parasite.

I can't get the goddamn strings loose, and so I just give the hell up and start heading for the dining room.

"You can't take that apron with you," Fred says.

"I'm going to give it to Drew," I say.

"You can't do that," Fred responds.

"Sure I can. He needs it more than you," I say. I mimic Fred's own ridiculous caricature of Drew. "He needs it to bake his soufflés and lime tarts."

"Where is Drew?" Fred asks.

"I thought you would tell me," I say.

"I have no idea," he says. "I have no explanation for those two or their whereabouts." Funny how he just goes right on ahead and scoops Jerry up in his prejudices.

Drew and Jerry are not where they are supposed to be. There is no explanation or there is. Who knows? It's either a coincidence or it's not. There are no such things as coincidences or everything is a coincidence. In any case, there is a particular abandon that comes over me when I realize that there is nothing stopping me from pushing open the flapping kitchen doors and bee-lining for the exit. Fred says a few more things, choice ones I'm sure, as I walk away, but I can't hear what they are. On my way out I knock over all of the little flower vases on each of the tables. It's not as satisfying as I'd like. All of the prickly daisies inside are fake and plastic, just like the rest of the joint. No water. No real life sustaining objects or forces or corresponding elements to speak of.

The Portable Pioneer Spirit (2003)

Lindy is still droning and painting when Dad gets home. She's been at it for almost three hours. We've stopped checking in on her, but last I saw she blended most of the random patterns together, so that now the wall just looks like one solid green color. It's almost like a regular job, except for the splatters of paint all over the room, on the floor and Lindy's hair, skin etc. This is what I assume Dad is noticing as he pauses in her doorway to gaze at the spectacle. Any second he will curse or throw something or both. It's only a matter of time.

For a long while he does nothing. He just stands there, staring, as Lindy chants. She swabs her hand back and forth, covering over the previous coats of green with her stained palm, and Dad just watches in silence. He brings the brown paper bag in his hand up to his lips and takes a pull from whatever's inside. He swallows heavy and loud.

"What is she saying?" Dad asks. He turns around, making an accusatory sweep of the apartment, implicating, willing to enlist anyone nearby, but there is nobody home except me.

I come forth, ambling my way out from my bedroom where I've been quietly reading for the past hour or so. My joints feel tight and creaky from lying in the same position for too long. It appears that I am the only one qualified or maybe willing enough, to comment. Granted, I am the only one home, but it's a moot point. Had there been fifty people in the house I'd still have been the only knowledgeable one in the lot. I've actually been waiting for someone to ask me about the process. I haven't been reading up on the details for nothing. There is a certain amount of honor and pride at being the chosen one. "It's the same one she's been saying for weeks," I tell him, approaching with an eager sense of duty. "It's been a month, I think." I traverse the hallway, join him in the doorframe like a tour guide. It's the same place where Mom and I and Maureen, before she became exasperated with our unseemly concern and went home, stood just a few hours ago.

"I'm not asking about the length," he says. "What is she saying?"

I yawn, stretch. "It's an abundance prayer," I say. "I think it's considered a Japa, technically, but I haven't finished studying that yet. What it means is, om and salutations to she who manifest—"

"Did she get it from Mexico!" Dad says. I'm beginning to feel that nobody will ever allow me to finish a thought again. His expression turns from frantic to infuriated in a few short, kinetic seconds.

"No, I don't think so," I say. I'm already backing away from him, monitoring the volume in his voice, the ferocity in his eyes.

"Did she mention anything about Dima or Liam's Higher Ground? The rocks and stones? The gems!"

"No," I say. Why would Mexico be a part of this? It doesn't seem like he is asking for any derogatory or intolerant reasons. On the contrary, there is a fanatical, fascinated aspect to his inquiries.

"No Liam? No Dima? Nothing about Guerrero, Mexico?"

"No. Nothing like that," I say. "Why? What is that?" There is no real reason for me to ask. I don't even know why I try. I may as well be asking why there are so many monkeys crawling on top of the refrigerator. I could say anything.

"Lindy!" Dad shouts. "Lindy, did anybody tell you about a small man named Dima who had a bone disorder, skeletal dysplasia? The little runty man who sold rocks on the beach? Did you meet him somehow? How? Was he here! How do you know…"

Lindy has not yet broken character. She is testing, waiting to see what else he comes up with during this tirade. She is intrigued, and although she wants to, is desperate to, she is not yet ready to give in. And so she recedes, feigns a penetrating interest in her task, intent on filling in the entire space with green strokes. She drops to her knees in order to attack one final white spot near the floorboards. It's obvious that she is waiting, still listening for Dad to setoff the right alarm on her reaction meter.

"Hey!" Dad says. His voice is searing now, white hot. "Answer me! I swear to God if you met Liam and he brainwashed you, I'll kill him!" He spits, perhaps forgetting that he is indoors, then flails about as if someone is holding him back, but I don't think there's anybody home… The bathroom door opens and clicks shut. A fan's whirring motor wafts out, and then is consumed by the swinging door. I have been wrong all along. At the sound of his latest outburst, Mom has come out of the restroom and into the picture. One side of her shirt is loose from her shorts, her face reddish and moist from heat. She is in the state of disheveled post-exertion that follows a grueling battle with one's own bowels. Strangely, I don't recall her staying, but I also don't have any concrete memories of her leaving. She must have been in there for a long time, and now that she is out it is as if she is recovering from a great slumber, slowly, dreamily. Her strides are more like lethargic drifts as she draws near. There is a heightened sense of caution in her movements but also a latent urgency. When she gets close I throw my arm out, keep her at bay. I don't want her doing something she regrets. He could be on something serious again, something ugly like LSD.

"Stop it," Dad insists. It strikes me as astonishing that he hasn't taken this stand earlier. Why has it taken him this long to get angry about the prayer? He stalks forward, hunching, lunging down at her. As he reaches out to make contact, I realize that this is the closest I've seen him come to Lindy in a very long time.

I feel Mom's body go tense and taut at the same time Lindy's does, but I'm not afraid. Something about the way he stretches for her is distinctly tender and gentle, the way someone might reach down to pet a cat. Lindy flinches as Dad juts his hand out in front of her face. He keeps the hand an inch in front of her lips, holds it there as if he hopes the words that come out will collide against his fingers and bounce back into her mouth. Squatting beside her, he places his other hand in the middle of her back. I watch as Lindy's knees go weak at the pressure, and she collapses to the floor in front of him. She's still praying, but the energy and vim behind it has been drained thin.

"Shhhhhh," Dad says. "Please stop, Lindy. You have to stop."

Gradually, Lindy allows her whole body to go limp and curl up at his feet. Dad continues massaging her back, holding his hand in place until her chanting winds down, then dims to a complete halt.

Mom strains against my arm, and I move it out of her way. She thrusts forward, but Dad catches her, freezes her with a steely look. "You can't do that again," Dad says. He's talking to Lindy, but he's looking Mom straight in the eyes. "What that prayer symbolizes is wrong. Wrong and devastating to things like compassion, vitality and prosperity. I don't know who told you to say it, but no more. That's it. I won't allow it."

Dad stops rubbing Lindy's back and removes his hand from in front of her mouth. The way he withdraws it is a cathartic action, a knife being torn clear from someone's back. It's subtle, but I see Lindy nod her head in agreement. She pulls her knees up tighter against her chest, brings her hand up to her own lips where Dad's used to be. I think she's going to put it in her mouth and suck it, but she just keeps it there instead, breathes into it. And as she nods herself off to sleep, Dad holds his glare on Mom. His eyes are interrogating her, asking her, *what's wrong with you*? How could you do this? How could you let this happen?

VI. THE SHORTCUT
TO RELATIONSHIPS

Toothache (2004)

The sex itself lasts less than two minutes. Max warned me it could go like this. I already know, I told him. I've read enough books, seen enough movies to know. My own diabolical intuition is plenty on its own. I don't need you feeding this beast. It doesn't stop him from going on. He's only "helping," he says. Helping? Whatever, the first time often goes awry, nothing to worry about he tells me. Relax. As if that is an option! I worry all afternoon. I worry like it's something to master, as if I'm preparing for an early-ejaculation job interview. I achieve a state of perfect worrying. I expect the worst, practically court it. God, I hate myself for listening to Max. The thing is, I could have avoided it; I could have left, walked away. We're a pair of sick bastards, the both of us.

April's arched and naked body seems to hover just above the sheets. Skin and bone, her bleached form takes up one whole side of the bed and then some, elbows bent, hands folded beneath her head. She exhales toward the ceiling, already lost in thought. I scissor the blankets, shake a cigarette out of her pack on the nightstand and light it.

"Oh, now you want to smoke? I thought you didn't like it," April says. She studies the way I hold the cigarette, the way I exhale. It makes me so self-conscious. As if what has just happened isn't aggravating enough. Nothing is ever as much fun when somebody else is watching. "It makes you seem old," she says, clearing her throat. "Well, older, I guess, anyway."

"I don't know," I say. She should know. She's the one who gave me my first cigarette. She got me drunk and high for the first time. Gave me my first screw… "I guess I'm a bit out of sorts. They say these things are supposed to calm your nerves. People smoke after sex, right? It's a thing I've heard about. I've never tried it before, obviously." Christ, I'm rambling. Forcibly, I make myself stop and take a breath. "Something about it feels fitting for the occasion. Am I doing it right? I feel like I am." I suck sharply, and my windpipe doesn't seem to be able to catch up, which results in the smoke rushing upward and swooping out my nose. I don't do this out of any sort of skill or showboating. There was nowhere else for the smoke to come out. If the ears had been an option, that would have been my first choice. I start coughing, and it's the kind of romping, galloping hack that you worry might never end.

"See, that's an old trick," she says. "You don't even see that anymore outside the movies. You're like from another era or something. I've thought it before. You have such a paternal soul or something."

I try to smile, but I can't stop coughing long enough to make it happen. After a few tries, I get it to stick. My eyes are watering like a son of a bitch, but after a while I pull myself together. The window is open, and I hear the distant whine of an ambulance siren down on Montrose Avenue. A crisp breeze sails through the room, raises the hair on my legs. Fall is coming. Regardless of the poor performance, this is a good moment, I think. After a series of nauseating, pain inducing and ultimately fruitless sexual endeavors over the past eight months, my virginity is gone, lost in the sweet smelling room of a pretty, skillful girl. It hasn't been easy. She called it "schooling me." I think she just liked the controlling part of it, the power, the domination over my manhood. To her, it was more satisfying to tease me than to succumb to the pleasure of intercourse. It's the summer before senior year, and this moment feels like a well-fought victory.

The weeping noise of the siren fades and disappears. In a matter of seconds the most meaningful cigarette of my life will burn out. Classes start on Tuesday, after Labor Day. This is a far cry from the chaos and turmoil that dominated last summer. With Lindy sneaking out every other night to see Barry, the eighteen-year-old ride operator from the Alpine Amusement Company, and Dad out drinking and doping all over the city, it's a wonder nobody ended up dead or in jail. The crazy thing is that Barry and Dad probably crossed paths. Well, I guess they did, sort of, unbeknownst to them, but that's not what I mean. What I mean is that with both of them having similar routines and hangout spots, getting wasted in the grocery store parking lot over by Roscoe Street or taking sloshy pisses under the Western Avenue overpass it's likely they came in contact with each other more than once. However, by the time Dad realized that the reason his daughter was hardly ever home was because she was shacking up with a greasy, aimless sex-offender, it was too late. Barry and the rest of his degenerate crew had packed up their soiled baseball caps, grimy Wranglers and illicit penchants for underage girls and hit the road, destined for another town in need of a sleazy, travelling carnival. Jesus, he really was a loser. What did Lindy ever see in him? Poor Lindy. Poor, lonesome, deprived Lindy. April officially took me to see him once when he was at work. This was after the amateur escape incident, I think. Officially. When April pointed him out he was standing next to the Ferris Wheel, one of those big cruddy numbers only two-bit mobile fairs use, those metal brontosaurus types that make those old rotted-out squeals at every revolution. Always makes you think the whole stupid thing is just going to come unmoored and go twirling down the asphalt, gunning for whatever crowd of morons gets in its path. Whatever, I remember he had a huge wad of tobacco stuffed in his fat lower lip, and his cheeks were all pocked up with acne and baby stubble. I wanted to go over to him so bad, just sock him right in that doughy little gut he had, but April wouldn't allow it. She was already in big enough trouble with Lindy as it was, and said she would never speak to me again if I ever did anything to mess with him or even told anyone about who he was or where he worked. I couldn't get a great look at him from where April was making me stand, but I do recall something about the badges he wore... There were some kind of safety pins or something stuck to the brim of his grungy red baseball cap. That hat was so gross. It looked like it had been tossed into a pigpen and then taken out only to be ground beneath the boot heel of some grimy, backwoods auto mechanic. I asked April what all those pins meant, and she said he attached one there for every girl he screwed. I was so disgusted I almost hurled right there on the pavement, but then she said she wasn't sure. It was either number of screws or how many hot dogs he could eat in one sitting. Lindy had told her that he ate so many hotdogs that she could see them floating around under his belly button. They made gurgling noises and felt like tiny sponges when she pressed on them. Good lord...

But why in the hell am I am even thinking about a fuckup like Barry at a time like this? Right now I have a hot, devilish woman lying right next to me wearing nothing but the corner of a bedsheet as underwear. The sheet only covers part of one leg, and through the crack in her legs I can see the outline of her beautiful, mesmeric pubic hair. Who would ever think that something so common, and some say unclean, as a wedge of brown follicles between a woman's legs could drive a man so insane? Oh, and April's are the best! They have to be, so defiant and untamed, just like April. It makes me so—

"Ouch!" I yell. I double over, clamp a hand over my mouth.

"What is it?" April asks. "Jesus! What's wrong with you?"

"My tooth," I say. My voice comes low and muffled through my fingers.

"You have tooth problems?" April says, popping bolt upright against the headboard. There is nothing less sexy than a woman moving fast to get out of the way of you in a bed. "My dad and grandfather both have those."

"It's been popping up for weeks… Ahhhhh!" I groan. I let my fingers go limp around the smoldering stub in my hand. When it singes my finger I drop it into the ashtray on the floor. "The pain never ends."

"Wait, hold on," she says.

April slinks herself off the mattress halfway. She leans over the edge of the bed and reaches underneath. She skims her hand around beneath the bed, clutching the covers to her, until she finds it—a hand-held mirror. Rocking back up into a seated position, she brings the mirror up close to my mouth.

She uses the rim of the mirror as a lever to help pry my hands away from my lips, then pops my mouth open. "I don't see anything," she says, twisting it back and forth, trying to get a better look at all angles of it. "Is it your tooth or your cheek? Is it your gums? Are you sure it's really there? I don't see anything other than pink and white. Your mouth is filled with saliva. It's dripping out. Are you certain?"

"Christ! Why would I lie, goddamn it?" Instinctively, unadvisedly, I grab the mirror from her and wing it across the room where it crashes against the wall and shatters to the floor. April pulls away in alarm, sits back straight against her own side of the bed again. She is stone still, ghostly pale.

"Okay," she says. She's over the whole ordeal already, packing it in. "Look, you can get it fixed if you want to or don't."

I close my eyes and moan, this time more out of humiliation than physical pain. "I'm sorry. You're nice for saying that. I know you saw it, but you're being nice. I know it's permanent. You don't have to do this. These sorts of things are eternal. They always are."

"Ooorrrrr," she drones, "you could get the fucker fixed," she says.

"Doubt it," I say. "I'll have to live with it."

This ends it. When I look back over at April she is motionless, a block of ice. The sight of her rigidness makes me grimace and shake my head. I can't stop shaking my head. There is not much else left to be done, I know it. I make sure my cigarette is out in the ashtray, and give one last look at April, hoping she'll show some new, sensitive emotion, but no luck. I make a final attempt, a gesture as if I am going to speak again, but stop. The pain is dissipating now, but I rub my cheek at the memory, the residual effects, then slide to the end of the bed and prepare for my fate. Once more I look back at April. Nothing. No change in her wooden posture or expression. Very slowly I turn away from her. I put my feet on the floor, wiggle the toes, try giving myself some other point of focus. I stare down at them for some time, waiting, before I pluck my underwear from the carpet and slide into them one inch at a time. Trying to buy more time, I move with langor, a hopefulness of sorts, halting and starting. It's on a loop again and again, a form of shameless and then shameful begging. I dress all the way, put my shoes on but don't tie them. There must be hope. I walk for the door, half-hearted and imploring. I bait her all the way to the door, dragging my feet. I put my hand on the knob, but not really. I'm hardly touching it. Still, she doesn't argue.

Flush (2003)

The color has returned to Randy's face. He's a new man. I ask him how old he is, and before he can even answer I yell out, "forty-seven!" Randy leans back on the sofa, waggles his spine deep into the cushion. He plunks his feet up on the coffee table and shows all of us his fresh white smile. "Forty-six," he says, and it's like you can see the newfound dignity just radiating off of him.

"I used to think you were fifty-five," I say, "no, fifty-six!"

"Clayton," Mom scolds, "don't say that. That's not nice. I'm sorry, Randy." She's carrying a tray of four steaming mugs, each adorned with its own wading tea bag. Ever since Randy got clean a few months ago, we've all been drinking tea like it's in danger of drying up, like it's some kind of magical potion in high demand, one that wards off temptation and illness of all kinds. Our level of devotion has grown so that now we have set aside special "tea times." Everyone's into it except Dad.

"That's okay," Randy says. He smiles, clasps his hands behind his neck. "It's like I've lost ten years off my waist line. I'm down to a sober size. A size sober! My belts are too big!" This really cracks him up. We all do our best to laugh too, but he must see the fakery show through. The mood he's in, though, he doesn't care.

"I think he looks great," Lindy says. She takes her mug from the tray, coils her legs beneath her on the recliner. Her mouth aims down to blow off the steam, but her eyes stay up, fluttery and trained on Randy across the room. This causes Mom to pause, and briefly she moves in front of Lindy's eyeline just long enough to break her gaze.

"Now we just need to get Neil back on the program," Randy says. He lifts his mug from the tray and sets it in his lap.

Two weeks ago Dad earned his silver chip for thirty days of sobriety. We celebrated by making hand-tossed pizza from scratch. Seven of his closest friends from work and AA were invited. He was so happy. We must have each drunk four cups of green tea and eaten three slices of apple pie for dessert. By the end of the meal we could hardly stand up from the table. Dad unbuttoned his pants and made a show of how bloated he was. Everyone laughed, and slapped his back. We made jokes about how he was going to gain a hundred pounds now that he was going to be around more often and eating Mom's home cooking. There were lots of jokes about Mom's inferior cooking skills followed by more laughter. The next day, Dad didn't come home from work. At around eleven that night we got a phone call from the police saying that they found him down at a bar called Fat Cat's on Broadway. He was lying out in the alley next to the dumpsters with a floppy ham sandwich clamped in his teeth and his pants down around his ankles. It was too much for any of us to process. Too many linked thoughts tethered to too many regrets. How many countless hours of sleep were lost to our private wonderings about implied failures, our doubts about if recovery would ever be possible? I thought of how when Dad put the token in my hand it was much heavier than I'd expected. It must have weighed six ounces on its own, and that made me think about how the physical heft must have been multiplied by a thousand to account for the mental gravity that weighed on his mind. At the end of all that, if you're like me, you're left to consider that the whole spectacle ended up causing the opposite effect we desired ... But I don't say anything, of course. Speaking in the past tense is useless.

We make this statement without stating it. This suppression has already been expressed in every form imaginable. Always imagined. Instead, we move forward. We invite Randy over to brainstorm while Dad stays out after work and gets hammered. We plan redos. Whatever we do, we do it with tea.

"That's why we're here," Mom says. She sets the tray down on the coffee table and takes a seat on the couch between me and Randy. She nestles in straight and erect, her rigid body creating a perfect right angle. "What do we do next?" she asks. She wedges her hands between her thighs so that there are zero remaining movements left to her narrowed posture.

"We create a space, an atmosphere of complete positivity, belief and faith. We purify," Randy says. He takes a sip from his tea, then plops it down on the coffee table with a thud for emphasis, as if this does it, this settles everything.

Randy is the one who suggested we drink green tea. It's brimming with ancient healing powers, he tells us. It's an anti-inflammatory. If you want to lose weight, drink it by the gallon, he says. Diabetes? Forget about it. You can't get diabetes if you drink at least four glasses per day. It's a proven fact. Oh, now you tell me, Mom says. Sorry, Randy says. He didn't know all of this until recently. He's had an epiphany. But, hey, he tells her, you're on the right track now! This seems plenty good enough to Mom, who sits breathing in the new information, cradling the mug in her thighs, losing herself deep in its possibilities, reveling in them.

"I've been praying," Lindy says.

Randy's so excited he spills hot tea down his chin. "Yes!" he says. "Yes, that's what I'm talking about."

"I am the violet flame," Lindy says. And right away she's slipped into her robotic, glassy eyed prayer mode. "I am the violet flame, to light alone I bow. I am the violet flame, in mighty cosmic power," she continues.

Randy nods his head vigorously. He gropes inside the pocket of his shirt as he fumbles for the right words to echo her response. A wrinkled paper is extracted from the pocket. Randy smooths it, flattens it out against the coffee table where he can read along. "I am the light of God, shining every hour. I am the violet flame, blazing like a sun." They are one, each word lining up, buzzing in unison. For the last verse Randy looks up from the paper and meets Lindy's eyes. Together they say, "I am God's sacred power, freeing everyone." When they are finished there is an intense, eerie silence left behind. Mom and I sit in that vacant wake, that muted, purring aftermath, waiting for whatever's next.

Mom moves first. She takes a chance. When she turns toward Randy, he pivots too, and their knees knock. "That's nice," Mom says.

"Isn't it?" Randy says.

"For about ten straight days I said it over and over again, like every second," Lindy says. It's like she's a little girl again, telling everyone she knows about how she's learned the ABCs by heart.

Randy bends forward, craning around Mom's legs. "Is that true?" he asks me.

"Mm-hm," I say. As Randy sways back against the couch again, I lean forward and pick up the paper from the table.

"Why did you stop?" he asks.

For a second I think Mom is going to step in and say something, but she only smiles, looks toward Lindy for a response.

"I lost my will, I guess. I felt… I don't know. I got sad."

"Hm," Randy says. "Why?"

"I wasn't seeing results."

"What were you looking for?"

"Warmth," Lindy says. "Comfort. Hope. Change?"

"You're looking for the wrong things," Randy says, "or rather, you're looking *at* the wrong things. You're looking in the wrong way. That's what's wrong."

I flap the paper open and hold it up to read. For a second I consider putting the paper in my pocket, hiding it and saving it for later. But nobody is looking at me at all. I look back and forth from face to face, and nobody returns my gaze. All of them are zoned out, locked in on some invisible spot at the center of the room. My eyes focus in on a bolded paragraph in the middle of the page.

The violet all-consuming flame is the seventh-ray aspect of the Holy Spirit; it emerges from the white-fire core as the omnipotent love of the blue that combines with the omnipresent power of the pink, refracted in the prism of the Christ consciousness, accomplishing the perfect work of the truth that makes every man free.

My eyes scan downward, back and forth, hungry to soak up all of the ink. It's like my brain is on autopilot, forcing me to keep reading, keep focusing against my will. I want so badly for it to make sense. I turn the paper over and see in the bottom right corner a miniature white box, with a thin black outline. Something about its contours, its unblemished interior makes my mind want to zoom in. I bring the paper up to my eyes and peer into the box. There is nothing inside of it but more dense whiteness. On the perimeter is the faintest of black lines... There is a sliver of space, an opening in the bottom right corner... Or is there? The letters WPI are stamped underneath in a fading gray font...

Randy's chirping voice breaks my concentration. He's been talking the whole time. "Do you see the sun on the windowsill?" he asks Lindy. She nods. "Do you see the light reflecting off the plant? Do you see the clouds moving across the sky, shifting, drifting? Do you see now?"

I re-read the passage. I read it a third time, a fourth. My brain begins humming. It's like the low whirring of an industrial freezer plugged into the wall at the far back corner of a quiet cafeteria. My eyes go crossed, turn blurry. I dig my knuckles into my sockets, try cleaning them out.

"You were looking for things to happen soon, like in an hour or tomorrow or next week. You weren't seeing the warmth and comfort all around you, right in front of you today, right now!" There is a genuine air of caring about him. Displaced or misguided as it may be, this is not a counterfeit type of fervor. It is not replicable in anyone other than true converts. He wants to help, passionately believes he is doing just that.

"I knew it," Lindy says. "I'm no good. I'm an idiot!" She makes a fist, hammers it down on the armrest with so much force that her mug goes flying out of her hand and sprays the carpet at her feet.

Mom gasps. She springs forward, leaping to her feet. At the precise instant she is propelling upward, Randy snaps his arm out and catches her across the waist. The momentum whips her back down, sending her tea gushing into the crevice between her legs. Her next reflex is to whisk the liquid away from her lap, disperse the hot contents away from her skin. This too Randy halts by grabbing her wrist.

"Look at the floor," Randy insists. "Look!" His conviction in what he is saying is evident. It gives him meaning, lifts him up, affirms him. To be in the room with someone like Randy, there is no denying it.

Lindy looks at the rug. Her shoulders start to shake and soon she is crying.

"Look at where the mug is laying, and look at what the water is doing." Just watching someone like him, observing and absorbing his strident vehemence is enough to take the wind right out of me.

We all look. The mug is tilted sideways, broken, leaking its clear liquid the way a cracked egg oozes its yellow yoke.

"Do you not see the way the fluid covers the sunlight coming through the window? Don't you see? It's blocking the light, cloaking it. Look at the bulbs hanging from the ceiling. Look at the rays dancing on your blouse. Look! Look in the kitchen! Look at how the reflection in the sink creates a tiny prism of colors. Do you see it? Do you?"

"Yes," Lindy says. She's sobbing. The tears pour down her cheeks. She seems almost too happy to just let them cascade. They ripple over her neck, pool around the collar of her blouse.

"Light," Randy says, pointing to the ceiling. "Light!" Pointing to the window. "Light, light, light, light, light!" He's breathing hard, chest heaving. "It's all light. It's all part of the same thing. It's all the same suit. We're flush with it! Hahahaha!"

In the wake of his hysterics, a pause follows. The tension inside me wells, whooshes. In order to displace some of it, put it toward something other than silence, I read the passage again, this time at hyper speed. Parts of it I say out loud. It's unconscious. It just comes out. Suddenly I'm chanting it, but nobody hears me because Lindy has started back up again with her prayer, much louder and with much more candor.

"Do you see it, Roberta? Do you?" Randy shouts. Mom gives an exaggerated, mechanical nod. "Yes! You see it. You feel it. It works every time. Every time! Never doubt, and it will never disappoint." He raises a single hand, shakes it up at the ceiling like a tambourine.

"I am the violet flame, to light alone I bow. I am the violet flame, in mighty cosmic power," Lindy roars.

The violet all-consuming flame is the seventh-ray aspect of the Holy Spirit; it emerges from the white-fire core as the omnipotent love of the blue that combines with the omnipresent power of the pink, refracted in the prism of the Christ... I read, half out loud, half in my own head. What does it all mean? Mom's wrist is still encircled by Randy's grip. There is a full cup of scalding tea sitting in the crease of her dress, stagnant in the divot of her crotch! I know what's coming. My heart throttles; it revs and rumbles until I can hear the pumping in my ear. Everything is churning together, the liquid, the voices, the humming, pounding... Make it stop!

"Do you see it?" Randy asks. "Do you? Clayton! Do you see it!"

NO! In my head I scream it a hundred times; I breathe flames when I say it, violet ones with lashing tongues of gold and white, and...

Heaven help me. Forgive me. I nod. Like a twitching, thrashing epileptic I nod and nod and nod until my teeth start to rattle and gnash. I grind them down. They practically disintegrate in my clenched and seething mouth.

A Functional Literacy (2006)

Lindy is the first family member Sasha meets. It's one of those forced-hand situations, which is Sasha's specialty. She has the power to persuade me just about any time, but never more than we are lying in bed together with little more than our underwear on and our inhibitions lowered. So it goes. Late one night, after a few too many Old Styles and a couple hits from some crazy potent weed (Sasha calls it "the bubonic chronic") I let it slip about Lindy and her hazardous sex life. As I talk, as each scurrilous detail is revealed, Sasha props herself higher and higher onto the pillow until she is sitting straight up against the headboard. She takes one more puff of the joint before leaning over and grinding it out in the ashtray. When she leans over, I take a peek at her breasts as they go bobbing downward, straining against her slinky tank top. Lord help me…

"Wait, she's had how many abortions?" she asks.

"I don't know," I say. "Two I know of."

"That you know of?"

"I'm not walking around asking my sister about how many babies she's killed."

"They're not babies!"

"Right. I know. Can we change the subject?"

"Call her."

"What?" I say.

"Call her up." And now she's bending backward, exposing the smooth, cocoa skin around her bellybutton. I'm stoned. She moves as if performing a routine, some choreographed aerobics just for me.

"Now?"

Sasha picks her cell phone up from the nightstand, stabs me in the ribs with it. "Now," she says. This, her forthrightness, is part of her appeal or her downfall, depending on your point of view. Me? I'm nuts for it, a real fiend. The rawness that she exudes in her speech carries over to all aspects of her character. It is reproduced in her brash style of dress, the aggressive way she drives, even in the subtle but triumphal way in which she slings a purse over her shoulder and barges into a room. For better or worse. Love it or leave it.

We set up a time and place for them to meet the next day. Lindy chooses a little German bakery called Lutz Cafe on Montrose near the apartment where we grew up. It's been a staple in the neighborhood since 1948, and most of the patrons look like they were born a decade before it opened. The place is filled with gray haired men and women with dentures and abnormal tremors, pitiful couples who buy cupcakes they can't get to their mouths without spilling half of it on their shirts. It's maybe the strangest place in the world to talk to your brother and his ex-stripper girlfriend about getting freaky too much, but nobody ever said that Lindy was conventional. On the phone, I tell Lindy she's weird for picking the place, but she ignores me, responds with nonchalance, as if I'd simply said, *see you there at four.*

When we arrive, we find Lindy sitting outside on the patio. She's seated at the same umbrella-shaded table where we used to always sit when Mom brought us as kids. I should have known. Walking out the back door, I feel a whir of emotions and memories come drifting back. The space is pretty impressive and whimsical in its own way, I have to admit. This is the same place, after all, where Dad used to feed the koi carps in the little fish pond, and where Mom once found a dollar bill laying in one of the garden beds filled, serendipitously, of course, with those wispy dollar plants. The table Lindy selects is the one closest to the little water fountain, the one beside the small stone statue that looks like cupid. I'll be damned if there isn't something nostalgic about the place that moves me. As we approach, Lindy stands and smiles. She makes a grand sweeping gesture with her arms, holds them out over the table like presenting us with some sort of feast from the gods, like she knows what I'm thinking, like *I told you so*.

Lindy reaches out her hand, and Sasha flings it aside. She grabs her, wrangles her into an exuberant embrace. Sasha's purse comes whamming around her waist, cracking Lindy in the stomach. As Lindy pulls away, Sasha catches her with a kiss on the neck.

"Sorry," Sasha says, "sorry honey." She rubs away the outline of lipstick from Lindy's skin, then pats her on the tummy. "Did I get you with my purse?" she says. "I'm so sorry. I'm just so excited to meet you."

"That's okay," Lindy laughs. "You're all right."

We all pull our chairs out and get situated in them. They're a bit cold and stiff, metal loops designed to hold you steady and compel you upward at the same time. Sasha looks down at the menu for two seconds, then immediately pushes it away. She clasps her hands in front of her on the table, creeps to the edge of her seat, and addresses Lindy with an expansive smile.

"What's good here?" She asks, then keeps right on going. "I love your nail polish. Where did you get those earrings? Sweetie, you have amazing hair."

"Thank you," Lindy giggles. She puts her hand up to her face in a modest attempt to hide her blushing. "My boyfriend got me these." She reaches up, tugs on the earrings and, as if this contact activates some internal trigger, her expression wanes. A pallor of sorrow washes over her face.

Sasha reaches across the table. She doesn't quite touch Lindy's hand, but leaves it resting there just a few inches away, letting her know it's there if she needs it. "Oh, honey, I know. They're a difficult lot, aren't they?"

Lindy nods in somber agreement, then reaches out and brushes Sasha's hand, a delicate sign of affection and gratitude. Lindy pulls back, but only to tend to her eyes, which are already showing signs of leakage. Sasha keeps her hand posted there, does not move a muscle. It is in this moment of calm, in that absence of movement, that their bond forms. I watch it happen. There is something beautiful and dazzling about observing as a connection expands, the extraordinary act of trust transferring between two people. Is there a greater gift in life than having a personality and disposition that endears people instantly, makes them feel comfortable and open in your presence with a simple offering of a hand or smile? I've known Sasha for only three months, and I've seen her perform this trick four or five times already. She is the real magician in the relationship.

The waitress comes over several times, but she can't make any inroads. She has my attention, but we cannot break the concentration of Lindy or Sasha. For a long time neither of them look anywhere other than each other's eyes. Within seconds they are engaged in a serious discourse about boys, relationships and now body language related to boys and relationships. The discussion is ceaseless and ardent, an impenetrable force. The waitress and I may as well not exist at all. I order a coffee, apologize and send her on her way again.

"I mean," Lindy is saying, "I know what certain things are supposed to mean."

"Okay, let's hear it," Sasha says. She leans back in her chair, folds her arms, squints. This is an expert level move in the art of conversation, a precise conveyance, an air of enchantment and intrigue.

"Well, like if a guy leans forward, uncrosses his arms, that means he wants to get to know you better."

"Go on," Sasha says.

"If he looks to the side or points his feet toward the exit that means he wants to get away."

"Sweetie, if he points his feet anywhere it means his bed is that way and he's getting anxious to move you in that direction."

Lindy's mouth falls open, and she neglects to hinge it shut. There is a mixture of shock and wonder in her eyes. "But then how do you know if someone really loves you?"

"Love?" Sasha says. Her eyebrows arch so high I'm afraid they may take flight from her forehead. "What is the longest relationship you've ever been in?"

Lindy shakes her head, sighs. "I don't even know."

"That's not love. Why are you in a rush for love? Baby, you're sixteen."

"Well, I mean, I want love. Doesn't everyone?"

"Yes," Sasha agrees. "You're right there."

"Yeah, and so I'm keeping my eyes open. I'm ready, just like being prepared, you know? Like, I know what to watch for. If a guy brings you chocolates or flowers that's lame, but if he shows up unexpected to your house and wants to take you on an adventure, that's a good thing."

"Just shows up, huh? Out of the blue?"

"Yeah, like rides up. I want a white knight," she says. She freezes, tenses up. I see her doing mental back peddles, trying to escape or reverse her choice of words. "I mean," she corrects, "not a white knight. That's not what I meant. He doesn't have to be white. I just meant… someone chivalrous!"

Sasha laughs. "Shit, white knights! I'd take some white, black or even purple knights! That would be something, wouldn't it? But that would also be a fairy tale, girl. If you're holding your breath for a white knight, you're gonna turn blue real quick!"

Lindy lowers her head, drops her shoulders. "But there's got to be something, some sign that means he's a good one, a romantic. What about the eye blinks? That's something, right? If he blinks fewer than six times in a minute… And his mouth, if it puckers when he speaks…"

Sasha stops laughing. She leans forward again, stretches her whole body across the table. The waitress comes by and drops off my coffee. She reads the angle and the intensity of Lindy and Sasha's postures and moves on without a word. "Let me tell you a story," Sasha says.

Lindy picks up her napkin, twists it into a crunched spiral around her finger. "Okay," she says.

"Do you know how many names I had when I was a stripper?"

"How many?" Lindy asks. She looks shy and sheepish, like a timid little girl.

"Three," Sasha says. "I had three names. I've got my stage name, Mercedes, that's one. I have my real name, Sasha, and there isn't a chance in hell I'm giving that out, and then I had my third name. The third name is the most important. I used my third name, Sherry, to convince men that I really liked them. Sherry only gave her name out to men who she *trusted*, who she *wanted*. See, if I told a guy that my real name was

Sherry, if I shared that little lie with him, then he was more likely to think we had something special, something exclusive. When a man thinks he has something exclusive, that man gives more money. All of a sudden he thinks I'm into him, right, his fantasy girl. See, a man isn't very likely to give Mercedes, the dumb stripper shaking her tits in your face, a wad of cash, but Sherry? Sherry, the girl who just shared her real name with you, the one who's working off the medical costs for her mother's cancer treatments? Oh, baby, you better watch out!" Sasha slaps the table hard. Lindy and I jump, catch our next breath as it sputters out. Meanwhile, every other feeble, grumpy customer surrounding us, all dressed in their best Sunday attire circa 1962, they all drop their pudding spoons and stare.

"And that worked?"

I listen to this conversation with one hand over one eye. This is what one does when part of him wants to observe and the other wants to avoid. I'm not sure why I seem to be the only one out of the three of us who feels this tension. Was she Sherry with me? Is she still being Sherry?

"Honey, like a charm. It worked every single time."

A pair of hoary, puckered ladies in their mid-eighties have been eavesdropping the whole time. One of them, the oldest, most shriveled looking of the two, is not even making an attempt to conceal her open, distasteful surveillance. She is either unable to hide her intrusiveness or she is past the age of caring. The other, younger only in terms of total viable teeth and suspect moles, attempts to obfuscate her intentions behind a hunk of spongy vanilla cake. A dab of white frosting on her right cheek, a consequence of her divided attention, gives her away as the spy she is.

"So, you could fool people?"

"There is only fooling. All that stuff you just said about lips and arms and feet, that's foolishness. Let me tell you something…" Sasha breaks off. She turns to face me, drapes her arm over the back of my chair. "Sweetheart, would you mind giving us some time alone so we can have some girl talk?"

It's then I realize how much I've been waiting for this opportunity. I've been sitting here all clenched and cramped, hoping for an escape, and I am not going to pass this one up. "Sure," I say, "no problem." I am careful to stand up slowly and with restraint, cautious not to show how anxious I am for release. I use the same self-control to keep myself from breaking into a trot as I head for the door. When I am almost out of earshot I hear Sasha say, "if he's not trying to put a ring on your finger, he's only trying to put a dick in your vagina. And as long as you know that and you own that, you're in control."

During the next twenty or thirty minutes, as I sit alone at a table inside drinking countless cups of coffee, I witness Lindy cycle through every mental state imaginable. For the first ten minutes she cries. Sasha hands her tissue after tissue until Lindy's tears dry up, and she is able to listen to whatever Sasha is telling her without falling into despair. The next five minutes are filled with laughter and smiles. Because I am facing Lindy's profile, I can't see Sasha's face, but judging from the way she tosses her head back and pounds the table in front of her, it's clear she is getting off some good one-liners. The final stage appears to be one of great concentration and sobriety. Lindy's eyes swim with acceptance and recognition as she nods along. It comes to a close the only way a monumental airing of honesty can, with an all encompassing grand finale—a long, genuine hug a few more tissues, some genuine smiles and appreciative head nods.

The two of them gather up their belongings and stride back inside where they find me waiting in restless anticipation.

Sasha comes right over and rests her hip against my shoulder. "Are you ready?" she says. She uses her hipbone to sort of lever me up and pry me out of my chair.

"Okay," I say. I stand, and as soon as I make it to my feet Lindy is there to greet me. She presses herself into me, wraps her arms around my back and squeezes.

"Thank you," she says. She tilts her head up and whispers into my ear, "I love her."

After a few more seconds, she discharges me with a vigorous pop, like tossing a fish back into the ocean. She and Sasha share one last gesture of salutation as Lindy lowers her sunglasses on her nose, making direct eye contact with a winking Sasha. It's a quaint, adorable sort of motion, like a tip of the cap, and then Lindy's gone, whisked out the exit. The chimes ring out above the door, and I look at Sasha standing next to me with what I can only describe as pure awe and veneration.

VII. THE SHORTCUT TO HEALTH

Quintillion Man (2004)

Randy Mullins calls me up about once a week. "You should tell your dad to quit drinking," he always tells me.

"I've begged him a hundred times," I say.

"Don't beg," he says, "trick him into thinking it's his own idea."

Randy's been off the sauce for almost six months now, and he's getting monumentally bored. Since I've known him, he's been eight different people. Now, he's got long hair like a Hell's Angel, a burly beard and a tattoo of a naked woman on his left bicep. This is the style he gets into *after* he goes on the wagon. It's confusing in an existential type of way, and I almost wonder if he's doing it on purpose, to fuck with people. Anyway, he's not the kind of guy you'd think would give up the bottle. Or maybe he's exactly the type; I'm not sure anymore, but the point is he wants my dad to get clean with him. Dad won't listen, says Randy's a fleabag and a traitor. He won't return Randy's calls anymore, so he calls me now.

"I'm getting so goddamn bored I went to the hospital the other day," he tells me over the phone. "I wasn't sick or anything like that. It was about the only place I could find air conditioning. I mean, I felt a little depressed and suicidal, but mostly I was just hot."

"Don't the restaurants and bookstores close by have A/C?" I ask.

"I wanted drugs, okay. Get off my back," he says. "Just kidding. You know I love you."

"I know," I say.

"Anyway, right inside the door is this poster advertising volunteer services. You know you can just walk right into a patient's room who doesn't get a lot of visitors and just start talking to them and keeping them company? Like, cheering them up and stuff?"

"I think so," I say.

"I didn't know, but anyway I thought it sounded pretty nice. I love to talk, and I like the idea of keeping some lonely person company. I've been lonely since I was about five years old, especially when I had people around. Having people nearby makes me super lonesome."

"You are a talker," I say.

"Tell me about it," he says, "So I went and asked at the desk, and the nurse assigned me to this paralyzed man named Oscar Cowling. She told me his room number and said he'd been in the hospital for about three weeks and nobody had visited yet."

"That's awful," I say.

"That's what I'm here for," Randy says. "I went to his room and lo and behold some young, attractive lady was already in there feeding him pudding!" He says. He makes it sound like the most shocking thing in the world.

"No way!" I say, sarcastically, but still trying to match his intensity.

"Yes! This blonde is in there sitting on a folding chair, and this man, Oscar, is propped up in his bed and she's spooning some lumpy slop into his mouth, only he can't really open his mouth so she's jamming it into his gums and most of it is falling onto his neck and chest. I looked at the lady like she was crazy and she just smiled and said 'you must be a volunteer too. Oscar is having a good day.'"

"Wow," I say. "She sounds forceful. He couldn't even open his mouth?"

"Couldn't even open his own mouth," Randy says. "He was a quadriplegic."

"That means that four of his senses don't work, right?"

"Not his senses, his limbs," Randy says. "I think."

"All four of his limbs, plus his mouth?" I ask.

"You're asking the same questions I asked the blonde!" Randy says. "I asked what the quadri part meant, thinking it meant four, remembering my geometry. I didn't know if his ears worked or his eyes or his toes. I was all confused. Oscar's eyes were looking at the ceiling the whole time, and it sort of looked like there was nothing going on upstairs, if you know what I mean. Picture a blind man with crossed eyes and his tongue out."

"Oh," I say.

"Yeah, so blondie, it turns out her name was Rita, she said that quadriplegic means both arms and both legs don't work. But I noticed his mouth wasn't functioning either and so I asked her what came after quadriplegic, and she said there was nothing."

"There's got to be something," I say. "What comes after four in Latin?"

"Well, Rita said it would be called a quintiplegic, but that was just silly."

"Silly to whom? You have five non-working instruments on your body; there's got to be a name for that."

"At least five," Randy says.

"Could be more," I say.

"That's right. So I asked her. I said, Rita, does Oscar's brain work? Can he hear me right now? Does he understand what I'm saying?"

"Good question," I say. I'm really starting to get interested.

"He can hear everything you say, and he can process it, Rita said. He just can't work his jaw to speak or respond," he says. "I said I was sorry and that I would shut up then, and she said that I should stay. So I stayed."

"Did you make friends with her? Did you ask her out?" I ask.

"Well, let me just tell you what I witnessed."

"Okay."

"Rita was clanking that pudding spoon around his teeth, and Oscar wasn't moving an inch or responding in any way. Rita turned to me and said, 'he can't swallow.' What? I said. What do you mean he can't swallow? That's at least six things now that don't work."

"That's like a seisipiligic," I say.

"He's not Spanish," Randy says. "Just listen."

"Okay."

"So Oscar starts moving a little. He's moving his head from side to side, just very slightly. In a few seconds the pudding comes sloshing out again. Then Rita turns around and I notice that she has a plate of chicken wings resting on a tray behind her. She picks them up and shows them to me. 'Chicken is his favorite,' she tells me."

"What?"

"Yeah, he loves chicken. 'I have to warm up his muscles with pudding but he loves to eat chicken the best. Watch.'"

"What did you do?" I ask.

"I watched," Randy says. "Rita tore off a piece of chicken and mashed it down in her palm until it looked like a glob of hair, then she held it up to his nose for a few seconds. After that she waved it in front of his eyes. She whisked it past his ears on the way to his lips and then crammed it into his mouth with her fingers."

"Did he choke?" I ask.

"You would think so, but no," Randy says.

"He could die," I say.

"You would think so, but not Oscar. Oscar sort of swished the meat around in his cheeks a little bit, like rinsing your mouth, and then he threw it up into a napkin that Rita was holding."

"Why did she do it?" I ask.

"Listen," Randy says. "This is what she told me. 'Seeing food, smelling it, hearing it and tasting the texture are the most important parts of eating,' she said. 'I even run it over his skin sometimes so he can feel it. That's the real pleasure in eating,' she said. 'Swallowing food is the boring part. That's where all the mechanical, tedious parts of eating come in. Oscar is a sensuous,' she said."

"A what. Ugh… Kill me now," I say.

"That's what she said," Randy says.

"And he could hear her?" I ask.

"He's not deaf," Randy says.

"She used sensuous as a noun," I say.

"That's all I'm telling you," Randy says. "That's what she said."

"He spits it out?" I say.

"You're just like your dad," he says.

"No I'm not."

"I'll call you tomorrow." He slams the phone down. It sends a crackling sound through the receiver that seems to splinter through my brain, spreading like a seismic shockwave.

Dangerously Well (2002)

Principal Davies calls home to tell Mom that Lindy's been hiding in the bathroom, skipping class to put on makeup and play dress-up in the mirror. Mom cloisters herself out onto our fire escape and calls Maureen. The ordeal is made worse by the fact that tonight is Mom and Dad's fourteenth wedding anniversary. Maureen tells her she'll be over right away. Her plan is to teach Lindy how to apply makeup together as a joint enterprise so that it ends up seeming less like an act of rebellion and more like a casual family activity. Kids are less inclined to act out, she claims, if they think their actions are preapproved by stuffy, consenting adults. Things will be fixed by sundown, so don't fret about the date night, Maureen assures her. Within the hour she knocks on the door carrying a makeup kit that looks more like an unwieldy toolbox. It's the extravagant kind that opens up and folds out into three different compartments, each tray another level of dusty, mottled instruments and vivid pallets.

Lindy's initial response to Maureen's plan is to lock herself in the bathroom. She wants no part of this contrived business about bonding and becoming a woman. As one could have predicted, she's onto them. It's possible she may have outlasted them too, but when Maureen threatens to remove the door with a screwdriver that she happens to carry around in her purse, Lindy relents out of sheer irritation. She'll get them back another time. As it turns out, she already has. She's been waiting for them. When she finally rips open the door, Mom and Maureen find her sitting on the commode lid with about sixty squares of toilet paper wrapped around her entire face like some sort of defiant toilet mummy.

Maureen kneels in front of her and begins unwinding the tissue. She snaps open her box and begins yelping instructions to Mom like a surgeon in an operating room. "Foundation!" she commands, "eye primer. Lip cream!"

Mom scurries through the slots and drawers, sifting and crashing about as Maureen scolds her to move faster. I watch Lindy's face transform from a neutral white to a plaster of coral red and chestnut brown. As Maureen dabs her brush in some sort of grainy rose-colored dish, Lindy stiffens up and begins to buck. When Maureen reaches up to apply it around her cheeks, Lindy swerves back, yanks her head to the side the way a dog might resist getting a collar buckled around its neck.

"It's face powder!" Maureen exclaims, as if that will fix everything. "Just relax."

Mom straddles the toilet bowl behind Lindy and holds her in place. "Sweetheart," she implores, "you look beautiful. We're almost done. Wait until you get a peek at how lovely you look. You can't even notice any of your acne or that fuzzy little sideburn hair anymore."

This sends Lindy into full shutdown mode. She clamps her mouth shut and squeezes her eyes closed so hard it looks like the lids might explode.

"There we go!" Maureen says, swaying back to admire her handy work. She stands, claps her hands off and takes a deep breath, like *job well done*.

"Oh, this is incredible," Mom says. "I want to get a picture of the two of you together. I don't know why," she says, near weeping. She clutches the tiny pendant on the end of her golden necklace, "but I haven't felt this happy in a long time. I feel like I could cry or scream or I don't know what!"

Mom leaves to go retrieve her camera from the bedroom, while Maureen and Lindy wait in a bubble of perturbed silence. As Mom nudges the door open, I catch a glimpse of part of Dad's left leg and his droopy left arm dragging off the side of the bed. Grasped lightly in his palm is an empty bottle of Jack Daniels, the round black lid laid out beside it like an incidental casualty. I hear his rough, grizzled snoring mixed with garbled sleep-talk and some kind of wheezy congestion coming from his throat. "Shhhhh," Mom whispers as she edges the door shut behind her. She returns a few moments later carrying Dad's old Canon 35 mm and twists the cap off the lens.

"Okay now," she says, looking through the viewfinder and adjusting the aperture, "look gorgeous!" She giggles, slides over beside Maureen and pushes her closer to Lindy. Now Mom is giving the orders. "Get in close beside her," she says, "put your arm around her. Lindy, open your eyes, honey. Open your eyes."

Maureen edges closer to Lindy, a hesitant, awkward smile beginning to creep across her lips. The two strike quite a comical pose together. Side by side, it's apparent what Maureen has managed to do. She's created a kind of waxy, delirious farce in her own image. Situated next to one another they form a portrait like someone might find on a poster advertising a comedy show outside a zany nightclub. *Come see the hilarious duo of Lindy and Maureen, two outlandish caricatures destined to turn your favorite cabaret troupe into a wickedly preposterous romp!*

"Oh, this is making me happy," Mom says as she clicks a few practice shots. "This is a thrill!" She checks the light meter, then rifles off a few more. Something has gotten into her even more than usual. She's practically erupting with joy, prickling and shivering as she dances about the bathroom. "Lindy!" she squeals, "Lindy if you don't open your eyes and allow yourself to take in this exquisite occasion, I am going to throw a fit!"

Lindy chooses that exact moment to flip open her eyes and throw her mouth open. It's a spectacle, half out of animosity and half out of reckless capitulation, an open display of her immense displeasure. Mom takes the opportunity to get it all in, frame it like a work of art. "Now we're talking!" Mom says. "Yes!"

What is captured is a middle-aged woman beaming like some queer harlequin performer and her young sidekick, eyes and mouth jacked open like a surprise attack, as if in horror. Both Maureen and Lindy's lipstick has been drawn on too wide and obtrusively so that the scarlet shade overlaps the lips and continues tracing up the sides of their cheeks in a bizarre arrow design. They look homicidal, like Jokers from Batman cartoons, and Mom loves it.

"Okay, one more," she says.

"This is the last one," Maureen says. She decides to place her hand on Lindy's shoulder for this one, and just as she does Lindy pounces up off the toilet seat. "Whoa!" Maureen shouts. "Okay, all right," she says, guiding Mom out of the room. "That's good. That's enough." She snatches up her kit as she shuffles for the exit.

"Okay," Mom says, "Well, that was wonderful. That was amazing!"

"We have to get you ready for your big date tonight," Maureen says as she scoots her out the door and into the hallway.

"Oh, yes!" Mom says. "Oh, yes, yes, yes! Can't you help me? Make me over! Make me look like Lindy!"

"Okay," Maureen says, "okay, just relax. I'll make you look like a queen."

"That sounds fantastic!"

Maureen slips around the corner, turns to face the open bedroom door. "Hey, is Neil okay?"

"Oh, yes!" Mom says, bopping the door shut with her foot. "He's fine."

"It looked like he was half dead," Maureen says. "Are you sure we shouldn't check on him?"

"Of course not!" Mom says. "He's fine. He had a long day. He's just resting up before we go on our big date to Gibson's tonight for some steak and lobster!"

"You're sure? Maybe we should wake him up now, get his blood flowing."

"No!" Mom shouts. "We have almost two full hours. Here! Here," she says. "Look. Look at this!" Hanging from a hook on the back of their bedroom door is a brand new suit Mom bought for Dad last weekend at Marshall Fields department store. It's a nice suit, tweed and navy blue, Italian cut with a shiny green tie and a white shirt with French cuffs. It was originally a six hundred dollar suit that Mom found on sale for under three hundred. "He's going to look like a king," Mom says, running her hands down the sleeves of the jacket. "So, you have to make me a queen. You said you would. Oh, wait until people see us out tonight! We are going to make a stunning couple. People will stop and look and wonder who are those celebrities!"

"Okay," Maureen says, gently tapping her on the back, "take some deep breaths. Grab a seat over here on the sofa, and I'll get started."

As they move farther away, Lindy comes at me, lunges for my elbow and hauls me over in front of the mirror. "Take this off of me right now," she says through gritted teeth.

"I… I don't know," I say. I try to take a peek outside to see if Mom or Maureen is watching, but Lindy won't let go of me. "I can't."

"If you don't wash this shit off of my face right now I'm going to punch you right in the mouth." She picks up a wash-cloth from the rack by the faucet and slams it into my hand.

"Lindy, come on," I say. "Wait until Mom and Dad are gone," I whisper. "They're going to leave in like two hours. I'll wash it off then."

"I can't even remember the last time I felt this... this well!" Mom says out in the family room.

"No," Lindy says. "Now." She makes a fist, cocks her arm back.

I pull with all of my might and break free from Lindy's grasp. I rush for the door, flicking it shut, and holding it closed with my foot. "Lindy," I say, trying to keep my voice down. She comes at me viciously, hands flying, slapping my shoulder, neck and ears. "Lindy. Lindy wait. Wait. Please."

"What's going on in there?" I hear Dad mumble from his room on the other side of the wall. I hear the bed creak, the bottle fall limply to the ground and clunk the hardwood floor.

"Nothing!" I say. "Nothing. Everything's fine."

"... and so I think I'm just going to get the most expensive thing on the menu," Mom's saying. "Because, who cares, right? I'm in charge. I'm a queen tonight. A queen!"

Lindy shoves me against the towel bar and when she backs up to get another swing, I grab both of her wrists and wrestle her down flat on the floor. I mount her legs and hips, sit down across her waist, press her to the cold tile. She's kicking and thrusting, struggling with everything she has. Her indignation is combustible, filled with so much passion and hostility. Her extreme righteousness hits me harder, delivers more pain than her actual blows. But I can't let her go. "I'm sorry," I tell her. "We have to... we just can't. It's too much. This hurts me too. I'm sorry," I repeat, "I'm sorry. I can't."

Apprehension Comprehension (2006)

To their credit, Drew and Jerry come right away when I call. Of course, Drew and Jerry are pretty much always up for some hard boozing and warped storytelling, but still. Meet me at The Wooden Nickel, I tell them, and bring your drinking shoes. I put my phone on the bar, swipe a few napkins and use them to mop the excess sweat off my brow. It's about a half hour before classes end for the night, so the place is still kind of dead. The great thing about The Nickel is not only is it the oldest bar around the campus, it's one of the oldest bars in the entire state of Illinois. It's got a musty, lived-in vibe that makes you feel like you're hanging out in your grandpa's basement. The faux wood paneling behind the bar features memorabilia from every Chicago sports team, buzzing neon lights, sooty, cobwebbed pennants, trophies of all sizes. A string of tiny white bulbs poke from the ceiling, draping from one tile to the next. Before the first drink of the night, or after the right amount, the little pinpricks of light are almost enough to make you feel like you're on vacation somewhere tropical.

"Another Old Style, Flynn?" Russ, the bartender asks. Russ fits right in with the rest of the décor. His black leather vest and handlebar mustache should be a requirement for all Wooden Nickel employees.

"Yeah, thanks, dude. Make it three," I say. "Drew and Jerry'll be in here in about two minutes."

"Uh-oh," Russ says with a chuckle, "those guys again!"

By the time Russ returns with three frosty steins, Drew and Jerry are sidling up, pulling out their stools. Drew sits to my right, Jerry my left.

"Perfect timing," Russ says. Drew and Jerry give him a high five. They both pick up their glasses and raise them in unison.

"Here's to…," Drew starts. He clears his throat. He elbows me, reminding me to lift mine high and join in the toast. Jerry and I chant along in harmony. "Here's to the breezes that run through the treeses, and lift girls' skirts up above their kneeses, to reveal something that teases, pleases and spread diseases, oh Jesus!" We clink glasses, take our slugs, and with that, the rituals and revelry of the night begin.

We bring our steins back to the bar with a thud, smack our lips with approval. "So, where's Sasha?" Jerry asks.

"Dude," I say, "that's not cool."

"Why? What?" Jerry says. He rakes his wrist across his lips, scraping away some suds.

"You can't ask about my girlfriend right after we say our 'Here's to the breezes' cheers," I tell him. "Where's your couth?"

"He's right," Drew says. "That's classless."

"Ha!" Jerry says. "Classless? We're in the goddamned Wooden Nickel drinking Old Styles from the same mug your grandma probably drank from during World War I. You can save your class for the Four Seasons, assholes!"

"That's not even the point, though," I say.

"What *is* the point, Flynn? Do tell," Jerry says.

"I told both of you on Wednesday that Sasha was coming up *next* weekend for a campus tour."

"He did tell us," Drew says. "That's not very considerate. You should listen more."

"Wait, wait wait," Jerry says. "Am I your girlfriend or is Sasha?"

"Damn!" Russ says behind the bar. He's working the taps in front of us. He's got two different droughts pouring at the same time.

"Am I right, Russ?" Jerry says. Jerry reaches up to give Russ another high five, but I knock his hand out of the air.

"Fuck both of you," I say.

Drew tips his glass all the way back, drains it dry. Jerry shrugs, follows suit. The two of them are always playing follow the leader. For example, both of them are wearing Hawaiian board shorts. Both of them have long hair almost down to their shoulders, and both of them look like they haven't washed said hair in over a week. Russ pours two refills from the tap and slides them back in front of Drew and Jerry. Someone waves at the end of the bar, calls something about "brewskis!" and Russ moves off in that direction.

"All right, are you guys ready for this?" I ask.

"Yeah, what happened?" Jerry says. "You sounded like quite a damsel in distress on the phone."

"Help me," Drew whines. He waves his arms over his head, imitating some limp-wristed queen in need of saving. "I'm Princess Leia. Save me from Jabba the Hutt!"

"That's so nerdy," I say. "You're such a dweeb."

"Yeah, and Leia was so much hotter. He's more like Jabba the Hutt."

"Okay, fine," I say, "I don't have to tell you about how Sasha and I almost got thrown in jail last night."

"Oh, ho ho, okay," Drew says, "Jerry, chill out."

"What? I'm cool as ice," Jerry says. "I'm a chilly Willy."

"Whatever," I say.

"All right, knock it off," Drew says. "That's enough."

"Oh, okay, fine. What is it? Tell us?"

I take a huge swig, finish my Old Style. I raise the mug up over my head, signal Russ at the other end of the bar to keep it flowing. He sees me, sends back a gesture to hold on a minute. "So, I told you guys about Deion," I say. The chugging gives me gas. I thump my chest, let loose a belch trapped deep in my gut.

"Sasha's ex-boyfriend," Drew says. "The one who's obsessed."

"Obsessed," I echo.

"Damn, you're good," Jerry says. "You two make a good couple."

"Well, shit got crazy on Friday."

Russ comes over and plops another full drink down in front of me. He whisks the empty one away, and flies back down the bar again. It's getting busy. A group of sorority girls has entered towing their fraternity brethren in behind. You can usually pick them out by their block shaped heads, their slack jaws or Birkenstock sandals. This crew has hit the trifecta. Jerry sometimes calls them the "Blockhead Bonanza," but he's a total prick.

"Anyway," I say, "he's losing his fucking mind. I think he's lost it already."

"Damn, what did he do?" Jerry says.

"Well, the first thing he does he just suddenly appears outside the Double Door in a suit and tie."

"What?"

"Why?"

"Very astute questions," I say. "That's what Sasha and I were trying to figure out. So, the reason we were going to the Double Door was to check out a Califone show. There was a rumor that they were going to play a secret afternoon concert, and I wanted to kind of show Sasha a sample of the kind of bands I'm into."

"I doubt Deion would be into Califone," Drew says.

"Dude, let him finish. And also, that's racist." Jerry says.

"So, yeah, well, I mean yeah to both of you. That's what we're thinking. That's not even the weirdest thing. He pretends he doesn't want us to see him."

"Wait, what?"

"What do you mean?"

"He acts like he's just hanging out, dropping by. We see him as we're crossing Milwaukee Avenue. Well, Sasha sees him first. She swears he looks right at us, and then walks up the street and starts hailing a cab. Sasha saw him right away. I saw him like a second or two later just sort of jogging south on Milwaukee in his pinstriped suit, whistling for a taxi."

"You're sure it was him?"

"Deion did this?"

"Definitely. Absolutely sure. We got a good look at him. It was like he wanted us to see him, but he didn't want us to say that we noticed him. He was acting all, like, professional and stuff, like he was a professional taxi hailer with a professional suit for the occasion, and he didn't want to talk about it. We were just supposed to get it, you know. Like... How do I put this? Like he had his fingers in his mouth, you know, like an expert whistler, like he was a master cab shagger, like he did this for a living. A professional, like I said."

"So, he just showed up and then took off?"

"Never said a word?"

"Didn't say a thing."

"That's really strange," Drew says.

"Well, how was the show?" Jerry says, "did they play the gig? Cactus Phone? What did you call them?"

"Califone. Oh yeah, they fucking rocked it," I say. "You've got to hear them play, man. It's like this whole garage rock cacophony mixed with like pop symphony and spoken word and they jam out… Whatever, anyway, that doesn't matter. Dude, I'm not even halfway done with the story. Shit didn't even get real yet."

"Whoa," Drew says. "What happened next?"

"Cacophony, Califone. I get it," Jerry says. "Sorry. Go ahead. This is getting good." He starts wiggling around on his stool like a little kid. "Hey! Can we get three shots of Jameson down here!" Russ hears him but he's swamped. He holds up two fingers like, *calm the fuck down and give me two minutes, bro!*

"So, then, next, Sasha takes me down to 57th Street Books for a reading by some poet she really likes. See, we've been doing this thing lately. We're going back and forth, taking turns showing each other the kind of different stuff we're into. I show her something I like, then she shows me. We're cutesy as hell, I know. I get it. Shut up. Anyway, she wants to take me to this bookstore in Hyde Park. This chick named Angela Jackson, this black poet, is reading her work. And man, she really kills it. She was awesome."

"Wow, that's insane!" Jerry says. He puts his hands to his cheeks and makes a shocked O face with this mouth. "You were right. It gets nuttier! Aaaaa! Run for the hills!"

"I liked the first part of the story better," Drew says.

"I'm not finished, idiots. Listen. So, she finishes reading, and Sasha and I get up to go shake her hand, say hello, whatever, and who do we see?"

"Maya Angelou?"

"Langston Hughes?"

"Wow, shit, you guys are ridiculous. Seriously? No, we see Deion. We see fucking Deion again, man! He's sitting in the front row! We didn't spot him until the very end because we were sitting near the back. This time I spot him first. He's got a different suit on! This one's like a mustard yellow, and he's wearing a purple tie!"

"Holy shit!" Drew says. "Okay, that's good."

"Yeah, purple and yellow are tight together!"

"Fuck you. He's in the front row. He jumps up as everyone is clapping at the end, and he rushes right up and shakes Ms. Jackson's hand. He's the first one up there. I smack Sasha to get her attention. I almost punched her right in the face by accident. I was so freaked out!"

"Damn! It was him?"

"I'm sorry Ms. Jackson. I am for real!"

"Yes. Shut up. It's definitely him again. Sasha sees him too. He's there long enough for us to see him. He knows what he's doing. I mean, he's up there bowing his head, giving one of those firm handshakes, a tip of the cap. He's hamming it up, like he knows her, like he might just kiss her hand or something regal like that. Some official bullshit. He's putting on a show again. When he's finally all done wooing her or whatever, we see him take a quick glance in our direction. It's just a real short, fleeting look, but it's clear. He wants us to take note. And then that's it. He's gone. He's out of there. He flies out the side door and takes off."

"Wait, he saw you guys?"

"Did he say or do anything to you?"

"Yes, he saw us, and no, he didn't do shit. I just told you."

"Okay, that's wild."

"Yeah, listen up. That's psycho."

"Yeah, so now we're flipping out, right? And that's when Sasha remembers she posted some of our activities for the day on her Myspace page."

"Oooooooh, I see."

"Right, right, right, right, right. Myspace."

"Yeah, right, so now we know how he's been following us. He's been tracking us down. We're onto him."

"He's got like his own personal map right in front of him."

"He probably printed it out."

"Yep, but, so, now we're onto him," I say. Russ comes back and slops the Jameson shots down in front of us. He's perspiring like crazy. His moustache is starting to look like an old, greasy dishrag. We salute him with our glasses, raise them, clink them together, and fire them down the hatch. We slam them down on the bar.

"You're onto him now."

"You've got Deion cooked."

"That's right. So, now we're headed to our dinner spot."

"Who picked the dinner spot? Whose turn is it? I lost count."

"Yeah. You both chose one spot each so far. Who's it gonna be next?"

"We chose it together, knuckleheads. We're going to Lao Sze Chuan."

"Good idea. Go someplace he can't pronounce."

"Throw him off the scent."

"Listen. It's probably the best Chinese food in the whole city, lame brains."

"Right. Everyone loves Chinese."

"What about Deion? Do Black people—"

"Okay, okay. Are you ready for this or what?" I ask.

Drew bends forward across the bar. He looks around me at Jerry, takes an exaggerated inhale of breath and makes a show of releasing it, blowing it all over the room in a steady gust. We all take hefty, hyper pulls from our glasses of Old Style. We're out of booze. We're ready for another round, but it's going to have to wait. Russ is frantically running up and down the bar, tossing coasters onto the bar like Frisbees and pumping four steins of beer at the same time. The place has been overrun by blockheads, all of them with their own guttural octave of grunts and chortles. Two of them butt their heads together on purpose. They ricochet off of one another, moan, cradle their heads. The girls look concerned but laugh anyway. Russ is laughing like a madman, but it doesn't look like he's tuned into anything in particular. He's laughing at something in his own head. He looks up at us, sticks his tongue out, gives us a thumbs up.

"We're ready. Fire away."

"Let's do this, Clay-*ton*."

"We walk in the entrance, and this time our eyes are peeled. At first we don't see him. He must have given up or maybe he hasn't showed up yet, right. Whatever, so, we take our seats. We have the table back by the kitchen. They gave us a booth, and at the end of the booth, sitting on the back of one of the benches is this shelf, and on the shelf is this enormous potted plant. I think it might have been fake, but whatever, it's gigantic. When Sasha gets up to use the restroom, she goes around the plant, around these huge oval leaves that have been blocking our view, and she lets out a scream. I hop up, come running. Deion leaps out of the booth on the other side, and he takes off in a full sprint."

"Oh shit!"

"Has he got on that mustard suit?"

"He has on the pinstriped suit again! He did a double, triple wardrobe change."

"That's incredible."

"That's extraordinary."

"Now, Sasha is yelling at the top of her lungs. 'Deion! Deion, what the fuck is wrong with you?' And the waiter, he sees him skipping out on the bill, so he charges out the door after him. Sasha and I run to the door, too, and we see him race down Archer like a bat out of hell. He's fast as lightning. He's got this terrific stride, no wasted movement. It's like Carl Lewis. He's a real pro."

"I bet he is."

"He's a track star, no doubt."

"The waiter yells, 'get him! Stop him!' And well, you might not know this, but Archer Avenue is swarming with cops, and so you know one of them hears him. This big, husky Irish looking motherfucker, CPD, starts chasing after Deion."

"He's running him down."

"Hot pursuit."

"He's chugging after him, radioing for backup the whole way, huffing and puffing like the tub of lard he is. Sasha and I are running too. It's like we don't even know what we're doing or why we're doing it, but there we are, just running as fast we can to keep up. Deion's got a pretty big lead on us, but when he goes to turn the corner onto Wentworth..." I pause for dramatic effect. "He's fucked."

"Wentworth is no good."

"That's trouble."

"Wentworth is teeming with pigs. There must be a dozen cops standing around, leaning on patrol cars, just chatting it up, shooting the breeze."

"Of course."

"This is Chinatown, right? Right? Am I right?"

"Sasha and I didn't get to see precisely what happened, but when we come around the corner, Deion's on the ground.

Two of them have their knees dug into his spine and two of them are yelling at him to put his arms behind his back. He can barely move enough to wiggle his feet let alone put his arms back, but they're still hollering at him. 'Put your arms behind you! Get your arms back here, fuckhead!' One of them says, 'what did he do? Tell me why we're arresting him. Give me a reason.' That's when old Irish Hulk Cop comes lumbering around the corner, and then he gives them their reason."

"He ran out on the check."

"Dine and dash."

"They've got him there, smashed on the asphalt like some kind of bug. He's lying there, flattened, and his suit is ripped and his shoes are all scuffed. I see him there, and I start to feel bad for him."

"He's fucked."

"They got him good."

"Sasha wants to go over and say something. She's pissed. She wants to give him a piece of her mind, let him know that this is the last time he'll ever show his face around her or me ever again. This is the last date he'll ruin. She's all worked up, pacing back and forth, pounding her fist into her palm, like ooooooooh, boy! But I tell her… I tell her no. I say, baby, no. Don't go over there. Please don't."

"She's asking for trouble."

"She may as well write a letter asking for it."

"So I hold her back. I calm her down. I tell her I got this. Let me handle it. I start approaching the situation, and as I'm getting closer, I feel worse and worse. I don't want this. This doesn't feel right. They don't have to hurt him. He's all dressed up, and I can hear him sort of whimpering and groaning. I don't want this. I walk up to the group of officers, and I come around right in front of them. One of them, she's this lady cop, right? You know what I'm talking about? Like Super Fucking Woman. She's got this voice, man, like really deep, like Barry White. It's not her real voice, but she's gotta do it. She has to be all Ms. Hardass and shit. Anyway, she sees me. 'What do you want?' she says. I tell her I know this guy. This guy is Deion. 'So what?' she says. 'What do you want us to do about it?' Hold on, I tell her. Wait. She looks at me like, 'I'm waiting, asshole, spit it out.' You don't have to do all this, I tell them. I want to take care of it. 'Take care of it?' she says. 'What the fuck?' I want to pay for him, I say. I tell all of them. Let me do this. Let me pay the bill. It's no big deal. I got this."

"No way."

"You're joking."

"I'm not. I go to pull out my wallet, and I hear Deion squirming around on the ground. They have his mouth like fucking nailed to the street with their stupid boots. 'Let him up,' one of the cops says. 'Let him talk.' Deion raises his head, spits some blood and fucking street grime from his mouth and he says… he says, 'get the fuck out of here.' He tells me, 'get lost!' And it's like I'm in a movie. He's straight out of some Boys In The Hood flick or something. He's got the cadence down, the lingo, everything. And, man…"

"Well, I mean…"

"What did you… I mean…"

"Wait up. Hold on. Hey, Deion, I say. Listen. What's up? Let me get this. It's all good, I tell him. Deion shakes his head. 'Motherfucker, can't you see I don't need your stupid cracker ass?' All the cops start laughing, like yak yak yak. Okay, whatever, right? Of course they would. So, I try again. 'You think you're better than me?' Deion says. 'Bitch, please.' He turns and takes a good look at all of the cops circling around him. His hands are all shackled and shit, and he smiles. He fucking smiles! He has like some blood and stuff in his teeth. This is really happening! He's like a real thug, like he's practiced for this, trained, like he's straight out of Compton! 'They can't hurt me,' he says. Then he spits, and he puts his head back flat on the ground. 'Man, get your honky, white bread ass out of my goddamn face. Can't you see you're making a fool out of your goddamn self?'"

"You probably shouldn't do his accent."

"That's a little suspect, yeah."

"And that's it. That's the story. Sasha and I went home."

"Then what?"

"That's it?"

"That's it. Craziest fucking night of my life."

Russ comes over and refills our drinks. "I'm in the weeds big time," he says. He points behind us, and when we turn around we notice that the line of people waiting for a drink is three rows deep. A guy in the back, hidden from view, throws a pickle that hits Russ in the eye. It hits with an elastic squish, sloshing light green juice all over his forehead, cheeks and neck. "Ouch! Hey!" Russ shouts. "What the fuck? Where did he even get that? I don't know what's going on. I'm losing track of shit. I don't even know how many you guys have had."

"Let's keep it that way," Jerry says.

"Nah, we got you," I say. "You know that."

"Thanks," Russ says. He puts his hands on the rail, hoists himself up off his feet. He perches over the bar, peers out into the crowd. "Hey!" hey hollers. "You trying to make some comment on my Italian heritage? Huh? You throw one more pickle, and I'm going to kick your fucking ass!"

We sit and think for a few minutes, each of us trying to process things in our own way. It's hard to think when the bar is so loud. Someone put Bon Jovi on the jukebox. Half the place tries to sing along while the other half boos their singing. It's a shit show. Jerry thinks best with his hands over his ears. He wears his hands like earphones. Drew likes to sort of stare off into space and nod his head, but when he notices what Jerry's doing he puts his hands over his ears, too. I'm more trying to think about what they're thinking. I've had twenty-four hours of non-stop thinking about the incident, and I'm worn out. After about five minutes, Jerry takes his hands off his ears. Drew sees him do it, and he falls in line. Jerry jolts up. He sort of pops up off the stool and smacks me on the back. "They shouldn't have done that," he says.

"They were way out of line," Drew says.

"I agree," I say.

"There's going to have to be some retribution," Jerry says.

"Yep," Drew says.

"Only you know that there won't be any," I say. "That's the real fucked up part."

"No, I know," Jerry says. "I mean for me, for us. We need something to take our minds off of this."

"For sure," Drew says. "That shit has got to be swept clean. Too much, man."

I wish they would take more time to think this through with me, sit with it longer, mull it over, though I guess I don't know what good it would do. The thinking and talking itself seems to be the means and the end, but that's okay with me. It's hard to find people who are willing to go to dark places with you and stay there. We all need a little light to come save us, keep us warm, even if the cold is trying to tell us something important...

"You know what to do," Jerry says. He makes a big display of glancing down at his jean pocket. He's fiddling his hand about down there and then he fishes it inside and shakes it all around.

I nod. "Stall number three," I say.

"That's right. Numero tres. Follow in right after me."

"Have a little of our own kind of 'over the *line*,' if you know what I mean. The Thin White Line," Drew says, winking at Jerry. "The White Line train!"

"Correct-a-mundo," Jerry says.

"Got it," I say.

"On it," Drew says.

"Then boys, meet me out back for some good old fashioned havoc and mayhem," Jerry says.

He picks his full stein up off the bar and places it to his lips. Drew and I pick ours up, follow his lead. We gulp. We do our thing. We chug and chug and chug until all the golden liquid is sucked clean from the bottom. Jerry slaps his down first, then Drew, then me, like some kind of routine, like a dive bar symphony. Drew rips a humongous burp, I plunk some bills down, and Jerry heads for the bathroom. One, two, three, one, two, three, one, two, three…

Tingle and Prick (1999)

I come home from Max's house and Mom's on her Tom's Natural brand soapbox again. Somehow she's managed to get Dad to sit still long enough to listen to her diatribe about homeopathic remedies for alcoholism. He sits across from her in his recliner with a sort of laidback air of condescension. It's like he's agreed to listen but with the bargain that he's allowed to form a grudge. There is a burning cigarette in his right hand and an empty Pabst can crunched between his legs that he's using for an ashtray. He's granted her at least fleeting sobriety, which is a small victory for Mom, but a bona fide one nonetheless.

"It's only about six needles, seven at the most," she's telling him.

I put my butterfly net in my room, and go in the kitchen to pour myself some iced tea. The tea is a decoy for eavesdropping, of course. I may as well have pretended I was constructing an improvised explosive device out of silverware and loose batteries from the junk drawer; they were so engrossed in their conversation they wouldn't have noticed.

"It looks like a lot more than that," Dad says.

"Well, it's not. Look it up," she says, "look up acupuncture under A in the encyclopedia."

"You realize that you are not a person who should be calling upon factual texts for assistance," Dad says. He flicks the cigarette into the can, crosses his legs. He sets the can down on the coffee table and clears his throat with excessive force. Next to the can is Mom's glucose monitor. It looks like a mini remote control with a white plastic tongue at the bottom for blood smears.

"You asked," Mom says. I notice she's sweating more than usual. She brushes a loose strand of hair from her eyes, curves her lips, blows a gust of breath upward toward her nose.

"Did I?" He's got the look of a man who's been drinking since sunup, crescent pouches of sodden skin beneath the eyes, blotchy red skin around the jaw like bruises from a fist fight.

"Well, you surrendered."

"Not yet I didn't. This is a disquisition." He drops the cigarette in the can where it reaches the bottom with a sizzle.

Mom shakes her head, lets out an exasperated groan. "It works," she says, "I don't know what else you need for proof."

"I'd like some literature, some science, some lab rats with a bunch of pins sticking out of their fur who have no more use for scotch or Bloody Marys anymore. What I really need is some engineering. If I'm trying anything, I'm getting on Antebuse."

"Antebuse! That garbage. Oh, you would. Drugs for drugs… You'd be the one to do that. That stuff makes you sick, you know. It's poison. Do you want to throw up all over yourself like some kind of sick child?"

"But you have to use to get sick. If you're clean you're in the green. You assume that I'd fail? You've got some negative thoughts about this one? This is fascinating."

"No. No! What I have is; I have all the positive thoughts in the world when it comes to natural, earthly solutions for ailments. That crap would probably make you puke even if you didn't use. How can you trust those pills? They're like little capsules full of venom. They're probably more toxic than the alcohol."

"One vote for alcohol!" Dad shouts, pumping his fist.

"Oh, you are impossible. How can you put your faith in something that makes you vomit?"

"Maybe vomiting is the point. I need a little shock to my system, a little punishment. I need to see the damage. Let me get a glimpse of the guts coming out. That's visceral."

"Acupuncture is sensory. You can feel it. It's got punch. It's sensual and it's sustainable. It's green."

"Punch? Not enough!" Dad says. "It's more of a little tingle. A tingle doesn't chase away demons—" He cuts himself off, changes direction. "Speaking of green. You're looking a little mossy yourself…"

"It got mine," Mom says. "It kicked my demons." Her eyes shift, move with purpose. Dad and I follow their side-eyed glance over to the table where her monitor sits next to the beer can. She's sneering down at it like her plot to overrun its reign of terror has been a rollicking success.

"Wait," Dad says. He looks from the monitor to Mom, then back again, like he's checking to make sure neither has run away or disappeared in the interim. "What are you saying?"

"That's right," Mom says. She is very satisfied with herself. "I won't be needing anymore pricks. I don't need to see the blood or the 'guts' as you put it. From now on, I'm strictly tingles. I'm on tingle street from here on out."

"You haven't tested your glucose today?"

"I don't have to," Mom says.

"What do you mean you don't have to? Have you eaten anything today?"

"I'm fine," she says. "It's a machine. It doesn't know everything."

"But how do you know?"

"I mean, I don't need to check on my glucose level because I already know that it's normal and stable. A man made that stupid meter. It's man made. We don't even know the man. Just like you don't know the doctors. Acupuncture is a ritual, an ancient, proven remedy from the Orient. I'm taken care of already. Forget about it."

Dad leans forward, puts his elbows on his thighs and studies the contours of Mom's face the way an entomologist might scrutinize the back legs of some rare kind of insect through a microscope. I look, too. I angle forward, bending over the counter for a closer view. Dad and I must be seeing the same thing because both of us have almost identical reactions. He squints and squints until he can't squint anymore. He stands and walks across the room where he puts a hand to her forehead. "You don't look so good," he says, and right away, as if words alone could turn someone diseased, the color leaves her and she grabs her throat.

"Why? What? What's going on?" she says. She runs her hand down her neck, letting it settle on her heart. Dad puts his hand on top of hers and together they clutch at her chest as it rises and falls with great heaving wheezes. She's trying to breathe and swallow at the same time, and neither one of them are turning out right. It's like watching a child try to fly by flapping her arms.

"How many fingers am I holding up?" Dad says. He's shoves a big, spread hand, with five fingers showing, right in her face.

And that's when she goes down. First her eyes go rolling back like some kind of rag doll, and then her body slumps and folds sideways like one too.

I come racing over just as Dad is slapping her face to wake her up. "Oh, you cunt," he says. "You stupid claw hammer.

Roberta! Roberta!" He yells, whacking her cheeks and chin with his palm. "Fucking mercy stroke!" he hollers. "Clayton!" He screams it like some kind of maniac, like he doesn't know I'm already standing right next to him.

"I'm right here," I say.

He lifts her off the sofa, wrapping one of her arms over his shoulder. "Get the other one," he tells me. "Hurry!"

"Okay, okay," I say, "I'm doing it." And I am. I'm already ducking my head under her other arm and helping to hoist her up. He keeps calling out orders to me like I'm still far off, like I'm not even there. "I got it!" I tell him, but he keeps going.

"Clayton! Clay, for the love of God, you're going to have to drive her to the hospital. I'm too drunk. Clayton!"

"I don't know how to drive!" I say.

"You'll have to drive, Clay. Clayton!"

Dad stands up so fast and with such brutishness that I am lifted off my feet. All three of us go crashing into one another like bowling pins. We right ourselves, and rush for the door. We carry Mom to the door and through it without even thinking. We're all the way to the car before we understand what we have done. "Clayton," Dad says. "You'll drive. Get in. Clayton!" He drags Mom into the back seat, slipping her inside like a loaf of bread in the oven.

"I'm right here," I say. I'm already sitting in the driver's seat. The chair is several feet too short. If I stretch my legs as far as they go my toes are still a good distance from reaching the pedals. When I try to look in the rearview mirror all I see is the top of my head in the dim reflection. I'm practically lying flat on my back, straining to touch the gas, when Dad reaches around me, twists the keys in the ignition and the engine turns on. "Dad!" I say. "Wait!"

"You fucking bitch!" Dad says, shaking Mom on his lap. "I love you. Why did you do this?"

"Dad, I can't drive," I say.

"Yes, you can," he says. It's the first time he's addressed me like a mutual person who is sharing the same space. His gaze becomes serious and determined. He wedges himself forward between the front seats. Mom rests on his lap like an immense, fleshy guitar. "You can do it. I have directions for you. There's a method to this. It's a concrete skill. I'll give you lessons."

"Is there anyone behind me?" I say.

With one fierce jerk of his head, he responds, "No. No, it's okay. Put your foot on the brake. Okay, good, now shift the lever until you see the needle on the dashboard turn to D. There you go, that's it. Now, slowly let the brake go and turn the wheel just a little bit to the left."

If there is one small blessing it is that there are no vehicles in front of me. I let go of the brake all the way, and the car drifts into the lane breezily, sweetly like a boat riding gently rippling waves.

"Clayton!" Dad says. I slam on the brakes, and all of us go sloshing forward. "No, no, no! Keep going. I was just going to tell you that I'm sorry. I shouldn't have called your mom those names."

"It's okay," I say, because in the scope of things the names mean nothing; the gestures themselves like nameless intimations. The fact that he even sees it necessary to mention them at this time makes my heart sink, and I almost lose control of the wheel.

"Hold the wheel straight," he says, and now his voice is calm and even keeled. "Grab it. Hold it tight. Feel it. Feel the road beneath you. See? That's it. Take control."

I straighten out. The car swerves briefly and then settles into a groove. If I concentrate really hard I can convince myself that I'm not driving at all but more like supervising, like a conductor on a set of train tracks already laid out before me. Whether my eyes are open or not doesn't seem to matter. I can't even see out of the window.

"It's okay, son," Dad says. "A little to the left. I'll be your eyes. You be my limbs, and I'll be your eyes. We know our appendages, don't we? Sure we do. These are things we understand."

Potshot (2004)

Practically every kid in Lindy's ninth grade class has a picture of her vagina. It's one of those tiny, pixilated photos that the cheap flip phones take, but it's plenty provocative for a freshman. It doesn't matter that it was taken by some lousy creep of a kid who spends way too much time at the Westfield Shopping Center. His classmates can't believe their luck. They crown him. They keep his handy work pressed between the pages of their math or history books like trying to flatten the leaves on a four-leaf clover. It's garnered her quite a following. She's got her own fan club now. Every day after school, a pack of ripe, rashy-faced boys with baseball caps and pubic-hair-beards flock outside her bedroom window. They hold the photos up over their heads like crucifixes, like trying to summon a holy spirit from our house. They move in busy, bumbling circles, like swarms of discombobulated gnats.

"This is the most confusing thing I've ever done," Lindy says. "Either it worked like a charm or it worked like a baseball bat to the head."

"That's true," I say. "Do you ever think that means it worked either way? Like, both ways...?"

She pulls the curtains back just enough to get a little peek, so that it only looks like the breeze is doing it. She kneels on the bench below her bedroom window. Like so much of her mangled adolescence, she assumes the dual position of either prayer or copulation. It was one week ago that she decided to put one of her murky, ill-advised plans into action. The idea started as a licentious proposition. What would happen if she wore a miniskirt to the mall with no underwear on underneath? Question number two, what would be the result of a well-timed, protracted bend to pick up a coin from the tiled floor? If she made it look accidental, then she wouldn't have to feel repentant or distraught about the ramifications, and she also wouldn't have to deal with the full wrath of her unwitting co-conspirator that day, April.

"Boys are so stupid. They're so much easier to handle," Lindy says. She closes the curtains. "The way the girls look at me," she says. "It's like they want to beat me to a pulp, spit in my face, then climb inside my skin, resurrect themselves and start over again as me. But they want to be the spitter and the victim and the whore all at the same time. They can't make up their mind."

"That's all in a look?" I say.

"It's a sense... like a vibration," she says.

The sound of boys' feet marching against the pavement reaches us through the closed window. Above the cadence is the chant, "Lindy, Lindy!" It's a murmuring, programmed type of inflection. "Lindy, come out and let us in!"

"It's going to be okay," I tell her. "They'll go away and forget about you eventually."

"That's what I want, right?"

"I think so."

"I spent so much time wishing and hoping and praying that I would achieve some kind of love and affection, that I would get all this attention... and then I did. I did it. What happened, Clayton?" She looks at me with raw, watery eyes. "I don't even know if I did it on purpose or not. I mean the whole thing, everything. I don't know what I'm doing. Did I do it right?"

"It won't matter much either way," I say. "People love failures and they love triumphs, but I think what they want even more than that is a rise from the ashes."

"Am I in the ashes or the air right now?" She pulls the curtains back again, looks out at the scene with a renewed sense of marvel. "Where do I go from here?"

"That's the thing," I say. "Ashes don't stay on the ground very long. They don't want to be grounded. It's not their natural state. They want to take off, soar."

She yanks the curtains closed fast, fearfully. "I think I may have done it out of revenge. I'm sick."

"You're not sick," I say. "And even if you were… You're not, but I don't know. Do you ever feel like you get comforted by sick people?"

"What do you mean?"

"Well, like sick people make me feel better. What I mean is that as long as an illness isn't terminal, as long as someone recovers, that's the best thing in the world. Do you know what I mean? It's like their recovery shows everyone that recovery, your own even, is possible. It's hopeful. I'm never more filled with optimism as when I see a recently debilitated person who has regained their health."

"So, you think I'll be forgiven for my vengeance against April?"

Her words startle me, buckle me like a sharp blow. I didn't know she still thought of the incident between me and April under the bridge. I mean, I knew she must still remember it, of course, but I was beginning to think that she would just bury it and never bring it up again. Probably just wishful thinking… She said that she forgave me. Well, she didn't say it directly, but it was implied. What she said was that she understood me, and she understood April, and that even though what she understood about us was sinister and dismaying, it didn't compare to what was inside of her, and she wasn't willing to lose the only two people in her life who could deal with her own disturbances. And then I told her that that wasn't true, and that there was nothing wrong with her, and that we didn't think of her like that at all, and it felt like everything was settled at that time, like we had a final determination, but now all of my guilt is coming back, flooding in. Maybe nothing is actually okay; nothing is resolved. Is all of this my fault? The foot of her bed is right behind me. I feel for it, find it with my hand and lower myself onto it.

"Is that what this was about?" I stutter.

"I don't know anymore," she says. "I need someone to tell me. I need someone to explain myself to me. I'm so lost. People look at me," she says. She comes toward me, frantically, and takes a seat next to me on the bed. "People look at me, Clay, and they ask things without asking them. It's like they're asking me, how did you do it? How did you get so amazing and so like ... extraordinary that I want to bash your skull in? They don't know if they love me or hate me, so how am I supposed to know? It's like my dream and everyone else's has come true, but they won't admit it. They want me to think it's a nightmare, and so I do. I believe them."

"You thought about what you wanted—"

"I brought it into being."

"You manifested."

"I put it out there, left it up to the universe."

We sit in silence for what seems like a long time. The boys' voices tire and sputter out. They lose velocity, grow wilted. Some of them cough, clear the chalkiness and hoarseness from their pipes and start back up again. A few give up and leave.

"I didn't mean for April and I… I didn't want to do it, but I couldn't say anything," I say. "She takes all the wind out of me." I can't look at her, and she can't look at me, so we just sit there staring straight ahead at the curtain and nod. It seems the nodding could go on forever, an eternal pendulum swung into motion. I free myself, free us. I stand up and start moving, just any old movement, a deep knee bend that cracks the joints. I kick my legs out, wiggle my back, crack my fingers. I'm knocking the emotions loose.

"I'm going to go tell them to get lost," I say. She stops nodding for a moment and swallows. She looks up at me for just a second and does one more long, gracious nod. "They need to get lost before Mom and Dad come home. I'll be right back."

As I walk down the stairs and approach the front door where the boys perform their incessant campaigning, my body fills with an extreme fury. The more I think about Lindy upstairs in her pathological, disgruntled state, the more the lathering continues. How is it that people can't recognize when someone is hurting? How do so many people keep laying grief and sorrow and insult at the feet of someone they know is toiling? I think of the way she looked as I got up from the bed, broken and adrift, and I know I have to do something to make things right about April. I know Lindy's watching from her perch upstairs. This is my chance to apologize. This is my display of remorse. It must be all encompassing. My fingers curl and clench. The hair stands up on my arms, and my biceps go into a series of involuntary flexes that I've never experienced before. I bang open the door, charge through it and growl, "Get your tiny fucking dicks out of here!" And it works. They yelp and scurry; they slam into one another, ricochet and panic. They locate an open path to exit and they flee. They scatter, migrate into the streets like a pack of petrified birds desperate for ascension.

VIII. THE SHORTCUT TO THE WORLD

If The Cat is Right (2004)

I always know when it's Randy calling because as soon as I answer the phone he's already mid-thought, as if we've had some extensive conversation leading up to this abrupt moment of intimacy. He starts right in with his chatty, haranguing delivery style.

"So, Elizabeth took her things and moved out," he sighs, "She's taking me for granted. That's what she's doing. She'll be sorry." He makes a sound like blowing onto a hot bowl of soup. "Yeah," he continues, "and I know if your dad was clean and sound of mind, he'd know just what to tell me in this situation. Your dad is a very wise man when he's sober. You know that, don't you?"

"I've seen it a few times, yes. Do you want me to go and find him? I think he's in the garage."

"Oh, no no no," Randy says, "the garage! Shoot, he's probably *under* the car by now, if you know what I mean ..." he interrupts himself with a cough and another sigh. "Man. That's sort of how I feel right now, too. Under the car..."

A long pause follows, and even though I can think of a few things that I could say to break the silence, I don't open my mouth. I figure if he calls a sixteen year old up out of the blue, and expects me to do all the work, he's even more cracked than I thought. It's not that I'm trying to teach him a lesson or anything, just trying to get him to sit with himself for a spell, and figure things out on his own. He can't keep relying on others to pull him out of his messes.

"There's a new cat just appeared outside the apartment below mine," he says all of a sudden.

"A cat?" I say. "Really?"

"Yeah, he's all crusty and mangled up. I have no idea how he found himself inside our complex, but there he is. Beaten up, starving, crying for affection."

"That sounds really sad," I say. "Has anybody called anyone? Animal control or something?"

"Huh? Oh, no. I don't know about all that. There's a place like that? I have no idea. No, we just all sort of say hi to it, and try to keep it company I guess you would say. I see him more as a reminder of all the lost souls out there. I couldn't turn him in or nothing."

"Well, I mean, you wouldn't be turning him in," I say. "It's not like he committed some secret crime. You'd be giving him a chance at survival."

"You don't think we can keep him living here on our own? We're not capable."

"I didn't say that."

"You know what the weirdest thing is?" Randy asks. Again, it's like he thinks we've already talked about other weird things previously during some imaginary discussion. "The cat doesn't know he needs saving."

"What do you mean?" I ask.

"Well, let me tell you. I'll explain. See, the first thing you notice about this cat is that he's missing an eyeball. You'd notice it right away, Clay! I know you would especially. You're always on top of that stuff. But, anyway, one eye is gone completely, just vacant, all covered over with some kind of puss and fur… It's not pretty. And well, the other eye, it's no good either."

"Jesus," I say. "He's got two missing eyes?"

"No, no no. Hell no. That would be crazy. The other eye is just like unable to focus or something. It's like it's always pointing straight up at the sky, like it's trying to tune in some kind of satellite frequency that might help keep it on balance. I don't know if that one eye is crippled or if it's actually got super powers, you know, like compensation memory muscles to help even out the other situation. It sort of looks like a blind man when he takes off his glasses, but this cat only has one eye."

"Wow," I say, "Yeah. That's really something. You've got some excitement in your apartment. Maybe that will help take your mind off of your girlfriend. What did you say her name was?" Randy's always going through women. The problem, from what I can gather, is that Randy has all of these heady, ingenious ideas about life and art, and the women he meets, against their better judgments probably, are totally into it at first. The real issue is that he won't ever return the favor. These women, literally dozens over the years, invest time in getting to know him, fostering an appreciation for him, even trying to *save him*, and when you ask Randy to tell you something about them, he's got nothing. What does Elizabeth like, you could ask. What is she into? You'd be lucky if he could tell you the way she likes her eggs. I don't think it's intentional, Randy is too well-meaning for that, but basically what he does is bankrupt them of all of their goodwill, cleans them right out. What will that do to them and the men in their future relationships? Randy wouldn't know.

"It's funny you bring up Elizabeth, because I was just about to say something about her. I'm getting there. See, the cat, the cat has this strange cockiness about it, like it thinks it's all high and mighty and worthy of love. It puts its nose in the air and struts around, comes in for hugs and kisses against your legs, even has the gall to bite sometimes, like as if it could even afford to bite a hand that feeds it! It's got nerve, man."

"That's what cats do," I say.

"Exactly! They don't know any better. That's what I'm getting at," he says. He shifts some papers around on a desk somewhere, slides them around until they go whisking right off of whatever surface they were on and hit the floor. "The cat can't see his own flaws. He literally can't see them."

"Oh, I see. You're probably right. If he knew about them, maybe he'd go get help."

"What?" Randy says, miffed and surly all of a sudden. "No! That's not the moral here! If the cat knew he was all busted up, do you think he'd even still be hanging around an old apartment buildings acting like a gift, like some prince of thieves? Hell no! That cat would be dead and gone by now. What this cat symbolizes is grit, determination and self-confidence, because of course it deserves love! The damn thing practically forces love right out of you, against your will and everything. Now, that's something. Elizabeth would have hated this fucking cat, but I don't. I'm starting to love the little rascal. I might even take it into my home and give it a name."

"Would you call it Randy Junior?" I ask.

"You're an odd kid, you know that Clay? But that's what I like about you. Yeah, you're all right with me."

There is another extremely long interval of dead air that follows. This time, I don't dare say what I'm thinking. I couldn't say it even if I wanted to. Randy would go nuts if I told him what I'm thinking. The quiet lulls on so long that I almost can't take it anymore. If he doesn't say something soon, I'm either going to hang up or end up blurting out something I'll regret. *You don't deserve the love people give to you!* Just as I'm about to put the phone down, I hear some papers start rustling in the background. I think he must be picking up whatever he dropped a few minutes ago.

"I'm going to go get that cat," he says. His voice is manic and racing. "I just need to fix up the place a little bit before I bring him in. I don't want him to think I don't respect him. He's been through a lot."

The papers are all off the floor, and now I hear him going through cupboards, moving jars to the side and crinkling old wrappers. In a few more minutes he's grunting as he tugs his shoes on. "Yeah," he says, "I was being all silent just now because I had an idea for a new painting. That cat is going to be my new muse," he says. He gets to his feet, stamps his shoes a few times so that they settle into place just right. "I'm going to put the phone down soon," he says, "okay."

"Okay," I say.

"I don't usually do this, but I'm going to tell you what I'm going to paint. It's going to be a masterpiece."

"I can't wait?"

"Do you want to hear it?" he says. "Was that a question or what? You're not sure?" I hear the door opening to his apartment, and then the sound of him descending steps.

"Of course," I say. "Yes. I want to hear about it."

"I'm going to lose you," he says. "My reception won't carry this far." I can hear the cat now. It sounds the way a cat might sound if it was trapped in a deep well for a long time and is now finally being pulled up, rescued out of the dusty darkness. It sounds happy and tortured at once. "I'm going to paint a picture of this cat, and it's going to be ultra realistic. It will actually be the cat. You won't even be able to tell the difference." The reception grows fuzzy and dim. "I'm going to call it The Beginning of The World is Nye!" And then we're cut off and the line goes dead.

Clean Break (2006)

She hadn't said anything back yet, not in the moment, not in the ambulance ride to the hospital and not during the X-rays either. Maybe she was in too much pain, or maybe her answer was in her actions more than her words. She had, after all, agreed to be my assistant, my "partner" as she insisted on being called. This partnership, as she put it, did involve coming on stage in front of a large crowd of imbecilic novices and volunteering to be cut in half by her boyfriend, some rinky-dink magician who hadn't practiced the trick in almost three years. Even three years ago I hadn't gotten it just right. I told her that. I didn't make any promises, and still she wanted to go through with being my sidekick for the show. She's the one who convinced me to do the show in first place! And now she's lying here on a hospital bed with her foot all bandaged up, and I'm sitting beside her with eleven stitches in my elbow, and she hasn't shown a single sign of wanting to curse me out or leave me for another man, any man who wouldn't accidentally snap her foot in two during a live magic act in front of a hundred people… Okay, so maybe that should be enough proof that she cares about me deeply, but still. The first time a man says he loves you he needs a quick, affirmative reply right away.

Her poor delicate, beautifully shaped foot looks so sad just propped there on top of all those pillows. There's so much gauze and tape and fabric wrapped round and round, and all of it that sickly beige color that only doctors use. The color doesn't even exist in nature or anywhere else outside hospitals, doctor's offices or medical supply stores. In a day or two she'll get her permanent cast, a thatched shaft of solid plaster, so firm and tough that she can use it as a battering ram if she wants. She says she's going to get hers in navy blue, which I like. It fits her. To me it signals midnight prowling, contains elements of deviousness... Right now, though, there's nothing symbolic or intriguing about it. Her whole leg is about three times the size it was this morning when we were still joking about "break a leg!" Hahaha... As it turned out, the whole spectacle really was a joke.

"Sorry I couldn't keep the coffin from spilling open," Sasha says. "I tried to catch it but I couldn't." She has the white bed sheet pulled all the way up to her chin, which makes her look like she's hiding from the outside world. It makes her all the more cute and also makes me even more paranoid about how much she's hiding from me and her feelings of disappointment.

"You're kidding, right?" I say. My chair is right next to her bedside, but out of shame and unease, I've been slowly inching it back. I just feel like she wants to be left alone. "You're worried about catching the coffin? I broke your foot."

"Well, I didn't want the trick to be revealed. Now, I've ruined it for everyone who saw it. They won't ever have that feeling, that fascination ever again."

"You?" I say. "You ruined it? How do you figure?"

"We were partners," she says, "remember?"

"Yeah, I bet you're regretting that now," I say.

"No," she says. "Did David Copperfield's assistant ever feel sorry about being his partner? What about Houdini? Did he even have a sidekick? Oh, I bet Houdini is rolling over in his grave right now, thinking about how badly we botched that trick."

"You want to know something crazy?" I say.

"You know you don't even have to ask me that," Sasha says. "I always want the crazy!"

"Clearly," I say, pointing at my elbow and then her foot. We both laugh. At least we still have that. "No, but it's funny that you mentioned Houdini and trick reveals."

"Why?" Sasha says. She lets the sheet down and shimmies her way closer toward me on the edge of the bed.

"Well, there's this story about Houdini. See, back in like 1915 he wrote a book explaining how to do all of his most legendary tricks."

"Shut the fuck up!" Sasha says.

"It's true."

"Why the hell would he do something like that?"

"Good question," I say. "He did it because the explanations were all fake. Phony. See, he penned the book under a pseudonym, and he invented these elaborate descriptions to throw off all of his competitors or any audience members who might want to cheat him out of his fortune. He was two steps ahead of everyone."

"Holy shit," Sasha says. "That's amazing. How do you know about this?"

"I'm one of his biggest fans. Back when I was a kid I read everything about him that I could get my hands on."

"Did you ever read his fake trick book?"

"Well, that's an interesting question. See, some people think he never had the chance to publish it. His wife insisted that he hold onto the manuscript. She was worried that his real identity would get out and it would ruin him, but apparently Houdini used to share the pages with his friends when they came over for dinner parties. There are fake trick books out there, though, and a lot of people think that Houdini is the author of a couple of them."

"Aren't pseudonyms grand?" Sasha says.

"Yeah, and some of those books made a lot of money! There are a lot of suckers out there in the world."

Sasha nods her head. She puts her pinkie in her teeth and wiggles it there, thinking about something.

"What?" I say, thinking she might bite clear through the thing before she comes to a conclusion about whatever she's contemplating.

She takes the finger out and smiles. It's a shy, coy smile, which isn't the type I'm used to seeing. It might be the pain medication the nurse gave to her before she left. I can't remember the name of it, too many letters and syllables. It seems like a very long time since the nurse left and promised to be back shortly. Sasha speaks from behind her medicated smile. "Your mom should have used a pseudonym," she says, drooling just a little bit as she tries to enunciate through her haze.

"I've thought about that," I say, and then a devilish little grin spreads across both our faces and we erupt in laughter. It feels so healing to laugh with her. Now, if I could just get her to say those magic little words back to me, I'd be fully redeemed...

She moves her broken leg by cupping her right hand under the left kneecap and hoisting. The heavy dead thing complies, but not without a muted groan and grimace. She tries not to let me see how much pain she's in, but I can't miss it. I can't take my eyes off of her. When she rakes her leg to the side, the covers peel back and creep up her thigh. She's still wearing that silky red outfit she had on for the performance. It's the same one that April wore when we did the trick a few years ago at the local YMCA. It makes me wince to think about how incredible Sasha looks in that getup, how much she wanted me to succeed, and how horribly I fucked everything up. We're here because of me. I'm the reason Sasha's lying in a stiff white bed under a bright yellow light. There's something about the watercolor hanging over the sink that makes me so depressed. It's supposed to have the opposite effect, I guess, but I don't see how. It's just so plain and dull—a collage of ordinary daffodils filling the whole drab frame. Couldn't they think of something more captivating or thought provoking? Is everyone in a hospital just supposed to be lying around thinking about nothing but boredom and flowers and blandness? How is that supposed to cheer anyone up? Sasha, in her hot red costume and her vibrant personality is the only thing with any color around this damn place. Only her personality isn't so vibrant at the moment. She's just sort of staring down at her cast and wondering how in the hell she's going to get around over the next six to eight weeks. There's nothing fun or lively about that, and even she can't jazz up that harsh reality, and that's making her look so sweet and melancholy... and she's so vulnerable right now... and why won't she say anything? Where is the nurse? She said she would be back with the prescriptions and a few ice packs, and that was over twenty minutes ago! And we're stuck here looking around at all of these tedious posters about CPR and breast exams, and stupid instruments like surgical scissors and packaged needles, and everything is so fucking tiresome... Doesn't anyone care that I'm trapped in this dump with a woman who I just professed my love to? I'm going to tear that shitty painting off the wall! It's too warm in here... stuffy. I have to do something to get some life back in this place.

"I had sex with Lindy's best friend," I say. I just say it before I can think about it. We needed something drastic.

Sasha moves fast, too, serpent style. Before she remembers that her leg is broken, she slithers herself forward on the bed, sending a volt of agony up from her ankle to her contorted face. The pain acts as a tether, slamming her back against the headboard. "You did what?" she shouts. If the nurse was dawdling before, this new explosive development will put an end to it. She must have heard her. The whole office must have heard. Now something's moving. At least now something is happening. She's responding.

I don't say anything, just creak my chair back farther in case she tries to hit me.

"You slept with … how could you? When? Where was I?" All of the hurt is gone from her leg now. It's all traveled north to reside in her slumped shoulders, her cloudy eyes, her broken heart. Sasha is the kind of person who can fight through whatever dose of drugs is in her system. She'll beat the hell out of morphine if it's what she feels she needs to do to get her point across.

She thinks it's happening now. In my rush to act, to trigger a reaction, I wasn't clear. "No, I … It wasn't—"

"Who the hell are you even?" Her voice has quieted down, which I take as a bad sign. She's already withdrawing, shrinking inward. I have to hurry.

"No, Sasha," I say, leaning forward a little bit but with great caution. "This wasn't recent."

Her eyes brighten just a touch. "How long ago are we talking?"

"I don't know," I say, "years ago. Before we met."

Sasha considers this new information. She shakes her head, lets loose a big gust of breath through her nostrils. Her body is facing the wall on the other side of the room. This is where she directs all of her agitated respirations and grunts. When she is ready, she turns on me with a different but none-theless fiery anger. "Now, why the fuck did you go and do something like that?" Her fury now is on Lindy's behalf. The aim has shifted, but the target is still the same.

"I don't know," I say, slumping back in my chair. "Because I was lonely, and I was lame. And April—"

"That's her name?" Sasha asks, crossing her arms over her chest. Does the name April make it worse? Would it have been better if it was a Jessica or Eleanor?

"Yeah," I say. "April was very... how should I put it? Persuasive."

"And you couldn't resist?"

"Not at the time, no. I was young and horny, and dumb and so unbelievably susceptible to something like that. I couldn't control myself."

I raise my head. The disgrace has gotten to me. I'd deliv-ered my last few statements with my chin, in shame, pointing toward the floor. I didn't want to see the displeasure on Sasha's face, but I see it now. Her eyes divulge mostly frustration, annoyance at having been put through not only a broken foot, but then a major relationship scare and now a faux scandal all in one afternoon. This is all my doing. It's not only that I wanted to get a rise out of her; I had some unselfish motives as well. She and Lindy have been getting close over the past few weeks, and I didn't want it to come up out of nowhere during one of their long talks. I've seen their discussions last long into the morning hours. Lord knows what they're delib-erating about. It's like some kind of peer counseling or therapy session. Sasha is great at those sorts of things. And that's just it.

She'd have gotten it out of her. Sooner or later it was bound to come out, and I didn't want Sasha to feel like I was betraying her trust or anything.

"Why did you tell me all this?"

"You and Lindy have become such good friends, and I didn't want you to find out from her or somebody else. These sorts of things always sound worse when they come from someone else, and I guess I thought that if I told you that I could control the way it was handled or explained or… I don't know."

Sasha puts her finger back in her mouth, only this time it's her index finger. She has a way of using her mouth and finger as devices of comfort, tools of thought. She moves the finger back and forth like brushing her teeth, then lets out a wet little raspberry of sound.

"And Lindy forgave you for this shit?" She says.

"Not right away, but yeah." I say.

"How?" she says.

"How?"

"Yeah, how? How the fuck does a sister forgive her brother for something like that?"

"Well," I say, trying to think about the best way to put it. "I covered for her."

"Really?" Sasha says, then waves her hand around in a rolling motion, impatiently gesturing for me to continue.

"I didn't tell anyone about Barry. I didn't judge her about him or about Randy or any of her other bad decisions she was making around the same time. I didn't say anything, even though, maybe I should have… Maybe she even wanted me to say something…" As I say this I am realizing for the first time that perhaps my silence and avoidance weren't the best methods for helping Lindy through that time. If I could have spoken to her in the right way or gotten someone else to speak to her, someone like Sasha or a psychiatrist or, I don't know… I could have done more than simply keep quiet. But that was the only strategy I had back then. That was what I could be counted on to follow through on. Secrecy… "Anyway," I continue. If I don't start back up again now everything will get lost and forgotten. "She knew how April was, and she knew how I was… I guess if you knew us both back then you'd have seen how our different weaknesses would have led us to lean on one another, and then leach off of one another. It all seems very inevitable looking back on it. Lindy understands that sort of thing because, if you haven't noticed yet, deep down inside, she's a total softie."

Sasha takes in these new facts, processes them in her particular way. Finger back in mouth, mouth gumming away, head nodding up and down, up and down…

"And who are Barry and Randy?" she asks, yanking the finger out with a pop.

"You'll have to ask her that," I say. "Like I said, for certain things it's best you hear it from the source, straight from the horse's mouth. I don't feel comfortable telling other people's business."

This reasoning seems to satisfy her. She unstiffens her back against the headboard, lets her hips slouch over toward me. There's those red underwear again, the hug of the fabric against her cool brown skin. It's a little chilly in here. Beneath one side of the blanket I can see a sliver of goose pimples covering her good, clean leg, the one I haven't sullied with my abject foolishness.

"I just didn't want to have anything between us," I say. I'm back trying to get a reply out of her even if it's not the exact one

I want. I need her to acknowledge my confession. I took a risk. I deserve an answer. "I don't want to hide anything. I know how big you are on being honest and forthright, and so... you know," I say, treading lightly at first and then just going straight to the point. "After what I said, and what it means. What it could mean... No more secrets. I wanted to come clean."

At first, what I've said hits her a little sideways. She dips back a little farther against the wall, but then on second thought sways forward again. She leans over and for the first time in a while looks me straight in the eyes. "So what you said wasn't just part of the show?"

I shake my head.

"That wasn't just some Houdini mumbo jumbo, some fake shit?" Her eyes and mouth are still fixed in a stern crescent of focus, but at the end of this question I see a crack start to form, a hairline fracture of humor that runs between her lips and makes her mouth quiver slightly.

"I wasn't faking," I say, trying not to blink. I don't want any sort of tick to mess up how serious I am about this situation right now.

"And we're coming clean today? That's what we're doing, right?" I nod. She takes a deep breath. She falls back against the pillow. "Okay, but you'll have to come closer," she says. "Some asshole broke my foot, and I have a hard time leaning on it. I need to see your face for this."

I stand up slowly, an expectant smile already forming. When I bow over her, and look into her eyes I'm surprised at what I see. She is not all giggles and lightheartedness like I thought she might be after the last facetious comment. Instead, she is somber and meditative in her expression, but also soft and hopeful. "This better not be a hoax," she says, and I think

I shake my head, but maybe I just stare blankly because I am caught up in this moment so intensely that I fear I might pass out. "I love you, too," she says. She whispers it so that only I can hear it, privately and sincerely the way such a declaration of this magnitude is meant to be delivered. I was the one who had done it wrong. She knew what she was doing all along. It was worth the wait.

She grabs my cheeks and pulls me toward her, and just as we are about to kiss, the nurse opens the door and comes back inside. I suppose we should have guessed as much. It's the moment you stop thinking about someone that they appear. Poof!

Aphorisms for Death (2005)

The next time Randy calls it's on one of the hottest days of the entire year. He wants to wish me a happy graduation, which is such a sweet gesture it almost makes me well up a little bit. Randy is one of those people who are impossible to get a concrete feeling about. It's like he's the kind of man who wrecks your car one day, and before you can start hating him for it, he gives you his great grandfather's watch as a heartfelt apology, and you start thinking he's the most lovable guy in the world. Anyway, he calls out of the blue, which for him must feel like a regularly timed function, and not only is it hot for this time of year, but it's an all-time scorcher, like one for the record books. It's so hot I drink three glasses of water before breakfast, and I'm so dehydrated my pee still comes out looking like apple juice. I mention this because I thought it was why Randy's voice sounded so gravelly and mushy when he first started talking, like he had sand in his mouth or something. It was all thick and raspy. Every few seconds he stops to clear his throat again. We're talking about high school and college, about the University of Illinois and Sasha, and all of a sudden he gets really quiet. He coughs a few times and then says *listen,* real abrupt and stern. I stop and go silent, just like he asked, and I start to wonder if what he wanted me to listen to was not what he was about to say next, but instead his choppy, wheezing breaths that go whistling through my ear, which did make me a little nervous.

"Are you okay?" I ask.

"No," he says, and then neither of us knows what to say for about the next thirty thousand awkward hours while he gathers himself for whatever is coming next. I listen as he gulps a couple glugs of water down. When he's finished he smacks his lips real loud and goes *awwwwwwww,* like he's seven years old or something.

"Ricky Simpson's family believed in reincarnation," he jumps right in. "Your dad would remember Ricky," he says, sniffling. "Anyway, when we were kids Ricky told me once that he was going to come back as a newborn tree behind the centerfield fence at our neighborhood baseball field, a chance offspring to one of the venerable maples that he would frequently splinter with his towering homerun balls. The kid was scrawny but also somehow strong as a fricking ox." He makes a sort of exaggerated hissing sound and keeps going.

"Ricky died when me and your dad were seniors in high school. I think he'd become Richard by then. One moment he was riding his rusty 10-speed with his signature bundle of newspapers bungied to the back and the next he was flattened beneath the tires of an old boat-sized Buick Park Avenue." More sniffling and snorting is followed by a thwacking spit into what I guess is a nearby trashcan or sink. "Even before the accident the baseball field had already been leveled to make room for a shopping mall, some chain restaurants and a mammoth parking garage. Because the parking garage was the first thing in town higher than four stories, we had very little to compare it to. The only thing I could think of was a gigantic concrete waterslide. All things considered, it was taller and wider than all the outfield trees put together, which I found depressing." His voice grows thin and labored. He takes another sip of water and soldiers on. It's clear he won't stop until he gets all this out.

"It was my very first girlfriend, Melissa Baumgartner, who asked me what my version of heaven would be like. Her family was Catholic, so Catholic they had a plastic statue of the Virgin Mary perched on the lid of their toilet tank. At the time of her question we were fifteen or so, sitting at the foot of her small, fluffy white bed. It was a remarkably soft, clean bed with plush, lacy covers and a knobby brass frame. Heaped against the pillows were endless stuffed dogs and bunny rabbits with blackened limbs. It was the kind of bed that only a verdant, demure midwestern girl could pull off." A series of coughs leaves him surly and frustrated. He pounds his fist down on the table, as if that will put an end to all this hoarse throat business.

"We were sitting with our backs against it, the bed you know, feeding the record player some Fleetwood Mac and maybe some Van Morrison or something. She had just gotten through telling me that in her heaven she would like to have a mansion set atop the highest mountain imaginable, close enough to touch the sun but not so hot she couldn't wear warm clothing and heavy blankets at night. I said I wanted a house situated somewhere near the middle of the Atlantic Ocean, low enough to hear the water slap its rocky foundation but high enough that I could see clear across to the northern most elbow of Africa if I felt like it. We argued for a while, playfully, about which was better, mountains or the ocean, and then we folded in on one another, collapsing to the carpet in a fit of young, sloppy kisses.

"Melissa died from a freak blood clot that had been blooming in her brain without anyone's knowledge, like the spidery cracks that lead to an earthquake. She collapsed outside her front door with the key still dangling in the lock. It seems like an odd thing to mention, but it's true. It's also odd but true that upon hearing the news all I could think about was how much she used to love socks. I remembered them wadded into pear shaped globs in the top drawer of her dresser. You couldn't even close the drawer all the way. She had socks for every occasion—Christmas socks, striped socks, zoo socks, running socks and socks for bumming around the house, skinny gray ones she didn't mind getting dirty. She used to tease me with them the way other girls might tease their boyfriend with different kinds of sexy lingerie. My favorites were the wooliest, fuzziest pair she owned, the peach ones I peeled from her otherwise naked body in her basement one winter morning after church… Thinking of it sends shivers through me. I recall just really, really hoping that wherever she was she was warm." He attempts a laugh, but it gets caught in his throat, and all that comes out are more roiling fits of hacking.

"Shortly after 9-11," he continues before I have a chance to interrupt for a wellness check, "I overheard a bunch of construction workers at a McDonald's talking about what sorts of things they'd crash their planes into if they were suicide bombers. One of them said he'd like to take out the abortion clinic here in Chicago. He even knew the exact address and everything. A buddy of his had told him that they kept the discarded fetuses out back in the dumpster and that some of them had fully formed arms and legs. 'If there's so much as a finger,' he said, the ropey veins in his neck bulging, 'one pinky…' and then he stopped. He was holding his pinky in the air and then he put it down to pick up his burger. He bit into the burger like it had wronged him, like he was getting even." He takes a pause to blow his nose. Afterward, he makes a moaning sound, and curses under his breath. "You don't have any idea where this is going, do you?" I start to answer but he shuts me up, talks right over me. "Don't worry about it. I'm getting there." A growing vibration of sound begins to expand into the phone. "Air conditioner," is all Randy says, then a few prolonged seconds later, "Goddamn it it's hot.

"What was I saying? Oh, right the guys at McDonalds. Well, one of them, one of them is saying something about how he would fly directly into the lobby of the Starbucks headquarters, wherever that was, because he thought their business model was 'gay.' Who is going to pay over two dollars for a cup of coffee, he wanted to know. 'Tinkerbells,' he said, that's who. They made a little toast then, tapping their Styrofoam cups together at the center of the table. The third and final construction worker said he'd like to crash into his ex-wife's forehead. They had deep, brutish laughs. Mashed onions and lettuce juice sprayed from their mouths onto the table.

"I wouldn't mind crashing into a completely empty field. Maybe I'd plow into that parking garage really late at night for Ricky. Or I'd try to find God. I'd track him down, man. I'd ram God in the balls with an enormous Airbus A380. Fuck it," he says. "You'll find out." I strain to listen as I hear him wriggle up from wherever he's sitting and go staggering about his house. He grumbles as he goes, talking to himself in what can only be described as childish, meandering babble. I can't make out whole words because they all run together, one long strand of burbling vowels.

He takes a seat again, flopping down with a shuttering sigh. "Here goes," he says, settling in. "When my doctor gave me the news that I had esophageal cancer, I thought about Ricky and Melissa and those three construction workers at McDonald's. None of them got to choose how they would go. This is assuming the construction workers are still alive or if they aren't, it's because maybe some random piece of metal or lumber came crashing down on their skulls before they had a chance to think. According to my doctor I have some time to think. He, Dr. Bowey, gave me anywhere from six months to a year to think about it.

"The last time I prayed, really, truly prayed, was with Melissa back in tenth grade." This is shocking. What is he saying? All that stuff about constant promising, pleading and evoking, that weird ceaseless ritual mediation he passed down to Lindy, was that all a big fraud? If that wasn't prayer, true prayer, what was it? "We sat on the edge of her bed and prayed," he says, and I can hear in his voice that this memory, whatever it is that it's bringing back to him now, is one of the most pure experiences he's ever had. "We prayed that she wouldn't get pregnant. She wrapped rosary beads around her fingers, made a fist and wept. I could feel the bed shaking, and I pretended it was God doing it. Kids are so good at make believe; it makes me jealous."

I look up at the sound of heavy footfall approaching down the hallway. Dad trudges through the room carrying a glass of whiskey, a cigarette and a stack of mail he intends to sift through over at the kitchen table. He must see my pained expression. If I'm not weeping outwardly, and I might be, I'm definitely starting to crack and ooze apart inside. Whatever the case, he must pick up on something, because he freezes right where he is, and his whole body sort of caves in, it's like a full body frown. Through a series of mouthed words and head tilts, he asks me what's wrong. I put my hand over the mouthpiece and tell him it's Randy. I'll tell him all the details later. I watch his arms go slack at his side, his chest deflate and slump forward. He stands there like that and waits, smoldering, looking like he's on fire from the cigarette smoke and heat, sweat sliding down his neck and shoulders, melting into the floor.

"The first few times I tried to pray after the cancer diagnosis, I prayed for recovery," Randy says, and his voice sounds like dried, dusty soil begging for rain. I want to just pour a glass of water for him and hand it right through the phone, rest it in front of him as a symbol of absolute sorrow. "It was a pathetic, delusional kind of whining and it made me feel horribly dull and proverbial. After a while I came to my senses and tried praying for a neat, happy death in general. I didn't know what that meant, but I thought praying would help me figure it out. The thing was I didn't have the faintest idea how to pray anymore. I'd close my eyes and try to picture something soothing or holy—stained glass windows with the sun shining through or a big wooden cross at the top of a hill with a great big shadow—but nothing would come. A few seconds into a prayer attempt my mind would start wandering all over the place. I kept thinking about my last visit to the doctor. Did Dr. Bowey's voice go up or down when he delivered his analysis of the situation? Did his brow or lips or nostrils suggest anything hopeful or dire? What exactly did he say... how did he say it? Why don't I ever pay attention? I've never been able to focus! Sometimes my grocery list or some other trivial thing will go wafting through my mind, and I'll be useless. A few times a certain celebrity has popped into my head. I don't know how it happened or where it came from. This was a celebrity, a man, that I had seen a thousand times on television or in a movie or on a billboard, in the pages of a tabloid at the grocery store, etc. I'd seen other celebrities do impersonations of him, so I'd seen copies too. I'd seen this man's face a hundred times more than I'd seen the face of Jesus Christ so it made complete sense to me." Dad is standing there, and he starts crying, just like that, like he's somehow extracted the grief, and all of its context, directly from my soul. I am his conduit for melancholy, and unlike so many other times in our history, he allows it to happen. He accepts the weight of emotions from my heart without the slightest hint of hesitation, lets them transfer over to his without ever questioning the motives. It's a meaningful, almost beautiful moment for me.

"I had reoccurring dreams with this celebrity in them," Randy continues. "I should say that this was a man that I had always greatly admired. He was the kind of man every other man wanted to be. If you weren't careful you could imagine this man capable of anything and then you'd wish you were capable of those things too. The man stood for impossible, unattainable things, which was maddening and also strangely inspirational in the most irrational of manners. He was unreal in ways he probably had no clue about. This was a guy, you'd tell yourself, who could pick out his favorite way to spend his afterlife and make it happen, which was ludicrous, but somehow plausible if you let yourself get caught up in things. I mean, not even Jesus got to choose his own death, but still, this celebrity, maybe… Anyway, he'd show up in my dreams."

I can't really talk or even move much at this point, so I just sit there and keep listening as Randy shuffles over to his sink and turns the faucet on. Thank God, I think, relief of some sort, and then I hear him slurping water straight from the spigot, lapping it up like a dog. The sound of the water flow changes from gushing to streaming as he sticks his whole head underneath and lets it just run all down his back and underwear. He talks over the stream. "There was one I had that totally scrambled my brain. This celebrity was watching a movie in my house," he turns the water off and growls with delight. "He was sitting on my sofa and he was looking at my TV. The movie was one that he starred in himself. He was sitting forward, leaning in with his arms on his thighs. I wasn't there. What I mean is that I wasn't physically present. I was watching this scene like someone watching a movie, like someone watching a movie of someone watching a movie, I guess. At some point I see the celebrity on my sofa put his head in his hands. He starts moaning. Something about his performance on the television is making him angry. He can't move his hands because if he sees the screen he'll just get more upset, so he sits there, rocking back and forth, pressing his fingers harder and harder into his eyes. It's then that I notice the most comforting thing. I realize that this celebrity is getting a little fat. I can see a bit of cellulite seeping out below his T-shirt when he rocks forward. His hair has lots of gray patches. And something else—he has really gross, long fingernails with dirt in them." There is a considerable pause, and I watch as Dad puts the mail down on the counter and flicks the cigarette into the sink. He uses the back of his wrist to wipe away some salty combination of sweat and tears. The way he looks, so vulnerable and earnest, I've never in my whole life wanted to hug a person more than I do right now.

"This changes everything for me. This makes everything okay. I'd like to have a little conference with myself, make some kind of peace, but I can't find myself anywhere. I've been misplaced or I'm invisible or faraway or non-existent and it's making me terribly anxious. I notice the television screen is fading. It's like somebody has hit the off button and it's taking an extra-long time to go dark. It's in slow motion. In my mind I am chasing that dimming light on the screen. I want to go where it goes. It's shriveling, the way your pupil shrinks when confronted with intense brightness, only this is the opposite.

This is the opposite of all those stories about glowing orbs of white light and heavenly gates. This is the anti-death and I like it. I want that perfect silence, that undiluted absence of magic and wishing... The screen is almost black. I watch the final dot go hurtling into nothingness and I am stricken mute and breathless. And then the news comes on gently by my ear or the buzzer comes alive, and it grows louder and louder, and the sun rises once more and with it comes my sensible, reborn body."

For a long while there is nothing but silence. I know what's coming next. In his clumsy attempt to keep me from responding or following up on any of his heavy, sulky emotions, he'll hang up before I have a chance to tell him how sorry I am. He won't allow himself to hear me blubber and snivel on about how much I'll miss him or how much I love him in spite of all his failures and blunders. He's done some regrettable things, and still, still I can't believe that this is the way his life will end. Nobody *deserves* to die, do they? I don't think so. Is that a flaw in my character, my unwillingness to accept horrible fates for anyone, even in extreme cases? Soon he will hang up without any space for me to express my sadness and despair, and for that, even for that, I should hold him accountable. I should yell at him. But I can't. I've been noticing that I've never really had it in me to hold grudges or drill down deep into my scorn... my ultimate judgements of others. What I've also noticed is how the people who do have the ability to lather up real rage and indignation over the shortcomings or indiscretions of others, those always seem to be the people with the most to be ashamed of in their own lives. It's like their extreme level of acrimony and their sense of righteousness; it's like a diversion. It's like if I get really loud and angry and I make a commotion about what's wrong with someone else, nobody will look at what's wrong with me. On the other hand, if I am reserved and measured, someone might start to wonder what I'm hiding. And what is so scary about that? Letting people in? We all know, deep down inside, the truth, that we're all hiding something somewhere. And that's human. Our shared burdens, those open secrets, if we allowed them to, should have the power to bring us closer together through our most honest revelations instead of tearing us apart in our most arrogant outrage.

The phone goes dead, just like I knew it would. And maybe that's his offering, his penance for all his wrongs. *I won't let anyone mourn my passing.* Sure, some might say that's a cop out, that it's not enough, but it's so hot, and I'm weak, and all I want is a final chance to say goodbye. In the end, I don't feel it's so much to ask.

Nothing's Too Big (2004)

Standing street level, gazing up at Max perched atop the rusty walkway flanking the huge billboard on the corner of Cicero Avenue and Irving Park Road, I wonder how I let anyone convince me this was a good idea. My only guess is that Mom's lectures on "inner-strength" have been falling on tin ears.

"Be careful," I call up to him in a half-whisper, half-shout that gets immediately swallowed by the vacuum of three a.m. darkness. The only response is a booming cackle followed by the low hiss of spray paint exiting the can.

I'm petrified. My shaking arm throws weak beams of light all over the space yawning between me and Max high above my head. Why do I even have a flashlight? Between the streetlamps, the looming Sears marquee and the glow emanating from the lit display window below, there is already enough illumination for Max to scrawl his ridiculous joke on the blank canvas. Besides, the flashlight is cheap and ineffectual, pulled from the junk drawer of our kitchen cabinets, purchased at the same store that Max now towers above in his freakish endeavor. I switch it off. When I'm less strangled by terror, I'll think more about how my simple, useless efforts feel like a metaphor for my impotent attempts to remedy situations after they've already been blundered, but for now I can't decide if I'm more afraid of being caught by the west side Irish mafia known as the Chicago Police Department or of Max tumbling drunk and leaden to the pavement in a mangled heap of blood and booze.

"Hurry up!" I holler. There is a tense clenching going on in my bowels that I can't control. A tingle runs up the sides of my legs and settles into a sharp pulsing in my groin. I take one more look up at Max. Even through the blackness, from twenty-five feet away, he still looks big and hairy, a clumsy bear bungling through a series of muffed movements far outside their natural habitat.

This is all because I told Max about what Mom said about dreaming large and asking for opulence. Telling Max something humorous or provocative while he is drinking is never a good idea. Once, I saw him drink thirteen bottles of Budweiser, then climb a tree so tall that he couldn't get down. He had to sleep up there until morning when we borrowed a ladder from one of the neighbors and coaxed him down. That time he'd gone berserk because somebody told him that it was possible to get "too high" and he wanted to prove them wrong. Max either doesn't understand the difference between literal and figurative language or he understands it so well that it drives him mad. I should have known better. Shoot, even sober he has an awful time trying to govern his impulses, but when he's drunk he turns into a maniac. So when I told him that my Mom's been talking to me about how God wants people to not just be mildly content with their mediocre aspirations, but instead wants them to be filled with the most bountiful rewards, his brain, which I should have already known, went right to satire and agitation. Those are his resting modes, for Christ's sake. Satire and agitation are the street corners on which Max dwells most of his life. Okay, so why then did I continue on, telling him that Mom's follow-up comment was something about how we should all, "be like an unapologetic billboard advertising our greatest desires?" Don't just ask for a new set of tires for your Chevy, Mom's line of reasoning went, ask for a brand new Mercedes with gold plated hubcaps. Ask for the grandest thing you can imagine. It's the only way you'll ever achieve the astonishing fortunes you deserve. This information was like kindling for the fire burning in Max's helter-skelter brain. I watched as Max mentally filed it away under "material too comical to ignore." You could see it happening. A wired, squiggly grin bloomed across his red face. He pulled the shot glasses down out of the cabinet, the ones shaped like cowboy boots from Wyoming, downed three or four shots of tequila, and an hour later he talked me into driving him here.

He's coming down. I watch as his lumbering body sways down the small ladder attached to the mammoth metal post. Each step is like another wish, a little prayer that he won't miss the next one and go sailing off into oblivion. It's chilly for early September, misty and crisp. An eighteen-wheeler barrels by under the stoplight behind us, oblivious and stern. Its roaring tires churn dampness loose from the pavement, turn the evening air moist and pale under the dim shine of neon bar signs and the brighter lights coming from the Sears' showroom floor.

"That was the most fun I've ever had," Max says, hopping down off the final ladder rung with a heavy thud. His momentum carries him forward and he slams into my chest. "Whoa, boss!" he says, as if he's accusing me of being the one who is acting too careless.

He's covered in sweat, his breath toasty with liquor and unbrushed teeth. The brim of his White Sox cap is covered in abstract stains caused by his animalistic capacity for perspiration. His eyes are wild and gleaming. He licks his lips and swallows. Using his right hand to jam the spray can into his front jean pocket, he smacks me on the back with the other. "Well," he says. "What do you think?"

The slap is hard and stinging. Hot pain shoots down my spine, spreading when it hits my waist, like a river being forked by an enormous rock. I gulp. Looking up into the moonlight, I take in the full breadth of his handy work for the first time. Laughing is the only reaction anyone could have, and against my best efforts, that's what I do. "Well," I say, "it's definitely unapologetic." Another vehicle coasts past behind us. It's only about the fifth one to do so in the past twenty minutes. Fittingly, it's an old Chevy with a rattling engine and dented fenders. Despite my worst fears, not a single driver seems to notice our shenanigans all night. Maybe they just didn't have the energy to care much. A few times I managed to look inside some of the foggy windows, but the only expressions I saw were ones of drowsiness and defeat, unfortunate hallmarks of this Portage Park neighborhood.

"Can you read it?" Max asks.

"Dear God," I read out loud, "Send me a space shuttle. Love, Abundance." I take a few steps back, spreading my hands out like a picture frame, making sure I can fit it all into the shot. He's no artist. It's shoddy but legible, a smattering of black painted letters, the edges of which run like sooty tears down a set of a gigantic white cheeks.

"I wonder where I'll put it when it arrives," Max says, breaking into hysterics. "Ha! Where do people put their space shuttles?"

"Shoot," I say, "I wouldn't worry about that."

"Worry!" Max practically screams. "That's hysterical. Good one!" It's loud and aggressive enough to make me jump.

"Shhh," I say, whipping back and forth to scan for anyone who may have heard him. Off in the distance, I spot what looks like a set of police lights drawing closer. The blue and red disks come flashing through the murky haze surrounding the 7-11 parking lot down Cicero.

"Worry?" he repeats. "Why would I do that? That would be stupid! You know better."

"Yeah, okay, I say, trying to placate him enough to calm him down a little. I'm just about to say, "You're right, let's just get out of here," when he slaps me on the back again. This one feels like a brick cracking against my shoulder blades, and I almost fall to one knee. Crumpling, I look up and still see the cop car getting closer. That's when I realize that the pain from the back slap goes away immediately. It's quickly replaced by the twisting, pinching ache in my crotch, the one borne of deep internal panic and dread. I'm trying to tell Max to run, but all the air is gone from my lungs, and I can't produce any sounds. I'd rather feel the physical searing in my spine instead of the psychological spasms squeezing my mind and balls like a vice, but I can't. The mental anguish is so much worse. Fear is a son of a bitch. It's not something you can outrun or outsmart. That's the craziest part, I want to tell Max; the craziest part is that it's inside you. It's inside me. I'm doing it to myself. I let in. I consented to this.

All Dolled Up (2005)

They've started recognizing her even when she wears her disguise. When I say "they" I mean Mom's new throng of devout followers. At first, after her appearance on The Ellen DeGeneres Show in July, a few people around Lakeview, neighbors we'd never met before, began randomly calling out her name as she got out of her car in the driveway. Once they caught her attention, most of them had no idea what to do next. They'd exclaim their affections without thinking of a follow-up plan. This led to awkward standoffs outside the garage as they both stood smiling at one another in silence until either the visitor turned and scampered away or Mom made an exaggerated show of jangling her keys out of her purse and escaping inside the house. Following her Today Show appearance in August her celebrity appeal fanned out. We'd be at a Shell station downtown and the woman at the pump across from us would approach and ask for an autograph. This usually set off a chain-reaction, and a normal five-minute stop-off for fuel would last an extra half hour as admirers flocked and hemmed us in. But none of this could prepare anyone for the insanity that happened after her interview on the Oprah Winfrey Show a few weeks ago. Now, we're lucky if we can even make it from the porch to the backyard without paparazzi firing off enough snapshots to make us go blind and dizzy from the exploding flashbulbs. Her book is in every window of every store in the entire city; its red emblazoned cover shimmering through the glass like a splash of crimson paint. It's as if everyone in the world is suddenly locked into a bobbing trance, forever looking from the photo on the back jacket to the open void in front of them, praying to glance up and catch a glimpse of the modern messiah known simply as Roberta Blaine. They can't keep enough books on the shelves. If you're not currently holding a copy of *The Shortcut* now it's only because you've either just finished reading it and passed it along or you have a spare one in your bag in case you run into the author. Mom just hired a bodyguard whose sole responsibility it is to make sure that pedestrians don't hurt themselves by walking into oncoming traffic once they catch sight of her. It's a mess. She can't even leave the house anymore unless she is dressed in a huge puffy coat, a large hat and a pair of thick sunglasses. And even still, people notice her. It's the most inconceivable thing. Perhaps they are able to pick up on some studied quark found in her hurried walk, her frantic arm movements or the way she sometimes hollers out in trepidation before she's even officially identified. Whatever the case, it's this issue that has led to Maureen coming over almost every afternoon, playing the role of deranged makeup artist for the stars.

"This blush is extra dark, isn't it?" Mom says. She's had her eyes closed for the past few minutes while Maureen pats on the mud colored makeup with her fat little brush.

Maureen has rolled her stool, with Mom still clutching and shrieking atop it, over in front of the closet door where she believes the full-length mirror will give them the clearest view of her striking profile. The whole space is bathed in fierce white light, beaming down from the ceiling, emanating from the brightest watt bulbs known to mankind. Under the burning glow, Maureen takes on an even greater look of focus and resolve, while Mom's meek posture grows in its reluctant pronouncements. Lindy and I are watching the whole spectacle from the hallway outside the bedroom. Maureen has made it clear that she'd like us to scram, but we (mostly Lindy) have already let her know, through a series of arm-folding gestures and head shaking, that we aren't going anywhere.

Mom blinks and fidgets as Maureen dips around beside her to touch up some of the coloring around her cheeks. "What is that?" Mom asks, referring to whatever is on the brush that Maureen whisks up and down her jaw.

"It's called bronzer," Maureen says in a hurry. The question is treated as a nuisance, something to be swept aside by the makeup brush in her nimble fingers.

"I've heard of bronzer," Mom says, "but this is darker. I look almost… brown." Her reflection in the mirror shows a confused, concerned woman searching for some recognizable word or familiar action to grab ahold of. Finding none, she continues. "Where did I even get this outfit?" she says. She holds her arms up, revealing the dangly sleeves that drape from her elbows and armpits. "I don't remember buying this." Her bewilderment is innocent, almost comical to watch. She looks like a wide-eyed child trying to comprehend Newton's first law of motion.

"I bought it for you last weekend," Maureen says. She puts her brush down on a pallet behind the stool. She scoots around behind Mom and starts crimping her hair, shoveling it up between her knuckles and flouncing it in her palms. "Trust me," she says, "they'll love it." Mom's hair blooms in volume as Maureen kneads away, blossoming into some sort of wild Afro.

"What are you doing now?" Mom says. Her head twirls and tilts under Maureen's motions.

"Please stop asking so many questions," Maureen says. "You asked me to be your stylist, and that's what I'm doing."

"But I've never looked like this before," Mom says.

"Have you ever gone on the Montel Williams Show before?" Maureen asks.

"Well, no, but—"

"You need to appeal to his audience."

"What do you mean his audience?" She is still examining her outfit. The top is gray and black, a bouncy number tied with a garish bow that lays across her breasts like an airy silk scarf. Beneath, a short black dress that hugs her thighs and a pair of knee-high boots with heels and open flaps at the top to allow for minor flexibility. A pair of brash, webbed nylons complete the bold ensemble.

""His crowd."

"What crowd?" Mom asks.

"Please tell me you're not going to make me say it," Maureen says. She stops moving. Her hands are dug so far up inside Mom's hair that it almost looks as if she's burrowed directly into her scalp with her nails.

"Ouch," Mom says, ducking her head away from Maureen's vulture grip.

"Hey!" Lindy says. For a second I think she's going to unfold her arms and attack Maureen, but she backs off.

"His crowd!" Maureen barks. "Jesus, his followers, his gang."

"Gang?" Mom says. "What gang?"

"You know what I mean," she says, "his … urban supporters."

"Oh," Mom says, like she understands, but it's obvious from the way she tilts her head to the side and curls her lips in contemplation, that she doesn't. She raises her arms again, let's them flap down. She looks down at her high suede boots. "But, but I look like … I feel like a hooker."

"Oh come on!" Maureen says. "Are you serious?"

"What?"

"You can't be serious."

"Why can't I?"

"You don't look... You look like... you look erotic, bestial."

"Bestial?"

"Christ, Roberta, you look Black, okay!"

"Black?"

"What don't you understand?" Maureen says.

"Well, I went on Oprah, and you didn't act like this."

"Oprah? Oprah!"

"Yes, Oprah."

"Oprah isn't Black," Maureen says.

"Yes she is," Mom insists. She turns around in her stool to face Maureen.

"Not like Montel Williams, she isn't."

"What does that mean?" Mom asks.

Maureen closes her eyes, clamps her teeth together. "You don't look like a hooker, Roberta. You look ghetto!"

Lindy lets out a cutting, audible gasp. Then, as if on pure reflex, she turns on me, stamps on my foot. People are always trying to hurt me in order to get a reaction, but it only makes me queasy and sad, reminds me how much it takes to awaken even the most basic of my deadened sensations.

"Ow!" I shout. The jolt comes as a two-fold shock, one part injury and one part astonishment at her belief that I will be the one to deliver some kind of recourse, some sort of confrontation. She knows that's her territory. I can't be trusted with these things.

The room is silent for a long while. Lindy folds and re-folds her arms over her chest. She stares acutely, severely at Mom, hoping to use her eyes as a crowbar, something to pry a stirring response out of her. I wiggle my smashed toes, looking on, hoping the same thing Lindy hopes but at my usual lower frequency. Maureen must sense some of our psychic heat because she feels stirred to say something.

"Those types are our primary target markets," she says. "There's nothing wrong with being upfront about who will need this book the most. We're doing them a favor. It's good for them."

"So you say," I speak up, shocking even myself. "You're telling them they need the book, convincing them."

"You're talking semantics here, Clayton. Stop being so strenuous."

Lindy clicks her tongue, raises her foot and holds it over mine, threatening. She is proud of me for saying something, but wants me to know that my job is not finished yet. I slide my foot out of reach. "No, it's not," I say. Lindy nods in support of my action. She cordially lowers her foot gently back to the floor. "It's bigger than that…"

But then I can't continue. I don't know what to say. What are the words for it? How does one explain that if anyone out there knows "what is good" for that population, it definitely isn't Maureen? It seems like when White people are left to decide, they teach self-reliance, optimism and morality. They write new books about overcoming obstacles with your mind. When people of color are given the task, they preach faith, God and resilience. They reach back to a book written thousands of years ago about a cosmic father and son who nobody has ever laid eyes on before. Both of these factions believe they are doing the right thing, but if belief was enough on its own, wouldn't everything be solved by now? According to Mr. Goodwin, nobody seems to be able to hone in on exactly who or what's to blame, and so the wrong people and things end up getting attacked all the time. Willpower is not the problem and neither is hedonism. Those things are byproducts of a much larger network of oppressive policies set in motion, strategically, by relatively few people who don't give a damn about any of the repercussions one way or the other. And that's capitalism on steroids, Goodwin would say. That's how we get the super elite. That's how we got here. Goodwin claims there's already a secret society of rich investors who people are going to start talking about soon, a circle of business owners who currently own an enormous percentage of the country's wealth and they aren't done siphoning it from the rest of us peons. Might never be done, he says, if the rest of us don't do something to stop them. They have more money than they know what to do with and still they cannot be satiated. How do I tell Maureen that she is becoming one of those rich and devious few, linking up with them, taking on their repressive mindset? It's too hard to have these discussions, and so we leave it up to our evangelists and entrepreneurs, which everyone knows are the same thing nowadays. Due to our perpetual fear and discomfort, myself included, this is the best we've come up with since the Book of Genesis. We've just tailored it to fit the next demographic, shortcuts to the same dead-end streets.

Maureen and Mom are frozen in time; Mom looking up at her like a sad young girl wishing to be consoled, and Maureen gazing down, challenging her to question the authority assigned to her by the same person now cowering at her side. We all know what will happen next. The answer is already preordained, the fate long since sealed. Mom turns back toward the mirror, puts her hands on her knees and sighs.

"Finish up what you need to do," Mom whimpers. "We have to get going."

The door opens up out in the family room. I let out a startled, wimpy yelp. Lindy sighs, uncrosses her arms and slaps her own thighs. Damn it, if I don't feel like the biggest idiot. I hate myself for all the times I've startled at the smallest of disruptions; I truly do. In a few moments Dad comes around the corner and into our sight. He takes three or four strides toward us, then stops to survey the scene. He wears a pair of soiled blue jeans, a faded white T-shirt with the collar stretched out. The stubble on his face is indicative of not just his casual thoughts about beard maintenance, but about so many other fastidious issues others deem worthy of the type of time he has no time for. As usual, he looks neither happy nor sad, but simply circumspect. Still, he has a keen eye for these sorts of plots and gatherings. All four of us watch as he looks from Mom to Maureen, than from me and Lindy back to Mom again. He seems to be calculating something in his mind, adding together the variables formed by Mom's odd attire, her strange hairstyle and figuring in the angle of Maureen's doubtless manipulative role in it all… He takes it all in, sums it all up. When he is through putting it all together, when he has reached a satisfying conclusion, he lets us know by issuing two distinct head nods. He transitions from head nods to headshakes. He clears his throat twice, snorts once, scratches the top of his head, then pivots to leave. There is a moment of hesitation where he almost speaks. But then, considering his central audience and the odds of reaching them, he steps back outside and pulls the door shut behind him.

The Other Side (2004)

It finally happens. Dad gives in and agrees to put his sanity aside for the sake of his marriage. It's been a grinding, seesaw battle of stamina and consciousness. At some point, while Lindy and I are sleeping or out of town, Dad lets go of the rope. It must have been different than a standard tug-of-war in that he didn't give up because she was stronger but because strength became secondary to some larger consequence. I picture him pulling harder and harder on his side, his length of realism and logic, hauling his end farther and farther afield until he realizes that one more step will result in yanking his opponent into a cauldron of existential tumult from which there is no escape. He has two choices, give one more tug and send his wife hurtling into a scalding bath of ruination or release his grasp and allow victory to take a backseat to compassion and modesty. He chose some perverse form of valor in the face of domestic anarchy.

To make a long story short, this is why I am now staring out the window at the garage where he roosts beneath a blazing sun, trying to install a skylight on the roof. He's agreed to carve a sunroof into the garage because Mom says he needs to, "let some light into his life." It's something he can handle—a chore that will at once make her happy and give him an excuse to spend more time away from her. It's a win-win or maybe a lose-win-lose-win ... I don't know, but he's out there making it happen. His expression, as he squares the dimensions across the shingles with his tape measure, is one of deep concentration, and also of both duty and artfulness. It's that final description that I choose to focus on as I watch him clamp his cigarette in his lips and hold an imaginary window out in his arms. He sets the hypothetical object on the roof's slant, cropping and patting it down with his hands, and as he leans back to pull the pencil out from his tool belt, I think I catch a brief shimmer of a smile. I'm chuckling to myself, noticing that there are more flasks and tobacco pouches inside the belt than hammers or saws, when Mom throws open the door and comes prancing into the room with two shopping bags in each hand and some sort of gay, rollicking song on her lips.

I don't know whether to call it galloping or skipping or prancing, but she's swishing her hips back and forth hopping from one foot to another with a high knee kick in between. She nearly takes out the lamp on the end table as she goes gamboling into the family room and drops the bags on the rug with a crinkling crash.

"Whoa," I say, "watch out!" She trips over the loops on one of the shopping bags and almost goes tumbling onto the floor.

"Oops!" she says, catching herself on the sofa. When she straightens up she goes right down again, this time doubled over in laughter. The laughter slowly subsides, and with it goes the last few bars of whatever song she'd been singing. "You are not going to believe what happened to me," she says.

"What?" I say.

"You have to sit down," she says. She feels her way around the coffee table and settles down onto one of the couch cushions. "Come on," she says. "Come over here and take a seat."

I do as I'm told. As I move in beside her I notice that there is sweat running down her cheeks and neck. She licks some beads of perspiration away from her mouth like it's no big deal. She waves a hand in front of her face to cool off, and I think I can almost see her heart pounding along to the same jittery rhythm.

"Okay," she says, "now that you're sitting I can tell you. Remember when I told you to dream big and ask the universe for all the riches you can handle?"

Oh no. Of course. I look at the shopping bags fanned out on the carpet. I should have noticed right away. All of them have the famous logo pressed on the front, the blue block lettering with the white stripe curving down the middle. They've added the little tongue of red underneath, just in case we didn't already get the Americana symbolism. Sears, they say, "Good life. Great price." Shit. How could I have forgotten.

"You know the Sears over at Six Corners, right? The big one on Irving and Cicero. Of course you do. You're not stupid. Anyway, I'm over there picking up a few things, and what do I see painted big and bright on the billboard above the store?" Her voice grows higher and more giddy with every syllable. I wonder how much more her heart can take.

I want to tell her that I know exactly what the billboard says. I want to tell her that Max and I chose that exact location because we knew that she'd be shopping there sooner than later. We knew that she'd been shopping at that same Sears for like forty years. It's one of the oldest stores in the entire city. Christ, it's situated on one of the most storied street corners in the history of the city. Six Corners is legendary, a hallmark of Chicago lore. When she was twelve years old, along with every other demure little girl on the west side, her mom used to take her to the exact location to pick up her coats for winter or her supplies for back to school shopping. Max and I knew she still shopped there, couldn't resist the nostalgic allure, the reliance, the loyalty. She'd have to see it. There was no other choice. That was the point.

"There," she continues, arching her arms high above her head for effect, "is this quote. It says something about 'I want a space shuttle.' Something about Dear God… What was it? How did it go? Something about, send me a space shuttle…"

"Dear God," I say, "send me a space shuttle. Love, Abundance."

"That's it!" she says, snapping her fingers. "You saw that too? Isn't it magical? What did I tell you? People are tapping into it, Clay. It's all coming together. They feel it." She puts her hand on my thigh and squeezes. "It made me feel like I'm doing exactly what I'm supposed to be doing. I'm on the right path. God is rewarding me for all of my positive thinking. It's a ripple effect, and…"

"It was Max," I say. I just blab it right out like that, no filter, no explanation. It just comes out.

"What?" She screeches to a complete halt. Her eyes grow big. I see the edges of her lips start to quiver just ever so slightly.

"Max painted that up there."

"Max?"

"Yes."

"Max is into positive thinking?" For a second she almost recovers. Perhaps her deep, dredging meditation has reached even Max, even the most walled off of the non-believers. She's ready to be lifted even higher by her powers.

"No," I say.

"Max? That big boy… the burly one? The one who's always hanging around, eating up all of our chips from the pantry?"

"Yes," I say. "He put it up there because he wanted you to see it."

She leans back, burrowing her spine into the cushions. She steeples her fingers into a prayer formation and rests them on her stomach. This is it, I think. She's ready to admit defeat.

I clench my fists, brace myself against the armrest. "Imagine all of the people who will drive by that and see that amazing message of hope and goodness," she says. "That note of optimism and levity." Her eyes are gone again, off swimming in some enchanted lake of fiction.

"It was a joke," I say. I might as well tell her now. It's already out in the open.

She doesn't hear me. I can tell. She's got her guard up. Nothing penetrates her gate of mysticism and faith when it's up. Instead, it looks like a drawbridge to her own private castle of spiritualism. Her lower teeth go out and over her upper lip as her eyes go blank and distant. Everything goes dim, and she closes up shop for the night. "It's a glorious thing, Max has done," she whispers. "People from all over will see that sign and they will feel the love and light of the world shining down on…"

There is a sound like a massive tree falling onto a car, a great wham of wood and steel crumbling. I jet up off the sofa and run for the window. I throw it open and poke my head outside. "Dad!" I call. He's right where he was before, perched on the edge of the roof with his tool belt, but now there is a gaping hole in the ceiling and the huge pane of glass that had before rested on the slant of the rafters is now missing, shattered somewhere down below.

"Son of a fucking whore dog!" he screams. He unsheathes his hammer from the belt and throws it across the yard where it disappears into a bush. "Goddamn mother fucking mercy stroke!"

"Mom," I say, turning away from the window. She's still just sitting there with that glazed over look, that ten-mile gaze that ends God knows where. "Mom!"

"It's all coming together now," she says.

"Dad broke the skylight," I say. "It's busted, crushed, gone."

"I told him to break through to the other side," she says. A smile creeps across her lips, stretches and grows in jubilation. She starts to laugh, slaps the pillow beside her. "There was something blocking his path. I told him..." she's laughing too hard. "No no..." she gasps, "He told *me*. He told me that he was going to break on through to the other side. Like the Doors! The Doors song. Jim Morrison! That's what I was singing when I came home. I was singing *break on through to the other side!* He did it!" she shouts. "He did it. No more will there be anything standing in our way. He broke the glass ceiling!" She brings her clasped hands up to her mouth and shakes them there in celebration. "We did it," she cries. "We did it, we did it, we did it..."

A Dressing Down (2005)

We find Dad in the shape and place where he can always be found; plodding for the garage, head hung low between two curved palms as he lights his cigarette, shoulders stiff and hunched against some invisible injury that he's either just recalled or imagined is soon to come. He's halfway to the door, hair snarling in the breeze, when Lindy comes shooting out of the house, tromping after him.

"Dad!" she calls. It's a warm day, but gusty, and so her words are blown sideways in the crosswind, diverted. "Dad!" she hollers again, and this time it reaches him. I can tell because he pauses slightly. He's got part of his sleeve up over his mouth to guard against extinguishing his cigarette, and he freezes like that, just for a second; a vampire tableau, cloaking his eyes from sunlight. The hesitation is long enough for Lindy to catch up. "I'm coming with you." In her characteristically blunt style, she tells him instead of asking. I've been catching up, trailing a couple yards behind, and the closer I get the more I'm grateful that Lindy is the one in charge of talking. Both of our desires to flee the troublesome scene of Maureen and Mom's cosmetic debacle were equal, but her ability to act upon them, as usual, far surpassed mine. And because of her audacity, we are now both standing right behind Dad, catching our breath, as he turns and gives himself over to our invasion.

"Okay," he says, or maybe he doesn't say it. Maybe it's only conveyed, an implied response made knowable in the way he shrugs or nods his head in the direction of the garage.

We huddle close in behind him as he opens the door and flips on the light. I think I let out a squeal. I must make some kind of noise because Lindy gives me a look like I've just said something awful, but I haven't hardly opened my mouth. It's just that we don't ever go inside the garage, and it's much more stimulating than I'd thought it would be. I hadn't thought of anything at all. One moment I'm watching Maureen give Mom a vexing makeover in her bedroom, and the next I'm standing inside this odd fortress, this forbidden place that has spent so much time infiltrating my dreams. In my dreams the garage is always a place filled with darkness, a den where all manner of perverse things happen. I picture strange drugs being consumed, weird books of conspiracy stacked on metal shelves, gasoline, dirty rags, pornography… In short, an eerie nightmare made of sinister yearnings. This is what happens when things are hidden from children. They build queer chimeras out of morbid fascination and innocence. Or maybe these things are peculiar, reserved for only the most unusual kind of child…

"You have a refrigerator in here?" Lindy asks with glee. Over in the corner there is a small brown fridge plugged into the wall. It makes a dissonant purring sound. Lindy approaches it without hesitation, swoops in and throws it open. Hungrily, she lurches inside.

"Grab me a beer, will you?" Dad asks. He shuffles over to a tall stool where he climbs up onto it and blows a puff of smoke at the ceiling. There is a wooden workbench beside him and he leans an elbow on it. It's a nice workspace, wide and sanded smooth, free of dust or debris. Above it is a shelf that holds several stacks of notebook paper anchored in place by mounded paperweights. A small radio with a long antenna sits on the top shelf. I wonder what he listens to. Everything is so mundane. In my dream there are no workbenches. No shelves or radios. In their place, I'd imagined some sort of locked chest filled with guns or voodoo dolls… I don't know, whips or chains… something horrifying.

Lindy still crouches in front of the fridge, letting the cold air out. The whole thing is only about two feet high and two feet wide, but she stares deeply into it as if its contents stretch on for acres. "What kind?" she asks.

"Pick a flavor," Dad says, "surprise me." Dad looks at me and laughs. He looks over at Lindy curled by the fridge and smiles, then looks back at me and shakes his head like what is she doing in there? "Are you hungry?" he says. He's looking right at me, but he's talking to Lindy. I don't answer.

"Sure," Lindy says.

"There's some cheese slices in there," Dad says.

"I see them," Lindy says.

"Grab a few for me and Clay."

"Okay," she says, straightening up and closing the door. In one hand she has a silver can of Pabst Blue Ribbon, and in the other she's carrying a stack of bright orange squares wrapped in clear cellophane pouches. She flicks one at me and hands one to Dad. She takes a few steps backward so that she can take in the whole panorama. Keeping her eyes up and scanning, she plucks the cheese out of the wrapper like peeling a banana. "So, this is it," she says, tossing the plastic husk into a wastebasket by the door. Dad doesn't respond much, just pops his can and takes a chug. Could this be it? Could the only thing that resembles malevolent forces inside this place be Dad's poor dietary choice to consume Kraft singles in private? He crosses his legs at the knee and ashes into an old coffee can at his side. Even the coffee can… so homey, so quaint. This is what I've been scared of all this time?

"What is this?" Lindy says as she strolls along the perimeter. She's decided to give herself a walking tour. Running her hand along all the available surfaces, she finds her way over to a wall filled with what look like a row of sharp, hanging weapons. Squeezed in her hand, she raises a forged knife handle attached to a huge, shimmering blade. *Here we go. I knew it.*

"That's a scimitar," Dad says, as if that explains everything. *Oh my God! I don't know if I want to hear this.* I stop just short of putting my hands over my ears… He leans back and inhales. "It's my butcher knife. You use it to cut large pieces of meat. When you see those big steaks sitting inside the cases at the grocery store, they've been cut by that instrument. Steaks don't just come flying off the bone and appear in perfect kidney shaped pieces all by themselves."

Lindy caresses the shank in her hand. She runs a single finger down the serrated edge, almost like she's teasing it. Even though she could easily slice her finger open, Dad doesn't say a word. He takes a sip of his beer. Lindy slips the tip of the knife into the center of the cheese and skewers it like a head on a stick. She forks it to the sky like a great conqueror of men, then clamps it in her teeth like a dog toy. Then she reaches up and puts the knife back where it was dangling. There's a magnetic strip holding it in place with the rest. They sway there, heavy pieces of shadowy steel, lynched implements of the slaughter trade. She bites a hunk out of the cheese and continues pacing.

She walks past the lawnmower and a pile of old newspapers that Dad says he uses to get a flame going in the fireplace come winter. There is a set of golf clubs, an old tire, a few cleaning supplies and a strange looking pole with a saw attached to the end. Dad explains how he uses the contraption to help cut down things called "bag worms" and "tent caterpillars" from high tree branches before they cut off oxygen to the leaves. Everything is ordinary and by the book. There's nothing warped or treacherous in the entire joint.

There is silence as Lindy completes her journey around the space. The only sound is that of the humming fridge and the scrape of Lindy's sneakers on the chalky concrete floor. It's a remarkably tiny space compared to the vast land that had been constructed in my sleep. In my mind it had taken on such monstrous proportions, both in physical dimension and spiritual animus. It's amazing what the brain can conjure left to its own devices. As Lindy makes her way back around the perimeter, she comes to a stop at the window by the door. She stands motionless in front of it for some time before reaching up and gathering something in her hand. Suspended from the lock, in the middle of the glass, is a long silver necklace chain with a little wedge of some sort attached. Lindy has it balled in her palm, cupped there like a fragile egg. She brings it in close to her eyes and studies it. Over her shoulder I see that it is a chipped rectangle of what looks like dried ice. Inside the ice is a series of multi colored flecks. Each color of the rainbow is represented in teeny specks of gravel. When Lindy holds it up to the window it sparkles, tossing beams of yellow, green and blue all over the drafty interior. It's like the little thing is generating heat. Right away it feels warmer inside.

"That's a selenite necklace," Dad says.

Lindy turns around, almost startled. Holding her arms and legs perfectly still; she rolls the pendant around in her fingers. "Where'd you get it?"

Dad takes a big gulp from his beer and sets it down. He wipes some suds away from his mouth with the back of his wrist and licks his lips. He takes a deep breath. There's something remote and reflective about the far off look in his eyes as he takes a few more preparatory swallows. "Mexico," he says. It's said with a sense of relief, like a heavy rock he's been holding onto for a long time and waiting to release.

"Mexico," I say, not knowing if it sounds more like a question or a simple repetition of his own word.

"There's a place in Mexico called the Naica Mine. It's in the Saucillo province." He mashes his cigarette out on the rim of the coffee can. When he's done, he folds his hands in his lap like a proper gentleman might at a posh dinner party. The hands do not fit there. They are rough and raw, as if he's worked them down to the second layer of skin, and has been dealing with them that way for some time. These are the extremities of a tough laborer, the bent, scaly appendages of a man who has spent the last two decades separating rib cages and whittling tendons from stubborn cartilage. "It's almost 136 degrees Fahrenheit inside the mine. Nobody can go down inside unless they wear a special suit and an extra tank of oxygen for emergencies. That crystal that you are holding was retrieved from those caves by a man who wore nothing but a pair of jeans and a soaked T-shirt wrapped around his forehead."

Lindy turns her attention back toward the window just in time to see Maureen and Mom come barging out of the house. Their voices are muffled, but it sounds like Mom is angry with Maureen, scolding her for something as they race down the pathway toward the car. Maureen, in her flowing dress and matching scarf, moves without impediment, practically gliding for the curb in her padded flats. Mom staggers and jerks on her flimsy ankles. The heels she wears are arched and pointy, stabbing the ground like fragile twigs. If she makes it to the car without toppling over, tearing a strap or breaking a kneecap it will be a documented miracle. Cursing and flailing she makes it to the door just in time. She clutches the handle, gripping fast to it like a woman bracing against the looming consequences of a sudden tornado. The only way to tell that this perturbed, flamboyant woman is Roberta Blaine is to have witnessed her coming out of the house led by her close friend and manager, Maureen Johns. There is no other resemblance to the mother I've known, most notably the out of place hat. There's some crude, chichi thing on her head. It's high and peaked with a golden buckle in the middle. Cocked to the side and resting atop a nest of mussed, frazzled hair, she reminds me of an aging pop diva who has spent the last few years strung out on too many Pepsi Colas and tanning beds. After a few awkward moments of Mom thrashing in the street as Maureen wrestles her inside, they are off for the O'Hare Airport then bound for New York City and the Montel Williams Show.

Everyone turns away from the window, recoiling in their own ways from the upheaval swirling just outside our modest sanctuary. None of us has adjusted to this new form of normalcy, and each of us falls into a moment of silence, processing the chaos and mourning the loss of whatever modicum of regularity to which we'd previously clung.

"Dad?" Lindy says in a low, almost somber tone, "when were you in Mexico?"

The distant, rippling look returns to his eyes as he uncrosses his legs and reaches for his pack of smokes in his shirt pocket. He taps one out and lights it. "I guess it's time I tell you guys where I was when I left all those years back."

Instinctively, I go into hyper mode. I find myself overcome with curiosity and enthusiasm. I can't be standing for this! Where can I sit? I dart around the space, shoving hefty jugs of motor oil to the side and wheeling a big toolbox out of the way until I clear enough space to reveal a grimy bucket with a suctioned lid on top. I resist the creeping notion that there could be chopped up body parts inside like in my nightmares, and slide it out. I sit down. Lindy leans on the windowsill, not out of relaxation but out of a fit of desperation in order to keep herself from fainting.

"For years my buddies at work had been telling me about a place called Guerrero Mexico, a little town on the southwest coast." He put his lighter down and re-crossed his legs. "They told me to come down and take a vacation with them. Five or six of them rented a house every year, went down for a week or two in November before Thanksgiving. It's a fantasyland, they told me. Cheap food, cheap clothing, cheap housing. Drink tequila all night long, sleep it off on the beach every morning. Beautiful women everywhere, begging for your affection, just begging for it, they said. You have to fight them off with a stick." He leans his elbows back on the workbench and smiles. Smoke pours from his lips, curls up around his eyes. "They were right. That was all true."

"You went to Mexico for two years," I say, again with no purpose or direction in my tone.

"I left right after the yard sale. You remember. It was 1993, the World Trade Center was destroyed, Waco was on fire ..."

"You had a three year old girl," Lindy says. "Remember that?"

"I do," he says, nodding his head. "Of course."

"You came back in 1995," I say. It would have been just as pertinent to mention that one plus one equals two. He knows how to count his own years...

"The year the death toll in Rwanda reached 2,000 and Bosnia and Croatia signed their first peace treaty."

"Your daughter was almost four."

"I couldn't take it anymore," he says.

"You missed us," I say, offering him some wiggle room the way someone offers to carry a star athlete's books to class. Meekly.

"I was sad and lonely and really, really angry." There is now a burning ferocity glowing in his eyes. He grits his teeth around the cigarette, then blows the smoke away and ashes into the coffee can. "See, the guys were right about all the beauty and fun, the surf and the parties, but they didn't tell me about the other stuff. I don't even think they noticed or cared. See Guerrero is also the place where cartels blow each other's legs and arms off in the middle of the street to mark territory. They didn't want to talk about that. Nobody wants to talk about how the only people with shoes in the whole town were tourists from the US and all the people with the most successful shops in the neighborhood were run by opportunists form Canada, capitalists from Asia or South America. Everyone from outside the country was living the high life while the natives delivered drugs to their beach cottages, polished their shoes in the town square or sold fruit from the back of a pickup truck. They died and went to jail for them, too. That's called colonialism."

"Colonialism?" I ask. I recall learning something about it in Mr. Goodwin's history class, but can't remember the details. Lindy lets go of the window ledge and slides down the wall. She sits on the floor with her knees up, settles in for the remainder of the story. I don't think we've ever heard Dad talk this much in one sitting before. The last time I saw him speak with this much emotion or passion, must have been at the yard sale twelve years ago. This fills me with a sense of mixed elation, equal parts excitement and doom.

"Well, let me tell you a story," he says, leaning forward on his stool. He puts his elbows on his thighs, aiming the cigarette at us like a smoking pistol. "The guy who found and made that necklace over there was an impish, squirrely little man named Dima. Dima was born and raised on the outskirts of Acapulco. His father taught him how to fish for food, his mother taught him how to sell trinkets to rich people from the north, and he taught me how to speak Spanish and drink liquor the way a camel drinks water in the middle of a desert!" He lets out a loud yelp of laughter, slaps his knee in hysterics. Lindy and I both respond with our own involuntary titters, more out of nervousness and confusion than any sort of mutual agreement.

"Dima became a businessman in his own right," Dad continues, "but unlike other entrepreneurs he was the kindest, most compassionate man I have ever known. He spent his days gathering pebbles and gems and crystals, tiny random slivers of colored rock the tide washed in. He picked them, polished them, smoothed them. He carried a suitcase with him lined in velvet. Inside were dozens of twinkling, twirling earrings and bracelets, necklaces … broaches for old ladies who liked to go home to Malibu and tell their grandkids about the 'authentic' Mexican man who custom made a real, tribal piece of jewelry with her name on it. Most of his money he made from selling basic little wedges of splashy sandstone. He was honest about their price, sold them by the handful for five American dollars, little sentiments from a vacation to take home and romanticize, wrap in nostalgia. People were happy to pay him and he was so excited to serve them. He loved making people happy.

True joy. Pure." He folds his hand into a fist, clenches it out in front of him like he himself has been trusted to keep his own sliver of joy safe inside.

He takes a swig of beer. "I got gonorrhea," he says. "One day I wake up on the beach and I feel this burning in my testicles, like someone had lit a match and thrown it down my underwear." This is where a normal speaker might pause or allow some type of reaction, but he doesn't let up. There would be hesitation at the prospect of speaking this way to one's own children, demureness, some signal of apology. But he is on a roll. There is no slowing down. Instead he keeps right on talking, as if he's engaged in nothing more than a discussion of basic breaking methods with a teenager out practicing driving for the first time. "And the urinating… forget about it. May as well have been trying to pass a piece of hot charcoal. Well, I have no experience with this. Foreign land, foreign problem, no reference. Of course I go to Dima. Dima will fix things. I know he'll understand what to do. The man is filled with this beautiful, cultural, practical… knowing. He's got the kind of knowledge a man could spend eighteen years trying to obtain at every ivy league college in America, and never touch his wisdom." He shakes his head, calling up the memory in his mind. He chuckles, puts his cigarette out. "Hot rocks," he says. "Dima gives me hot rocks to mend my hot crotch. Fighting fire with fire. For the next three days, Dima tells me to lie on my back, a mummy in tomb he says, and place two smoldering pieces of something called hematite, straight out of the oven, directly on either side of my groin. Hematite is like this dusty, gray, flaky rock that looks like it comes from the bottom of a volcano. But I take my diagnosis. I perform my prescribed corrective. " He lies back, sticks his feet straight out in front of him, and crosses his arms over his chest. "I lie like this for three days, hot rocks setting fire to my testes and penis... meditating. Meditating, Dima tells me, means thinking and chanting, 'stay healthy, stay healthy, stay healthy...' Stay," he intones, shaking his head. "Stay. *Stay* healthy. I've got some festering STD and... Oh, man. Wow, Dima." He pulls his legs back in and sits up straight. Closing his eyes, he takes one enormous breath and releases it slowly. He opens his eyes. "Three days later I can hardly pee without screaming. My nuts are the size of baseballs. Nothing. Dima believed." He says it stressing the "lieve" part with anguish. "I couldn't tell him that it was a crock. He believed with honesty. His truth was rocks. I couldn't say anything. Day four I go to this little drug store and speak just enough Spanish for the pharmacist to take mercy on me and hand me this white bottle of pills with no label. Charges me four American dollars. I pop em', and in five days I'm healed. I'm pissing with so much ease that I can't even remember what it was like to have pain. I'm pissing like it's my duty, like I'm performing some kind of God given right! But it was too late."

This is when I realize that I have been stuck in some sort of stoned silence for the past five minutes. I find that at some point, I began biting into my cheese slice, but never completed the process. I've got one small corner of the orange square in my teeth, and the other half tweezed in my hand, a freeze frame of a boy in shock. I clamp down, releasing the soft, waxy cheese, and begin chewing. The digestion comes just as slowly as the gnashing and comes with its own detail. It's a thought with a side-thought, attached to a deep rumination that has never occurred to me before. This is the food of the dispossessed, the poor and earthy. Dad eats this cheese, not because he loves the taste, but because it suits him, says something about his rustic, gritty stance against flamboyance and decadence. It's practically a protest meal. Kraft singles are the food of the dissidents, the guerillas, the Dimas of the world.

"What was too late?" Lindy asks in a hushed reverence. She squeezes her knees up tight against her chin, creating a sound like a broom whisking the hard floor.

"See, what I had noticed when Dima first spoke to me on the beach about my ailment, when he gave me that primitive advice… what I looked back later and realized, was that there was another rubberneck nearby. This day-tripper, some guy named Liam. Liam was from England, I think. He came to Mexico to unwind and unplug, so he said. He wanted to experience the real Mexico. Fuck Cancun and Cozumel, fuck the tourist traps and spring breaks. Yeah, that was Liam." He takes another sip of his beer, then crushes it in his fist and sets it behind him on the workbench. "Two weeks go by after my talk with Dima about healing crystals and sacred rocks. Two weeks. Liam opens his own 'Rock Stand' on the beach. Only a visitor would say rock stand, only a phony. He opens this stand right on the eastern point of the peninsula, where all the big spenders settle in. This asshole has no idea that the rocks I used didn't work. He never checked back in to find out. He doesn't care. Why should he? He's on a mission. See, what shady little Liam with his pseudo accent, his London Fog hairstyle and brown teeth didn't tell us, was that he wasn't there as an admirer like he claimed, he was there as an investor." Dad holds his hands high above his head, frames them there like holding a wide wooden sign. "The placard read, 'Liam's Higher Ground. Rocks and Gems to suit all your theological and therapeutic needs.' He makes this really elaborate sign, this perfectly square design, all whitewashed in this thick white paint and edged in this slender black line with just a teeny crack at the bottom…" He is transfixed, reimagining the display, half admiring the artful delicacy, half cursing the unearned arrogance. And for a moment my mind goes there with him. There is something oddly recognizable about the composition, this description of a bleached white cube that seems to extend downward and inward forever with only one tauntingly small entry point. Or is it a point of exit, of escape? It's all so tempting and yet restrictive, as if it wants to lure you in and keep you out at the same time.

"Shit, this guy, Liam…" Again he goes into his head shaking and eye closing. This is taking a lot out of him. He puts his hands in his lap and looks down at them, perhaps contemplating all the things they have seen and done in the past fifteen years, before Mexico, during, after… "That motherfucker was so *proud* of himself. From the core of him he believed that he had done something good and pure and true… He thought he was helping people. Jesus Christ, the jerk hired Dima. *He* hired Dima. People bought his rocks, ate them up. They bought his promises of health and soothing, gobble, gobble. Made a goddamn fortune! Puts his pretty sign up and smiled his stupid rotten British smile, and… and all of a sudden he's the fucking mayor. What a guy. What a fucking piece of work."

The story is over. That's it. His body is spent and stooped the way one's body is sapped and wasted at the end of a long, harrowing surgery. It must have taken every single ounce of his effort to remove that story, to take out that piece of himself and offer it to us. I've never, ever seen or heard anything like that from him… never. It will take me days to process this, put it into perspective. Right here in this garage, in this his private fortress, he took his greatest risk, with us, with his kids. He is our father. This is happening. Neil Blaine… Neil Blaine simply did not open up this way. Nobody would believe this. It is a marvel beyond all scope and history. It takes everything I have not to just fall apart. I want to hug him and weep, bury my face in his tobacco scented shoulder and bawl. I can hardly contain myself. The cheese is gone. I've eaten all the rest of it in a fit of anxiety and sorrow; something to put in my stomach in hopes it will keep anything else from coming out… This is too much.

"You could have at least called," Lindy says. She stands up in a hurry, making a racket as her shoes clang against an old paint can by her feet. She grabs the doorknob in her hand, using it as a threat. Her emergency exit could not be more convenient. Did she plan this? She is heaving, pulsing. Some sort of fervor and fanaticism courses through her. It's in her eyes and then it streams downward, flexes in her elbows and knuckles. "I wish you would have died from your gonorrhea." And she is already twisting the knob and stepping outside, hurling the door shut in one swift motion. The necklace, swayed by the force, clinks against the window, casting flares of light across the now empty, cavernous space.

Once again Lindy has responded to upsetting stimulation with anger and fury. This is an acceptable response. It's natural. I, on the other hand, am not natural. I am not normal. My reaction is of deep sadness and misery. On the inside, I am withered and exhausted, I am a parasite for his suffering, his empath. I am everyone's empath. And just when I think I cannot take it for one more second, alone here with my father, a man who has just spent the past half hour spilling his guts about a matter that has clearly left him hollowed out and beaten… I see the broken glass on the floor behind him, under the rafters. It's the leftover shards from the skylight project Mom asked him to undertake a few months back. It's just a few pieces; a triangle or two in one corner, a spray of fine crystallized dust sprinkled at his feet. It's right there under his feet, the remnants, the reminders of his failure.

And now this is the dream I'd pictured. I'm inside of it now. This is the nightmare, the one where the garage is simply a vessel, a receptacle for my father's fiendish misfortunes. A garrison of grief I cannot penetrate. What am I going to do? If my sister's rough, blunt measures are of no match, how might my soft, rounded edges prevail as a weapon against this melancholy? They can't. All I can do is look on as he toils away. And nobody would voluntarily submit themselves to this, a waking nightmare? There is only one way to escape the churning agony welling up inside of me. There is only one exit, and for the Blaines, for us, it is the most natural action in the world.

IX. THE SHORTCUT TO YOU

One Way or the Other (2006)

April uses her special, secret cunning on me. She convinces me to come check out her new store in Humboldt Park. It's some kind of gypsy shop, she says, and I don't even ask. I don't ask her what that means, what it's like or why it is, and I definitely don't ask her how she afforded the startup costs. If there's anything I've learned it's that April has her ways, and it's best to just leave it at that. Whatever the case, she hooks me and reels me in. She's calling the place "Leafless," which, I don't know, might be part of the allure. Whatever, the word does something to me, she does something to me…. I'm not sure what I mean by saying her cunning or secret ways… All she really does is call me up and tell me that it would mean a lot to her if I come by and tell her what I think of the space. But there is something in the way she says it. Whether that something is real or imagined, it's enough for me to keep the visit a secret from Sasha. I don't know, maybe it can't be avoided, the lusty implications, the conjuring. Maybe there will always be, for everyone, an unavoidable, erotic button wired to the voice of the girl with whom you first had sex. Perhaps there is a filter that acts as a speech modulation device, so that every word your first-lover speaks, regardless of tone or intent, comes out sounding like an arousing invitation for savage copulation. There's almost no chance of anything happening. April is on the straight and narrow, and I'm in love with Sasha, but that doesn't keep me from fantasizing how the whole dirty spectacle might go down, and for some people, simply the hatching of the idea, means that it may as well have already happened, so I keep my mouth closed.

It's a damp and dreary day, which makes all of the boarded up windows and warped gates along west Division Avenue look even more decrepit and forlorn. The only thing I know about this part of town is that all the 5-point crowns that are spray painted on the side of buildings aren't there because the residents feel like pampered royalty but to signify Latin King territory, one of the biggest, scariest gangs in the whole city. It's all I can do not to reach over and hit the automatic lock function on my console. But, I shouldn't be like that. Sasha has taught me not to jump to any conclusions. Besides, locks won't matter when I come out from April's little gypsy store and find my car's been stripped clear down to the primer and left teetering on cinder blocks. I wish Sasha was here. What is April thinking?

The address she gave me can't be right. If it is, then April's store is nothing more than the garden level apartment of a two-story flat that sits in the middle of what looks like the housing equivalent of a junkyard. There are no livable, workable properties in sight, just broken down remnants that have been scrapped for spare parts. I coast up to the curb, keep my engine running. To my right, a ramshackle Dollar General has been gutted, but not before someone salvaged the clothing racks inside. On the opposite side of the street, a floating door sits fifteen feet off the ground, waiting for someone to return the brick steps that used to lead to the porch. I unfold the paper from my pocket and take one last look at the scribbled address I wrote down last night. I hold it up in front of the dilapidated residence that matches the street number and shake it back and forth, as if I wave it enough times it might start working like a magic wand. But nothing happens. There's still nothing there but a rotting set of stone stairs leading down to a plate glass window draped in cheap bamboo beads and encircled by the type of blinking tube lights usually reserved for seedy liquor stores.

There is no turning back. Once the key is turned off, and the comforting heater with it, I slowly make my way out of the car and onto the craggy surface of the sidewalk. The sensation is like stepping out of a warm bath directly onto a rusty, jagged nail. Everything tells you to recoil, turn back. But I have already been tempted, and am drawn, more or less like a magnet, to the front door where I linger before proceeding. There is a small stenciled sign above the doorframe that reads "Leafless" in gold and orange, which does offer a sort of autumn appeal, and I'm admiring the care she took with this detail, if only because it may be the lone thing I can offer in the way of praise, when I realize that the place is empty inside. I've got my forehead pressed up to the window, and I see a shaggy maroon carpet, a crooked table lamp, some curled posters... a small glass showcase where a cash register sits... but there are no people. A thought occurs to me that maybe it's closed because she is still remodeling, maybe even considering moving locations, and then I spot a large piece of canvas hanging far down in the back corner. It looks like a tarp of some sort... frayed and billowy... what is it covering... I move closer, mashing an eyeball up tight to the pane.

"Ahhhhhhh!" I leap back. High, peeling laughter erupts from beyond the door, and then I see the body attached. It comes popping out from behind a coat rack like some kind of spider woman. It's April. That part is clear. That part is too clear. She's fully naked, and so all of her parts, everything is abundantly clear—from the tangled, knotted hair on her head to the bristly hair below her waist, matted there like a small bird nest tied between her legs, to her hairy knees, her blackened feet and toes… It's all… right there.

She wrenches open the door, some chimes ring out overhead, and she swoops in for a quick bear hug. Despite what I may or may not have pictured before this moment, this is not a seductive encounter. There is far too much confusion and alarm for any sort of amorous exhilaration. She pulls me inside by the wrist and spins me across the carpet in a jolly twirl of elation. Sometime during our second twirl she releases me and I settle where I am launched, dumbfounded in the middle of the enormous Persian style rug with soiled tassels. She stands across from me with her arms spread wide, like what do you think, like tuh dah! There is an absurd moment that follows, one in which I look deeply at her every contour and also try hard to look away at the same time. She still has the firm, streamlined body that I remember admiring so much, but where once the skin ran smooth and silky, it is now covered in course, swirling thickets of black hair. There was even some peeking out from beneath her armpits.

"Well, what do you think?" She asks, bringing her arms and hands clapping back together.

There is a song coming from a small speaker behind the counter. It's a popular one that everyone knows, but one that it takes me a while to figure out in my current dazed state. Sinead O'Connor. That's it. "Nothing Compares 2 U."

"I'm doing a whole thing," she says when I don't reply. "It's a whole marketing and performance thing. It's a blend of different forms. I dig it." Her voice is so steady and sure, that I'm almost comfortable with it for a second, but then I go right back to my state of disarray. There are a few white shelves along the walls, a couple round tables in the back and some low pedestals up front by the window. Almost all of them are completely bare. Maybe her nudity is supposed to match the décor or the other way around…

"It's minimalist," she says. "It's a new promotional strategy. All of the hottest places are doing it."

I bet they are. There certainly won't be any other hot girls willing to take their clothes off and prance around in front of a crowd. Or will there? Am I out of touch? Has the whole world passed me by, gone crazy? I walk over to one of the shelves and pick up a single pair of suede boots. Well, they are more like moccasins to tell the truth. Maybe this is what she meant by "gypsy." The soles are made of soft fabric, I guess for sneaking up on elk in the woods, and there is a turquoise pendant on the side with frilly red sequins. Over in the showcase there are exactly two sets of purple earrings, one feathery, beaded headband, and a handful of stretchy necklaces with chunky plastic peace signs on the end. It's like she's collected the left-over pieces from a small-town art fair and arranged them like insects pinned to some kind of mounting board.

"It's a power move," April says, striding back in front of my view. She basically pirouettes herself so that she's standing face to face with me. "Once people get over the fact that I'm naked, they will feel good about buying things from a strong, confident woman. It's a bold move, but why be any other way? I mean, do you think people thought Playboy would ever make it big when it first started?"

Astoundingly, I'm not thinking about her nude, shapely body. I'm thinking about the store, which is why she asked me to come here in the first place, and not about the tantalizing curve of pale skin that runs from the nape of her neck down to her wonderfully perky breasts with the pinkest, most erect nipples you have ever… Okay, now I'm thinking of her naked-ness. I take two steps back and one giant deep breath. I shake it off, first my head, then shoulders, then hips, legs and feet…

"What is going on in the back there? With the tarp?" I ask, changing the subject.

April smiles, licks her lips, and without even turning around she says, "no roof, no limits."

"You don't have a roof?"

"Does it look like I have a roof?" she says, forcing my gaze back on her, as if she herself is a building in disrepair, missing her own floor, ceiling etc. She stands there motionless for a while, only her mouth and jaw sort of adjusting behind her cheeks, then she slides her hands up onto her hips and poses.

"I don't know what to say," I say. "I'm not… I don't think I'm the one to tell you if this is working or not."

"Then you're the perfect person," she says. "You've always been the perfect person, Clayton. Anytime anyone wants to hear something good and nice and weird, they come to you."

"That doesn't make me want to keep doing it," I say.

"But you will. You always do," she says.

"You might have the wrong idea about strength," I say. "I mean, I guess I don't know about femininity or…"

"That's right, you don't. See, right again. Perfect."

"Is it like feminism? I mean, is it supposed to be…"

""Now, see, now you're messing up," she says. "I'm feeling powerful, and you don't want to… you don't want to…"

"I'm taking your power away."

"You're taking my power away."

"Got it." I nod my head. After a few nods, I just keep my head facing down at my shoes. I make circles on the rug with the tip of my sneaker.

This new idea about feminism, the notion that women should not only be able to but should be encouraged to flaunt their bodies for cultural, political or capital gain seems to me, counterintuitive. Didn't the last wave of feminism ask women to put their clothing back on and concentrate more on sculpting their minds? I understand that they want both things, to be appreciated for their bodies and minds at the same time, but I don't know if the world works that way. In rare cases I'm sure it does, but those are the exceptions rather than the rules. How much time and effort should we all be dumping into the exceptions the world has offered us? Isn't that like focusing all our ingenuity on the one case of a baby being born with three arms, insisting that all future children from now on should be determined to reap the rewards of a three-armed lifestyle? Americans have a knack for looking at irregularities, and attaching an unhealthy, detrimental significance to their liberalizing singularity.

"Now," she says, "let's try this again." She drops her pose and comes toward me, moving in so close that I can smell the sour scent of incense mixed with sweat and oil. "What do you think of the place?"

We don't even take the time to ask if a person with three arms is actually a superior option! What if three-armed people suffer mental anguish and physical abuse as a result of their good fortune? We don't wait to make sure the qualities we are holding up as the ideals are even good things! And what about the fact that women's fixation on beauty is a win for the patriarchy? Oh, you want to make it important that men accept hot women with tight bodies who look good naked? You're going to shove that in men's faces and make sure they take note? No problem. Isn't that what they already want, what they already expect from their women? What kind of progress is that? Do you want the right to take your clothes off or do you want a seat at the table? Choose one. Perhaps some women already tried and lost the argument. People like to talk about the battle of brains versus brawn, but in the end, unfortunately for those with high levels of education, it isn't much of a contest. If it makes them feel any better, it's not much different for men. How many linebackers do you know who have cured diseases or broken down social barriers with their brains rather than their fists?

Sinead O'Connor's voice sounds so broad and soaring, so filled with passion and beauty. *It's been so lonely without you here/Like a bird without a song. Nothing can stop these lonely tears from falling.* "This is such a sad song," I say.

"Awe, see, that's it. You noticed. It's all part of it, the whole thing. This is a special playlist. You could be like one of my little advertising assistants." She walks over behind the counter where the stereo sits and turns the volume up. "Did you know that people are most likely to buy things when they are at their saddest moment?"

I shake my head.

"It's two for the price of one," she says. *All the flowers that you planted mama, in the backyard…* "Well," she says, stretching both palms out on the counter in front of her, "what will it be?"

I move over in front of the glass counter and peer inside the showcase below. I look past the bright, dangly earrings with their cascading wampums, beyond the sparkly discs smeared in constellations, and my eyes settle on a plain brown bracelet. It is one simple strand of brown yarn with a series of tan balls circling the outside like tiny chestnuts. It's the only thing I could see Sasha wanting to wear. I point to it and she bends to reach it out. She holds it out in front of her like somebody asking their dog to lick a treat from their hand. I pluck it up carefully, using my fingers as tweezers. April reaches below the counter and hands me a small paper bag. "How much do I owe you?" I ask.

"The first one is on the house," she says and winks.

"Thanks," I say. And then we just stand there for a few seconds, gaping at one another. "Okay, so, well..." I say. "I guess," and I start hedging toward the door.

"You deserve it," she says, calling after me. I pause and look back at her. "You earned it, Clayton. You're a good kid." We are silent again. I have no idea what to say. "Hey, you just reminded me of something," she says. "Everyone deserves something for free. Come in now and receive your first purchase under ten dollars for no cost at all. Let Leafless lure you in. You're worth it! I have to write that down!" she says, and then she dips below the counter and starts rooting through some paper and pens. Her gnarled hair bobs above the glass top, and through the case below I can see her contorted ribcage and jagged hipbones. She is so completely lovely... Someone is going to hurt her so badly, and I can't be around for it.

I take this moment to make my getaway. I scamper for the door and right as I step across the threshold I try turning to say thank you one last time, but between the bells ringing above, the song's trilling chorus inside and the wind's suction outside... it all gets lost and swept away.

Son of Soothsayer (2000)

Mom's compulsive collecting habits, thank god, have never regressed back to those obsessive years of full-throttle hoarding, but there have been moments of worry. I'm in the middle of one right now. I don't know if anyone else has noticed, but under Mom's rocking chair in her bedroom a warped material structure is taking form. First there was a thin foundation of cheap clothing, a few pairs of underwear from a fire sale at Sears, some wool socks half off for springtime, a garish Hawaiian shirt with a missing button... It's that missing button that concerns me the most. She's gotten to that point again where the allure of a bargain outweighs any sense of practicality, and that is a danger zone for sure. One day it's a missing button on a shirt, the next a broken motor on a blender, then a spare set of snow chains two sizes larger than any tires we own, and after that it's best to just nail some boards over the windows and leave town. What is actually happening is that Mom is slowly adding to that clothing foundation. Atop the shirt lays a level of insulation, a large cardboard case of generic shampoo bottles, then a layer of budget brand ketchup and mustard containers, and then a roof of boxes carrying what appear to be some kind of disposable cameras. It's to the degree now where the seat on the rocking chair has been banked by the mounting debris below, tipped back at a thirty degree angle so that anyone who sits on it finds their knees suddenly raised to chin level, feet arched back so that their soles face the ceiling. This is where Mom reclines in discomfort, bent limbs splayed akimbo, as she yells into the phone.

"It's lost its purpose, Mother!" she shouts. She's got the phone gripped tight in her palm as she wiggles about, trying to find a comfortable position that doesn't make all the blood pool down by her hips. It's Grandma Shirley on the other line, which explains the uproar. Actually, there isn't much of an explanation that I've nailed down or anything, just that when Mom talks to Grandma there is always a certain amount of requisite yelling and agitation that comes with the interaction. I've grown used to it without getting to the bottom of it, which I guess is sort of like a metaphor for everything else in my life if you really think about it... "If it has holes in it, and it doesn't keep the food fresh anymore, what in the hell are you keeping it for?" Mom hollers. She hits such a high pitch that the tremor causes a crack in her vocal cords, and she spends the next few seconds trying to clear the scratch from her throat. "Let's go through this one more time. Now goddamn it," she sprays. She only swears when she talks to her mom. It's just a thing that happens, I guess. The truth is, I don't know what the deal is. I'm not close to Grandma Shirley. Never have been. In fact, I don't know if we've even gone to visit her or vice versa more than ten times in my entire life. "You have five more sealed boxes of freezer bags under the sink, right? Right, okay. Those boxes may or may not be from the disco era, but they're down there if you need them! Christ, and so, in the meantime, you've been using the same fucking freezer bag for two months! That freezer bag has at least three holes in it, you said, but you don't want to just throw it away because, quote, it's not all the way worn through. Do I have that right? It's doing more harm than good, Ma. You are hurting the food. Do you understand that? The thing you want to keep most safe is actually being harmed by the very thing you keep in the house! Do you understand what I am saying?" There is a pause as I assume Grandma Shirley attempts to answer this most loaded of questions. What could the correct answer possibly be? I can only imagine how carefully she chooses her words. Perhaps not. Maybe she likes verbal abuse? She must. This routine has been going on for decades. "Throw it away!" Mom shouts in response to whatever Shirley came up with. "Or... or, you know what? Keep the motherfucker. Keep it. Keep putting your broccoli and carrots and your meats and cheeses in there. May as well use it ten or fifteen more times. The harm's already done, right? Why start caring now? Yeah, why not? Just ignore the fact that every single thing you put in there turns out rotten in a few hours. Try not to think about how one of those goddamn bags costs a nickel, but all the ruined food you've wasted costs fifty dollars, Ma! Do you understand what I'm saying? I can't take this anymore. Ma, Ma, I have to hang up. This is too much. Call me back when you're ready to talk some common sense. Good bye now," she says, and pushes the button to hang up the phone.

Experience tells me that she will need some debriefing time to process and recover, and so I stand up from where I've been eavesdropping in the family room and make my way over to her bedroom door like I've just all of a sudden remembered to ask her something important. "Hey Mom," I say, leaning in the doorway.

She leaps right into action. "Can you believe her?" she snaps. "I mean, can you even imagine? Re-using a fricken plastic bag," she's back to her non-swearing, "for two months with holes all over it." As she squawks and shakes, she begins trying to hoist herself up out of the chair at the same time. "I mean, of all the ridiculous, asinine ..." she is really struggling, feet flailing, elbows digging for purchase on the armrests as the whole apparatus keeps swaying back against the mound of refuse below. "What kind of a moron would keep buying more bags when they already have five more boxes of bags right there in the kitchen? Doesn't she understand basic supply and demand? Can she not tell the difference between cost and value? How many stupid plastic bags does one idiot need?" With this last syllable, she puts all of her might into sling-shotting herself up out of the chair. As her momentum carries her up off the seat, the rockers catch on the pile underneath and by the time Mom comes crashing down, the chair is tilted even farther back, this time jammed up against the wall so that it's not budging any which way. In the end all of her efforts have literally landed her exactly back where she started.

All of the air and anticipation is sucked from the room. In the absence, all that is left is the pure essence of spectacle, and there is no way that anyone could have witnessed it without at least a slight chuckle in response. Well, what starts out as a little chuckle blossoms. I can't stop myself. All at once I'm heaving with laughter. For a moment I am bent over, eyes watering, and when I look back up I am certain that I will be joined by Mom, two hysterical participants caught up in a performance of folly unleashed. By now she must be appreciating either the stark irony involved in her wayward anger at a mother whose ludicrous issue so closely mirrors her own battle she's been waging for years, or at least she has recognized the comical effect of a middle-aged woman trapped inside an unwitting torture device of her own making...

She has not. Instead, she is stone still and fuming, cradled like a small child inside the cruel arms of an inanimate object made for soothing. If there is an opposite expression to one of recognition and connection, that is the one Mom wears on her pale, zapped face. It's a frozen, bug-eyed look that says, "If what you are laughing about is somehow at my fragile, explosive expense, I'd rather die than have you tell me about it."

"Help get me the hell out of here!" she yells.

And if she didn't initially perceive the paradox of the situation, she must have slowly realized it as I came over and gently peeled her from the chair's clutches. She must have been coming to terms with the satire as I bodily hiked her up into my arms and lowered her onto her feet like a baby from its mother's embrace. As she waddles to the bathroom, sniffling and shuffling down the hallway, she must be struck by the whimsical tragedy that has just played out at her own hands. When the door shuts behind her, and she sits on the commode or peers into her own reflection above the sink, she must be thinking about the odd but concentric turn her life has just taken. There is no other conclusion to be drawn, is there? She must be.

St. Joseph (2003)

After about two grueling hours of Mom's grunting and hacking away at the frozen ground with her small, flat shovel, the hole is finally large enough to bury the statue. She wipes the streams of sweat away from her brow and rocks back onto her butt with a thump. She's about all the way worn out.

"I told you I could do it," she says, trying to catch her breath.

I'm not sure if she's talking to me or Dad. I've been pacing around the garden patch, watching the entire spectacle go down. In preparation for the event, I'd wrapped myself in about four layers of sweaters, scarves and coats, hoping to fend off the January wind as it tries to freeze me solid. Dad just showed up about three minutes ago. He's sort of just bobbing over her, letting the wind whip right through his light jacket. The thing is paper-thin. What was he thinking coming out here like that? He's in the mood for acting tough, I guess. Got his spring jacket on, no gloves, pretending that the can of beer he's holding hasn't already turned to ice in the short time he's been outside. Mom shakes her head at him, clucks her tongue. I'm pretty sure now that she's talking to him.

"Guess I'd better go up and call 811. Yep. Better let the utility companies know you might've plowed down so far you struck some oil!" He laughs, takes a swig of beer.

"Don't do that," I say, waddling up beside them. "Don't get us in trouble." My hands have become permanent balls of flesh, molded to the inside of my pocket. I can hardly feel my toes.

"Oh, he's only joking," Mom says. "He likes to give me a hard time about everything." Big plumes of vapor come billowing from her mouth.

I nudge in beside Dad. It's not much of a hole. Looking down at it, I can't believe the size. It must be no deeper than six inches, maybe five inches wide. That's what all the fuss was about? Dad peers down into it, tenses his shoulders as a chill runs down his spine. He's got to get back inside. I can't believe he's made it this long.

"Well, dear," he says, blowing steam into his free palm, "you really showed me. You showed that damn tundra even more. That'll be the last frozen earth that ever messes with Roberta Blaine."

"That's right," Mom says, rolling onto her side to get up. "I'm the boss around these parts."

One more shiver rips through Dad from head to toe and he's had enough. "Okay, well, I have to get back to the Bears game," he says. "It's not as important as making a million dollars or feeding the poor or finding eternal life…."

"It's for the house…" Mom interjects.

"The Bears aren't even playing. This is playoff season. They stank this year!" I reprimand.

"Yeah, okay, okay, well," he says, swatting us both away with the wave of his hands, "you'll have to tell me about it later," Dad cuts us both off. "I'm colder than a bear with no hair. The miracles will have to wait!"

He turns and heads for the lobby door, and right as he reaches for the knob a huge gust of wind comes thrashing through the courtyard, pummeling all of us pretty good. "Aaaaaaaaah," Dad groans, wobbling as he fights booth booze and breeze to the door. "Shit!" he says, and right before he slips inside, "fucking mercy stroke!" The door whams shut behind him.

Mom struggles to her knees and crawls back over the hole. I watch Dad climb the stairs back up to our third story apartment. I can see him through the windows on each floor, hiking faster, taking two or three steps at a time, leaping farther at every turn. Old Mrs. Jergovic, the Polish woman on the second floor, still has her Christmas decorations wrapped around the railings outside her entrance, and as Dad trudges up to her landing, he shakes the whole place, making the green and red lights rattle and fall free from the post as he passes.

Mom unzips her jacket just an inch or two, and fishes her hand inside. When she brings it out there is a small white figurine lying in her fingers. It looks like a tiny man carved from soap. "Saint Joseph," she says, all proud and congested. She lifts it up to the light like a big sparkly coin, then holds it out to me. "Go ahead," she says, "do the honors."

I take it into my fist, squeezing it for warmth. Like the diminutive hole, the statue isn't much to write home about either. "Who was St. Joseph again?" I ask, rolling it around inside my gloves.

"Jesus's father," she responds, a little shocked.

"Oh," I say. "I didn't realize they were the same. I thought you had to do something extra special to be considered a saint."

"You mean like give birth to the most powerful being ever created?"

"Well, he didn't give birth," I say.

"He's the stand-in father," Mom says.

"I know, but technically Mary didn't even give birth. Not the traditional way..." I open my palm and look at it again. Joseph is carrying some kind of water jug in one hand and what looks to be a hamburger in the other. "I didn't even think we were Christians."

"We aren't Catholics."

"So we are Christians, though?"

"Okay!" Mom blurts, "just give me back Joseph."

"No," I say.

"Well, if you're not going to appreciate him, then why are you the one burying him in the ground?"

"Tell me again why we're burying him?"

"He's good luck."

"For growing plants or something?"

"No! Clayton, I told you this already. He looks over your house, makes sure it is sold quickly and by the right owner."

"Because he was Jesus's dad?" I ask.

"Because he just is. He's holy and pious and he doesn't ask so many questions!"

"Shouldn't we at least wrap him in a bag or something? It seems disrespectful…"

"It's fine, Clay. Now come on. It's freezing out here."

"We aren't even selling this apartment. It's not ours. We're trying to buy a house, not sell one," I say.

"Oh, for Pete's sake!" Mom shouts, falling back on one of her non-denominational expletives. "Give me the statue, you little practical brat!" As she swipes for it, I try to close my hand, but she's too fast. Part of her finger catches the statue and when I jerk away, the thing goes flipping up into the air. After about two rotations it comes sailing down and plops right in the hole!

"That's amazing!" I say. "Did you see that? It went right in the hole!"

Mom growls and hisses. She dives for the hole with both hands.

"No!" I say, batting her away. "Don't touch it! That was perfect."

"Clayton! It's standing up!"

"Perfect!"

"It's supposed to be upside down. It won't work unless it's upside down!"

"That doesn't make any sense," I say.

"Would you knock it off!" she screeches. She elbows her way back at the hole, but I manage to stop her again.

"Let me do it!" I say. I pluck the statue out and in one swift movement, I flick it upside down. "There!" I say. I start covering it with the rock hard dirt beside the hole.

"No!" Mom says, and she actually hits me. She swats me right in the ear with the bony part of her knuckles. "He has to be facing toward the house. Toward it!" She wrenches it out of the hole, brushing the dirt away furiously, and pokes him back down at the right angle.

My ear is ringing, but the physical pain is nothing compared to the immense and utter confusion I feel at the fact that my own mother has just struck me! I could have never even imagined! I'm stunned. I bring my hand up to my ear and just sort of touch it, mostly just to check if I'm dreaming, and I see a look in Mom's eyes that lets me know that she is just as surprised as I am, but neither of us has a chance to fully process what has just happened because at that exact moment Dad comes bursting out of the door behind us.

"Earthquake in Mexico!" he hollers. "Colima. Seven-point-six. Just a few miles from Guerrero." He is dressed only in his jeans and T-shirt, and even though he is shaking all over he doesn't look cold. The shaking is from something else, some kind of hysteria. A light goes dim in his eyes. He's not here anymore. Somewhere between the family room and the garden he has removed himself from this place, this temperature, everything. His mind has already carried him south. "Everything is lost," he says. He wags his head slowly back and forth, then looks down at his hands like they have done something to betray him. "Everything," he repeats.

Mom stands straight up from the ground and rushes toward him. She looks steady and almost calm, like she'd been preparing for this moment for a long time. She knows just what to do. First she takes her wool hat off and puts it on his head, then she wraps her arms around him, pressing her whole body into his like a giant blanket. "I'm sorry," she says, I think, but I can't quite make it out. What are they saying? What is going on?

"Dios mio," Dad cries. "todo se ha ido."

"Dad?" I say, but he doesn't answer. I don't know if he can hear me. "Dad?" I say again, but there is no response. He is still talking, jabbering about something. I can't make out any of the words. He's drunk, but this isn't drunk babble like I'm used to. It's like he's speaking in tongues. I've heard about speaking in tongues before. It's something that only the holiest of people are supposed to be able to do. It's reserved for the most glorified... Maybe the St. Joseph statue brought it out of him. Maybe it really does work, just not in the way that Mom thought. My ear hurts. What is happening? "Mom!" I scream. "Dad!" Why won't they answer me? Even in the rarest moments of genuine emotion, the suffering is in a different language. Why? I scramble to the hole and start shoveling dirt over the statue as fast I can. Maybe if I cover it up all of this turmoil... whatever it is... maybe it will all go away! Yeah, it will disappear! I've got the thing totally buried when it hits me … Or does it only start working when it is covered … ? Does it lock things into place? What if once it is completely hidden it just pauses time, keeps everything exactly the way it is right then? Maybe it needs to come out. Oh no. Get it out. Hurry. *Get it out!*

Mercy (2004)

Max counts off four stiff, elongated steps across the worn grass, then pivots and snaps into attention like some kind of rigid soldier, which makes me laugh quite a bit because the similarities between Max and a trained soldier begin and end with the black combat boots they both wear in the summer.

"Don't laugh," Max says. He takes two hulking breaths then puffs his chest full of air and strikes a pose sort of like a slouching gorilla at rest. He doesn't actually say *go ahead and hit me,* but he kind of implies it by the way he nods his head, points his chin down at his stomach and smirks.

"You don't have to do this," I tell him, but he only closes his eyes and takes another breath.

"Do it," April says.

"Yeah, I want to see this," Lindy says.

There is no doubt that a good part of the reason why Max is grunting and posturing in the middle of Horner Park is because Lindy and April are around. He's been talking for weeks about how he knows a special meditation technique that monks use to block out pain. He knows this will get Lindy's attention because of all the praying she has done for comparable reasons, and April will want to see it because she gets amped up about anything that causes torture. This display is a perfect match for all of them. It's like Max is a magician performing a disappearing dog trick for an audience of cats.

"Don't do it like a pussy," April says. "Really hit him."

Of course Max is not the only one on display here. If I mess this up, April will never let me hear the end of it. I still haven't decided if she likes me because she believes she can mold me into the image she has of a virile ass-kicker or because she knows she can't.

I come charging forward, shoulders lowered the way a bull does with its horns. My fist comes swooping from my waist, swinging up like a bag of rocks. The feeling of bone striking Max's abdomen is firm but plump, like punching a frozen pillow. The wind leaves Max's lungs in a sharp gust, like cannon fire. He takes two bumbling steps backward then catches himself on his heels and growls. He opens his eyes and takes a bow.

"Wow. Damn," Lindy says.

"I gave it all I had," I say. "That's as hard as I can hit."

"Well, that leaves a lot of things open for interpretation, but still…" April says, "That was no joke."

"I want to try!" Lindy says.

"Give him a chance to recover," I say.

"No!" she says, disgusted with my suggestion. "I mean, I want to get punched."

Max looks at me and shakes his head, but his words are meant for Lindy. "I don't think that's a good idea," he says.

"I'm not going to hit you," I say.

Something about the way Lindy is dressed, her skimpy white shorts, the New Kids on the Block T-shirt she bought at the thrift store last weekend, her long braided ponytail; it all makes the whole idea seem even more absurd. She can't take a punch looking like that. Has she lost her mind? April isn't much better, leaning up against the swing set in her stone-washed jeans, popping her bubble gum. She's got a lime green Fanny Pack around her willowy waist that looks as if it was made especially for girls like her to put mace and condoms inside. Early nineties fashion is making about its third resurgence in the past decade. One more time and people won't understand the reference anymore. Then what will it mean? No, this isn't something these girls want to mess around with. This is real and present and daring stuff, and we have to make that clear.

"It's not going to happen," Max says, still a little winded, but all in all pretty recovered already. "We're not hitting a girl."

"April can do it," Lindy says.

April stops popping her gum. She reaches into her mouth and stretches the gooey pink gum with her fingers, loops it around her index. "I don't know," she says.

"Come on," Lindy says. "You have the easy part. All you have to do is punch me."

"That's not a good idea," I say.

"Oh, what do you know," Lindy says. "Stay out of it."

I could say that I know a lot. I could remind her that I was the one who just performed the stunt two minutes ago, but it won't matter. Max and I both know that once Lindy and April set their minds to something there is no use trying to change it around. Lindy gives April a look like *are you chicken?* And I already know April won't let that stand.

"If you really think you can handle it," April says. She stabs the gum back inside her mouth and struts over onto the small patch of lawn where we are all waiting. Max has chosen the part of the park where there's plenty of obstacles—a couple of sliding boards, some swings, a set of monkey bars and a tether ball court. Basically, he picked the area where there is the most foot traffic. He's a total exhibitionist, and this style also matches Lindy, but just in a more disconcerting manner. Max wants attention because he feels good about himself, and Lindy wants it for the opposite reason. A few kids have already been hurried away by their disturbed guardians. Only a few parentless children remain behind, stunned and impressionable in their forsakenness. This can't possibly go well.

April rolls the sleeves up on her sweatshirt. It has a bunching and tightening effect on the rest of the garment, pulling it taut across her small but perky breasts. What is wrong with me? Am I more turned on by her animalistic potency or horrified by the prospect of a best friend knocking the guts out of a girl who can't take one more count of abuse? It's all happening too fast to think.

"Okay, well, whoa," Max says, rushing over to get in between them. He looks so huge and beastly towering between them with his arms flapped out, a vulture flanked by two baby robins. "Let's just chill here for a bit. I have to tell you what I did. Let me get you ready."

Lindy could not be more offended. She takes three flailing steps backward, guffawing harder with each step. "You don't think I know how to prepare for this? Have you lost your mind? You're talking to the master," she says. She looks at April for backup, and she does the best she can, shaking her head, tossing her arms up in disgust. "Ephesians 6:18," Lindy says. "Do you even know what that is?" she asks Max.

"No, I don't but…" Max says.

"Exactly. You don't. I've been planning for moments like this for months. I've already lived and survived this moment about eight hundred times. There is nothing I haven't seen or heard already in my devotions or incantations, and you have fake mumbo jumbo crap you saw on a talk show or heard about from some gross cousin, and, and…" Lindy stutters, working up a real fervor, "you don't even know Ephesians!"

There's nothing any of us can say or do. We don't know Ephesians. She has us there, and once Lindy has you on any one, singular point, there are no further points that matter. There is no other discussion to be had.

Lindy clasps her hands together and bows her head. She breathes in through her nose and makes an ostentatious show of cracking her neck. She does something else with her eyes, like some kind of flickering thing with the lids. If she could make her eyes roll back and disappear, this is when she'd do that too, but she hasn't perfected that illusion yet. There's a sort of natural magicianship that I feel she's always had inside of her, but not a professional one, more of a raw, unrefined instinct. She rocks from one foot to another, creating some rhythm to match the prayer that comes next. "Praying at all times in the Spirit, with all prayer and supplication," she begins. She nods her head in time to some deeper beat playing inside her head. "To that end keep alert with all perseverance, making supplication for all the saints."

She repeats this two more times, eyes shut, feet rocking. It is unclear what the rest of us are supposed to be doing. The chanting grows louder and more insistent, like someone calling out for initiation, signaling for something to commence. Still louder it goes, more insistent and agitated. A small Hispanic girl with two skinned knees, an old mealy jacket and two bright blue ribbons tied in her long, dark brown hair, hops up off the swing she's been sitting on and comes bolting for Lindy with her own hands clenched in prayer. She comes toward us pleadingly, like she's petitioning for adoption or something. Where are her parents? April first looks at the little girl in alarm, then at me in a panic and finally at Max for guidance. Max shrugs his shoulders, gives her the same beckoning, triggered look he gave me right before I socked him one. There is a sense that if we don't speed this thing up we'll all regret it. Or maybe if we don't stop we'll feel remorse. Something needs to be done. Motion is imperative. Catching the essence of this perception, April acts on the urge. She turns and, in one decisive blow, rifles her fist directly into the ribcage of Lindy.

There is first a cracking sound from April's shot, followed by a whimpering yowl coming from Lindy, and then Lindy is curled up on the ground bawling.

We all go sprinting to her on the grass. "Are you okay?" April says. "I'm sorry!"

"Lindy," I say. "What's going on? Are you hurt?"

"Can you breathe?" Max asks. "Breathe, Lindy. You're not breathing. Breathe!"

Lindy rolls onto her side and vomits. It comes hot and fast and leaves her groaning in agony. "It hurts," she says. "Oh, it hurts. It wasn't supposed to hurt like this. Not like this." The Hispanic girl takes off like a rocket, barreling up the mossy hill behind us and disappearing over the crest on the other side. A billow of dust lifts from her jacket, trailing behind her in a gray cloud.

"I tried to tell you," Max says, but immediately backs off this line of engagement when April and I glare at him.

April kneels, takes a piece of tissue out of her Fanny Pack and lightly wipes Lindy's lips with it. She must be the first one to notice the change in Lindy, because all at once she stops dabbing and freezes. I wrangle past Max and peer down over April's shoulder. What we both see is an expression of sheer collapse and ruin. She makes a wincing gesture with her lips that reaches all the way up to her eyes. Her whole body sours and shrinks as she works her way up to a seated position. Only now can she breathe with any sort of regularity. A single tear trickles from her eye. "I'm not doing that again," she says, her voice thin and sucked of life.

"I tried to tell you," Max says again, but he's not down there at Lindy's level. He doesn't see her. She's not talking about the punch. She doesn't mean the punch at all.

X. THE SHORTCUT TO LIFE

The Front Door

Saturday morning I have a dream about a wide, glorious field somewhere I've never been before. I am alone in the middle of a brilliant comb of golden wheat, rolling prairie in all directions. Despite what is obviously a splendid, appealing scene, I take on a posture of opposition. I am a portrait of stark contrast, the human antithesis to a patently serene ambiance. For whatever reason I have a premonition, an intuition about some pending calamity. This sensation results in me ducking, crouching into a defensive posture, hands folded above my head as a shield. Then, uncertain if I have brought this on through my own backward, catastrophic mesmerism or if I have merely reacted to an omen I picked up on first, the landscape begins to shrink. Where once was a huge, sprawling meadow, there is suddenly a dissolving wrinkle of black edges, sizzling and rippling toward me, like the sides of a piece of paper curling in on their own lit and burning center. As the rectangle around me diminishes into a square and then nearly a speck, I am consumed by thoughts of whether or not I brought this on myself through unfounded fears or if my cunning instincts simply foresaw the inevitable doom and sounded the alarm. Does it even matter? The fading panorama will soon devour me in its own indifferent deconstruction, its eradication of space, and I am wondering about the motives of an impartial, inanimate universe…

Sounds of someone tripping out a door and banging down the back staircase rouse me awake. I jostle out of slumber, and get to my feet quickly. Before the person has even made it to the second landing, I'm out in the hallway, which is where I hear Lindy moving around in her bedroom. There are sounds of drawers opening and clothing rustling, feet scuffling across the floor. I come around the corner, unsure if my reaction to whatever is going on should be defensive or offensive. Her door is cracked and I nudge it open.

"Whoa!" We both shout in unison. I whip away from the door, pressing myself to the wall outside, as Lindy wraps a bed sheet around her naked body.

"What are you doing?" Lindy asks.

"I don't know. What are you doing? Are you okay?"

There is silence as we listen to whoever is rattling outback, descending the final steps and hopping down to the porch. I hear Lindy stretch into a shirt, then slip into some sweatpants, and then she steps outside and gives me a sort of softened, forgiving look. She doesn't say anything, but goes back inside and leaves the door open. I take this to mean that she is accessible to talk about whatever it is that has just taken place. First I check the surroundings. I'm still a bit groggy, but I'm able to decipher that the coast is clear. Nobody else is stirring in the apartment. Coffee is warm and sitting in the pot, but the liquid is settled and stewing in a way that lets me know it hasn't been touched in awhile. The whole place has that kind of gentle wafting stillness that only comes with the absence of certain adult family members.

I worm into her room, still unsure of what I am about to encounter. "What is going on?" I ask. "What was that sound? Who was that?"

"That was Barry," Lindy says very cool and off-handedly. She's folding up some pillowcases and tossing them into the hamper. I've never heard the name Barry before.

"Who's Barry? Do I know him?"

"I mean," Lindy sighs, "if you've never heard of him, you probably don't know him. He's not somebody you really need to know. I don't even know why I let him in."

"He came by this morning?" I ask.

"He came in last night."

"Last night?" I say. "Where was I? Where was Mom and Dad?"

"Here," she says, "I assume."

"Do Mom and Dad know?"

Lindy rolls her eyes at me, shakes her head. She throws the pillows on the floor. "He came right in through the front door."

"Right," I say, "stupid question. Where are Mom and Dad right now?"

"They're right outside," she says. "Out front." She sort of nods her chin toward the window, and I walk over and peer out. Mom and Dad are both standing right outside on the sidewalk. They're talking to a random woman who has stopped walking her dog, some sort of yappy little Maltese, long enough to chitchat. They are a comical sight. Dad is smoking away as Mom jabbers on, the lady and the dog both edging away, the woman to escape the smoke and the dog anxious to drop the babbling and pick back up with his walking. I'm about to laugh out loud when I see what must be Barry, stumbling and lurching as he tries to put his shoe on. He's got a coat in one hand and a baseball cap in the other, and this is what's making the shoe situation cumbersome. Barry is wearing a pair of ripped jeans and a tight T-shirt that fails to reach the bottom of his jiggly belly. When he manages to get the hat fixed straight it goes on low over his ears, giving him a kind of sun scorched farmer look. There's no way he's from around here. He's the type of dense, rural hick who goes beyond what is reared in even the feeblest of suburbs here. You'd have to go far south to find someone like Barry, Springfield maybe or Johnsonville. In short, this is not at all Lindy's type, and there is humor to be found in this mismatch, and the blunder that is her bumbling lover floundering past a set of parents who could not be any less aware of the production. When I turn around I expect to see Lindy sharing in the awkward but hilarious mishap. Instead, Lindy is crying. She has the comforter wadded up in her hand, and she is leaking tears all over it. This startles me.

"Hey!" I say, coming in close to her. I put my hand on her elbow. "Are you okay? Did he hurt you?"

"We just woke up," she says through sniffles. "It was like almost ten. We slept in for fuck sake. We both just sort of forgot that he was here. We didn't even have an escape plan. We should have needed an escape plan. It should have been a thing." She lowers the blanket to her breasts, then grits her teeth. She pulls at the seams, trying with all of her might to rip it in half. "We woke up, and the sun was shining, and Mom and Dad were right outside the window, and we were like oh shit!" She throws the comforter down on the bed. "I mean, who… how… how the fuck does that happen?" She sits down on the bed, rakes her hands over her face. "I mean, he didn't even have to run out. That was for show or some shit. He could have just put his clothing on, poured some of Dad's coffee and eaten a bowl of Mom's cereal, and what? They wouldn't have even noticed. So, no he didn't hurt me. But that hurts. *That* hurts. The fucking obliviousness. Do you know what I'm saying?"

I don't know what to say or if the question even really needs a direct response, so I just nod my head. I sit down on the bed beside her, and just sit there as she cycles through different emotions, mostly ones of annoyance and wrath. I've learned that during these times it's best to just sort of be around to listen and comfort quietly. She has a way of winding herself down on her own, and sometimes words just get in the way, block the clearing of bad energy.

"Shit," she says after awhile. She stands up, shakes her shoulders back and forth, shimmying about like a tree trying to rid itself of rotten fruit. "Barry," she says. "Ugh. Fucking Barry." I don't say anything, unclear if this is the end of my distant soothing duties or if there is more to come. "I mean, you saw him," she says. "Come on," and then I see a smile start to creep across her face, and I know it's okay.

I laugh, but just a little bit. "He did look like a Barry," I say. "He has that sort of bumbling, dimwitted quality of a Barry. That's unfair. I shouldn't be so hard on a Barry like that. Why do I think that about Barrys?"

"Because you just saw one," she says, trying to hide a smile. "A good magician always trusts his eyes." Now the smile is out in full effect. "Shut up," Lindy says, and she allows herself to laugh along, which is a good sign, and a big relief. "Do you want to make breakfast?" she asks.

"You know I'm good for eggs, but you'll have to make anything else beyond that magnitude."

Lindy smiles and laughs some more. She clears away the last remnants of tears and mucus from her eyes and nose. "You are a lousy fucking cook."

"The fucking worst," I say.

We are on the way out of the room when Lindy pulls up short, causing me to crash into her back in the doorway. It's a very jarring collision. There is something about the prostate

angle of her head and shoulders that I don't like. Uh-oh…
After a small pause in which I quickly, almost artfully, manage
to cycle through dozens of horrible scenarios in my head,
Lindy says, "I didn't have sex with Randy. Nothing happened
at all. He was a total gentleman. I mean gentle in the most
literal sense. It was just that…" She leaves her head hung low,
covers her eyes with both hands. "I just didn't want to tell
Dad, because he was so angry, and, and… I kind of enjoyed
that." She slides her hands up her face, rubs her forehead. Her
posture goes soft, almost mushy. "Do you think I'm insane?"
she asks, and I can hear the tears get caught in her throat.

The release I feel is not merely abstract. It comes with
its own movement and tenor. Bowels disentangle, a knot
unfurls in the pit of my stomach, gurgles to a rest. Thank
God! I knew it! I mean, I had a doubt or two, but I knew it.
Thank God Dad did not slug him, and Mom allowed him to
re-enter the house again. And most importantly, Lindy does
not have to carry any pain or hate around for Randy. Always
trust your eyes…

I take a deep breath, put a light hand on her shoulder. I
squeeze just enough for it to translate, for her to decode my
response, and then, just in case, I squeeze harder. She removes
her hands from her eyes, puts one of them up and grabs my
hand, and we stand like that for a few seconds, smuggling our
mutual affections from one another.

"Okay," she says, already removing her hand before I can
fully soak up what I need from it. She sweeps some hair back
from her ears, smooths it flat on her neck, then right away
goes about tidying herself up, putting herself in order. She
sucks in and then expels a swift breath, claps her hands. "I'll
make pancakes."

Following her own bodily straightening, she walks into the kitchen and immediately goes about squaring things again in her surroundings. Within seconds she has a skillet down, some oil and a spatula. "None of this red meat, violent, hostile bacon or ham bullshit." Her voice has already changed back into its sassy, confident frequency. "According to the psychology of color," she says, spraying the bottom of the pan with extreme gusto, "white is symbolic of progress. Pancakes are a transition food!" She grapples our biggest mixing bowl out of the cabinet, clanks it onto the counter, and I know it's going to be okay. I don't have to say a word, and everything is back to normal again.

A Stitch in Time (1997)

It's confusing. She's either trying to beat the disease or she's attracting money. I guess you could sum up her whole life like that. Today she spends the entire afternoon talking to one of her two cactuses. The other one she ignores. It's another insider trick she's learned in her *Woman's Day* magazine. Her deep belief in the publication's personalized attachment and attention to her needs has long seemed to disregard the fact that it is also viewed by twenty million other readers. She tells the cactus she *does* like all about her diabetes and how much she has always wanted to feel what it was like to be rich before she dies. The other cactus gets none of this monologue. It is forced to sit alone on the windowsill in the bedroom and act like it isn't royally offended.

At night she spends six hours sewing magnets into all of her favorite dresses. *Woman's Day* again. She is quite handy with a thread and needle, and each pocket is only about one inch by one inch in size. Dad brushes his teeth and prepares to climb into bed, but there are dresses all over the mattress. Hold on, she says. Wait. He's peeling them off the comforter anyway, one by one, and draping them over the back of her vanity chair. There's something else, she says. Please wait. So Dad stops. She's contemplating adding more pockets for coins.

"Won't that just make the dress stick together? Won't it all just fold around you like a roll of carpet?" He asks.

"They aren't that kind of magnets," she says.

"I won't ask," he says. "Isn't it heavy?"

"Yes, very," she says. "That's the point. It leaves an impression. Memory."

"I thought the point was recovery," he says.

"Well, if you can't feel it…"

Dad can't bite his tongue. I can see him trying, pressing it up against the inside of his cheeks like a wad of bubble gum. But he can't do it. It's something he's working on. We had a long conversation about it last weekend during our morning breakfast and errand outing. Sometimes he just has to say things that are on his mind, can't help himself, which might be part of the reason why I usually don't say anything. My Dad's role in the family is mess maker, lawbreaker, and mine is innocent bystander.

"You literally work for a healthcare facility," he tells her.

"So?" she says.

"Don't be so stubborn. Use your health insurance. You're making the rest of us feel like liars and snakes. Give us some ammo at least while you can."

Mom walks to her dresser and brings her purse back over to the bed. She opens it and pulls out a bundle of twenties.

"Touch it," she says.

"You know I won't," he says.

"Smell it. Go on. Touch it. Smell it."

"I need to go to bed, Roberta. Not that I'm not glad you're making magical clothing… I am, but… But still. No."

"This is why you're unhappy," she says. "You fight it."

"I'll take the money to the mall tomorrow and spend it if that's what you want. I could use that kind of satisfaction."

"That's not the point," she says.

"Yes it is. We sound like children," he says.

"Here!" she says. "Take it!"

So he does. Before she can even finish her sentence he snatches it right up. "Thank you. Now I can smell it and touch it and rub it all over my body." He starts to. He does a little rumba step, pressing the bills to his heart like a dance partner. Mom turns away, dejected. She picks all the dresses up, folds them over her elbow. "Roberta," Dad says, and he stops dancing. There's a trace of regret and repentance in his eyes. If he had the ability to apologize, the stomach for it, this is when he'd do it. But apologizer is Mom's role. "I really hope you feel better soon." he says. It's the best he can do. "I'm pulling for you. You know that. Look, if there's something I can do to help that's more… tangible… or…" He fails to go on. Instead, he lifts the dresses off the chair and lays them back down again on the bed. "Here," he says. "I'm going to get a little snack and go to the bathroom. Maybe you could get one or two more done, but then I'm going to sleep." Mom doesn't say anything, but it's clear she hears him. Her acknowledgement comes in the form of an ecstatic gesture. As soon as Dad's done talking, she swings her arm down, releasing the dresses, sending them fluttering onto the bed. Then she races to pick back up her needle and thread and begins suturing.

In the kitchen, Dad pours himself a glass of milk. He takes the box of Fig Newtons down from the cupboard above the sink. He pulls three out, stacks them directly on the counter like a set of Lincoln Logs. When he tries to slide the tray back inside the packaging, he can't get it to go. The plastic edge keeps getting caught on the bag's frayed opening. This is the only way he shows his drunkenness tonight. If not for the way he wrangles with the casing, swearing and mumbling as his wobbly knees thump the cabinets below, I could have almost thought he was sober. Some nights are worse than others. After a few minutes of struggle, he gives up, rams the mangled package back up in the cupboard and closes the door.

For the past few minutes I've been standing in front of the fridge with the door open, pretending to look for something to eat. The thing is, I don't know what I'm doing other than just trying to stay close to him, I guess. Maybe part of me wants him to say something, even yell at me for letting all the cold air out, but he doesn't seem to notice. When he washes down the final cookie, I charge him. Something in me wants to pummel him, but in a loving way. It's a confounding compulsion, but there's nothing I can do to stop it. I plant a hug on him before he can protest. He's shocked at first, but pretty soon he gives in. It's not his idea of a good time, but he lets me do it for a little while before pulling away. When he goes in the bathroom, I head into the bedroom and give Mom a long hug, too. Then I walk back out and go over to the neglected cactus. I want to comfort it. *There there* I want to tell it. I want to grab it, wrap my whole body around it, burrow my face into it. What would Mom say? Or Dad? The urge is almost overwhelming. Almost.

For My Final Trick

In order to saw a woman in half you need a standard hand saw, some fake plastic feet for "flashing," a few strategically placed sight markers only visible to the performers, a six foot wooden box with a false edge halfway inside, and some spiffy outfits that make the magician and assistant look legit, something with bowties, cummerbunds and cleavage. But, most importantly, you need an incredibly encouraging and understanding sidekick like Sasha.

"I can't believe we painted those silly ass white feet black," Sasha says as we are standing backstage at the Raven Theater in Rogers Park. The hilarity of the situation has picked a weird time to dawn on her. We have fifteen minutes until show time, and she's doubled over, hissing giggles through her clenched teeth. She tries so hard to keep the snickers in that tears start dripping down her eyes, messing up her mascara. "I'm sorry," she says, blotting her eyes. She's taken the liberty of adding some gold and silver glitter makeup to her cheeks. I don't know how she came up with the idea, but it works. She looks so superstar. "But look, look," she whispers, pointing at the clunky fake feet shoved inside the box's spring-loaded end. "The paint is chipping off. Motherfuckers look like Michael Jackson's feet." I can't help but laugh at this too, but I'm also nervous and anxious as hell, and so I try to shush her and validate her at the same time, which kind of makes me feel like I'm going to pee my pants.

Sasha is the one who made me sign up for this thing in first place. We saw a flyer posted at The Grind café in Lincoln

Square about two weeks ago. Sasha took one look at the corny poster tacked up on the wall, all glossy and schlocky with a cartoon man pulling a rabbit from a top hat, ripped off the little tag at the bottom displaying a phone number and email address, and didn't drop the issue until I said yes.

"You have to do this," Sasha insisted as we sat down at a table by the window. Outside a line of middle-aged foot traffic mosey on by, many of whom are young parents pushing strollers. It's a quaint part of town, but one that most often brings images of yuppies or bourgeois to the mind, but they also tend to be the wealthy philanthropist types. According to polling data, last election ninety-eight percent of them voted democrat. Historically, older German immigrants were the ones that took up residence here, but the only things left from that era are a kitschy sausage restaurant and a plaque in the center of the square with Dutch writing. Anyway, all of these categories, including some old dragging German couples, are represented on this day, but Sasha doesn't notice because she's facing the counter. She wouldn't have cared much even if she had noticed.

"I haven't even worked on any tricks in like... forever."

"It's gotta be like falling off a bike," Sasha says. "You don't forget that shit."

"I can only really do like one impressive trick," I say. "And I don't have an assistant anymore." I crossed my fingers, hoping I wouldn't have to tell her about how April was my previous assistant. Try explaining April's and my relationship in any sort of coherent or condensed manner.

"What is it?" Sasha asks. "What's this big trick?"

"Saw a lady in half," I say.

"What? What?" Sasha yelps, tapping her chest. Her voice is too loud for this low key, Caucasian brunch crowd, and she relishes every look she gets. She shrugs, throws her arms up. "Am I not a lady? I can't get my ass cut in two?"

I laugh, reach across the table and grab her arm, yank it down. "Shhhh," I say.

"Naw, don't do that. Don't shush me," she says. "If I'm going to get chopped in half, I don't need someone telling me to keep the noise down. That's not cool."

"Okay, okay," I say, laughing. She puts her hands down and takes a sip of her coffee. I take a sip of mine too, shake my head. "Jesus, I thought you said that you didn't want to be like my great Black savior or whatever."

"I'm not," Sasha says, "Don't, okay. That's not what I'm doing. You got this twisted." She puts her mug down. She reaches her hand across the table and I take it. "Listen, for real," she says. "This is your dream. And first of all, I don't want you giving up on that dream for anything, especially not me, Ms. Black Mother Teresa. You heard? Secondly, I think it's kind of sexy to be a magician. That shit turns me on." She flutters her eyelashes, winks. I laugh again, and she shifts back into her serious mode. "Seriously, though," she says. "I really want you to do this. It'll be good for you. You'd do the same for me." She squeezes my hand extra tight so that I'll agree to her statement. I nod. Of course, I tell her. Of course. "We can work together, you know, share in the experience."

I'm overwhelmed with how much I love her in this moment. "You are something else," I say.

"Don't forget it," she says.

"I'll do it, but you should know this gig is no walk in the park. The box you're going to be stuffing yourself into is no prize. You don't know what you're agreeing to. That thing is old and crusty, filled with cobwebs. You might catch a splinter in one of your tits or something."

Sasha laughs. "You'll have to suck it out if I do." We both laugh, and then Sasha lets go of my hand and folds her arms. "I'm not going to be your assistant though. That word makes me feel weird, like I'm your servant or something. Makes my historical, ancestral senses go all tingly and shit. I want you to call me your partner."

"That sounds like we're gay lovers."

"Don't care."

"What, like Batman and Robin, like partners in crime fighting?"

"I'll fight the fuck out of you right now if you don't agree." She pops her fist in the air as a threat, arches her eyebrow.

"Okay, okay," I say. "Partners. Let's shake on it." I offer her my hand and she takes it. She pulls my whole arm up to her mouth and licks it from wrist to fingers. There is no saying no to this woman.

"We'll have to paint those phony feet," I tell her.

She gives me one of her lathered up looks of impudence. "And do you mind telling me what the hell you're talking about…"

A squirrely looking lady with buckteeth and a clunky headset that's way too big for her face, peeks behind the curtain and tells us we're on in two minutes. Sasha asks me how she looks, and I tell her she looks gorgeous, because that truly is the best word to describe her. She's wearing the same shiny red negligee that April used to wear, only she's filling it out about ten times better, so much better that it's a wardrobe risk. Her boobs are tumbling out of the thing. They look like two big cantaloupes about to spill out of some lacy, scarlet fruit basket. A half hour ago, when I handed her the cape, she put it on without a single quibble, just flapped it over her shoulders without hesitation, and when I asked her to carry the ridiculous wand as a prop, she grabbed hold of it, wrenched it right out of my hand in an instant. I know how much she must loath this charade, but she cares about me so much that she's willing to go on stage dressed like some kind of saucy porno maid, and, well, it makes me so happy that, honestly, I want to cry. She comes toward me, maybe sensing that I'm about to crack, and breaks the tension by leaning into me with her head. What I mean is that she sort of bucks into me, mashing her forehead to mine, and then she kind of scoots me around a little like she's steering me through mind control. It does take my mind off of things because I have to concentrate just to keep from falling over. She wrangles me against the wall and plants a kiss on my cheek. "You're going to rock this," she says.

"Ladies and gentleman," we hear the announcer proclaim, "our next act is going to dazzle and amaze you. If you have a queasy stomach or you just don't like to be blown away by some stellar magic, then I suggest you head for the nearest exit pronto! Because, because… what you are about to witness is a real life man saw a real life woman directly in half right before your very eyes! Everybody give it up for Clayton the Conjurer and his partner, Sasha Spellbound."

As soon as I step in front of the curtain, I can't feel my legs anymore. Sasha comes bounding past me, hooking me in the ribs to get me going. She vaults forward to the edge of the stage, waving and blowing kisses to the audience in grand style. The applause is amplified, ferocious. It just keeps coming, more clapping, more hooting and roaring. It's like one big cascade of noise; so thunderous and jarring that I start to get suspicious of their motives. Are they trying to rumble me right down off the stage? Can't they see that my knees are about to buckle?

The box is right beside me, and I lean on it for support. It sways under my touch, slides to the side on its rolly casters. I didn't tell them to put wheels on the bottom supports. Why did someone do that? Is this even my box? It looks way too small. What kind of a table is that? It looks more like a gurney? What are those legs even made of, Slinkys? That will never hold Sasha. My God. Breathe. Breathe, Clayton…

Picture the audience naked. What kind of advice is that? Who the hell could picture someone nude when they are in the middle of a nervous breakdown? I've never understood that. Picture someone? I can't even see straight. For all I know the entire front row has already stripped down to their underwear and thrown their clothing on stage. My eyesight is so blurry… Is that guy looking at Sasha? Of course he is. Of course he's looking, why wouldn't he? Relax. What is Sasha doing? Something with her hips… some loopty-loop… That's going to really rile them up. Don't do that. Lord, how long have they been cheering? Oh Jesus, Sasha! I never even thought about it before. The last time she was on stage people were throwing bills at her from the seats! How could I have not considered that before? What is wrong with me? I rub my fingers around in both eyes, dig them in good. I have to clear this out. Get a hold of yourself. That's better. I can actually see now. Christ, everyone is white as daffodils. Every single person. This is too much. I know Sasha must be thinking about it. Back on display for all these ignorant, gawking imbeciles. This is too much. Are they still clapping? Is that asshole getting out a dollar from his wallet? I'll kill him! I can't…

"Clayton," Sasha says, circling back around to whisper into my ear. "Here, are you okay?" She twists her back to the crowd, tips her hip to the side like bumping a door shut with one of her butt cheeks. She hands me something that I can't see *because I'm still trying to stare down the piece of shit in the back row with the orange lumberjack beard and the fucking black wallet!*

"Aw!" I scream. Something pierces my elbow, something sharp and searing hot. I leap out of the way, eluding whatever has just burned me, and I come down directly on Sasha's ankle.

"Ouch!" she squeals. She goes down hard, toppling backward into my chest. I'm no match for the momentum. Knees crumble, feet sail free from the floor, and both of us are flailing backward onto the box.

The box comes crashing down so cleanly and with such efficiency, that it's as if we had taken the time to plan the whole thing perfectly. The rolling table takes off across the stage, pushed by some invisible hand, and smashes into the sidewall. The box hits with a resounding shutter, a tree collapsing in a forest, and the lid pops right off. If we had wanted to reveal the entire trick to the audience on purpose, we could not have done a better job of disclosing to them the inner workings of the illusion. It lies open facing the audience; everything exposed, divulged. It's over. On one end they are seeing now the plank where Sasha would have crouched… the board to crunch behind, curling up to avoid the blade. And on the other side, dear viewers, you have the little spurious black feet, flaky and quivering out in the open like two sad, shameful hunks of plaster. There you go, everybody. Good night.

"I was trying to give you the saw," Sasha says, looking up at me from the ground. Her face is contorted in pain, but she still has enough fortitude to give me a little smile. God bless her. Out in the middle of the stage, where all of the ruckus began, there lies the stupid Sears and Roebuck hacksaw. It's the same one Mom bought me ten years ago for my birthday. I look at my elbow. There's a trickle of blood running down my wrist and drizzling onto my absurd magician pants. The wound looks small but angry, a series of jagged, barbarous teeth marks.

My body is flattened next to her ear on the deck. One more inch to the left and I'd have sat on her nose. I pick my leg up and swing it over her torso. I scramble to my feet, crouching over her. The ankle I stepped on does not look good. It's bent upward at a strange angle, like someone's tried folding it in half. "I am so sorry," I say.

She reaches up and grabs me by the collar of my shirt. I brace for impact, but then she glides her finger over to the bowtie on my neck and straightens it. "Don't be," she says, wincing a little. "We had to try. Shit happens. This is life."

The crowd is cycling through the various stages of shock along with us. At first there are a few giggles and applause, then oohs and ahhs, then outright distress and concern. Somebody calls out, "Call 911!"

I fall forward onto my knees, everything drained out of me. It's melodramatic, and she'll hate me for it later, but I can't help myself. I reach down and scoop a hand in under her head. Raising it there in my palm, I gaze deep into her glitter speckled eyes, and tell her I love her for the first time.

Smart Asses (2006)

The Wooden Nickel bar is not accustomed to feisty black women or patrons in wheelchairs, so when I roll Sasha inside with her big blue cast and her penchant for striking entrances, everyone in the bar stops to stare except Drew and Jerry who are in the back by the pinball machines waiting. Drew stands up and whistles.

"Yo, Flynn!" He shouts. "Sasha! Over here."

"Why is he acting like we don't already see his pasty white ass?" Sasha asks as I wheel her inside. Drew and Sasha have what could be called a spirited relationship. They love to bust each other's chops, but it's usually all in good fun. The place is not setup for wheelchair access. I have to loop her around a scattering of chairs and stools, each cluster sloppier than the next. It's a pub-crawl obstacle course. It's pretty crowded for nine o'clock. The floors are already smattered with shucked peanut shells and warm beer. The wheels stick to the tiles as I squeeze her around the pool table. Her foot is wrapped in hardened navy gauze, propped on the foot brace like a pugilist's rod. "Watch out for that Garth Brooks jukebox," she demands. Just for fun, I bang her right into it on purpose. "You are such an asshole," she says, laughing over her shoulder at me.

We pull up alongside the circular table where Drew and Jerry await our arrival. Jerry stands up and comes around the side to greet Sasha. He puts his hand out, but second guesses himself and pulls it back, then he decides to come in for a hug but backs out of that attempt, too. Finally he settles on sort of grabbing her shoulders and giving them a quick little pump. "Have you lost your mind?" Sasha says. "I hurt my ankle, not my hand." She offers her hand to him, but when he goes to take it she rips it away. "Psyche!" she says.

"Oh, good one!" Drew says.

"You know damn well you'd have gotten the same treatment, Drew, so don't even front."

"True, true…" Drew says, slinking back down into his seat like a scolded puppy.

We all take our seats and settle in. Jerry tells us that he's already ordered two shots for each of us and some bottles of Miller Lite as chasers. "That sounds like a horrible idea, Jerry," Sasha says, "wouldn't have expected anything less from you."

Jerry proudly salutes her. "I'm full of horrible ideas."

"The man doesn't lie," Drew says, and the two of them clang their glass steins together for a cheers.

Just as Jerry promised, in a few moments the waitress comes over and sets down all of our drinks. This must be a new girl. I haven't seen her before. She's pretty, but only in that foxy sort of way that all young skinny blond girls are. And those provocative knee-high socks she's wearing, that's cheating. It's an easy trick, an effective one, but still a ploy. She's got that obvious sort of beauty that always makes me question girl's motivations or work ethic. It's not fair, but I can't help all the thoughts that come into my head. She unloads each item one at a time. It takes a long time. When she's finished, she calls out the total price, and everyone just sits there. There's a few seconds of silence before Sasha speaks up.

"Oh hell no," she says.

"I'm the man with the good ideas," Jerry says. "I can't do everything here. Someone else has to be the money man."

"Ha!" Drew says. "Too funny, man."

"We'll figure it out," I tell the waitress. It's too awkward having her just stand there and stare at us. Her eyes are so big and blue. "We'll take care of it, just come back in a little bit." She walks off, and Jerry licks his lips. He's such a pervert. Beside him, Drew rolls up his sleeves, and I think he's about to take charge and offer to pay the bill, but it turns out he's just prepping to move onto a new topic. Not surprising. I wonder how many hits of E he and Drew already took tonight. From the looks of his bloodshot eyes, at least two or three.

"So, old Flynn almost killed you," he says, nodding at Sasha's foot. "That's crazy."

"Bogus," Jerry says, knocking back his first shot. Drew follows right after him. They both slam down their glasses, sigh, and wipe the suds away from their lips with the back of their hands. "Was it right after he said abracadabra?" he asks.

"Didn't even get that far," I say, and I take my first shot. I can't resist the allure of the pattern. Drew pulls a cigarette out of his pack, then Jerry pulls one out, and they both light up at the same time. I want to follow along so badly, but I hold off. It takes every bit of my will power.

"Oh, shit," Drew says. "Not even an abracadabra? That's rough!"

"That's not even a real thing," Sasha says. "That shit's for amateurs."

"No, no," Drew says, "that's legit. That dates back to Old World?"

"Oh, give me a break," Sasha says. She slams back her shot, then chases it right away with a swig of her beer, breaking the pattern. She has no idea how exhilarating that is. I take a drink of my beer, too.

"I was just telling Jerry," Drew says.

"He just told me," Jerry repeats.

"You don't know about abracadabra?" Drew asks me. He takes a stiff pull from his cigarette and blows the smoke out. Somebody has put a few quarters in the pinball machine beside us, and all kinds of bells are going off. There's a tall lanky guy with a leather jacket on who smells like a moldy shower curtain standing right over my left shoulder. I try breathing more through my mouth.

"I don't know what you're talking about," I say in a stuffy voice.

"Abracadabra?" Jerry says, astonished.

"I know what it is," I say, "but that doesn't mean I know what you're talking about." Sasha laughs, and that makes me feel good. Her sense of humor has worn off on me so much over the last few months. I'm even surprising myself.

"Well, okay," Drew says, "you're being smart, fine. But I'm going to tell you about it anyway. Abracadabra is a word that comes from ancient Rome. There was some sage, some guru named Serenus Sammonicus in the 2nd century AD."

This is something new, this Queen's English. I've never heard Drew talk like this before, and neither has Sasha. "Oh, shit. Okay, now!" Sasha says. "Let's go. Go on." But nobody moves. It's like we're waiting for her to give us some added permission… but she's already granted it… Sasha picks up her second shot and tosses it back. We all do exactly the same, being careful to even set the glasses down in unison. When Sasha goes to lift up her beer, we all follow suit, and it is this gesture, this raising of the bottle, that has unlocked the consent. "Keep going!" she says, swishing the beer down her throat.

"Yeah, okay, so this guy," Drew continues, "he writes a book about healing powers. It's called *Liber Medicinalis.*"

"Where did you hear about this?" I ask. I'm totally flabbergasted by this academic jargon. Three weeks ago he was talking about dropping out of school and becoming a plumber. "Are you making this up?"

"You know I take a class on Hebrew languages," Drew says, and it really seems like he's offended. He looks truly hurt. "I'm not an idiot."

"Sorry," I say.

"But you are an ass," Sasha says.

"Boom!" Jerry says.

"Yeah, okay, whatever. Do you want me to go on?"

"By all means," Sasha says.

"There's this disease, and it isn't clear which one exactly, but it's killing a lot of people in this dude's village, so he comes up with a plan. Keep repeating this word, abracadabra. Not only repeat it, but write it down. Start with all of the letters at the top of the page and then keep reciting the word, removing one letter each time you write it below. Continue on until the last letter makes the apex of a cone."

"Freaky, right?" Jerry says.

"Shut up, Jerry," Sasha says.

"When you see that design, wind the paper around some linen cloth and hang it around your neck."

Drew goes to take another swig of his beer, but it's all gone. Jerry picks his up, but when he realizes that he still has some left he gets confused. How come we have different amounts left, he seems to ponder, before pushing it to the side. Moldy Curtain is cursing the pinball machine, humping his hips into the front panel.

"What else? That's it?" Sasha says.

"Oh, come on," Jerry says, "that's pretty good."

"Yeah, but," Sasha says, "that's so, I don't know…. It sounds dumb. I'm sorry, but it's like something out of Harry Potter."

"Harry Potter isn't dumb!" Jerry shouts. He pounds the table for emphasis, and even Moldy Curtain looks over, but he gets no backup from anyone else at the table, and so he gets quiet real quick. You can tell he wishes he hadn't said anything at all. He puts his hand over his mouth, then stares down at his beer, wondering how he's going to get the remaining amount through his covered lips.

"Oh, no, there's more," Drew says.

"Don't be a smart ass," Sasha says.

"I'm not!" Drew insists. "There's an alternative possibility. That's not the only origin story for the word."

"Well, you have to tell us now," I say. I'm really impressed with Drew tonight, and I know everyone can hear it in my voice, but I don't care. It's not often that I feel proud to be friends with these guys, but I feel it now. The thing is, it isn't that they're stupid. They really aren't. They're just very immature. It seems to be a product of our generation. A lot of our parents filled our heads with ideas about being special and unique. They told us things like, "You are perfect just the way you are." The problem is that when they first started telling us, you know, "just the way you are," we were only like thirteen years old, and so we believed them. We stayed just the way we were, thirteen forever. We never changed or grew up. This pertains to many of us, but especially Drew and Jerry.

"So," Drew says, "Its etymology may have also come from an Aramaic phrase, one that uses a particular root form of the word, abraxas, which means 'I create as I speak.'"

This is phenomenal. Even Sasha looks enraptured now. I can tell. She's sort of unwound a little, let her joints hang loosely in her chair. She sits up, takes another lazy sip from her beer.

"You didn't tell me this one," Jerry says.

"Well this theory is a little bit fringe," Drew says. *Fringe?* Look at this guy! Who is he?

"You've really been learning a lot," I tell him.

"It came to pass as it was spoken," Drew responds.

"What does that mean?" I ask.

"Abracadabra," he says. "It came to pass as it was spoken."

"That's incredible," I say. "I really like that."

We are silent for a while, each of us letting the language lesson sink in. Jerry takes his hand away from his mouth, but waits to drink until Sasha and I take a gulp. Drew's eyes are darting all over the bar. I turn and follow his sightline. He's trying to track down the waitress with the blond hair and high socks. He crushes his cigarette in the ashtray. Jerry remembers that his has been smoldering in the tray for a while too, and so he picks his up and mashes his out also.

"You guys want another one?" Drew asks. I do. I really do, but I also don't. I don't think I want the other commotion that goes along with it tonight. I'm not in the mood for all the hijinks and disregard that comes along with accepting another drink. I look over at Sasha. She's still deep in thought.

"But what all that boils down to," she says, "It actually seems pretty simple. I mean, of course everything happens as you speak, right? And also nothing happens, too. It either happens as you speak or it doesn't or it happens in silence. What does it all amount to? Really? Things happen while you are alive and you can pretend they happened because of what you said or because of what you didn't say. Take your pick."

"You make it sound so trivial," Jerry says.

"It's not trivial at all. Life is hugely, vastly consequential, so much so that it seems trivial to try and label it," Sasha says. "Why do we have to profess to control everything all the time?"

"Because we're all a bunch of scared children, right?" I say, wrapping my arm around her.

"You said it," Sasha says.

"I mean, that's cool, fine, if you want to be a smart ass about it," Drew says. Whoa! I can't believe he's challenging Sasha like this. He knows better. The last time he tried to make fun of Sasha was during a game of darts. He told her that she couldn't hit the broadside of a barn door, and so she threw one at his leg and it nicked him right in his thigh. "I guess you're a barn door," she said, and we all laughed like crazy. So now, it's on. In my mind, even Moldy Curtain spins around in utter shock and repulsion at Drew's audacity. There's a whole choreographed production that plays out in my head, one where Sasha flips over the table and sprays Drew in the face with the ketchup bottle … She spins around in her chair. I steel myself in preparation. Jerry covers his ears.

"I do, Drew," she retorts. "I really do." She glides back and forth, gripping the wheels in her firm hands. She twirls once, then leans back to pop a wheelie. This is her favorite trick, an impressive one that it took her all but five minutes to perfect in the hospital hallway. It's quite a subdued response for her. She's proud of herself, you can tell, but aside from the wheelie stunt, she's pretty reserved about it. It's as though she's aged ten years in the few short weeks that have passed since the dart incident.

"Nice!" Jerry says.

After the light, obligatory laughter dies down, there is a stretch of calm. If not for the pinball machine guy or the louder patrons up at the bar, you'd be able to hear Drew and Jerry gulp from their glasses or listen to Sasha as she absently plays with the zipper on her jacket. It's nice, actually. We've reached that point in our relationships when silence is not a burden but a blessing. It's a comfortable, pleasant stillness. And is there anything more comforting in life than that level of familiarity, that intimacy?

"I miss Max," Drew says. The beer moustache coating his upper lip lessens the impact of his confession, but it's still sweet.

"Me too," Jerry says.

Sasha and I agree and nod. We spend a few extra seconds alone with our own thoughts of Max, our images of him as he was and as he is now, a blurry figure in camouflage with a helmet and gun somewhere in the deserts of Iraq.

"He'll be fine," Drew says, still deep in his imagining.

I hope Drew is right of course, but I'm not as sure. The last time we all hungout together was the weekend before Max left for boot camp. He seemed ready for the challenge, resigned to it if not emboldened by it, but he was also scared. Max said he was scared, actually said it out loud, which kind of put the whole evening under a sort of solemn, gloomy pall. I didn't think soldiers were supposed to admit that out loud. Nobody did, but then Max can't help it. That's who he is. Max is probably the most honest, upfront guy we know, which is why we all love him and miss him so much. It's weird because looking back on it, the army seems inevitable for a guy like Max. We all agree on that, but we don't agree on whether or not he'll survive it. Drew and Jerry think that his gung ho attitude mixed with all of his bravado and his adventurous spirit will carry him through, make him an unstoppable moving target, but Sasha and I worry that that these are the same qualities that could lead him to his demise. Sasha and I don't talk about that with Drew and Jerry, but we confide in each other about it all the time. Does being brave make someone more or less likely to encounter death's wanton clutches? I don't know, but if I prayed, I would pray for Max.

"Yeah," Jerry says, "He's going to be just fine. Nothing can stop that guy."

Sasha catches my attention with one of her side-eyed expressions, and I know it's probably about time we get going before she can't hold herself back from saying something that everyone will feel is too blunt or brazen. It's that kind of look…

"I'm getting another drink," Drew says.

"Me too!" Jerry shouts.

Sasha looks over at me and shrugs her shoulders. "It's up to you. I'm good."

"Are we running out the front or the back door tonight?" Jerry asks, sanding his hands together in anticipation like some cartoon villain. There is so much boyish glee on his face…

"My smart ass is going right out the front door," Sasha says, "so you just let me know when you're feeling squirrely." She wheels herself farther back from the table, ratchets into getaway position.

"I'm good, too," I say. I put my hand on the back of her chair and hold it there. The handle is my rock. I put so much pressure on it my knuckles turn pink.

"You are?" Drew says, shocked.

"You're good?" Jerry says, mimicking even his tone.

"I'm good," I say through clenched teeth.

"Are we good?" Jerry asks Drew.

"I don't know, are we?" Drew says.

Everyone pauses in time, waiting for someone to be decisive. I'm thinking Sasha will be the one, but then Jerry speaks up.

"Hey," he says. "How much did you make for that magic show?"

"I don't even want to say," I say.

"How much?" Jerry asks.

"Twenty-nine dollars," Sasha says, smiling. She puts her hand on top of mine.

"And all you got to show for it was a broken ankle. And old Flynn took a couple stitches in the elbow," Drew jokes.

"That's right," I say. And then I get an idea. I stand up, and move behind Sasha's chair. "I'll tell you what. What if I give you the money?"

"Why would you do that?" Drew asks.

"I don't know. I guess because I'd kind of like to get rid of anything attached to the memory, and you guys are short on cash. It's a win-win. You did entertain us tonight with that story," I say. I look down at Sasha, and she reluctantly nods her head in agreement. "And so you earned it." I take out the bills from my wallet and toss the small wad onto the table.

"You sure?" Drew says.

"You don't have to do that," Jerry says.

"Save yourself some danger and foolery tonight," I say.

"That's a hell of a nice gesture, buddy," Drew says.

"That's my man," Sasha says.

"Abracadabra," I say, and everyone laughs.

"Good-bye Jerry and Drew," Sasha says. "You had me going tonight. I admit it. You almost had me. You know I'm a tough crowd."

"The toughest," Drew says.

"Nails," Jerry says.

"Hey, Flynn," Drew says.

"Yeah?" I say.

"We love you, man," he says. He holds his beer up for a toast, and Jerry does the same, and it dawns on me that that is the way I will forever remember them, frozen in a boozy salute.

"I love him, too," Sasha says.

"All right," I say. "You all know I'm awful at this sort of stuff. We should go."

"Are you feeling awkward, Flynn?" Drew teases. "We all love you sooooo much."

"Okay, that's enough." I say.

"I love you," Jerry says.

"We love you," Sasha says, joining in. She's getting a real kick out of this.

"Okay, okay!" I say. "Okay. I'll see you guys later."

"We'll be waiting," Drew says. They are still posed in place, heads and arms fixed in that fresh-faced, exuberant silhouette. It's so American in a way, like a Norman Rockwell if Rockwell did freshman drunkard debauchery.

"I know you will," I say. I nod and begin the process of leading Sasha back through the slalom course of stoned and sloshy teenagers with fake IDs. The cracking peanut shells beneath us sound almost like an added bass rhythm to whatever song is playing on the jukebox, something old but catchy that everyone can sing along to and make fun of at the same time. I steer us all the way to the exit, and right before we go out the door, I stop and look back.

"Oh, Flynn," Sasha says, suspended in the threshold. "You can stay, you know." I know she means it. She wouldn't stop me. Neither one of us are trying to save the other. A few months ago I probably would have gone back and joined them.

Maybe I would have taken Sasha home first and then gone back out and found them at another late night bar or twenty-four hour diner. I didn't have the determination or resolve on my own before I met Sasha. I didn't have the balls. Whether she knows it or not, she has saved me in a way.

"I know," I say. "I know you mean that." I put my foot on the back of the pegs near the base of the tire and tilt her back in a wheelie. "And call me Clayton," I tell her as I roll her clear of the door. I intentionally knock her foot against it one last time to make her laugh, and then we head out into the street, sealing the noise and lights and youthful intoxication behind us.

Stone Garden (2006)

Mother disappears from the garden around 2:30 in the afternoon. I know this because I check the microwave clock as I pour a glass of lemonade, intending to take it out to her as a peace offering. We'd had a bit of a dust up regarding President Bush's veto of the stem cell research bill. My point to her at breakfast was that the research could have helped cure or at least soothe the very disease, diabetes, which had been plaguing her half her life. Why would anyone want to block a procedure that could lead to the end of one's own suffering? Her argument was that messing around with stem cells amounted to playing God, and that nobody should ever tinker with what she called "God's perfect divine creation." If there is to be a cure for anything, her line of thinking goes, then it shall come from our own realm of nature, spirit and alignment, things she deems within the innate boundaries of God's rightful kingdom. The fact that stems cells are the very essence of internal pureness and that they are made of our own raw material, seems to have no effect on her. "It's blasphemy!" she hollered. "If we are made in the image of God, which we are, then we are impeccable already, and there is no reason to look elsewhere outside our own mind or body for anything science cooks up in some test tube laboratory!" At this point she reared back, astounding even herself I think, and hammered her fist down on the table. The problem was that she missed the topside and caught the rigid edge with the rim of her hand, slicing it wide open. Blood poured down her right pinky finger, like yoke trickling from a cracked egg. The red line surged the length of her arm, pooling onto the white shirt she wore beneath her dingy pair of denim overalls.

It wasn't surprising that the gash was so sharp and flayed. For months she's been losing weight, so that now her knees and elbows look more like whittled domes of bone and her fingers are so gaunt that they themselves have begun resembling a set of narrow kitchen knives. The action itself was shocking and regrettable, but not the result. However, it was her next gesture that really filled me with guilt and adrenaline. She raised her hand high over her head again and brought it swinging down for a second round, like an axe going in for another chop at a hunk of wood. I would have tried to stop her, but it caught me so off guard that I didn't have a chance. Just before the hand made contact she pulled up. She brought the hand to a vicious halt about one inch above the table, and then all in one movement, as if it were part of the same mechanical circuitry, she slid the chair back and stomped outside. My shame and sympathy reflex, which I will never be able to fully eradicate from my mind, kicked in immediately, and it was right then that I decided to bring her some kind of apology gift. It was only a matter of time.

Mom's been working in the garden every single day for about three straight weeks now. She does it with some kind of single-mindedness, some sort of compulsion. What I mean is that the activity does not seem to have a calming effect, as most would assume, but almost the opposite. Despite the fact that she sings while crouched over the lilies or whistles as she trims the arborvitae bush, there is a tight-lipped, arch-browed mania that shines through. Instead of casually massaging or tilling the soil, she goes at it with pounding and stabbing motions, acting out some kind of unspoken vengeance. Dad calls it her, "aggravated harmony with the earth." I'm thinking how wonderfully poetic that description is when I take the glass of lemonade out to the garden and find nothing but a pair of crusty leather gloves, a soiled tulip trowel and a few droopy dandelions, weeded and stacked in an oddly meticulous pile at the edge of the grass.

Sometimes the long walk from one side of the house to the other feels insurmountable and almost too ostentatious to bear, but I feel certain that she couldn't have wandered too far, and so begins my orbit around the olive colored siding and double chimneys. I only make it past the first chimney before I hear what sounds like an animal scratching its claws along the backside of the second one. I freeze, lemonade sloshing in my hand. Whatever is back there is big and loud and, by the sound of the hollow thuds clunking against the stone wall, angry as hell. One more second and I'm going to run, shame and reputation be damned, but just as I am about to pivot and flee, a small orange object comes launching out onto the grass. It's cylindrical and rolls for a few feet across the newly mowed lawn before coming to a rest under the bright afternoon sun. I'm still not convinced that a raccoon or badger isn't behind this. Perhaps a large rodent has dislodged some plastic trinket from the ground. I'm still poised to take off, but then I hear a voice. "Shit!" it says.

"Mom?" I say, easing forward. My steps are syncopated and clumsy, two steps at a fast speed followed by two more in slow motion. There is someone crouched, hiding behind the chimney. What is going on? The orange object in the grass is definitely a pill bottle of some sort. I can see the white label wrapped around the side. It's a big bottle, the kind someone might receive who needed more than two months to recover from something like a major car accident or a heart attack. There is a large shadow swaying behind the edge of the chimney.

"No," the voice says, "I mean, yes. I mean… Shit!" Another pill container comes spilling out into the light, and all at once, like some kind of circus performer fired from a cannon, my Mom comes bowling out after the bottles, tripping over one of them and tumbling to the grass. I drop the lemonade and the glass shatters on impact. Her hair is long and matted with leaves sticking from every angle. One of her elbows is caught and bound in the strap of her overalls, making it look like she's missing an arm.

"Mom, what are you doing? What's going on?" She scuttles to her knees, crawling to gather up the bottles into her one free arm.

"I don't… Um, it's just that. Shit!" she's out of breath, and I can't tell if she's been crying or drooling or both, but her words are all moist and slobbery.

"Let me see that," I say reaching down and snatching up one of the bottles before she can grab it. The label says "Klonopin" which gives me no insight into what the hell is going on. I have no idea what that is. The pills are small and round and blue, and it looks like they are almost half gone. I catch a few more descriptions, "500 mg," "take once daily," before she rips the bottle out of my hand.

"Give me those," she says. Her eyes are wide and buggy, full of frenzy and fear.

"What are you doing?" I demand. "What is going on?"

She struggles to her feet, where she stands, insecurely, in the middle of the yard. She does manage to wiggle both arms loose from the restrictive fabric. The bottle is clenched in her fist like some kind of weapon. "I was…" she says, and then all the life goes zapping out of her. She folds in on herself, head swinging down between her knees, and I lunge to catch her, but then she's flailing upright again. "I was abused!" she bursts. "I was molested by my neighbor, and my father never did anything about it."

"I'm sorry?" I say, more out of sheer reflex than any sort of processed response. Did it come out as a question or a command?

"Your dad knows I was abused already."

"Okay?" It strikes me as strange that her first thought is one of mistrust and precaution. As if I was already planning an assault on her character. It stings.

"His father used to abuse him, too. Not sexually, but with his fists." She shakes her fists out in front of me. The one holding the pill bottle makes a rattling sound like a maraca. Her state of being is something I would describe as hyper alert, as if someone has recently jolted her into consciousness using a cattle prod. "Your grandfather once beat a horse to death with his bare hands."

"That doesn't sound possible," I say.

"Exactly!" She shouts. "Can you imagine that kind of strength? Your poor father…"

"You're talking about Dad's dad?" I say, clarifying.

"Obviously," she says, upset that I would ever even inquire about something so ridiculous. "Grandpa Blaine was in the Korean War," she says. This memory takes a lot out of her. She stumbles back a few paces, leans herself against the chimney.

"I know," I say. "What does this have to do—"

"He had horrible nightmares! He had nightmares every night. He still thought he was searching for and killing Koreans."

"Is that why he hit Dad? He thought Dad was a Korean?" I say.

"God only knows what *his* father saw. What kind of horror did your great grandfather know?"

"I don't know," I say. I want to pick up the other pill bottle, but I don't want her to know that I want to. I take a half-step forward and lean down just a little bit.

"And my mom," she says. Her eyes take on an even deeper, darker quality. She is seeing and speaking from the bottom of a very wide gorge somewhere inside her soul. "My mom never even inquired about anything. She never even asked why I suddenly shut down, went from a happy, energetic little girl to a shy, despondent block of wood." Her eyes flutter and twitch as her mind begins the difficult ascent, digging its way upward out of the pit of despair.

I don't know what to say to this. How long do people go on repeating the frailties and failures of their ancestors? Where does it all stop? When? How can we make ourselves aware? What will cause us to wake up?

"Ever hear of the Cherry Coal Mine disaster?" she asks.

"No," I say. I bend a knee, trying to stoop just a little closer to the ground.

"Two hundred forty-seven men died! One of them was your great great grandfather, Marcus Malloy Blaine! 1909. Men are always hurting others and being hurt. I'm just trying to get you to safety, sweetheart." She comes toward me, intending to give me a hug at the same time I reach for the bottle. We almost smack heads. "Whoa!" she says, leaping back. "You want that other bottle, don't you?" she snaps.

I nod my head. I picture my great grandfather Blaine—a sepia toned photo, crinkled and fading, depicting a rugged man with a Stetson and a bushy moustache. I imagine his weathered nickname, "Mad Dog Marcus."

"I'll save you the trouble," she says. She stretches her foot out, covering the bottle, stamping it down into the earth. "I was abused," she says. "They're for my abuse. Your mother was molested when she was five years old, me, and when she was six, seven, eight, nine … It's so painful," she moans. Tears fill her eyes. "You have no idea how hard it is to keep your head up when all day long your thoughts keep going to nightmares. Can you have some sympathy?"

"I do, Mom!" I cry. I'm starting to shake. I can't catch my breath. "I know." I have a sick churning in the pit of my stomach, a mixture of heartbreak and betrayal. Imagine the person you thought you trusted most in the world has just shot you in the gut. "Why didn't you just tell me? I would have understood."

"You can't understand," she says. "How could you possibly?"

"Because I'm your son. I'm me!" I shout. "You should know. Have you even been paying attention? You know I'd be sympathetic. You know I'd support you. How could you do this? After everything. After you told me, in sixth grade, that you couldn't put me on the medication Ms. Morrow suggested for my anxiety because it would turn me into a sissy and an atheist. How long has this been going on?"

"I'm trying!" she shouts back. "I told you I'm trying." I can see the mental breakdown happening inside her head. It shows on the outside, manifests itself in the way she claws at the collar of her T-shirt, how she clamps her teeth down on the fat part of her upper lip.

"I can't believe you," I say. I look down at my wet, sticky hand that used to hold the glass of lemonade. "I was going to apologize."

Astoundingly, she smiles. She snorts, wipes her runny nose on the top of her wrist. "Your father wanted me to treat my depression with magnets!" she laughs. "Magnetism," she says.

"He wanted me to use real magnets, real science. Something called transcranial magnetic stimulation. Said he read about it in The Smithsonian. There was a word he used, what was it... opto something... optogenetics. I said that if I couldn't pronounce it, I wasn't going to use it. Isn't that incredible..." she says. Her voice lowers, softens. I watch her eyes flutter and close. "He used my own words against me," she whimpers. Her eyes are still closed. "We couldn't get our communication straight. Just look at us. Two doped turkeys. Look at what great solutions we came up with for our problems. Might as well have been speaking two different languages. It's like we were at two opposite ends of the field," she says. "Ha! Magnetic fields..."

"It didn't have to be that way," I say, but she's too far gone to hear me.

"Fields," she says, drifting, "The Field Museum. The Field Museum of Misery..." She slinks sideways, takes a seat on the grass.

She picks up the other bottle in her free hand, so that now she is gripping both orange cylinders to her chest, and then she slowly lowers herself onto her back. It's a strange tableau, a middle-aged woman splayed out on the ground, arms and legs spread in a star-shape of submission. It's like a painting of a madwoman holding two sticks of dynamite to her breasts in the middle of a gorgeous afternoon. And it's then that I know she's been taking the pills for a long time. I remember the last time I saw her like this, flung out on the ground in a pose of raving fatigue and failure. It was many years ago, after her father was laid to rest in the cemetery. That afternoon her embrace of the lawn was more mournful and repentant. She was face down, more like a hug. But there was still the similar current of punishment and mercy, an odd torrent of trapped emotions. "An aggravated harmony with the earth."

Incidentals (2006)

For better or worse, I'm a man of my word. When I promise my mom that I will accompany her to the final show on her big book tour, even when that final engagement is held in one of the shittiest states in the country and even after I observe that her entire adult life has basically amounted to an unmitigated fraud, I keep my promise. I don't run and tell anyone about anything. I don't go gushing to Dad or Lindy or Maureen. I don't even tell Sasha, whom I owe it to, seeing as how I've already convinced her to join me on this Florida excursion, this blasphemous caravan of heresy. In hindsight, my reaction was completely irrational and unexamined. It was pretty much a given. The patented reaction goes: trauma, push it aside, move forward. This happens involuntarily, void of angst or meditation, like an action carried out on autopilot. Get busy doing something banal, the tiny message inside my head says. Carry on. Damn it if I'm not standing right here, fifteen minutes after the bomb drops, packing my idiotic best suit for the occasion, wondering if Oprah will find me fetching or if Sasha will be proud to call me her man. Is my ability to move past deception or plow through betrayal without first throwing a fit or putting up a fight a good quality or a bad one? Better or Worse? I have a feeling I don't want to overthink it right now, so I force my attention toward making sure that all of my underwear is folded and pressed into tight neat rolls at the bottom of my suitcase. I am also a man of maximum efficiency. This is the incredible nonsense I'm contemplating when the phone rings. It's Sasha.

"You have no idea how happy I am for this distraction," I say as soon as I pick up the phone. There is sniffling and throat clearing coming from the other end. Shallow, shuttering breaths. "Sasha? Are you okay?"

"Not really," She says.

"What's wrong? What happened?" I close the suitcase, sit on top of it, as if whatever will be said must be kept secret from the contents inside.

"Everything went to shit as usual."

"What are you talking about? Why?"

"That's exactly it," she says, fighting back another surge of emotion, "for no fucking reason at all."

"Okay, sweetie, well, what are we talking about here? Are you okay? Do you need help?"

"I'm okay," Sasha says, snorting, almost laughing a little in her overcorrection. "It's Deion."

"Deion!" I say. What the hell did he do now?

"He was shot last night. He's in pretty bad shape."

She says it so curtly, with such efficiency, that it leaves no room for an offhand response, and since that is the only type of reply that could possibly result from this stunning news, I don't say anything at all. It's probably best that I don't react because I have no idea what to say. My first instinct is to comfort her, but then right away that thought gets forcibly replaced with notions of hostility and antagonism toward Deion, as though his audacious intentions all along had been to go and wreck our trip and the whole promising relationship with it. Part of me doesn't know that it wasn't...

"He called last night. He was super wasted," Sasha says, enduring, persevering in her reliable way. Her voice shifts from sad to angry.

"You talked to Deion last night?" I say, catching myself. This is not about me and my knee jerk jealousy. "I'm so sorry."

"He said a lot of things. He said that he loved me. He hated you. He hated white people. He threatened that if I didn't let him take me out and be his girl that he was going to go back and join the gang he used to run with. He said that he'd tried picturing all these wonderful, beautiful images in his mind that he'd learned from the book, about kissing me, hugging me, feeling loved and comforted, but that it didn't work. Nothing ever came true. It was all a lie. He said the only things he pictured that seemed real to him were the violent, rage filled images. When he pictured hurting someone, that felt real and true and it gave him some actual relief. He didn't know what to do."

"My god," I say. "That's so scary. That's awful. You should have told me."

"I was worried that he was watching me. He was already so angry at you. I didn't want to get you any more involved than you already were. I didn't want him to hurt you."

"I'm lucky he didn't, I guess. I'm so glad that he didn't hurt you!"

"It doesn't make any sense. Nothing makes any sense. Thank God!"

"So he shot himself?" I say, and I swear I want to follow it up with *Thank God*. It's horrible, but I feel relief.

"He shot a rival gang member dead on the street."

"Oh no!" But it's not like the words actually come out, more like a gasp with a few stray vowels thrown in. *Thank God.* "Why did he do that?"

"He was so angry at you," Sasha says, and she starts crying again. I almost start to cry. My body doesn't know how to respond. I'm so relieved but also confused and shaky and fired up. "He got in a shoot-out."

"That's insane."

"It was right in the middle of the park. This was broad daylight. This morning. Children playing, moms out walking, dad's running, school kids just chilling, minding their business. It's such a mess!"

"And he was angry at me?" I ask.

"He hates you."

"And you told him that I wanted… I told him I wished him the best."

"You told him. I told him."

"You told him that all of that positive thinking was madness."

"I tried to tell him," she says. "He wouldn't listen. He said you were nothing but a rich, jungle fever cracker. A phony."

"I don't… I'm not."

"He knows who your mom is."

"Yeah, but…" I forget sometimes who my mom is. It's like waking up from a dream every morning but still walking around half inside of its fog all day long. You can't escape it. It's supposed to be a good fog, like a warm mist, but I can't quite process it that way. For me it's a dark haze of disorientation and guilt. And then I just get angry at myself for ruining what should be an enjoyable life. And then it's time for bed again, and… I tried explaining it to Sasha, and she said she saw what I was saying, but that it was a luxury and privilege to even waste my time on such frivolous thoughts. She was completely right, of course, but it's still something, it still nags at me. "I don't even feel rich. I don't feel anything."

"I told him. But he doesn't get that. How could he?"

"I mean, I understand. Yeah, I understand, but I'm not... he could have talked to me."

"He had such a hatred for you. He can't talk to you about this. He doesn't see you as anything other than the enemy."

"I could have lived with that. No hard feelings."

"I tried telling him. Am I supposed to tell him to shoot you instead?"

"Well, no, but, I mean he knows, right? Does he know about all the crooked politicians and the fat cat billionaires that run this town? I've never met them before. I hate them, too. They live in Highland Park and Gold Coast and they eat their steaks and drink their whiskeys downtown. and, and, and... they have addresses with guarded gates out front, but they can be found."

"How could he know about those things?"

"I guess he couldn't. How can anyone, really?"

"It's not that he's incapable," Sasha says, "but they're too far apart. They're from different worlds."

"I'm surprised he didn't try to kill my mom or Maureen," I say, suddenly feeling flush and panicky, as if I need to whirl into defense or attack mode despite the fact that the threat is half dead somewhere in an intensive care unit.

"That's a horrible thing to say!" Sasha says.

"Of course. I know that, but it crossed my mind. I can't help it."

"I'm sure it crossed his mind too, but..." she pauses, trying to find the right words. "I don't know how to say this," she says. "I don't even know if I know how to describe it. I don't think Deion knew... He can't kill what he doesn't see or feel. I mean, he knows they're out there, but he doesn't know who they are or what they are... he has no concept of their role in his life. He looks around himself and all he sees are walls and wolves and he either wants out all together or he wants to be one of the wolves so he can survive, and so he... he shoots himself... he shoots his way out."

"That's so true," I say.

"As much as you might want to you can't go after what you don't see or can't reach. And then it gets so that you resent the stuff you can't see so much that you just stop caring or you tell yourself that it's all bullshit anyway."

"Of course," I say. "It's not a matter of intelligence, but a lack of imagination."

"How could they imagine... other men, in the same city? They don't teach that school."

"Are you kidding? The schools are scared shitless. Most of them don't even teach music anymore because they're worried the kids might end up discovering Miles Davis, Chuck D, Nina Simone or Zack de la Rocha and burn the whole place down. Slippery slope and all that."

"They can't risk that."

"They won't. And Deion is not the only one. Far from it. The more I learn, the more I see that it's like an entire generation. Everybody's been duped. Mom and Maureen just tapped into it, packaged their own brand of distraction." I'm rambling again, but I can't seem to stop myself. I've been thinking about so many things lately, and it's exhausting. It's hard work trying to figure out what's behind everyone's discontentment and loneliness. Maybe that's why nobody wants to engage in the process. "Nobody seems to understand the root causes of... you know... or the inside men, the top dogs making everyone's lives harder, pulling the strings, cutting everyone's securities, uh, um, raising prices on everything from heating bills to highway rides while they get off scot free, you know? But Deion… he's not… They especially can't allow him to know—"

"Look, why don't you take out the pigs at the top yourself? Why aren't *you* going after the lying, cheating root causes in their hidden mansions?"

"Yeah, but they're not affecting me as much."

"Passing the buck!"

"Well, no, but—"

"But nothing. It's just like the Black on Black crime myth. Everyone wants to wash their hands of it, and so they bend the data. When you bend the data, you bend the meaning, the responsibility… Black on Black doesn't exist. It's bullshit. People commit violence because they're wounded in some way. It's all just some disastrous cocktail of proximity, rage and affliction. There's no color involved. If there were a bunch of abused green people running around the south side they'd be doing the same thing to one another. Just some broken, fucked up loons murdering the unlucky bastards who happen to cross their paths. You stop the trauma, you stop the violence. But that's too much work. It's too costly. Shit, in the end, none of us ever kill or save the right people!"

"Yes," I say, my thoughts slowly forming around this fresh intelligence as they recede and dribble away at the same dreamy pace. "I guess some colors are just born into more dire dimensions…" The harder I try, the more my thoughts refuse to fully crystallize…

"Okay. Well, who's going to be the one to tell these colored kids all that? *Hey younguns, gather round. I know you think that slavery is over, but it's not. Those motherfuckers just shifted the shape of it, switched the game on you. Because for every Black boy or brown girl the rich White men let into their society, there are hundred more that they lock up.* Who's going to tell them that their hopes and hearts are still shackled?"

There is a rippling silence that follows this biting assessment, a wave of stillness. We are at its peak. As rough as it is to hear, it must have been ten times harder to say out loud. She has emptied her arsenal, worn herself out. We are past the point of pulling or saving any punches for later. Later is now and now is later. I admire her, but do not envy her position. She takes a moment to reach for more Kleenex and blow her nose. In the middle of her blowing she gets pissed at herself for crying again and starts cursing the tissue. This is the wave's trough, the valley. As upset as I am right along with her and for her over this travesty, I wish more people would speak up about all this injustice and cruelty. Say something. Where are our priorities? Our society seems to be okay with telling the oppressed that they have a hard life. We tell them *what* they are, but not how or why. I wish someone would have told Deion, explained the chain reactions linked to trauma. I know it's tough, it's devastating, but it seems to me that the devil you know is a lot easier to overcome than the devil you don't even know exists.

"I don't know," I say, catching the final current of quiet as it washes ashore. "But..." I say, hesitating to respond. "What's the alternative?"

She honks her nose one last time, and I hear her open a trash can lid and slam it shut. "Baby," she says, "we're living it."

There is something so final, so conclusive to the resonance and scope of this statement, like the ending lines of a poem, and yet still she is not done.

"It's hard to talk like this about my own people," she says, starting to sniffle again. "But, that's the problem," she says.

"I'm sorry," I say. "I'm really sorry. We don't have to talk about it."

"Yes we do," she says, trying to rally and keep going. She blows her nose again, and I wonder how many boxes of Kleenex she must have gone through. "Anyway, Deion didn't know the right enemy, and he'll probably go to his grave not knowing."

"But he knows what they represent to him?"

"He knows they're white."

"He thinks he knows—"

"He knows they always seem to win and he always seems to lose."

"I guess that's enough," I say.

"There is no guessing," she says.

"And so the guy he killed, he was a nearby resident. Was he a local kid?"

"He shot an eighteen year old high school student, drop out, I guess, right between the eyes at around nine this morning. Family lived about six doors down from him on the next block over."

Right away an image comes to mind—a poor Black boy, flexing and feigning hardness, playing at invincibility, certain that everything short of a savage scowl is a sign of weakness, but having little frame of reference or model for comparison. "And then one of them shot him back," I say, so sure of the answer.

"A police officer shot him."

Shit. That's so much worse. I don't even have to ask. I know the police officer must have been white. Most likely with an Irish last name like Murphy or O'Connor, a stout barrel-chested blockhead with a penchant for chaos. Not necessarily a hideous guy, but someone who gets off on playing a hero even when there is no real, definable villain around to match his illusion of one. "And what is Deion's condition exactly?"

"Stable at the moment. He's coming around. Earlier they were worried he wouldn't make it through the night."

"It doesn't make any sense."

"That's what I said from the beginning."

"Yeah, but it doesn't."

"That doesn't mean anything."

"It should."

"It doesn't."

Part of me wants to keep arguing, pleading, *"But it should!"* I can't get over it. I want so badly for things in this world to make sense, to add up. There is a touch of casualness that comes into Sasha's voice as she tells me that this will be the second child that Deion's parents have lost to gun violence. The first one dead, the next one probably on his way to life in prison. There is an air of normalcy, of *nothing can be done.* It isn't that she's cold or heartless about it. In fact she's extremely sensitive and caring, more so than most people would be in her situation. When Deion's mom asks for her to please come by and stay with her at the hospital for a while because she is so lonely, Sasha agrees right away. She is getting ready when she calls me. She wanted to contact me and let me know what was happening.

"As we're getting off the phone," Sasha tells me, "Deion's mom is explaining what the doctor said while he was going over his recovery. 'He's very lucky,' he told her. 'He is going to pull through. Get some rest. He's going to be all right. Everything is going to be all right.'" There is an abrupt end to her description, as if someone has cut the line dead. I wait to see if she's going to continue, and just when I'm about to ask her if she's okay she says, "Lucky? What is wrong with him?"

"Who?" I say. "Deion? The doctor?"

"The doctor was Black," Sasha says. "Deion's mom was very clear about that. You could tell that she was happy about it, proud. And okay, so go ahead. Be happy, but what about being rational and honest? He's not going to be okay, Clayton. We're not all right! Everything is not okay!" Her tone takes on a high, soaring quality, untethered from all restraints and decorum. Her anguish is palpable and it hurts that I can't do anything about it.

"Yeah," I say, thinking about the depth and complexity of what she's just said. "I guess he had to say something. The doctor has to offer some words… There's nothing else to say." But I don't like what I've said. I don't even believe it myself. It's just so hard. I understand her frustration. There are so many hard and awkward and intense conversations about reality that are not happening every day. And so instead, as our neglect and avoidance have dictated, here we are…

"Clayton," she says, putting herself back together, "I can't go with you to Orlando tomorrow." Her voice has turned tender and full of remorse. I know she is sincerely sorry, which is why I tell her that everything will be okay. I understand. Do what you need to do, what you feel is right. I comfort her, let her cry some more.

"Are you sure I shouldn't just stay here and make sure everything is all right? Is there anything I can do?" I say.

"There's nothing you can do. You should go. I'm sorry."

For a few seconds nobody says anything. I can hear the echo of my own breath in the phone. On her end, I can hear her over and over again start to cry and then stop herself and then start again.

"Do you at least think that my plane will crash and explode into a million pieces?" I ask. As I often do in times of extreme sadness and gravity, I make a joke. A few weeks ago, when I told Sasha about my morbid sense of humor and my acute fear of flying, we decided to have a little fun at each other's expense. Our joke goes that if you talk about the worst-case scenario, if you verbalize your worst fear, then it can't happen. We both know how ridiculous and counterintuitive it sounds, but in our way we are making fun of the opposite line of thinking that so many others, especially my mom and Maureen, subscribe to, and so it makes us giddy to thumb our noses at the whole absurd notion of blind optimism. Wide-eyed pessimism is the way to go! We both agree that horrible things have a tendency to catch absentminded people off guard, and so if we stay on our toes, the farce goes… In our own quirky way, it comforts us.

Sasha laughs a little bit, as much as she can. She at least appreciates my attempt at levity. "I think you'll probably collide with another plane midair," she says, a touch of spunk coming back into her voice. "And you'll all have to jump from the plane and fall five thousand feet. And you'll end up smashing onto the sharpest tip of the highest mountain around."

"I'll be skewered?" I say.

"Skewered!" she says, and then both of us allow ourselves to laugh for a few brief moments before each of us comes back around to the solemn task at hand.

"Well," I say. "Good luck with everything. I hope you can find some peace."

"Thank you," she says. "Hang in there, okay. I know how irritating and baffling things can get for you around these types of events and people. I wish I could be there to help."

"Yeah, thanks. Me too." And then it's time to wrap up. I know I'm supposed to say something comforting and consoling before I hang up, but what? I come very close to saying, "Everything will be okay," but I manage to stop myself, thank God. I search for a different set of words, and by the grace of whoever or whatever, they come to me. "Sasha," I say. "We'll get through this together."

"Yes," she says, and I can tell that she approves of this salutation, this solution. We'll get through this together. I like it more the more I think about it. The world would be a better place if we all said that instead of "everything will be okay" without ever fully processing why or how the statement will ever come true on its own.

"And I can't do anything to help?" I ask one more time.

"Nothing can be done," she says.

After a brief pause, I take a deep breath. "Okay," I say. I don't want to hang up, but I know it's coming.

"I love you," Sasha says, and this helps a lot. I immediately feel better. Not great, but better.

"I love you too," I say.

"Good bye," she says.

"Good bye."

And then she hangs up, probably knowing that I wouldn't be able to do it myself, and the silence feels unbearable. I let the phone dangle in my hand. I put it between my legs and squash it there. I want to crush it. I want to destroy something. I want to scream…

Why can nothing be done? Who decides these things? How can we all just accept that these things happen, that people just die in the middle of the day from gunshot wounds, that boys kill each other out of some raw, intense buildup of rage, and nobody ever stops to track down the birthplace of such hostility? How is it that my girlfriend won't be able to share an important moment with me because one of her friends is in serious condition following some crazy morning of gang warfare? I can't accept it! I won't! But where do I go to appeal? Who wants to hear me go on about such harrowing, depressing shit? I want so badly for the world to make just a little bit more sense. It doesn't even have to make perfect sense or always work out to some rosy scenario, but maybe it could just like produce a few more logical, reasonable conclusions based on facts once in awhile. Is that so hard? Is that too much to ask? That my girlfriend comes with me and comforts me in my time of need, when I need her most? Can I have that? Can you give me that one small thing, world? She's *my* girlfriend! She's not some depraved gangbanger's girlfriend, some lunatic who can't tell the difference between his ass and a hole in the ground!

Fuck!

I throw my shoe against the wall. It bounces back, bangs the carpet with a thud. And that's it. Nothing else. A shoe crumpled on a bedroom rug. Silence. What's the point? A quick bang, a limp clunk against the floor, and nothing to follow. Deadness. Game over. For what? I pick it up to throw it again. I want it to crush something, put a dent in the wall, something. I raise it up over my head, and I almost let it fly before I realize that I'm not angry at Sasha or Deion. I'm angry at society at large, and that realization is so vast, so daunting and consuming, that I can do nothing but put the shoe down, lie back on my suitcase and try to cool out a little. The strangest thing, the stupidest, nuttiest, most fucked up thing, is that once I start to unwind a bit, as soon as I take a few deep breaths, my mind goes immediately back to pondering the most trivial, mundane shit again. Should I pack my toothbrush or just buy one at the hotel? I need a new one anyway, but… I mean, it's right here in the bathroom. It doesn't make much sense to buy a new one when the old one still works. I should go online and check the weather down there. Did the White Sox win last night? What's wrong with them this year… ?

Jesus, what is wrong with me? What is wrong with us? What is wrong with people? Aaaaaaaaaaaaaaaaaa! Fuck.

The Desired Effect (2005)

My phone's been going off for the past five minutes. He calls, lets it ring a few times, then hangs up before the voicemail comes on and calls back again. Prior to this moment I kind of liked my ringtone. I chose a zany one with this upbeat, jangling tempo; real electronic sounding, like Kraftwerk or something. It's called *City Streets*. Now, three or four consecutive listens in, all I can think about is some nerd with a synthesizer trying to imitate the soundtrack from an Atari game he used to like in fifth grade. I don't want to answer it. Randy's called about ten times in the last few months, and every time it's something else, something warped or harrowing or incoherent. He says he's not back on the wagon again, but he must be. The last time he called he talked for two straight hours about some new organic kind of fertilizer he was using on his grass. Said it was so fresh and pure that he was thinking about sprinkling some on his cereal. I don't even think he has a lawn, which means it must have been some kind of cry for help. But that's just it; everything's a cry for help with Randy. Nevertheless, I've got a soft spot for the guy. I can't do anything about it. He has this way of using his charisma and graciousness as a misdirection of sorts, like a decoy. You're looking at this guy's kind eyes and easy demeanor, laughing along with his wit, and meanwhile he's setting you up to be his sympathizer and confidant when things go sideways. Before you know it, you're wandering around in this dark weirdness with him, knee deep in it, holding his hand, trying to help him find a light at the end of some endless black tunnel. Magicians have a name for this type of craftiness, "a manipulation of interest," they call it. I'm convinced that if Randy had wanted to, he could have been one of the best showmen in the business.

"You know, usually when somebody doesn't pick up the first four times, it means they're too busy," I say when I finally answer.

"You're not," Randy says.

"How do you know?"

"You picked up," he says.

"I'm trying not to lose my mind over here," I say. "One more ring and I felt like I was going to scream."

"It's a tactic," is all he says. He sounds remarkably crisp and lucid, but it's early in the conversation. I wonder what kind of medication he's on. Mom said he'd been on something called lorazepam. I guess she found a bottle of it in his coat last time he came by the house. She explained that it alleviated pain and anxiety during the later stages of cancer, but that it also caused disorientation and amnesia in many patients. This could explain the strange phone calls. It seemed a little funny that she knew so much about a medication like that, the synthetic pharmaceutical type that she eschews, but then she did follow it up by saying that she had advised him against it, and suggested fish oil capsules instead. That sounded more like her. Apparently, according to Maureen, mixing alcohol with lorazepam is a death sentence, but I'm not even sure if Randy would care about that at this point. His final sentence has been handed down already.

"You're filled with tactics," I say.

"They work, don't they?" Randy asks.

"Well, here we are, right?" I say, "I'm talking to you."

"I'm actually really glad you say that. I was going to ask you to confirm with me. I've been really out of it lately."

There's a timid, tender quality to his voice that makes me quiver a little. He has a way of breaking my heart. I'm such a dick for ignoring him. The guy's dying for God's sake. Dick. That's April's word. I'm sure that not only her vulgar words but her lewd imagery will stay with me for a long time yet. Shit. "How are you, Randy?" I ask, and then it occurs to me that maybe he's toying with me again. Maybe he's completely fine.

"I'm actually better than ever," he says.

"Really?" I say. "How come?"

"Have you ever come to the realization that your entire life you've been putting something off, denying something that's been right beside you the whole time? Then one day you just have this flash, this epiphany, and you think, now why the hell didn't I listen to myself years ago? I could have had everything fixed and taken care of before it ever got all twisted and broken?" He runs a faucet, clinks some kind of pots or bowls around on the counter. My guess is he's either chosen this time to make a giant helping of spaghetti or he's gathering materials to concoct a homemade explosive device. A cat's soft meowing in the background quiets my worries. It must be waiting for fresh food and water dishes. Totally normal. I'm thinking that when the clatter dies down I'd actually like to answer him about the realization stuff. I want to tell him that I think I might have experienced something like that, help validate him, but he starts talking again before I have a chance. "Hey, take it easy little fella," he says. The meowing grows louder, more insistent. Randy squats, letting out a deep down belly groan. He sounds awful. On his creaking ascent back up from the floor he says, "Sorry, kitty still needs to be taken care of. It's not his fault."

"His fault about what?" I ask.

"I'm going to kill myself," Randy says. He says it breezily, offhanded, like asking for someone to pass the breadbasket at a dinner party.

"That's not funny," I say.

"I'm not joking," he says. The cat's purring and chewing sounds like his mouth is right up against the receiver. I suddenly picture a stark white creature with red eyes and spiked fur. Demon cat.

"You can't... Randy, you can't be serious."

"I am. One hundred percent serious."

"This is why you called me?" I ask, animosity and indignation boiling up inside of me. "You can't do this to me."

"Why not?" Randy asks. "You are the best person to call in this situation. You're the perfect one."

"Excuse me," I say, furious as hell.

"Don't be so upset," Randy says, "it's a compliment."

"You are complimenting me on my ability to field suicide threats?"

"Well, not in so many words," Randy says.

There is a long pause in conversation as Randy coughs and hacks, clearing the malignant phlegm from his windpipes. All of the life has been ripped out of me. My mind is a swirl of anger, sorrow and dizziness. I have to sit down.

"What words are you referring to, Randy?" I say. I'm worried I already know the answer.

"You are a giver and an eternal satisfier. You're basically one enormous shoulder to cry on."

I don't know whether to be honored or disgraced. There is a kind, friendly warmth that comes from being known as a comforter and confidant, and then there is the flipside, the side where you are the enabler, the stepping stone, the weakling.

I don't want to be that guy anymore. I'm tired of his syrupy sweet self.

I already know what he wants from me, and I'm not going to give it to him. "What do you want from me, Randy?"

"I want you to tell me that it's okay. That you'll still love and respect me, and so will everyone else. Everybody will understand and accept my leaving. I need your reassurance on that."

I take a huge deep breath. I dig a knuckle into my parted lips and gum down. I close my eyes. "You can't put this one on me," I say.

"I'm not putting it on you. You're taking it off of me. You're lifting a weight off of my chest."

"Weight removal. It's not a service I offer anymore," I tell him.

"Why not? Since when?"

"Since right this second."

"Seriously!" he protests. "Now? You choose right now to stop soothing the afflicted, assuaging the guilty? That's your best quality. That's your ace!"

"Remember when you said you had a realization about wishing you had come to terms with something sooner, that you could have avoided a lot of trouble if you had?"

"You little rascal! You're using my words against me."

"I'm just opting out. I'm letting your words and your actions be yours and yours alone."

"You're abandoning me?"

"That is so unfair."

"Clayton!" Randy says. He's pleading, begging. "Why now? Why are you choosing now to do this to me?"

"Can you think of a better time to make a huge change than in the middle of a life or death situation? Please, explain. When exactly would be a more appropriate time?"

Randy is silent for a while, and then he starts laughing. The laughter leads to more coughing and wheezing. I wait for it to die down, feeling proud and distraught at the same time. Why can't I ever feel one emotion at a time? Just let yourself feel free for once! It's so exhausting! It's all right to feel unburdened, unfettered, I try telling myself, but it's hard. Let yourself go, man.

"You little son of a bitch," Randy says when he's able. There's still an edge of laughter to his harsh, gravelly voice. "How am I supposed to argue with that? You can't fight that."

"Please don't," I say. "I don't know if I have much more defenses left in me."

Randy lets out a long, wet groan. It sounds like he's either easing himself onto the floor or a very low mattress. "You're saying I'm in this alone."

"Nobody has to say it," I say. "It is what it is. Nobody else is in this with you. There's nothing that can be done to change that. Do what you think needs to be done, but know that this decision lives and dies with you alone. I mean, in a way... You have help. Many others have gone down this path before, if that makes you feel better. It should. They've been where you are. It would help me to know that, but they aren't here to tell you their story. Use your imagination. You're an intelligent man, Randy. A philosopher. I'm not telling you anything you don't already know. You have the strength to make the decision all by yourself."

"You went back on your word just now," Randy says.

"No I didn't. How?"

"You soothed me," he says. The words come out drained and breathy, like a worn out body slipping into a big, hot bath. "You did it again. Thank you," he says, "goodbye," and then he hangs up.

Paramount to the end (2006)

"Maaaaaaaaaaaw!" I keep screaming through the pouring rain. "Maaaaaaaaaw!" The crowd of vehicles is growing, gaining in force and ferocity, their horns blowing like trumpets of war. The drivers, every desperate one of them, want blood.

"Maaaaaaaaaaaw!" I stretch one leg out from under the garage roof, and suck it right back in; its denim surface already black with condensation.

I don't even know what I'll do if she sees me. What is my plan? Do I go sprinting out into the deluge and start hollering at all the pumped up, freaked out motorists? Come to her rescue? Rescue from what? Her own fans? Her followers? Her fate? Should I stomp in their taillights, challenge them to get out and fight me like the crazy zealots they are? *Come on, motherfuckers! Let's see if you know a shortcut out of a swift kick in the teeth!* How bizarre and prophetic is it that her disciples, not knowing they have encountered their own messiah, want to tear her limb from limb for a parking space to the very event in which she will bestow upon them the secret to eternal life? It's almost too much to fathom. Or maybe it's the most fitting, climactic scenario possible. The age-old myth of wrath and crucifixion come home to roost. There's something so epic, so biblical about the whole lush, primitive scene!

Through the streaked window of the Jaguar I see her head dip down beneath the dashboard on the passenger's side. It seems only proper that she's wearing that silly Chinese bandana. She's always said it was her good luck charm. It bobs there atop her head like some absurd expression of surrender. She was wearing it twelve years ago when Dad came back through the front door and into her life. That's what gave it the magic and charm, she believed. I recall her explaining that the Chinese symbols stood for fortune and abundance, a long vertical slash with smaller lines bisecting horizontally in quick strokes. Jesus, it even looks like a cross. The satirical part was that she bought the chintzy thing at a Dollar General on Montrose Boulevard. Of course the irony was completely lost on her. It was always lost on her, which I guess is her best and worst quality. It's carried her to this point. It's really why she's here right now... being all lucky in her little Chinese handkerchief.

She's been under the dashboard for a long time. I can't see what's going on. There must be something inside the glove box she is searching for. The rain is coming down sideways now, lashing upon the cars as if struck by a giant whip. Police sirens wail in the distance. Somebody stuck inside a trapped minivan, pinned by flanking motorists on both ends, shouts out, "holy hell!" so loud that even though the voice is locked inside the cabin, it still rings out sharp and alarming on the outside world. Lightening cuts through the black, tumescent sky, jagged like a handsaw. This is what Noah might have felt like during the flood had he ever been alive, had he been real.

The Chinese bandana, along with Mom's pale face, pops up from below the seat. Her hand follows, one bony fist clenching an empty pill bottle. She hoists it up at the window, either to get a better view of the label in the light or to curse its vacant contents or perhaps to use it as some sort of garlic clove against the approaching zombies outside. Whatever the reason, it doesn't work. This new gesture, this audacious maneuver has only served to rile them up even more. How dare this woman! She must be destroyed!

"Mooooooooooooove!" somebody yells. "Move your ass!"

The impatient vehicles are coiled in one single-file serpent around the lot. In front, at the mouth of the beast, are a line of luxury automobiles, your Lexus SUVs, Mercedes Benz C-Classes, Volvo S60s and Audi A4s. These are the closest to the prize but the fewest in amount. Each car farther back in the row is a little less fancy. In the center are your mid-class models, Subaru Legacies, Mazdas and Nissan Altimas less than six years old. There are more of these than the extravagant brands, but they are dwarfed by the number of low-end models—Chevys, Fords and Toyotas more than a decade past their prime with rusty doors, sunburned hoods and missing hubcaps. This section, the neediest, is also the angriest. This is expected, but their course of action is not. The Chevys and Fords are not upset with the drivers in front of them but with the ones in back. Heads in Chevys crane backward out the windows, over their shoulders, to quarrel with Fords. The Fords turn and shake their fists at Toyotas and so on back in the procession.

There are no pills left. She turns the orange bottle upside down, shakes it at the floor. *Why are they doing this to me?* The question is right there in her moist, sorrowful eyes. I can see the anguished expression flush across her face. How can you not have compassion, she asks them. She wants an answer. She pounds the bottle against the windshield, mashes it against the glass. *Why? What's wrong with you?*

This motion, her desperate plea, has been received as a threat rather than entreaty. It has pumped anger and venom into the parking lot like a needle into a vein. Someone, a few rows back, comes charging out from one of those industrial utility vans with no windows. It is a heavy-duty rectangle of a van, all blank white and steely with little to no other distinguishing features. At first it is unclear whether the blitzing driver is a man or woman. It is round and stout, one massive boulder of flesh. It's like the entire body is one continuous stomach from neck to knees. The crewcut makes it appear masculine, but there are two doughy boobs and soft pink cheeks that throw everything off. It is plaid and ragged and pissed off. It grabs the front of the Jaguar's grill, either in an attempt to rip it off or use it as a lever in which to roll the thing upside down. There is a distinct bankrupt, ruined quality about this person, a sense that there is nothing left to lose. It rattles the car, rocks it back and forth until all the wind has been exhausted, and it is at that apex, that pivotal moment, that their eyes meet. I can faintly make out Mom's expression. Through the windshield her eyes are forlorn and pleading. She is at the end of a journey she has been on for a very long time. This is the last bend on the road to Damascus, only it is this hulking person, gripping madly onto her bumper, who is most like Saul in this parable. Here is the misguided judge come to persecute my mother, but God has chosen to remove the scales from her eyes rather than its. There is a look there on my mother's face that I know I will never forget. It is reborn and transcendent, the end of an era. Never again will she be the same. How cruel, that here in the city meant for wondrous, childlike dreams, hers has ground to an abrupt halt. Here in this land, a region known for endless streams of outlandish, grotesque news, she has been caught up in the current. Tomorrow, alongside reports of the latest baby being delivered in a Walmart bathroom or another severed foot found on Jupiter Island, there will be the story of Roberta Blaine, debunked guru stampeded in an Orange County parking lot.

I look back at Crew Cut's van, and once again I see the white sticker slapped to its drenched bumper. There is something so omnipresent about this square emblem, so familiar, as if the basic mold of it, the fundamental scheme has been there forever. It's everywhere you look these days. It's taking over. What is it that people like about such a simple, primitive design? Perhaps it is the suggestive modesty of it that makes everyone feel that they can be a part of its prestige, its inherent eminence, as if we have all had a hand in its creation. And maybe we have. But if everyone feels they are included in the process, then why the need to put a sticker on something? Isn't a sticker to standout, convey uniqueness in some way? What is the point of announcing to the world that you too are a part of something that everyone else is already involved in? Why advertise that you are an advertisement? Because everyone wants to feel that if they think or dream or declare enough that they too can get a piece of the royalties. But it should already be clear that they can't. The publisher of Mom's book, along with the administrator and architect of the vast modern world isn't taking any new applications. It says it right in their name, *Whole Pie Inc,* and yet we have two billion people all convinced that they can squirm their way through that narrow, exclusory crevice at the bottom, that sliver in the white box sticker. Crew Cut and the rest of the cronies could hardly fit through the doors of the Ponderosa Steakhouse, and yet they are the biggest believers. Such a filthy, conniving trick we have all allowed ...

Involuntarily, my eyes fill with tears. I should be at home with Sasha. I should be cheering Mom's demise, hating her for all the lies and deceptions, but this is not a time of gloating or seething. She is still my mother, and though I am partially inflamed with malice, there is a real and present danger unfolding right before me that cannot be denied. There is a level of authenticity too stark and chilling to ignore. This is extraordinary to the point of feeling false or hallucinatory. This is otherworldly. If ever I was to believe in supernatural forces it would be now. And just when the discord hits a pitch sure to cave the whole mess down on top of itself, things get even realer. Mom rolls down her window. She opens her mouth so wide that it is as if one can see all the way down her throat, deep into the esophagus.

"Aaaaaaaaaaaaaaaa!" she screams. Her head tilts all the way back, drinking in the rainwater, gargling with it. "Aaaaaaaaaaaaaaaaa!" she hollers, and she lays her hand on the horn at the same time.

The person in front of the car reciprocates. "Aaaaaaaaaaaaaaaaaaaaa!" it howls. "Aaaaaaaaaaaaaaaaaaaaaa!"

And then I, uncertain if I am joining sides with the behemoth or Mom, join in the screeching. "Aaaaaaaaaaaaaaaaaaaaaaaaa!" I yell. I've never yelled so hard or loud. "Aaaaaaaaaaaaaaaa!"

The horns and sirens rise to meet our octave, and the whole lot, the entire godforsaken place is engulfed by our cries. We are completely and totally awash with our fury, and it feels good. It feels so good. This is our cleansing. This is our baptism back into reality.

Wide Angle Lens

Mom decides to make her move as soon as he arrives home from work on Monday. She ambles out into the late afternoon sun, halting his pickup halfway up the drive like a petrified traffic cop. Dad says that from the way she looked, all haggard and frayed in her old bathrobe, he thought something awful had happened to me or Lindy. There was a look in her eye, like she had been searching for something extremely important all day but had reached a point, after tearing the house asunder, where she gave up, and now had to deal full bore with the implications of her wreckage. And as she stood there, spending the final seconds still hysterically rummaging through her mind for whatever has gone missing, Dad realizes that it is words she's been seeking all day, and right then he already knows what she is about to say. He doesn't know exactly how, he tries telling me and Lindy, but a moment before she reveals her indiscretion, he gets this psychic flash about hospitals and medication, a little brainstorm of illness related imagery. When she finally unloads her confession, it comes out ecstatic and gushing. Dad explains that it felt more like an invasion rather than any sort of admittance of wrongdoing. Perhaps she was trying to apologize, but in the tumult of announcing her perilous declarations, it came out sounding like she was attacking him with her words, blaming him for making her keep such toxic secrets inside for so long. Intentional or not, these connotations are not lost on Dad. The fact that these suggestions would even accidentally slip into her tone, after all that she has put him through, turns his stomach sour. Any warmth or compassion he might have had under different circumstances freezes over, and the rest of whatever else she says, her sorrys or various ablutions, are lost on him. He keeps thinking, he tells us, about the little blob of spit glistening on her cheek. Every time she downshifts in her pleading, switches pitch or changes facial expression for dramatic effect, Dad is not listening. He sees only her movements, absorbs none of her language, like watching a silent film. And all the while, he keeps thinking to himself, poor Roberta. Here she is during one of the biggest moments of her entire life, on the day her husband leaves her forever, and she has this hideous pearl of sudsy, infantile drool just clinging to her quivering cheek like that. She doesn't even know it's there, taunting her. She probably thinks he's looking at her face for a different reason, for something sturdy to hold onto as he takes it all in. There is so much injury in this world, he says, and then the universe has to go and pile on all that insult, too. What a life. He shakes his head.

We are in the garage, me, Lindy and Dad, clearing out all of his tools, wiping down individual canisters of lube and fertilizers, and packing them in boxes he brought home from work, cardboard crates usually meant for shipping purple slabs of meat across the city or state.

"Are you drunk," Lindy asks.

Sometime between Mom's confession in the driveway, and her whirling, weeping exit from the house, I tell Lindy about my and Mom's altercation in the backyard. The second she comes back from the mall, amidst Mom's moaning and thrashing about upstairs, I pull her into my bedroom. There is no careful preparation or jittery hedging, just straight to it. Though I had tried to plan for how I might tell her, there was not enough time. It had to be done now. Even if I had been afforded hours, days for that matter, it is doubtful that I could have hit upon any prudent or shrewd way to report such an intensified, momentous event. Perhaps it was better that I didn't have the means to concoct some dubious, half-baked explanation. These things are best handled efficiently and with great, masculine mettle… So I tell myself, anyway. In any case, I couldn't be sure how I'd deliver the news, breathless and terse or maudlin and protracted, but we both found out right then and there, wedged as we were between my childhood bed and my oversized poster of the Great Houdini taped to the back of my door. There's no telling what I said or how I said it. That grave, historical reenactment is lost forever in a blur of fever and spasms, but I recall that it must have hit her in just the right way, because all at once there was a tremendous whoop, followed by a shuttering brace, and a slow, warm release of clenched breath trailing off into silence. And then, pressed tight against the wall, color already rebounding, eyes returning clear and fresh, she says, "Do you think Dad is out getting drunk?" I inform her that Dad is currently in the garage, and we both spend a few mute moments nodding back and forth, eyes locked in a sort of wordless but understood transmission of joint uncertainty and fear. There is no telling what state we will find him in out amongst his own plot of ghosts and gambits.

"Lindy," I say, upset that she has launched so quickly into strike mode. "Give him a chance to breathe." It's still astonishing to me how forward and contentious Lindy can be. It's like we are from two different sets of parents. Which of us could have been so lucky to be adopted into this thorny imbroglio? Probably me. I was the one who watched out the living room window for ten combustible minutes, cloaked inside the heavy patterned curtains behind the sofa, as Mom and Dad tussled in the driveway. I could have practically exploded I was so charged with curiosity, so desperate for information about what transpired during the encounter, and yet I would have never dreamed of coming straight out and approaching the situation so directly, so brazenly. Lord knows I may have *never* gained a single scrap of knowledge from the confrontation, too meek to so much as attempt a feeble inquiry. No, it's Lindy who is adopted. She is the only confrontational one of us in the bunch. Lindy is like that little cartoon devil that sits on everyone's left shoulder in times of harried contemplation. Jesus. Thank God for all those Lindys not too spooked by the appearance of their own dark shadows.

"No, no, no," Dad says, twisting tight a lid on top of a jar filled with dirty, miscellaneous bolts and screws. "She can ask. It's a valid question." He wraps the jar in newspaper, slips it into the corner of the crate. He locates the pack of Camel cigarettes atop his workbench and taps one out, lights it. "I'm not drunk. I should be. If ever there was a time to get and stay plastered, it is now. I could stay wasted for a whole month and with god's own permission, too. Nobody could have said a thing. But it didn't seem right." He flicks the ash on the concrete floor. He nods to himself, smirks. The way he clamps the smoke in his teeth, readjusts his crotch with a dusty hand, there is no piety here. "I thought about it. Don't get me wrong. I thought long and hard. I considered going to 7-11, buying one of everything. I started walking to my old hangout, Ten Cat. I got halfway there, and I could almost taste the beer on my taste buds. I could swish it around in my mouth!" He says, filling his cheeks with air and shaking his head back and forth. "But the crazy thing was that even the imagined flavor, even the thought of it ... it didn't taste right. In my mind it had this rusty, metallic blend, like a handful of pennies. It just didn't feel like ... well, I guess it was the aftertaste, actually, the regret. You know like when you think about eating an entire pizza, but you don't do it because the bellyache afterward will sit like a bonfire in your gut?" He looks at us, willing us to agree, to nod our heads at least. "Of course you don't. You're too young. This ability to process three steps ahead ... it's an adult thing, boring maturity settling in for a long and tedious residence. All I can say is that I didn't do it because I have, for better or worse, achieved a certain clarity about risk and reward analysis. It's a real son of a bitch, but it's, I don't know," he literally grasps the air, squeezing the vacant space before him like an invisible sponge. "It's the opposite of pretending." He blows a sort of ambiguous puff of smoke, the cloud and his face behind it still probing for precision. "I knew that if I made it through this moment without having a taste, I could probably go the rest of my life, and that prospect was too enticing to pass up."

Lindy is nodding her head, contemplating her level of faith in this pronouncement, considering her next line of action. She ponders, lips drawn downward, brows paused in pensive arches, and it is through my observance of this pose that I decide we are safe to trust him. I locate my faith in him through her vision, her discerning eyes. She would not lead us astray. Her steadfast, instinctive expressions do the hard work, make the miscalculation improbable.

It is quiet for a stretch as Dad mashes out his cigarette. One of the cardboard boxes over by the tool chest is full, and it is the sound of Dad spooling and ripping packing tape that breaks the silence. This is when I notice that his clothing has changed since I saw him walk out to the garage earlier. Well, it's not a full change exactly... The tan T-shirt he wore an hour ago is still present underneath. He's got the same jean shorts on and sandals, but it's the top shirt. There's this light, wispy button-down shirt with ocean waves and palm trees just kind of dangling from his shoulders. It looks old and well-worn, like at some point it may have been a favorite shirt of his, though I've never seen it before. It's blue and green and white, draped wide open from top to bottom. It's the type of garment a certain type of older man might wear on a beach holiday. And like those older gentleman, it appears that he has pulled the thing out of some dank and cobwebbed trunk stored inside a sooty location such as a basement, attic or... garage. Putting it together, my mind travels the short distance between hidden vacation attire and his Mexico adventure. Is he taking off for Mexico again? Is this his way of feeling closer in an abstract sense, putting him in the mood before he actually makes the trek south of the border? It would seem to make perfect sense. He's had a hard year. I wonder if Lindy has the same question. If she does, she's not showing any concern yet. Again, I am reminded of how freeing it is to know that if the question does come to her, she'll be the one to pose it instead of me. For now, seeing him there, bent over with his shirt fluttering easily in the light breeze drifting through the door, I recall my own Florida vacation tomorrow morning, and that notion promptly makes me want to avoid the situation altogether.

Lindy has moved over to the area reserved for camping gear and coolers in the back corner. She's made herself at home, rooting around behind the folded up tent. She crawls behind the apparatus, stepping high to get over the rolls of bedding stacked on the floor, and comes clambering back holding a large canvas.

"I thought this was still crammed behind all my shoes in the back of the closet," she says, holding it up in front of her. The image is facing toward her. She looks at it with something like reverence, but also a new found puzzlement.

Dad stands up, cracks his back. He lets out a low moan, half out of muscle relaxation, half out of sorrow. "It was there until about a week or two ago. I pulled it out one night, because I was thinking about Randy."

At the mention of Randy's name, all of us bow our heads and observe a moment of silence. It must have been almost exactly five months ago, back in late February, that Randy took his own life. I can see from just a quick glimpse that it's the painting Randy did about three or four years ago during one of his infamous spells of sobriety; those times when his sweeter, more poetic side took center-stage, and nobody was immune to his captivating performances. Part of me does recall putting it in the back of Lindy's closet, but I don't remember exactly why...

Lindy sighs. She rests the painting against the front of our old washing machine, situates it against the crusty door as if she's preparing it for a gallery showing. The decrepit washer's been sitting there for years, waiting to be used for spare parts or to achieve antique status or something. The portrait's painted space points toward all of us now, a big nostalgic set of eyes resting in a rectangular cranium of sorts. It looks almost like one of those propped bedroom mirrors if not for the colorful brush strokes.

"I can't believe he did it," Lindy says. She steps back, puts her hands on her hips. She peers deeply into the bright lines, investigating its contours as if some satisfactory reason for his morbid decision might be coded somewhere inside.

"I know," Dad says, and for a moment, based on his slight stride toward her and his stooped posture, I think they might embrace.

"He must have really wanted to do it," I say. I say it because I feel it might alleviate some of the second-guessing or feelings of regret, letting them know in the only way I can that it wasn't a kneejerk decision. Dad and Lindy both turn and look at me with denouncement, like I've just taken some great leap of liberty with my explanation, but they don't know what I know.

I've never told anyone about the phone conversation I had with him about his wishes, and I never will. The guy did too much for me; changed my life, really. The disrespect and betrayal it would take to divulge his thoughts … it's too much to risk. After all, he did me such a profound favor. In a sense, Randy allowed me the most peace out of anyone, and because I was never anything more than a confidant or a set of open ears for him, it does make me feel a little guilty or unfairly blessed. His family should be the ones to have this kind of closure. The real blessing though, was the way he put my mind at ease. It was like he knew how much I'd beat myself up if he hadn't left things the way he did at the end of that phone call. In an almost impossible feat, in the midst of his own worst tragedy, he made sure my relief would go on to outweigh my remorse, and for that gift I will always remember Randy Mullins with love.

"It must have been bad," I say, "that's all I'm saying." This doesn't help much. Lindy scoffs at me, while Dad scratches his scalp in stiff defiance. Perhaps it was too obvious an observation. I try clarifying. "I mean, he used a gun. Randy. Randy Mullins," I say, as if the use of his full Christian name makes everything crystal. "Where in the world does a guy like Randy Mullins get a gun?"

"At the gun store," Lindy says, leaving off the *numbskull* comment at the end.

This off-handed wisecrack does a grand disservice to what actually transpired on that fateful day. As far as suicides go, Randy's must rank high on the list of most considerate incidents in the history of mankind. Not only did he do it in the bathtub with plastic sheets coating every possible inch of the surrounding tiles, he did it naked save one disposable diaper around his private regions. But that's hardly the half of it. He left a note, sure, but he also called the police and the coroner a few moments ahead of time to let them know what was coming. He ordered a maid service to show up the next day at precisely seven in the morning for mop up duty. There was also a handwritten will, but the crowning touch, the real jewel was that he left special instructions for the maid service, reminding whoever came to please clean all of the tricky, hard to reach areas of the entire house, behind the refrigerator and stove, for example. He left an extra twenty dollars for the assistance, as though this duty, this pesky business of cleaning troublesome areas, was the most important part of the whole humiliating ordeal.

"No, I mean, Randy didn't own a gun. He'd never want to own a gun. I doubt he'd ever even want to hold a gun. Probably never thought about a gun once in his entire life."

"It does seem bizarre when you think about it," Dad says, and I catch a glimpse of the grin I'm looking for, the signal that says he's at least starting to understand where I'm coming from. "I guess when you really want something," he says, staring off in the distance, "you're willing to do anything."

"Exactly," I say, and I look to Lindy to see if she's caught on yet. She is too busy gazing at the painting. She's really fixated on something.

"This doesn't even make any sense," she says. She keeps her hands on her hips but leans far forward with her upper body, like she means to kiss the thing on the nose.

"Hey!" Dad exclaims. His eyes bloom wide and alert, a sign that he's just been hit with some sort of revelation. "Didn't Randy leave you his cat in the will?" An odd thing to bring up now. I wonder how long he's been wondering this.

"Nah," I say, "he made a joke about it, but he was just playing. Something about how he thought I could fulfill both my dream of being a veterinarian and my goal of being a magician at the same time by simply taking in that one stray pet." I pause to laugh, remembering the eccentric, offbeat way he had of saying just about everything. "The next lines after that made it clear that he was only kidding. Then it said something about how I was bound for much bigger, more profound things…" I start to tear up remembering how sweet the message was. He didn't have to do that. "I forget how he put it… Anyway, just a little wink from Randy."

"What a guy," Dad says. "It does beg the question, though" Dad says. "What is your next idea for how to spend the rest of your life? Who will you try to become next?"

"I have absolutely no idea," I tell him.

"And that doesn't bother you? Really?"

"Not much at all, surprisingly. I'm not obsessed with figuring anything out at the moment. I'm trying to let things come to me on their own time, trust my instincts, you know? Too much pressure will give you an aneurism. I'm a different person now."

"Randy was right," Dad says, and the two of us share a brief smile before Lindy interrupts.

"What does this thing even mean?" she asks. She's got an eyeball pressed all the way up to the surface of the canvas.

"Have any of you ever even stopped to ask yourself what all of this means?" She unglues her cheek from the tacky sheet and straightens up.

"Not really," I say.

"Not much, no" Dad says, "I just always assumed it was something from the abyss inside the mind of Randy Mullins. Best not to wade too deep into that water."

"Yeah, well, this thing is weird," Lindy says. "Look, I mean, what is the point of this painting?" She steps closer to the canvas, laying her index finger on the strokes of color that make up Dad's bloated but lifelike figure. It doesn't take much of an effort to recall the first time I saw the painting, especially with the unearthed thing sitting right here staring us all in the face. It all comes back to me. There he is, fishless Dad in the back of the boat with his meat cleaver in his fist, pumping it at a clear blue sky. In the front of the boat sits Randy, happy as a lark, fish dangling from the end of a glimmering rod, sun smiling down on him. "Dad," Lindy says, fairly barking for his attention. "Dad, what are you doing here? Did Randy mean for you to look angry at the heavens for not allowing you to catch a fish or was he trying to make it look like you were waving at the heavens, thanking god for allowing your friend to catch a fish on this fine day? Are you happy or sad?"

"I have wondered that before," Dad says. "I don't know. I don't think it's up to me to determine. I'm too invested, too much a part of it. I can't get the right distance."

"Yeah, and why is Dad in his butcher outfit, but Randy's not?" I ask.

"Oh, who cares about that!" Lindy insists. "That's too evident. That's child's play. What I want to know is, is this an optimistic or pessimistic painting?"

A light flicks on inside of Dad. "Yeah!" he shouts. "Hey, I see why you ask. It's like, is this about bad luck for the fish because one of them got caught or is it good luck because all of the other fish are still safe and alive?" He walks up very close to the picture and runs his hand over the full span of it, from top corner to bottom.

"Well, I was thinking more about the luck of the people, you and Randy. Good luck for Randy, bad luck for you?" I say.

"See, now we're talking!" Lindy says. "Now you get it. What the hell does this damn thing mean?"

"Do you think Randy meant to have us all confused as shit, walking around like this, making guesses like some kind of idiots?" Dad asks.

"Obviously," Lindy says.

"Clearly," I say.

"What an asshole," Dad says. Lindy moves close behind Dad, and gently puts an arm on his back. Dad's shoulders begin shaking with a rumble of passing laughter. In response, Lindy, as if tethered to the surging sensation through touch, lets a little titter out herself.

"We could add to the painting," I say.

"What, like change it?" Dad says.

"We could paint over it, make it clearer, make the point *for* him," I say.

"We could paint a whole bunch of little fish down below swimming through the water with big smiles on their faces, like hey! Look, this is a positive painting! We're in a utopia down here! We're free!"

"Well, shit," Dad says, stepping back from the painting and deeper into Lindy's embrace. He rests his hand on his chin, stroking the knob of it in mock rumination. "In that case... If we're going to go that far, we may as well go all the way! Let's just paint a huge fucking gumdrop over the sun and call it the tenth planet!"

"Fucking mercy stroke," Lindy says.

"Fucking mercy stroke!" Dad repeats, a little louder and with more vinegar.

There is some sputtering and hissing as we all begin the process of allowing ourselves to relinquish our inhibitions. We stretch open our diaphragms and limber our mouths for what will become the most raucous, cathartic release of our whole lives. And then we are all laughing, howling our approvals and appreciations for such a well-timed comment. It seems to somehow sum up everything we've experienced in the past five if not fifteen years, and we unleash our cleansing roars. We topple over with our mirth, lean on one another for support, allowing each other the full strength of projection. This may be the closest we've ever come to a group hug and right when it is needed most. I think about all of the marketing consultants, the claim adjusters and hedge fund managers up and down Greenview Street. I think about how some of them must be hearing us right now, listening to our merry, thunderous voices carry through the open garage windows. They must be thinking to themselves, *Now there is a festive, satisfied family! I knew we were all living the right way! This certainly supports my way of thinking! Everyone is happy!* And no matter what the cost, they will go on telling themselves this for the rest of their lives. Are they aware of the illusion? To what extent? To what end? It's unclear whether they like their fantasies, whether they openly choose to cling to such stubborn, murky virtues or perspectives. But it is certain that they *need* to rely on them, rely on some backward sense of righteousness that they themselves have defined. How else could they go on living the way they do with their luxury houses, cars and boats while others live in poverty? Their bounty is owed to them, they believe. *We deserve it!* And so in their backroom dealings and in their most private moments before they fall asleep at night, they must overestimate their generosity, overlook their fraudulence, and conclude that they are… right. *We are good.* Don't look back, they must whisper to themselves. Don't look down, never to the left or right, and never, ever, whatever you do, peer inside. See only what is in your immediate field of view; never zoom out… It's all for the best… Just believe, they tell themselves. They must. They absolutely must. Anything else would be bad for business.

SIMON A. SMITH

A Chicago novelist, teacher and script writer, Simon holds a BA in fiction writing and a MAT in secondary education. His fiction has appeared in many journals, including *Hobart Pulp*, *Whiskey Island*, *Juked* and *Curbside Splendor*. His journalism has also aired on *Chicago Public Radio* and appeared in the *Chicago Reader*. He lives in the Albany Park neighborhood with his wife and son.